GREAT
BIG
BEAUTIFUL
LIFE

TITLES BY EMILY HENRY

• • •

Great Big Beautiful Life

Funny Story

Happy Place

Book Lovers

People We Meet on Vacation

Beach Read

GREAT BIG BEAUTIFUL LIFE

Emily Henry

BERKLEY ROMANCE
New York

BERKLEY ROMANCE
Published by Berkley
An imprint of Penguin Random House LLC
1745 Broadway, New York, NY 10019
penguinrandomhouse.com

Copyright © 2025 by Emily Henry Books, LLC
Penguin Random House values and supports copyright. Copyright fuels creativity, encourages diverse voices, promotes free speech, and creates a vibrant culture. Thank you for buying an authorized edition of this book and for complying with copyright laws by not reproducing, scanning, or distributing any part of it in any form without permission. You are supporting writers and allowing Penguin Random House to continue to publish books for every reader. Please note that no part of this book may be used or reproduced in any manner for the purpose of training artificial intelligence technologies or systems.

BERKLEY and the BERKLEY & B colophon are registered trademarks of Penguin Random House LLC.

Book design by Alison Cnockaert

Library of Congress Cataloging-in-Publication Data
Names: Henry, Emily, author.
Title: Great big beautiful life / Emily Henry.
Description: New York: Berkley, 2025.
Identifiers: LCCN 2024050180 (print) | LCCN 2024050181 (ebook) | ISBN 9780593441299 (hardcover) | ISBN 9780593441244 (ebook) | ISBN 9780593954171 (Export edition)
Subjects: LCGFT: Novels.
Classification: LCC PS3608.E5715 G74 2025 (print) | LCC PS3608.E5715 (ebook) | DDC 813/.6—dc23/eng/20241028
LC record available at https://lccn.loc.gov/2024050180
LC ebook record available at https://lccn.loc.gov/2024050181

Printed in the United States of America
1st Printing

The authorized representative in the EU for product safety and compliance is Penguin Random House Ireland, Morrison Chambers, 32 Nassau Street, Dublin D02 YH68, Ireland, https://eu-contact.penguin.ie.

For my mom and my three grandmothers.
Life is complicated. Your love never was.

GREAT
BIG
BEAUTIFUL
LIFE

THERE'S AN OLD saying about stories, and how there are always three versions of them: *yours, mine, and the truth*. The guy who first said it worked in the film business, but it holds true for journalism too.

We're not really supposed to take sides. We're supposed to deal in facts. Facts add up to truth.

Fact: Robert Evans—producer, studio exec, and actor, who coined that catchy mantra about the truth—was married seven times.

Fact: I, Alice Scott—staff writer for *The Scratch*, aspiring biographer, not much else—am not even officially the girlfriend of the man I've been dating for seven months.

Fact: At five feet and nine inches tall, Robert Evans was the exact same height as I am.

Fact: My entire life is quite possibly about to change, and instead of sprinting up the walkway to the quaint picket fence separating me from a lifelong dream, I'm sitting in my rental car, blasting air-conditioning and reading the IMDb page of a man whose name I'd never heard three minutes ago, because his quote about stories popped into my head and also because I'm stalling.

I'm more excited than nervous, but there are still a *great* deal of nerves vibrating through me. With one last deep breath, I turn off the car and pop the door open.

Immediately the dense midday heat of a Georgia summer hits me from all sides, a familiar and deeply loved sensation that's only improved by the salty sea breeze sweeping in off the water surrounding Little Crescent Island.

I double-check that I have my notebook, voice recorder, and pens, then bump the door shut and stoop to check my rapidly dampening bangs in the side mirror.

I try to school my grin into an expression of neutrality. It's important that I play this cool.

Fact: I have never played it cool in my life.

I open the gate, my sandals slapping the stone walkway as I follow its curve around a wall of foliage: black needlerush and cabbage palm, prickly pear and glasswort, and—my favorite—live oak.

Eleven years in Los Angeles, but every time I see a Georgian live oak, I still think, *Home*.

A charming turquoise house on wooden stilts comes into view, and I climb a handful of worn wooden steps to reach its hot-pink front door, every inch of which has been hand-painted with white swirls.

I'm rewarded with a suitably eccentric doorbell. I mean, it looks like a normal doorbell, but when I hit it, it sounds like wind blowing through chimes.

I'm still mid–preparatory breath when the door swings open and a short, gray-haired woman in a faded flannel shirt and jeans scowls out at me.

"Hi!" I stick my hand out. "I'm Alice. Scott."

She stares back, her eyes pale blue and hair cropped short.

"With *The Scratch*?" I add, in case that jogs anything.

She doesn't even blink.

"I mean, not *with The Scratch*. I'm on staff there, but I'm here about the book?"

Her expression remains placid. For a second, I'm forced to contemplate the possibility that all of this has been an elaborate ruse, perhaps orchestrated by this woman's middle-aged son, from his computer in her basement, where he spends his days shooting off emails and phone calls to gullible writers like me, pitching his voice upward and adding a light shake to pass himself off as a woman in her eighties.

It wouldn't even be the first time.

I clear my throat and refresh my smile. "I'm sorry. Are you Margaret?"

She doesn't *look* like her, but then again, the last pictures I've seen of the woman I'm supposed to be meeting are easily three decades old. So for all I know, this *could* be the once-glamorous, nearly legendary (at least to a certain subset of people, including me) Margaret Grace Ives.

The Tabloid Princess. Known as such both because she was the heiress to the Ives media empire *and* because of those years when her own celebrity status earned her near-constant attention from the paparazzi and gossip columnists.

The woman barks out a loud, genuine laugh and widens the door. "I'm Jodi," she says with the faint hint of an indeterminate accent—German, maybe. "Come on in."

I step into the cool foyer, the smell of lemon and mint in the air. Jodi doesn't pause or even slow for me, just marches straight into the house, leaving me to pull the door shut and bound after her.

"This place is beautiful," I chirp.

"It's hotter than hell, and Dracula has nothing on the mosquitoes," she says.

I spare a thought for Robert Evans: *Yours, mine, and the truth.*

At the end of one narrow hallway, she turns down another, the house an airy, bright labyrinth of whitewashed beadboard and sea-glass-colored accents ending in a spacious sitting room whose walls are seventy percent window.

"You wait here, and I'll go grab *madame* for you," Jodi says, with a detectable edge of amusement in her voice. She unlocks one of the glass back doors and steps into the yard, a vaster and wilder garden than the front, with a small swimming pool set off to one side.

I take the opportunity to make a slow lap around the room, still buzzing *and* smiling big enough that my jaw has started to ache. I set my things down on the low rattan coffee table and cross my arms to keep myself from touching anything as I wander. Art crowds every inch of the walls, and plants hang in clusters in front of the windows, still more in clay pots on the floor. A thatched fan twirls lazily overhead, and books—most of them about gardening and horticulture—sit in messy stacks and face down with cracked spines, covering every antique-wooden surface available.

It's beautiful. I'm already mentally drafting how I'd describe it. The only problem is, I'm still not convinced I'll have a *reason* to describe it.

Because so far there's nothing to indicate this is Margaret Ives's house. No photos of her illustrious family. No copies, old or new, of any of their dozens of magazines or newspapers. No framed illustrations of the opulent "House of Ives" where she'd been raised on the California coast, and none of her late husband's Grammys on the mantel either. Nothing concrete to link her to the now-collapsed media juggernaut, *or* the joys and tragedies the Ives family's competing publications had so loved to catalog back when Margaret was still on top of the world.

The door swings open again, and I spin to face Jodi, working myself up to demand answers about who exactly invited me to do eleven hours of air travel plus forty-five minutes in a rented Kia Rio for this meeting.

But then I see the woman standing just inside.

She's shrunk a few inches, gained some weight—much of it muscle, I'd guess—and her once jet-black hair is now a mix of mousy brown and silver.

She's been scrubbed clear of any glamour, or air of money and power, but that sly sparkle in her blue eyes is exactly the same as in every photograph I've seen of her, the elusive, unnamable *something* that had turned her from *heiress to a newspaper fortune* to *princess of the cover page.*

"Well, hello there." The warmth in Margaret's voice surprises me, just like it did during our few brief phone calls in the weeks leading up to this trip. "You must be Alice."

She shucks off her gardening gloves and tosses them across the arm of the nearest white rattan chair as she strides barefoot toward me, dusting her hands off on her caftan before stretching one out to shake mine.

"You're her," I say. Every eloquent or even *serviceable* sentence I've ever put together has been typed out slowly, over time. The ones that come directly from my mouth usually sound more like this.

She laughs. "I was under the impression that was the point."

She gives my hand a little squeeze, then drops it and gestures for me to sit.

"No, it is." I lower myself to the couch. She takes the chair opposite me. "I was just trying not to get my hopes up! It didn't work. Never does. But I keep trying."

"Really?" She sounds amused. "I tend to have the opposite problem. Can't help but expect the worst from people." She flashes a smile. It's both dazzling and sad. Sazzling.

That, for example, would *not* make it to a typed-and-edited sentence. But the point is, I can see it hidden back beneath those sparkly irises of hers somewhere: the truth. The one we've never heard before.

What it was like to be born into a world of silver spoons and golden platters, of actors drunkenly swimming fully clothed through your indoor pool and politicians making handshake agreements across your antique dinner table.

How it felt to fall in love with rock 'n' roll royalty, and for him to love you back, wildly.

And, of course, about the *other* things. The scandal, the cult, the trial, the accident.

And finally, twenty years ago, Margaret's disappearance.

What happened, but also *why*.

And why now, after all this time, she's open to finally telling the story.

Behind Margaret, the door squeals open and Jodi reenters the house, toting a bucket of lemons. "Thank you, Jodi," Margaret calls, without turning around.

Jodi grunts. I could not *begin* to guess whether the two women are friends, romantic partners, an employer and employee, or mortal enemies who happen to be roommates.

Margaret crosses one leg over the other. "Cute nails," she says, jutting her chin toward my hands in my lap.

The moment of connection makes me near giddy. "They're press-ons." I lean forward so she can get a better look at the little strawberry-printed designs.

"I'd bet you're the kind of person," she says, "who tries to find beauty in everything."

"Don't you?" I ask, intrigued by the soft, sad smile that feathers across her lips.

She gives a half-realized shrug that reads less like *I don't know* and more like *I don't like that question.*

Then, like the Ives she is, she neatly reroutes the dialogue: "So how exactly would this work? *If* I agreed to do it."

I don't let the *if* discourage me. I know she isn't one hundred percent in just yet, and I don't blame her. "However you want it to," I promise.

She arches one brow. "What if I want it to work how it would usually work?"

"Well," I say, "I haven't done anything exactly like this before. Usually I'm doing features and profiles. I spend a couple days, or weeks, with a person. And I write about my observations, crack some jokes. It's an 'outsider looking in' perspective. This would be different.

"It'd be about getting *your* experience onto the page. 'Insider looking out.' That would take a lot longer, months probably, just for the first round of research to be able to write a draft and figure out where my holes are. I'd rent a place nearby, and we'd have a schedule, times for sit-down interviews, but also time for me to just shadow you."

"Shadow me," she repeats thoughtfully.

"Follow you around in your normal life," I clarify. "See what you grow in your garden, who you spend your time with. Hang out with you and Jodi, and any other friends you've got in town."

Margaret's chin juts forward, her eyes closing on her own quick, blunt laugh. "Do me a favor and say that again when she gets back in here."

Mere seconds later, Jodi comes streaming into the room, carrying two glasses of lemonade. She plops them both down on the coffee table.

"Thanks, Jodi," I say, determined to win her over.

She marches back out the way she came in.

"I'd die without you," Margaret calls teasingly after her.

"Don't I know it," Jodi shouts, before disappearing through the doorway.

I take a tiny sip of the lemonade, which turns into a long gulp, because it's amazing, fresh and crisp with torn mint leaves swirling around along with the ice cubes.

I set the glass down and force myself to get back to business. "Look, there are a lot more experienced writers you could pair up with. There are hundreds of people who would push me in front of a bus to get this job, and honestly, I'd understand it if they did."

"Troubling," Margaret says.

"My point is, if you're ready to tell your story, you deserve to have it told exactly how you want it to be. It needs to be yours, no one else's. And that only works if you're doing this with someone you completely trust. But I can promise you, if you end up wanting to write this book together, *your voice* will be front and center. That's my top priority. Making sure it's your story."

Her smile fades, her face sobering. The crinkles at the corners of her eyes and the folds at the edges of her mouth deepen, proof of an entire life lived, not just those first thirty-three years she spent in the public eye, but the thirty she spent as a recluse after that, and the twenty since she vanished.

"What if," she says slowly, "that's not what I want?"

I shake my head. "I'm not sure I'm following."

"What if I don't want it to be my version of the story?" she asks. "What if I want the whole awful truth? What if I'm done living with my version of events, where I'm always the hero, and I want to sit down and see things in black and white for once?"

Her question catches me off guard. If anything, I'm used to having to reassure my subjects that I'm not there to twist everything they say into a brutal takedown piece. That I *want* to see the full picture, right down to their humanity.

Margaret's brow arches at my hesitancy. "That a problem?"

I scoot to the edge of the couch. "It's how *you* want it told," I repeat. "If that's what you want, that's what we do."

She considers for a long moment. "One more question."

"Anything." She could ask for my most embarrassing sex story, and I'd trot it out right now. I need her to understand she's safe with me.

Her gray eyebrow arches wickedly again. "Are you always this perky?"

I let out a breath. This is too lengthy and important a job to kick things off with a lie.

"Yes," I say. "Yes, I am."

Her chortle is interrupted by a sound like wind blowing through glass chimes. Margaret glances at the driftwood clock on the Grammy-free mantel.

"That'll be my two o'clock." She sweeps onto her feet. "You've given me a lot to think about, Alice Scott."

I bounce up onto mine too, grabbing my unused notebook and recorder. "Either way," I say, "thank you. Seriously."

"For *what*?" she says, sounding genuinely baffled as she leads me back through the maze of hallways.

"For today," I say. "For giving me a chance." For the fact that I *finally* have something work related to tell my mom that won't make her eyes glaze over with disinterest.

"It's just a chance," Margaret reminds me as we reach the front door. "Don't thank me for that. Everyone deserves that much. And I've still got a couple other branches to shake, see what falls out."

"I completely understand, but—" My words drop off as she swings the bright pink door open, and I realize how wrong I was.

I did *not* completely understand.

Margaret's two o'clock is standing on the top step in slate-colored chinos and a white T-shirt.

It's not the outfit that makes my heart sink and all the blood drain from my face—though the idea of wearing long pants in weather like this certainly does give me pause.

It's the hulking, dark-eyed, hawk-nosed man wearing it.

Hayden Anderson.

Four years ago, you might've said *Hayden Anderson the music journalist*, and that would've been a fair summation. But if he were *still* just a music journalist, I wouldn't know his name, let alone what he looked like. I have a decent memory, but I don't make a habit of memorizing *Rolling Stone* bylines.

However.

He's no longer just *Hayden Anderson the music journalist*.

Now, he's *Hayden Anderson the Pulitzer Prize–winning biographer*. The one who wrote that doorstop-length gut punch about the Americana singer with dementia.

Now he's the Hayden Anderson that Margaret just referred to as another branch to shake. A more successful, more well-known, more *more* branch.

His dark eyes cut from me (expression blank, he doesn't recognize me; why would he? I am an unimpressive branch) to Margaret (in whom he is only marginally less disinterested) as his low rumble of a voice says, "Am I early?"

"You're exactly on time," Margaret says warmly. "Alice was just going."

I would describe the expression on Hayden's face as a distinct mien of *who the hell is Alice*, like he's already forgotten there's another person standing immediately in front of him, or possibly didn't actually register me the first time our eyes met.

"Hi!" I recover enough grip on my organs for my heart to be pumping blood again, my lungs to be pulling in oxygen, and my hand to be reaching out to shake his.

He lifts his slowly, as if he'd like some more information before he agrees to physical contact.

"I was just leaving," I promise, and that seems to do the trick. Finally, his very large, very warm, very dry hand folds around mine, dips once, and drops back to his side.

"Thanks again," I tell Margaret over my shoulder as I hurry out onto the sidewalk.

"I'll be in touch," she tells me, and I force a smile, like my heart isn't a little bit breaking and I'm *not* on the verge of tears over the dream job I'm ninety-nine percent sure I've just missed out on.

2

I SPEND MY first night at the Grande Lucia Resort eating Twizzlers and googling Hayden Anderson while convincing myself the world isn't ending.

First I read a dozen rave reviews of his book. Then I stumble across a *Publishers Weekly* article that estimates its first year's US sales to be upwards of two million. Lastly, just to torture myself, I watch an interview with Hayden and the book's subject, Len Stirling, wherein Len informs the interviewer that he'd already considered nine writers before Hayden even threw his hat in the ring. Hayden, without any trace of humor or irony, leans forward to add, "I'm very competitive."

I cut my own groan short.

There's still a *chance* Margaret will choose to work with me.

Maybe she'd rather work with a woman. Maybe she always roots for the underdog. Maybe she just has a natural distaste for tall, muscular, talented men who write the kind of biographies that not only *don't* make a person fall asleep but also go so far as to make said person weep multiple times while she's reading alone at the bar of her neighborhood taqueria back in Highland Park.

There could be lots of reasons why she doesn't want to work with Hayden, and surely there could be at least *several* why she *would* want to work with me.

I nod to myself, more enthusiastically than I feel, as I flop back on the cheery gingham bedspread, gazing out the window, upside down, toward the beach beyond the hotel's courtyard.

I should've known a secret like Margaret's whereabouts couldn't last forever.

It had all started four months ago, when my profile on the former child star Bella Girardi came out. That piece was *the* thing I was absolute proudest of in my career thus far. I had a full folder of sweet emails from former colleagues and glowing screenshots of online chatter about the story after it went live.

And all of that, in itself, would've been *more* than enough to make the weeks of writing and rewriting and back-and-forths with my fact-checkers and editor all worth it.

But at the bottom of one very short email there was also a little something extra.

Loved the piece, LindaTakesBackHerLifeAt53 wrote. P.S. That Cosmo Sinclair song about Margaret Ives that u and Bella talked about is one of my all-time faves. Did u know Margaret's living down on an island in Georgia now, selling art under a fake name?

That was it. No more information. And when I emailed Linda back, I got no reply.

I spent two weeks researching any connection Margaret might have to Georgia (none that I could find), and googling combinations of her name with "art" and "island," to no avail. Margaret Ives vanished entirely from public view in the early two thousands, and mostly the rumor mill seemed to suggest she'd married an Italian olive farmer half her age and settled down on the opposite side of the Atlantic.

At first, I was ninety percent sure Linda was lying or misinformed.

There was no way Margaret Ives was in Georgia, on a little island that survived on local tourism, within a long day's drive of the west Tennessee hometown of her late husband, Cosmo Sinclair.

But the idea wouldn't let go of me. The rumor had to come from *somewhere*, I thought, even as I tried to talk myself out of my innate optimism.

I started trawling online message boards. Anything to do with Cosmo's music, with the illustrious Ives family, with Margaret's disappearance.

Nothing. On any of them.

And then I found the conspiracy theorists. People posting pictures of "Elvis" at a mall in Tuscaloosa. Or JFK wearing a bucket hat and a barely buttoned shirt, white chest hair spilling out around his gold chain necklace, in Miami. It took a while to find the Margaret post, just because the *mystery* of what happened to her had faded with time.

People knew about Ives Media, and they knew about the family's palatial estate (now owned by the state and open for tours). They of course knew about the whole snafu with Margaret's sister and the cult, and they could probably instantly call to mind the famous black-and-white photograph of Margaret and Cosmo running, hand in hand, up the courtroom steps the day that they eloped, his blond hair slicked back and hers teased into the beehive style of the time.

But after Cosmo's tragic death, his widow had largely retreated from the glare of the spotlight. So that when she disappeared altogether, twenty years ago, no one was quite so interested as they might've been.

Most people had simply accepted that we'd never find out what happened to her. Just another Amelia Earhart, a woman lost to time.

But there were still some active Margaret Ives online communities dedicated to the rumors surrounding her vanishing. To debunking or proving them, depending on the poster's point of view. They were treated like true-crime-junkie communities, bits of old interviews trotted out as evidence for or against a favorite theory.

Those specific message boards got me nowhere.

The Not So Dead Celebrities message board, however, led me here, to Little Crescent Island.

And if *I* could find her through that post, there's no telling how many other Hayden Andersons might be flying cross-country to Little Crescent Island this very minute.

My phone buzzes on the mattress beside me, and I feel around until I find it. My stomach rises expectantly—maybe Margaret's already made a decision—but then I see the screen.

Theo. Now, a different sensation rumbles in my stomach, that anxious flutter I *still* get when I hear from my on-again, off-again not-boyfriend.

How'd it go with the heiress? he asks. I'm touched he remembered. Probably too touched. I haven't talked about much else the last few weeks. But still! He reached out to check in—that's something!

I hesitate over how to phrase it and settle on: She's intriguing and her house is a dream and I want the job so, so, so badly.

All true. It wouldn't do me any good to add *and I'm terrified I'm not going to get it, because a six-foot-three rock face of a man with a Pulitzer and a scowl to freeze a Gorgon is on the scene.*

I watch the phone for a minute, two, three. I set it aside. I was drawn to Theo for his easy confidence and his laid-back, carefree way of moving through the world. There's something so appealing about a person who doesn't take anything too seriously. Until you have to text with one. Theo's terrible at it. To be fair, I'm not amazing myself, but he's the *king* of sending a message, to which I immediately reply, and then waiting a full day to acknowledge my response.

By then I may have lost my dream job and also fully melted into this bed, the puddle formerly known as the writer Alice Scott.

"Get yourself together, Scott!" I cry, pitching myself back onto my feet and slapping my laptop shut.

"You're on a beautiful island with a growling stomach and an open schedule," I tell myself, snatching my phone and stuffing my feet into my sandals. "Might as well make the most of it."

• • •

LITTLE CRESCENT ISLAND is a vacation destination, but it's *not* a nightlife hot spot. Most of the people here seem to be either retirees or families with kids, and it's nine o'clock on a Tuesday night, so pickings are slim on the main drag.

The first open restaurant I come to is called Fish Bowl, and the menu posted out front seems to be ninety percent alcohol and ten percent seafood.

Inside, it's cramped and wonderfully kitschy, with bamboo wall paneling and fishnets suspended from the ceiling, all manner of colorful plastic fish and glow-in-the-dark seaweed caught in them. A ponytailed server in a tight white shirt and short shorts whisks past me, tray in hand, and says cheerfully, "Sit anywhere you want, hon. We're slow tonight."

There are plenty of open tables, but two older gentlemen in matching bowling shirts are sitting at the bar, and I'm feeling kind of chatty, so I head their way. Right as I'm sidling onto a stool two down from them, though, they're tossing money onto the glossy, dark wooden countertop and standing to go.

One catches my eyes, and I flash a smile.

He smiles back. "Highly recommend the Captain's Bowl!"

"I'll take that under advisement," I promise, and he tips an invisible hat before shuffling off after his companion. On the way out, the two of them stop to have a word with the ponytailed server, and she gives the lover of the Captain's Bowl a peck on the cheek, so either they're all locals or this place just has over-the-top service.

I go back to perusing the menu, resuming a practically lifelong debate of mine: whether to order fish tacos or fish and chips.

I'm still working on this when someone plops a massive bowl of startlingly blue liquid, ice, and roughly five fruit spears down in front of me. I look up, surprised, to find the ponytailed server smiling at me from behind the bar. "Captain's Bowl," she says. "Courtesy of the captains themselves."

"Oh?" I glance toward the front door, the gentlemen from earlier long gone now. "What are they the captains of?"

"Uncle Ralph is the captain of the bowling team, and Cecil is the captain of this restaurant," she muses. "Each has his own seat of power, but Cecil's carries a bit more weight here, understandably."

"Well, next time you see him, thank him for me," I say.

She nods once. "Will do. Now, are you eating too tonight or just swimming?" She tips her chin toward the gargantuan bowl of violently unnatural blue, and I burst out laughing.

"What's even in this?" I ask.

"Everything," she says. "Plus some Coca-Cola."

I take a tiny sip through the neon-pink straw, and it feels like I just inhaled sugar, then poured gasoline down my throat, but in a fun way.

"Food?" the woman—her name tag says Sheri—asks again.

I tell her my predicament, tacos versus fish and chips.

"Tacos," she says decisively. "Always go with the tacos."

"Perfect." I set my menu down, and she whirls off through the door behind the bar. I look down at my drink and burst into laughter again. I've never been a big drinker, but I'd give this concoction a ten out of ten on presentation alone. I snap a picture and text it to Theo while I start nibbling on the first spear of fruit. *You as a drink*, he replies immediately. *Have fun!*

I will! I tell him, then set my phone down and give the restaurant another once-over. Other than me, there are two parties present at the moment: a family of five at the table under the front windows, and a guy nursing an ice water and eating a salad at the tiny booth back by the bathroom hallway.

He looks up from his water at that exact moment.

Nearly black hair, angular nose, a stern brow.

I whip back around to face the bar, nearly capsizing my stool in the process. I grab the edge of the counter to steady myself, heart racing. It probably isn't even him. It's probably my mind and the glow-in-the-dark ceiling playing tricks on me, forming Hayden Andersons out of random shadows.

I take another small sip of Captain's Bowl to steel myself and then slowly, casually, throw a glance over my shoulder toward the booth.

He's no longer looking this way. Instead he's staring down at something in front of him, his brow tightly furrowed. Hunched over the tiny table like that, he gives the impression of a bear at a tea party, everything around him just a little too small and breakable.

Definitely him.

And seeing him now, a not-so-small part of me wants to run and hide. Which makes *no* sense.

He's not a grizzly. He's a guy who happens to want the same job as me. A guy who wrote a book I *loved*!

It's ridiculous to treat him like some kind of enemy, just because we both want to write Margaret's story. And it's ridiculous to sit here and ignore him when we're ten feet apart.

I should say hi.

Just one more sip of Captain's Bowl for good luck, and then I hop down from my stool and cross the restaurant to stand in front of Hayden's table.

He doesn't look up. I give him a second to finish his page, but even after he taps to the next one, he doesn't peel his eyes off his e-reader.

"Hi!" I chirp.

He flinches at the sound of my voice, then slowly, very slowly, drags his eyes up to mine from beneath a creased brow.

"We met earlier?" I remind him. "I'm Alice."

"I remember," he says, his voice a flat rumble.

"I actually already know who you are," I say.

One of his dark eyebrows arches.

I slide into the booth, across from him, our knees bumping together. I'd always wondered why it seemed like enormously tall men tend to date adorably tiny women, and now I have my answer, apparently: A man as tall as Hayden Anderson can't comfortably sit opposite anyone over five three. I'm about six inches into the red here.

I turn to perch sideways instead. He's still staring at me with that brow arched, the visual equivalent of a question mark.

"Because of your book," I explain. "*Our Friend Len.* I loved it. I mean, obviously. Everyone who read it loved it. After the Pulitzer, hearing that from a random woman in a bar probably feels a little anticlimactic, but still, I wanted you to know."

His shoulders relax, just a bit. "Are you a friend or family?"

"What?" I say.

"Of Margaret's," he clarifies.

"Oh, neither." I wave a hand. "I'm a writer too."

His gaze dips down me again, sizing me up now that he has this new information. His irises are lighter than I thought. Still brown, but a pale shade of it.

"What sort of things do you write?" he asks.

"All sorts," I say. "A lot of human interest, and pop culture stuff. I work at *The Scratch*."

His face remains completely impassive. I try a different tack: "Have you ever been to Georgia?"

"First time," he says.

"Really?" I say, surprised. "Where are you from?"

"New York," he says.

"The city or the state?" I ask.

"City," he replies.

"Born and raised?" I say.

"No," he says.

"Then where'd you grow up?" I ask.

"Indiana," he says.

"Did you like it?" I ask.

His brow sinks into a scowl, his wide mouth still keeping to an utterly straight line. "Why?"

I laugh. "What do you mean *why*?"

"Why would you want to know if I liked growing up in Indiana?" he says, face and voice perfectly matched in surliness.

I fight a smile. "Because I'm considering buying it."

His eyes narrow, irises seeming to darken. "Buying what?"

"Indiana," I say.

He stares.

I can't fight it anymore. The amusement wins out, and another laugh escapes me. "I'm just trying to get to know you," I explain.

He sets his forearms on the table, his posture very nearly a challenge. His head tilts to the left, and he says, quite possibly, the last thing I'm expecting: "This isn't going to work."

I draw back, surprised and confused. "What isn't?"

"You, trying to throw me off my game," he growls.

"And what 'game' exactly are we talking about here?" I say, glancing around the now totally empty Fish Bowl. "Wait, *Sheri*?" I spin back to face him, our knees colliding again.

"Who is *Sheri*," he says, with some distaste.

"Our server!" I drop my voice, in case she pops out of the kitchen. "If you're trying to make a move, all you had to do was say so, and I would've gone right back to my fishbowl—"

"Not the server," he interrupts. "The book."

"The book?" I repeat. Then it dawns on me. He means *the* book. Margaret's book.

Hayden goes on: "I don't know what this"—he waves one large hand between us—"is supposed to accomplish exactly, but this is *Margaret Ives* we're talking about. I want this job and I'm not going to back off, so you can stop."

At first, it stings, being talked to like this by a stranger. That someone whose work I admired has just accused me of trying to somehow professionally thwart him when I actually was just trying to get to know him.

But underneath the sting, there's another feeling growing, getting traction all through my limbs.

Hope.

In life, I've learned there's almost always a silver lining. Here's one now.

Hayden's brow furrows, his arms sliding off the table. "Why are you doing that?"

"Doing what?"

"*Smiling*," he says dryly.

I snort out a laugh and slide out of the booth to stand, practically floating back to the bar, because his reaction has told me one important thing—I mean, aside from the fact that he's a mistrustful cynic. "Because," I call to him, "now I know I still have a chance."

He rolls his eyes, and I plop back down on my stool, buzzing with excitement, just as Sheri bumps the kitchen door open with one hip and marches out with my basket of fried fish tacos. "I see that Captain's Bowl got you grinning," she says.

"It's great," I tell her with another big, appreciative slurp. Probably one of the last few I'll be able to handle, honestly, unless I plan on being hospitalized or arrested later.

"Glad to hear it," she says. "You're not driving, are you?"

"No, I'm over at the Grande Lucia, so I'm on foot tonight," I tell her.

"Aw, my husband, Robbie, and I honeymooned there," she tells me.

Sheri doesn't look quite old enough to be married, but I guess that's going by Los Angeles standards. Most of the girls I went to high school with are married now, and my mom and dad were married by the time they were twenty-three, though they didn't have my sister or me until much later.

"Get you anything else?" she asks, one hand on her hip.

"Actually," I say, "I'd like to send a drink to someone, if you don't mind." A little something to brighten *his* mood the way he just brightened mine.

Sheri's eyes wander over my shoulder and back to the corner, locking onto the only other patron in this fine establishment. "What are we thinking here? Whiskey? Beer?"

"Do you have anything bigger or bluer than *this*?" I ask, pointing down toward my bowl.

"Aside from the freshly cleaned toilets, no," she says, "but I can throw in some candied hibiscus to spice things up if that helps."

"That," I say, "would be perfect."

3

I WAKE WITH a splitting headache. There's no way I'm hungover—I might be a lightweight, but my five sips of liquor last night couldn't have made quite this impression.

No, this is a kind of headache I am all too familiar with: caffeine withdrawal.

Before I collapsed into my freshly laundered hotel bedding last night, I'd turned off my alarm, cranked my volume up all the way—in case Margaret decided to call—and shut the blackout curtains.

The clock on the bedside table reads 9:32 a.m. A full hour later than my usual first cup of espresso. I stumble out of bed and throw open the drapes to find brilliant sunlight, a clear blue sky, and turquoise waves crashing against the shore below.

It's interesting that Margaret's property is on the far side of the island, backing up toward the marshy waterway that separates Little Crescent from mainland Georgia, rather than out here, where—judging by the string of resorts near the main drag and the mansions farther to the east and west—all the tourists and the millionaires seem to favor.

Maybe that's because she wants to avoid people, or maybe there's more to it than that. Either way, I make a note in my phone to add it to the list of questions I'll ask if and when she agrees to the book.

The last note I made, sometime late last night, reads *play with structure???* After several seconds of casting my mind backward, I remember what I was talking about.

The idea came from *Our Friend Len*, Hayden's book.

Len Stirling had decided to authorize the biography shortly after his dementia diagnosis. He'd hoped it could help slow the progress of the disease, but more than that, he thought it would be a comfort to his family and friends after he'd gone. Not died, necessarily, but lost his memory of them.

Hayden had told the story in reverse, each section focusing on the Len of a different era as his short-term memory faded, and then, gradually, his old memories too.

In one of their final conversations in which Len remembered Hayden, he'd shared his fear of losing himself, of reaching the point where not only did he not recognize his old band, or his wife, or his daughters, but he no longer knew who he was.

Hayden had asked Len what he ought to tell him, if Len should ever ask the question *Who am I?*

And in a way, that question had been the scaffolding for the whole book, the thesis of who, ultimately, is the legendary Len Stirling. What, in the end, matters most about a person's identity.

After some thought, Len had answered Hayden, "Tell me I'm your friend Len."

By then they'd been working on the book for four years, only Len's manager and most intimate acquaintances aware of the diagnosis that led to it.

And that final section, the portion of the book concerned with Len's childhood in the Mississippi Delta, beautifully stripped away the legend and the mythos to present just that: a loving portrait of a friend, of a boy who'd rescued snakes from torture at the hands of the neighborhood kids, one who'd hung his head in shame after shoplifting taffy on his younger brother's birthday, a more human Len than he'd probably gotten to be in a long time.

Obviously, I wouldn't emulate the structure for Margaret's book, but finding some other device like that might help to achieve something similar, to scrape away all the labels and rumors and stories piled atop this person and reveal the *person* herself.

Before I can think through it any further, though, I'll need coffee.

I take a quick shower and get dressed: a pink skirt that's technically a tiny bit too short, big watermelon earrings, and a white knit top. I step into my sandals; grab my purse, sunglasses, and room key; and step out into the cool, breezy morning, a layer of salt coating my skin almost instantly.

I jog down the steps and get into my car. I grabbed a coffee at Main Street Bean yesterday before my meeting with Margaret, and it left a lot to be desired, but I found a spot online with rave reviews, a ways back toward the bridge to the mainland.

Punching the name of it—Little Croissant—into my phone, I start the car. The Cranberries song I was listening to on the way home from Margaret's yesterday automatically starts playing, and I crank my windows down as I pull out of the hotel's parking lot.

Within a few minutes, the palm trees that dot the road at regular intervals are replaced by more wild foliage: cypress and live oak and massive century plants, the shaggy grass beneath them dappled in shadow by the rising sun.

I take a left onto the four-lane road that heads out of town and off island, eyes darting from the GPS to the narrow cross streets as I pass them.

Ahead, a wide dirt turnoff flanked in more palm appears, a grid of candy-colored wooden signs posted there beneath a larger sign for the Little Crescent Enclave.

Little Croissant Coffee Bar
Two Dudes Pizza
Turquoise Turtle Antiques
Esmeralda's Fine Art & Jewelry
Sisters o' the Sea
Booze Hound

I turn down the drive and find myself hemmed in by twin rows of squat shops, each as brightly painted as its respective sign. Both sides of the enclave are built atop graying wooden platforms—protection against flooding—and every single shop has its door(s) propped open, shoppers milling in and out with coffee cups in hand.

The road ends in a round, white-graveled parking lot, a huge gnarled tree at its center, and I take the closest spot I can find, leaving the windows open so the car doesn't bake. I hop out, admiring the charming little nook tucked away by woods for a moment before picking my way toward Little Croissant.

The line is all the way down the platform steps, but it takes only a few minutes for me to put in my order, and since I'm just getting drip coffee, I'm waiting only a moment beneath the upper seating area's sun-sails (there's also a stone patio down off the side of the platform) before the teenage barista at the shack's serving window calls my name.

"Thanks!" I call inside as I grab the cup.

Two decades' worth of tongue burns, and I still haven't learned to be cautious with that first sip, which is why I find myself with a *very* full mouth of something that is *definitely* not coffee, and thus somewhat disgusting.

I almost spit it out, but at the last conceivable second force myself to just hold it in my mouth long enough to turn the cup around and read the name and order scratched on its side.

Green tea. (Instantly less disgusting now that I know this.)

Hayden. (Instantly more embarrassing.)

"This must be yours then," a low, rumbling voice says behind me, and I turn to find a large expanse of chest in front of me, a gray Purdue T-shirt clinging damply to it.

My head tips up past a collarbone, Adam's apple, and strong jaw to an angular nose and glowering light brown eyes.

It's a marvel I remember to swallow the gulp of tea before blurting, "Why are you so wet?"

His glower deepens as he holds the paper cup in his hand out to me, my name clearly written on the side. "It's called sweat. It happens when you run."

I take the cup and pass the one in my hand to him. "What were you running from?" I ask guilelessly.

"Boredom," he says dryly. "*And* sloth."

"I had no *idea* there were sloths here!"

He stares at me, trying to determine whether I'm serious. I feel my smile growing.

Either way, he doesn't get the chance to acknowledge what I said, because his watch starts ringing with a phone call. He eyes the screen, and I see something like satisfaction flare in his eyes before he drops his arm and meets my gaze again. "I'll leave you to your morning," he says curtly, and turns, tapping the call over to his earbuds as he stalks down the steps toward the lot.

"See you around!" I shout after him, forcing myself not to check out his butt. Or legs. Or back.

He glances over his shoulder as if reading my thoughts, and I look away right as I hear him answer the call: "Ms. Ives, hi."

• • •

I TELL MYSELF that her calling him first is a good thing.

Obviously she'd want to get not-quite-firing-but-definitely-not-hiring one of us out of the way *before* sharing the good news.

But still my heart is in my throat the whole drive back to the hotel, and singing along at the top of my lungs to "Linger" feels less celebratory than desperate. Like doing jumping jacks to stem off a panic attack.

It will be okay, I promise myself. *Either way, it will be okay.*

I've been through way worse than losing out on a dream job. And since I barely told anyone aside from my literary agent, a couple of work friends, and Theo about this job, there'd be hardly anyone to let down.

Thank *god* I didn't tell my mom. I almost did, multiple times. The temptation of *finally* working on something she was remotely interested in was nearly too great.

I love my mom, and I definitely respect her, but the list of things we have in common is short. In the Venn diagram of *things she thinks are worth writing about* and *things I might actually have a chance to write about*, the history of America's most influential media family might actually sit in the middle.

In her mind, I'd be contributing to history, and for me, it would be a chance to find the love story inside all Margaret's family's tragedies.

Really, Dad's the one I wish I could tell. He was the one who first introduced me to Margaret, when I was a little girl. He used to play all of Cosmo's music while he and Mom cooked dinner, but he especially loved what the superfans called the "Peggy Quartet." The four love songs Cosmo wrote for Margaret.

My father, the only other romantic in the family besides me, adored their larger-than-life love story. He used to call Cosmo the "Great American Storyteller"—*He gives you just enough to leave you champing at the bit to get the rest.*

A phone call interrupts the song playing through the car speakers, and I yelp like someone just grabbed me from behind, flicking on my turn signal and pulling into the parking lot of a small strip mall, the smell of sunbaked blacktop wafting in through my open windows.

I check the caller ID: *Margaret!*

Is it good that she called so fast after speaking with Hayden?

Or does that mean *his* call didn't require the requisite apologies that came with passing on an offer? Was it, instead, only a quick *see you on Monday, cowriter*?

"You can do this," I remind myself. Whatever *this* is. It's just a job.

I take a deep breath and answer the call on speaker. "This is Alice Scott."

"Hi, Alice," a brusque, not-at-all-Margaret-like voice blusters through. "Jodi here."

"Oh! Hi!" I recover. "How are you?"

She blows right through that: "Margaret was wondering whether you could come by for another meeting today. Maybe at dinnertime?"

"Yes! Definitely!" I say. "Around five or six, then?"

She snorts. "Good lord, I wish. She's over eighty, and still eating dinner like a twenty-five-year-old in Rome. Eight p.m. But cocktail hour's at seven thirty. Don't be more than five minutes early. Or late."

Frankly, I can't imagine Margaret caring whether I landed in that precise ten-minute window, but I'd guess Jodi might care quite a bit, and that's good enough for me.

"I'll be exactly on t—" The phone line clicks before I can finish my sentence. "Hello?"

No answer. She's already gone.

The Cranberries blast back into song, and this time when I sing along, it's fed by sheer joy.

4

AT SEVEN TWENTY-NINE, I shift the bottle of wine and bouquet I brought into one hand and ring Margaret's doorbell with the other.

Heavy footfalls answer on the far side, and then the hot-pink door swings open to reveal Jodi in a different but nearly identical flannel, T-shirt, and jeans. "You're on time," she announces.

"And bearing gifts!" I thrust the wine and flowers toward her.

She eyes them skeptically. "Margaret hates trimmed flowers. They make her sad."

"Oh." I frown down at them, then meet her gaze. "What about you?"

Her square face softens a bit. "I don't mind them."

"They're yours then," I tell her, and because she did me such a solid, I add, "and if you tell me she hates wine, this is for you too."

Her mouth turns up in an *almost* smile. "Sadly, I'm no liar. She loves wine."

"Well, just tell her it's for both of you then," I say, handing it over. "But I should warn you, I don't really drink, so it could be disgusting."

Jodi jerks her head over her shoulder. "Come on in," she says, back to all business. "They're already out back."

They. I'd assumed this was just a get-to-know-you dinner. If Margaret has friends over, I really should've brought my recorder. I always use both it *and* my phone, in case something goes wrong with one of the recordings, and I feel a little irresponsible for not tossing it in my bag before I headed over from the hotel.

In my defense, I'd been distracted combing through a list of Little Crescent Island's monthly furnished rental properties online. Just in case.

At the back of the house, Jodi leads me through the glass double doors and down a flagstone path that winds around a wall of brush, the sound of cicadas, katydids, and crickets pulsing through the night.

A wide flagstone patio sits ahead, globe lights strung back and forth over the long wooden table in its center, and more still wrapped in a spiraling pattern up the side of a huge tree that partially hangs over the far end of the table.

Twelve people could easily eat here, but there are only three high-backed wooden chairs, two of them occupied.

"Well, hi there, Alice!" Margaret calls cheerily, pushing to her feet as, to her right, a rigid behemoth of a man essentially snaps to his.

Hayden doesn't look surprised to see me, but he doesn't look happy either.

I understand, of course—I'm not thrilled to find him here myself—but it still trips an old wire in me, a need not just to win him over but to root around until I find out what's under his cold exterior.

I push my rising disappointment aside as I follow Jodi to the table.

Ultimately, I am still dining al fresco with the only remaining member of one of America's most storied families—someone who has fascinated me since childhood.

"Good to see you both!" I say, reaching out to take Margaret's hand. She holds my palm briefly between both of hers, her warm cookie scent engulfing me and her eyes as sparkly as ever. Which is to say, exceptionally.

"You too, sugar," she says. "Thanks for coming on such short notice."

"Thanks for having me," I reply.

Her gaze tracks sideways to Jodi, and her smile falters.

Jodi heads her off. "The flowers are for *me*, so don't you go getting any ideas."

"And the wine's for everyone," I put in.

"Well, aren't you sweet," Margaret says, gently squeezing my forearm. "You remember Hayden, from yesterday."

"Of course," I say. "I'm a big fan." I specify, unnecessarily, "Of his work."

"That's very kind of you," Hayden says, before lowering himself stiffly back into his chair.

"Sit, sit," Margaret says, waving toward the open chair across from Hayden. As I take a seat, she asks, "What would you like to drink? Jodi's an excellent bartender."

"Oh, I'm good with water," I say.

This seems to displease both Margaret and Jodi.

"Don't deny a gal a chance to show some Southern hospitality," Margaret says. "At least have some sweet tea or something."

I look toward Jodi. "Coffee?" I say. "Decaf if you have it, regular otherwise?"

She nods and disappears back down the path, leaving the three of us to settle awkwardly around the table.

"So!" Margaret folds her hands together and slides her elbows onto the table. "I'm betting you two are wondering what exactly is going on. Well, you anyway, Alice. I was just telling Hayden here what I'm thinking."

Hayden here takes an extremely terse sip from his water glass, eschewing the dark cocktail also sitting in front of him.

"I am a little surprised," I admit.

"I know, I know," she says. "I tried to make a quick decision, believe me, but I kept thinking about what you said, Alice."

"What *I* said?" I say.

"This only works if it's with someone I completely trust." She shrugs. "And seeing as how I'm not the most trusting gal, determining who that might be will take some time."

I cast a glance toward Hayden. He's staring at his water, as if he's trying to make the glass shatter with only his brain.

With a quick clearing of my throat, I look back to Margaret. "That completely makes sense. We should spend a few more days getting to know each other before you commit—"

"A month," she says.

"A *month*," Hayden and I say in unison.

She smiles cheerily, but the expression flickers when she reads something in my face. "Now, don't worry," she cries. "I'll pay you both for your time, of course. Jodi's inside working on some paperwork for you two to sign." I look to Hayden again, take in his frown and the tension in his brow.

"I'm still not sure I'm following," I admit.

"It's like this." Margaret sips from her frosted martini glass before going on. "I'll pay you both, for the month, and provide a reasonable housing stipend. Jodi can send first offers to you or your agents, as you prefer. I'll negotiate within reason, and in the end, you'll both be paid the same. You'll sign NDAs, and I'll meet with each of you throughout the month. At the end, you show me what you've got so far. I choose one of you to do the book with, and we go off and sell it to the highest bidder."

"Ms. Ives," Hayden begins.

"Margaret," she says, with a wave of her hand. "Just Margaret. Or Irene. That's what everyone around here knows me as. Swapped my first and last initials. Guess I should've waited until *after* the NDAs to cop to that."

She winks at me, and some of my unease about this arrangement fritters off, as if by magic.

"Don't you think it would be easier to just—"

"Maybe," Margaret cuts him off, smiling all the time. "But if you want something done right, you don't go with easy. I've thought about it, and this is how I want to do it."

"And what if one of us just bows out?" he asks.

She stiffens at this, the humor leaching from her eyes. "Well, I'm not just going to choose someone by default. I want options. So if one of you drops out—which is of course your prerogative—I'm still going to finish this monthlong trial with the other, before committing to anything. If I like what you've done, we'll go from there."

"So you're saying," Hayden bites out, "that we could both put a month of work into this, and you might not even decide to do the book?"

I'm surprised by how blunt he's being, bordering on combative, but the gleam returns to Margaret's eye and the corners of her naturally pink lips turn up. "That's the deal."

For the first time since I sat down, his eyes flash to me. "All right" is all he says. Not a word more, but somehow his tone makes it evident what he means: not *All right, I understand* or *All right, I'll consider it*, but *All right, I'm in*.

Margaret's smile widens as she spins toward me. "Miss Alice, what do you think?"

I think it through, ask myself whether there's any reason *not* to stick around a few weeks and shoot my shot.

Who am I kidding?

I would've said yes even if she *wasn't* paying. I would've drained my savings and put my job at *The Scratch* on the line and stood on my head while doing the YMCA with my legs if she asked.

I would've done just about anything for this opportunity.

"I'm in," I tell her.

She claps her hands together. "Wonderful! This calls for a toast!" She hefts her martini glass into the air. Hayden, visibly skeptical, lifts his rocks glass to join her, and right as I'm about to point out that I don't *have* a drink yet, Jodi drifts out of the shadows to set a tray down on the table.

A silver coffeepot. A steaming mug. A saucer of creamer and a little white bowl of brown sugar cubes. And next to it, a stack of tabbed documents.

Contracts.

I take my mug and lightly clink it against Margaret's and Hayden's cups.

Margaret lets out a refreshed sigh after she sips. "Now," she says, "who's hungry?"

• • •

AFTER DESSERT—LEMON meringue pie—Margaret is the one to walk Hayden and me back through the house to the front door. Only a couple of lamps are still on, and there's no sign of Jodi, lending a bit more credence to my theory that she's on the clock when she's at Margaret's.

"Now, you've both got your paperwork?" she double-checks as she opens the door for us.

"Yep!" I brandish the folder she gave me, and Hayden simply nods. He barely spoke at dinner either, just sort of glowered at whatever he was eating. I don't know if it was *my* presence, or if this is how he always is, but it's hard to imagine a man like *this* coaxing Len Stirling's breathtaking, heart-squeezing story out of him, let alone finessing it into the beautiful version I read.

Then again, I know better than most that you can rarely tell who a person really is, or what they're going through, just from looking at the surface of things.

For all I know, Hayden came straight to dinner from getting unwelcome personal news or arrived on Little Crescent straight off a breakup. In my experience, it's best to give people the benefit of the doubt.

"And your pie?" Margaret asks.

Now both Hayden and I lift our little Tupperware containers of leftover fluffy meringue in confirmation.

"Well then," she says with a wink. "My people will be in touch."

"I can't wait!" I tell her, going in for a hug before I can think better of it.

Luckily, she reciprocates with a tight squeeze across my back. "More to come, more to come," she promises, then turns, with her arms wide, to hug Hayden. Only, he's already lifted his hand to shake hers.

She laughs a little, but takes it warmly, between both palms. "You two get home safe," she says. Then: "Where are you staying?"

"The Grande Lucia," I say.

Hayden's eyes cut sideways toward mine, his mouth twisting down for a brief moment before he faces Margaret again. "Grande Lucia," he bites out.

"Oh, good!" she says. "Glad you won't be far from a friend, if you need one."

I flash Hayden a smile. He doesn't look over.

"Anyway," I say brightly, "we'll get out of your hair."

"And you get that paperwork back to me, so we can get started!" She ushers us through the front door and waves as we make our way down the path toward the road, so I wave over my shoulder every few feet or so, a game of Southern Hospitality Chicken, both of us waiting to see who cracks first.

Hayden, meanwhile, is stalking ahead, eyes on the prize (the prize being getting the hell away from me, apparently).

I throw one last wave over my shoulder as I follow the bend in the path that leads to the gate.

Hayden has left it open for me, and I hurry after him to the quiet, moonlit country road beyond. "So," I say, "should we talk schedule?"

"Schedule?" He doesn't slow his pace.

I jog to catch up with him by our cars, his parked in front of mine.

"I was thinking we could divvy the days up, so you work with her Monday through Wednesday, and I take Thursday to Saturday."

He stops and faces me so suddenly I nearly collide with his chest. Instead, I screech to a halt close enough that I have to tip my head up to meet his eyes. "Then you would get the weekend and I'd only get weekdays."

"Okay," I say. "Then I'll take Monday through Wednesday, and you take Thursday through Saturday."

"Then *you* only have weekdays," he points out.

I laugh. "And that's a problem for you?"

"I assume you're still writing for *The Scratch*, and I'll need time for my freelance work. We'll both need some weekdays free," he says. "Plus, to get a full picture of a subject, you'll need a more complete view of her schedule."

I feel my brow inch up toward my bangs. "So, what, you're looking out for me? Instead of just taking the upper hand?"

Just more proof that there's always more to people than what you see first.

He rolls his eyes and turns away from me, stalking toward his car. "Trust me," he calls as he pauses to unlock his car door, nothing but a huge shadow against the moonlight, "I don't need an upper hand."

5

DESPITE BEING IN his car with the door shut, headlights on, and engine purring, Hayden doesn't speed away until I'm in my car with the door locked.

Maybe he actively doesn't want me to get murdered on a dark country road out by the marsh, or maybe it's just coincidence, but I'm choosing to be positive.

He can't be as bad as he seems. And even if he is, it's not like we'll be spending time together.

I roll my windows down and pull away from Margaret's house, listening to the soothing hum and murmur of a Georgia night.

Briefly, I consider calling my mom to let her know the news. But it's after ten, and she's always been an early bird. Besides, it's probably best to wait until I see how things shake out. I'll let her know I'm close by for work, schedule a time to visit her, but wait to divulge anything else until I know which way the scales are tipping.

I glide back onto the mostly empty four-lane road that connects the mainland to Little Crescent and slow to a stop at a red light. Hayden's in the next car over. He notices me too. I wave. He frowns.

The light turns green and we both pull through.

It feels like we're both trying to *not* drive side by side, but the stoplights keep foiling us. We pass Little Croissant and the other shops, and I get into the lane behind him so at least we aren't taking turns passing each other anymore.

At the Main Street intersection, I follow him through a right turn back toward tourist town and into the parking lot of the Grande Lucia Resort.

He turns left down an aisle, so I turn right. In the end, we wind up parking three spaces apart.

He takes the same staircase that *I've* been taking to and from my room.

I slow my pace, but surprisingly, he pauses halfway up the first set of steps when he realizes I'm behind him.

Not only does he pause, he actually *turns* toward me and makes eye contact. Huge progress for us. Friendship bracelets incoming, surely.

"Monday, Wednesday, Friday," he grunts.

"Good days," I say.

"Or," he says, "Tuesday, Thursday, Saturday. You choose which you want. You'll be able to spend Friday or Saturday evening with her that way, if you want, and we'll either alternate Sundays or take them off, depending on what she prefers."

I stop on the same step as him, considering the plan. "When would we start?"

"I plan to get all of this"—he lifts the paperwork—"wrapped up tomorrow. Friday and Saturday can be our first research days."

"How did you find her?" I ask.

His brow knits at the question. "I'm not telling you that."

"Really?" I ask. "Why?"

"Because you don't need to know," he says.

"I'll tell you how *I* found her," I say, dangling the offer like a carrot.

"I'm not interested." He resumes climbing, and I follow.

We reach the first-floor landing and both keep going. "You're already here," I point out. "Knowing how I got here doesn't do you any good. Just like *you* telling *me* how *you* found out about Margaret wouldn't give *me* any kind of edge."

"I really don't see why you care," he says.

"I'm curious," I say. "It wasn't easy figuring this out."

He casts me a suspicious sidelong glance as we reach the second landing. "So you're impressed," he says dryly.

I ask, "Is that so hard for you to believe?"

He snorts and goes back to staring straight ahead as we climb. "You're doing it again," he grumbles without looking over at me.

"What?" I ask.

"The maniacal smiling," he says.

That surprises a laugh out of me. "I'm not sure how you can tell. You're not even looking at me."

That earns me a dart of his eyes to mine. "And yet I see now I was right."

"It's just exciting," I say.

"This breakneck race up the stairs?" he deadpans.

"Working with Margaret," I reply. "You have to be a *little* excited, somewhere inside that block of marble."

"I wouldn't call *not* getting a job *exciting* to me, personally, no," he grumbles.

"But you're in the running," I say.

"Yes," he says. "And so are you."

"Right," I say. "Thus the *excitement*. Can you imagine the stories she has to tell? She's met *everyone*. She's been *everywhere*. This is the job of a lifetime."

"I'm aware of that," he says. "Thus my irritation at being strung along for a month before even finding out whether I have it."

We reach the third of four floors, and he hesitates a moment, waiting to see which way I'm going. I step off the landing onto the walkway. With a sigh, he follows.

"What are the odds?" I say as we fall into step, side by side.

He doesn't seem amused. That's okay. I'm amused enough for the both of us.

He pauses at one of the pale blue doors, something like relief seeping into his bold features. "This is me," he says.

"Ah," I say, walking past him to the very next door. My room.

"You're kidding," he says.

"I'm not," I say. "Sorry in advance. I've been told I snore."

He shakes his head, muttering to himself, "Of course you do," as he fishes his room key out of his back pocket.

"Tuesday, Thursday, Saturday," I say.

His eyes slice back to me, his hand stilling on the doorknob.

"If it really doesn't matter to you," I begin, "I'll take Tuesday, Thursday, Saturday."

He looks at me silently for another moment, then gives one slow nod. "In case I don't see you again, then . . ."

"It was nice meeting me?" I guess.

The corners of his mouth twitch downward. "*Enjoy your stay, Alice*," he corrects me.

It's the first time he's said my name, and for some reason it feels like a win.

As he steps into his room, I can't help but call out, "Sweet dreams, Hayden! Use a white noise app!"

His only reply, as the door swings shut, is a grunt.

Or maybe . . . surely it wasn't a *laugh*.

I unlock my door and go inside, ready to scour my list of furnished rentals.

For Hayden Anderson's sake, I'll shift my search far away from the Grande Lucia Resort.

At least, as far as you can reasonably go on a six-square-mile island.

• • •

I SLEEP BADLY and wake up early. It's dark out, but I can't seem to grab hold of the tail end of sleep as it escapes from me, so I might as well get up and fill my body with coffee.

I pull on shorts and a tank top, then grab my laptop bag and step out into the blue morning, my arms and legs prickling from the sea breeze.

The roads aren't as empty as they were last night—there are locals heading into work and tourists driving down to stake their claim at the beach before things get too hectic—but the world feels quiet and still, and when I pull into the little enclave of shops back toward the mainland and Margaret's street, the lot is sparsely populated. Most of the shops on the left are shut tight. All the restaurants on the right, aside from Little Croissant, also sit dark and empty, the striped umbrellas over the patio tables snapped closed.

There's only one customer in front of me, a man with a horseshoe pattern of white hair around an otherwise bald head. The back of his salmon-pink T-shirt reads *I Got My Sea Legs at FISH BOWL LITTLE CRESCENT ISLAND*, complete with the street address, in smaller font, just below it.

"*Captain Cecil?*" I say, recognition hitting me.

The older gentleman turns around, revealing a gap-toothed smile. "Well, hi there!"

"I'm glad I ran into you," I tell him. "I wanted to thank you for the drink the other night."

"Pretty tasty, huh?" he asks.

"Extremely," I agree.

The barista waves the good captain up to the window to order, but I head him off. "Let me get this for you."

His wispy, curly gray brows pinch together. "Now, why on earth would I do that?"

"To make a visitor very happy?" I say.

He chuckles. "Well, can't rightly argue with that."

"I should hope not."

He steps up to order: "One large iced brown sugar and cinnamon latte with whipped cream on top, please."

The barista nods and scribbles CAPN on one of the to-go cups, before turning to me.

"Same thing," I say, "but no whipped cream, please."

"I'll take hers," Cecil puts in.

"Oh! And a large iced green tea," I add on a whim.

"You got it," the barista tells us, and I hand my card over to pay, punching the tip into the tablet when he swivels it toward me.

"So," Cecil says as I step back to join him. "What's a gal like you doing flying solo on our little island?"

"I'm here for work," I tell him.

He frowns at this. "Work? This is the wrong place for that!"

"Well, I love my work," I say. "So it's also kind of *for pleasure*."

"And what is it you do?" he asks. Then: "Actually, who is it you *are*? You seem to know my name, but I don't recall yours."

"Oh! Sheri told me who you were," I say, holding my hand out to shake his. "I'm Alice. And I'm a writer."

"Charmed to meet you, Alice the Writer," he says, pumping my arm twice before dropping my hand.

"Same to you," I agree.

"And what is it that you write? Is our fine home to be the locale for a murder mystery?" He seems delighted by the thought.

"No, no. At least not one written by me. I'm a journalist."

He whistles through his two front teeth. "How about that. An article about Little Crescent. Finally getting our due."

I don't correct him. I gave the NDA a quick read last night before sending it off to my lawyer (read: friend from college, who is now a lawyer), and while I'm not confident I understand the full scope of it, I *am* fairly sure Margaret wouldn't appreciate having her presence on the island revealed before she's even agreed to do the book.

"We had one once, you know," he says. "Travel journalist from *Rest and Relaxation*. But frankly, she wrote more about her travel companion than she did about us."

"Two iced brown sugar cinnamon lattes," another barista calls from the next window over. "One iced green tea."

Cecil and I step up to collect our respective drinks. "You extra thirsty?" he asks, eyeing the tea. "Or are you meeting someone?"

"Meeting someone," I say, then add, "maybe. I'm not sure." If Hayden happens to run past again, I'll give it to him. If not, I'll drop it by his room after.

Cecil frowns. "Alice! If you have to wonder whether he'll show, he's not worth it! That's my two cents, not that you asked."

I feel myself smiling. He's way older than my dad was, but there's still something in this man that reminds me of my father. The confident but relaxed posture, or the barrel chest.

I appreciate the little ache that sends through my throat, the reminder of how lucky I was to have my family, how lucky I've always been. "I'll definitely keep that in mind."

"Well, I'm afraid I've got a long day ahead of me," Cecil says, fishing his wallet out of his pocket. "But if you need anything while you're around, here's my info." He tucks a business card between my fingers and the cup of coffee.

"Thanks! I really appreciate that," I tell him.

He waves me off as he heads toward the steps down to the dirt drive. "And, Alice?" he shouts over his shoulder.

"Yeah?"

"Don't wait *too* long." He juts his chin meaningfully toward the green tea.

I lift it in salute to the captain, and he chuckles as he shuffles off.

I carry both cups down to the stone patio off the side of the platform, setting them on a wrought iron table nestled between a bunch of lush potted plants. A matching wrought iron gate rings the patio, ivy and kudzu crawling over it to give the space an enchanted feeling.

A couple of women in workout gear chat over croissants at a table in the far corner, and once I set my laptop up, I go back to the window to order two myself.

The coffee shop has decent Wi-Fi, so I pull up all of my bookmarked Margaret Ives sites as well as my preliminary notes document as I nibble on the pastry, dividing up the almond center bits so that each bite is the perfect ratio of buttery to sweet.

Assuming my lawyer friend and my agent both give their approval in the next two days, I should be able to start interviewing Margaret by Saturday, and I want to be prepared.

I also fire off an update to my group chat, Itchy Bitches, with my closest friends from *The Scratch*. The last message was from Priya, last night, a blurry bar selfie, her raven hair twisted into a topknot and a guy sitting behind her with the caption Does he look like Pedro Pascal?? (I've had five beers.)

The message came in after two a.m., and no one's replied, though both Bianca and Cillian thumbs-upped the picture in apparent approval.

His face is barely visible, I point out, but I can tell he has a certain je ne sais quoi.

Then, in a separate message, I add, BTW M agreed to give me a shot. One month audition, basically.

HELL YEAH, Bianca writes a few minutes later. Though you should probably tell your editor . . .

Putting it in a formal email rn, Ms. Ribeiro, I write back, then pull up my inbox on my computer. I type *bribeiro@thescratch.com* into the *To* field to make my formal request. I'll still be working here, just mostly on stories that can be done remotely, by phone and email. Nothing too intensive.

After I send the email, I go back to the group chat.

Unfortunately, I say, there's another writer auditioning too. Hayden Anderson.

Priya sends a picture of herself still in bed, squinting, last night's makeup blurred around her eyes. Someone tell my editor I'm too sick to come into work today.

Should've thought of that before you sent the five beers text to her, Bianca points out.

Cillian replies to my text: I've met him. Rather unpleasant sort, isn't he?

I frown. Rather unpleasant sort? Didn't realize I was texting a regency era gentleman.

What? Cillian says. He IS unpleasant. Hot though. SAD.

I don't think he's that bad, I reply.

LOL, Cillian replies. Duh.

Meaning? I say.

You like everyone, Priya says.

I take a long sip of my latte. Once again, Cecil didn't steer me wrong. It's delicious. I'm just saying, I type out, he probably has his reasons for being the way he is. People usually do.

Bianca and Cillian both like the text, and Priya says, Hot people are usually somewhat unpleasant. They don't have to play by the rules. Hotness is wasted on the hot. Like me!

As a pleasant hot person, Cillian says, I'm offended by this.

Putting you on Do Not Disturb to get some work done, but love you all. I silence my phone, put my head down, and pore over my notes, adding thoughts as I go.

After about thirty minutes, though, my laptop battery is on its last legs. By then the sun is all the way up, the back of my neck beginning to sweat and tingle with an oncoming burn, so I pack my stuff up and head back to the hotel. Late last night, I managed to book a place for the month, but it's not available until tomorrow, so I've got one more night at the Grande Lucia.

One more night as Hayden Anderson's neighbor, which I'm sure he'll be relieved to know.

Rather than interrupt his morning by knocking on his door, I leave his green tea and the paper bag with his croissant outside his door, then let myself into my own room.

I plug my computer in to charge, then take a scorching shower, mostly because my bangs are too greasy for dry shampoo to have any shot.

Afterward, I towel dry my hair, my bangs falling into messy pieces across my forehead, and slather myself in sunscreen before getting dressed. Since this is, ostensibly, one of my last free days before I dive into work, I decide I might as well do something fun. Like go to the beach or rent a bike and ride around the island. I put on my bathing suit, just in case, and pull on a floral yellow-and-pink romper with a sixties-style collar, along with the Simon Miller platform sandals Priya gave me for my birthday.

If my mom could see this outfit, she'd faint. When I was a teenager, she'd insisted that, because I was tall, everything looked shorter on me than on other girls, and while she was very likely right, I'd always so desperately wanted to be allowed to dress like the other girls I went to school with, which is probably why I still style myself, in Bianca's words, *like a little scamp*, or as Cillian put it, *like a 1990s animated Nickelodeon teenager.*

Both compliments, in my opinion.

I leave my laptop behind but slide my notepad into my bag along with my sunglasses before stepping out onto the walkway.

I'm already past Hayden's door when I notice the green tea and croissant still sitting there.

I backtrack, check the time on my phone. Surely he's up by now.

For a second, anxiety spikes through me. I check the long-dormant impulse to panic. For the most part, I'm grateful for the things my childhood gave me—optimism, empathy, an appreciation for life—but the unease that still comes from a shut door isn't one of them.

The urgent ping of *did something happen*, and the thought that always follows: *What if I'm too late this time?*

I shake myself. Hayden is *not* my sister. I have no reason to suspect he might not be okay, and furthermore, no reason to feel responsible for his well-being.

Still, I find myself knocking on his door, needing to be sure he's all right.

When there's no immediate reply, the anxiety deepens.

Never mind that he could be out running, or at lunch, or anywhere else on the island.

I just have a *feeling* he's the sort to stick to the same basic schedule every day, and if that's the case, he should've been back from his run by now.

I pound again. "Hayden?" I shout.

I hear a muffled grunt from deep within the room, and instantly something in me relaxes.

I mean, for all I know, he's duct-taped to a chair inside, but that *sounded* like a fairly typical Hayden grunt, from what I've witnessed so far.

"Grunt twice if you're okay!" I shout.

Instead, I hear the rattle of the dead bolt, and then the door swings open.

"Is there a fire?" he asks.

I can't answer immediately. I'm focused on prying my eyes off the bare expanse of chest at face level to look up into Hayden Anderson's very nonplussed expression.

6

I SWALLOW THE lump of heat that's risen to the back of my throat. Now that I know he's fine, I'm embarrassed.

Now that I see he clearly responded to my pounding by running straight from the shower to the front door, a towel wrapped around his waist and a scowl set deep into his brow and jaw, I'm humiliated.

My whole body feels hot and tingly, that burgeoning sunburn feeling times a hundred.

"Alice?" His expression wavers. "Is everything okay?"

I step back abruptly from him and bend to grab the tea and croissant off the ground, holding them out at arm's length. "Didn't you see these when you got back from your run?"

His gaze dips, then rebounds to my face. "Yes?"

I balk. "Then why didn't you take them?"

"Because I didn't know where they came from," he says, "and I'm not in the habit of eating and drinking things I find on the ground."

I feel myself wilting. "I brought them for you."

His dark brows flick upward, the light catching his eyes for a second, turning his irises the color of whipped coffee. Despite the latte sitting in my stomach, it sends a burst of thirst across my tongue.

He clears his throat. "I didn't realize." He reaches out one hand to accept the cup and bag from me, his other still clutching the towel against his damp hip.

Which, of their own accord, my eyes drop to, before snapping back to his face.

"Thank you," he says.

"No problem," I force out, keeping my eyes pointedly *not* on his water-speckled chest. Or the rivulets running from the dark hair tucked behind his ears down his neck. Or his stomach and hips and legs and towel and whatever's under the towel and— "Anyway! Today's our last day as neighbors. I booked my rental for the month."

He opens his mouth as if to say something, then closes it on a nod.

"Sorry again, if my snoring kept you up," I say.

He hesitates before answering. "It was actually sort of soothing."

I guffaw. "Are you serious? You could hear it through the wall?"

He lifts one shoulder, my eye tracking the motion, my body impolitely informing me that I might have a shoulder fetish. "I'm a light sleeper," he says. "Don't take it personally."

"Oh, I try to take almost nothing personally," I tell him. "I actually could probably afford to take a little *more* personally."

The corners of his mouth twitch, and I have no idea whether it's a gesture toward a smile or a grimace.

I take a half step back. "Anyway, in case I don't see you again . . ."

"It was nice meeting me?" he says, parroting my words from last night, with one brow hooking upward.

I break into a grin. "Enjoy your stay."

As I walk away, his low thunder roll of a voice says, "Nice meeting you too, Alice."

That, I decide, is *definitely* a win.

• • •

THAT NIGHT, I awake to a screech. To flashing lights. To sheer confusion.

I jolt away from the sound and half tumble out of bed, bleary eyes darting around the dark room.

On the wall behind the bed, a mounted device flashes and blares, alternating strobes of red and white streaking across the room. My first thought is *ambulance*. My second is *Audrey!*

My sister. Pain spears through my chest right alongside the panic, and then I piece my surroundings together.

Fire alarm, I realize.

You wouldn't think that would trigger such a wave of relief in me, but it does. My chest loosens, my heart very gradually slowing as I clamber to my feet and snatch my laptop and phone from the side table on my way to the door.

I step into my sandals, grab my room key, and dart out onto the walkway, joining the crowd of sleepy kids and grumpy adults stumbling toward the stairs.

The night is sticky and warm as we make our way down to the parking lot, hotel staff spilling out from the lobby, a manager shouting for us to "REMAIN CALM. THE FIRE DEPARTMENT WILL BE HERE SHORTLY."

I join a group of guests standing on the sidewalk. With my laptop tucked under my arm, I check the time on my phone—just before four a.m.

Someone stumbles into me, and I look up to find a man about ten or fifteen years older than I am, swaying on the spot, his red-rimmed eyes fixed dully on me.

I reach out to steady him. "Are you okay?"

His toothy grin blasts me with the smell of liquor. He's drunk, not simply tired. "Better now, baby." His gaze drips down me like slime.

I'm wearing a blue nightgown from the sixties, loose and long enough to cover my knees, but he manages to make me feel like I'm naked, and not in a good way.

I try to step back, but he's latched on to my elbow now. He seems more solid, steady, than I first thought. "I think we might be neighbors," he says, squinting at me. "What room are you in?"

"I . . ." I look uncertainly over my shoulder, hoping for a friendly face, or even just proof that there's anyone else watching, but no one's looking this way. "I don't remember."

His expression darkens, the smile melting off his face. "You don't *remember*?"

"There you are," says a low, cool voice behind me.

I spin around, the drunk man's grip loosening on my arm but not entirely letting go.

Hayden towers over me, his face stony. "Hi!" I try to signal with my eyes what's going on. I'm not sure whether it's working, because Hayden's face remains exactly the same.

He turns toward the interloper as he asks, "Who's your friend?"

"He's our neighbor, I guess," I say.

"I thought you were here alone," the man says, either too drunk or too clueless to realize how horrifying that is to hear, as a woman who is, in fact, frequently traveling alone.

I open my mouth to try to excuse Hayden and me from the conversation, but Hayden's faster: "Nope." He curls an arm loosely around my waist. "Not alone."

The man's face slackens, his hand finally sliding off my arm. "You should've said so," he slurs at me irritably.

Yes, I'm the one at fault here.

I shrug like, *Whaddya gonna do?*

"If you'll excuse us," Hayden says, "I think we'll take this break from our room as a chance to go get breakfast."

The man swats an annoyed hand in our direction as Hayden turns and steers me deeper into the parking lot, his arm falling away.

"Thank you," I say. "I'm really bad at that."

His gaze lances over his shoulder at me. "Bad at what?"

"Avoiding drunk people," I say. "Avoiding creepy people. Not starting conversations with strangers. Getting *out* of conversations with strangers. You name it."

The corners of his mouth tighten. He stops beside the passenger door of his rental car. I look back the way we came, and find our inebriated friend leaned at a nearly forty-five-degree angle against a tree.

"If we give it five minutes, he'll be asleep and we can go back and wait with everyone else," I say.

Hayden's frown deepens.

"I mean, not that you have to stay with me!" I add. "Honestly, now that I know his whole deal, I'm fine. I just won't engage again. I know we already said our farewells this morning, so."

His head tilts like he's puzzling over something. "I was serious, about going to get breakfast. If you want to join."

"It's four a.m.," I point out.

"These things always take forever, even when they're false alarms," he says. "We'll be out here at least another hour. Might as well go somewhere more comfortable."

"But it's *four a.m.*," I repeat.

"So you're not hungry?"

"I'm famished," I say, "but nothing will be open."

He turns and unlocks the passenger door. "Something," he says, "is always open."

HAYDEN PUNCHES RAY'S Diner into his GPS once we're settled in the car. It's twenty-five minutes away, back on the mainland.

"Maybe I should've mentioned," he says, "the *something* that's open is toward Savannah. Closest thing I could find. That a problem?"

I shrug. "Not for me. Like you said, these things always take forever anyway. But if you wanted to go back to sleep—"

"I can never go back to sleep once I get up," he tells me, starting the car. "Thus why I know about Ray's Diner."

When we get there, a few trucks and cars are already littered throughout the lot. Bells tinkle over the door as we let ourselves in.

A server in a mint-green dress and apron is mopping between the tables, and oldies play quietly over the crackly speakers. A grizzly bearded man looks over at us, noticing that we're in pajamas—or rather, *I* am; Hayden's in black sweats and a white T-shirt, so he's more discreet—but then goes back to eating his eggs.

The server looks up from mopping as we pass and nods a greeting. "Be right with ya," she promises, and we settle into the corner booth.

"You're a real corner-booth guy," I say.

His brows pinch. "What?"

"You took the corner booth at Fish Bowl too."

"The corner booth is objectively the best booth."

"Says who?" I ask.

He shrugs. "I don't know. No one needs to say it. It's obvious."

I gesture toward the other few diners, most of them likely long haulers or people getting off third shift. "None of them chose this booth."

"It was probably occupied when they got here," he says, unfolding one large plasticky menu and sliding another across the Formica tabletop toward me.

"How many times have you been here since you got to town?" I ask.

"Four," he says, not missing a beat. "Counting today."

"And how many of those times have you scored this booth?" I ask.

His eyes slowly peel up from the menu to meet mine. "You're doing it again."

"Doing what?"

"Smiling like you've just walked into a surprise birthday party," he says. "When almost nothing is happening."

"Something *is* happening," I counter. "I'm getting to know your idiosyncrasies."

"*My* idiosyncrasies?" He scoffs a little, sets the menu down. "You're the one who sleeps in an *I Dream of Jeannie* costume."

I devolve into laughter at that.

The server sidles up, her notepad ready and waiting. "Get ya anything to drink?"

"Coffee," he says, then looks to me.

"Me too."

"What about food? Ya ready to order?" she asks us.

Hayden tosses another quick look my way.

"I can be," I promise, flipping open the proportionally gigantic menu.

"Egg whites, wheat toast, and the seasonal fruit, please," he tells her, and her large brown eyes swivel to me next.

"Peaches and cream French toast," I tell her.

"Have that right out for ya." She walks away.

"Did you notice she never starts speaking at the *beginning* of the sentence?" he asks, ducking his head and dropping his voice.

I mirror his posture. "How many times did you get the corner booth, Hayden?"

His lips twitch downward. "If you want to move tables—"

"Oh, *I* don't want to move tables," I say. "I'm just fascinated by the way you see the world."

He leans back against the shiny pink banquette. "It's the most protected seat in the house. You have a view of every entrance and exit."

"You're by the toilets," I add.

"You can see the server, anywhere in the restaurant, if you need to flag them down."

"You're by the toilets," I say.

"Or alternately, if I sat where *you're* sitting, no one would be able to see my face without trying pretty hard," he says.

"You're by the toilets," I say, "and also, are you on the run?"

"I'm private," he says.

"And I'm the one with the idiosyncrasies," I tease.

One of his brows arches upward. He opens his mouth to retort, then shuts it again as our server reappears, flipping our mugs right side up and filling them from the steaming pot in her hand.

"Thank you," Hayden says stiffly.

"'S no problem at all, sweetie." She retreats again, pausing at the counter to top off the bearded man's mug.

Hayden hesitates, considering something for a while, and I fight every impulse to rush him. He really does remind me of some huge, wild animal. Not *dangerous*, but skittish.

"I grew up in a sort of . . . public family," he settles on.

Now I can't help it: I lean forward eagerly. "Please tell me the Andersons had a reality show."

He cracks a smile. At least I *think* it's a smile. It could also be a wince. "Not *that* public. My dad was the mayor."

"The mayor," I repeat. "The mayor of Indiana!"

"Well, since states don't have mayors," he says, "no. But the mayor of a small town *in* Indiana, yeah."

I scoot to the edge of my seat, only to remember that our combined height makes such an arrangement inadvisable. Instead, I pull my legs up onto the bench and sit cross-legged, as far forward against the table as I can. "So you learned to be private from them?"

"No," he says. "I learned to be *perfect* from them."

I must be making a face—probably another *is this a surprise party, just for me?* smile of delight, because what he's just said is so utterly ridiculous.

"I didn't say I still *do* it," he says.

I stifle a laugh.

"Oh, come on." He scoots forward now, our knees knocking even with my adjusted posture. "I'm not so bad that you can't *imagine* me making a good impression."

"I didn't say you were bad at all!" I cry. "But no one's perfect."

"Oh, trust me," he says. "My dad is. And my brother."

"Is your brother the mayor now?" I ask.

"Worse," Hayden tells me. "Louis is the local pediatrician. And his wife is the head of the school board."

Another cackle of delight escapes me.

"Unless I joined the Peace Corps," he says, "I was never going to live up to that."

"Okay, well, *one*," I begin, holding up a finger, "you won a fucking Pulitzer. I doubt they're wringing their hands over how to shepherd the Anderson family black sheep back onto the right path."

"Maybe not now," he allows, "but for the ten years prior, yeah, I'm pretty sure they were."

"And two," I cut in, "that's pretty much a perfect segue into the fact that my sister actually, literally is in the Peace Corps."

He stares at me. "You're kidding."

Another round of exhausted giggles ripples through me. "I'm not. She's, like, helping combat food shortages in another country right now, and I'm—to quote my mother—'still doing that celeb gossip stuff.'"

His forehead wrinkles. "But you don't write celebrity gossip."

"Right, but what I *do* write is close enough that I can assure you, my mother will never feel a pressing need to understand the difference."

He shakes his head, evidently confused. "But she reads your work."

Inside my chest, it feels like a pinprick puncturing a balloon. "No, not really. I mean, the first couple pieces when I got the job, yeah. But it's just 'not really her thing.' And I get it. I mean, I'd actually probably prefer she *not* read it, rather than force herself to and then pretend, badly, that she liked it."

"*The Scratch* is a prestigious outlet," he says. "They pay well and have great subscription numbers."

I shrug. "It's just not her thing. I get it."

He studies me for a moment, so intensely that he—and frankly, I—jump when our server returns to plop our plates in front of us.

"Hot, so be careful," she says, and then she's gone again.

I clear my throat. "So," I say, meeting Hayden's gaze once more. "Are you excited for your first interview with Margaret?"

He shakes his head.

"You're *not*?" I say.

"No," he says. "I mean, don't ask that."

"Why not?" I press.

"Because I'm not going to talk about it with you," he says.

I roll my eyes, slide my feet back down to the floor, scooting forward again. My knees wind up caged in by his, but I don't retreat.

"What do you possibly think I could *steal* from your answer to that question?"

He stabs his fork into his eggs and leans in too, his thighs pressing gently against mine in the process. He drops his voice to match my tone. "*Alice.*"

I feel a flutter of anticipation under my collarbone. "*Hayden,*" I say.

"I'm not going to answer that either," he says.

Then he takes a huge bite.

This round, I think, is a draw.

7

"I STILL CAN'T really believe we're doing this," I say on Saturday morning.

"Sitting in a living room, drinking mint tea?" Margaret teases, eyeing me through the steam lifting off the mug in her hands. "Alice, dear, I think you should aim higher."

She sits in the rattan chair across from the sofa where I'm perched, all the windows flung open and the smell of sun-warmed greenery drifting in toward us every time the wind blows, broken up by the occasional burst of brackishness from the marsh behind her property.

"Are you kidding?" I say. "This is my Everest. After this, I'll be ruined for celebrity profiles. I'll have to retire early or, like, get really into fixing up old cars or something. I honestly didn't think you'd agree to this."

"Then why'd you go to all the work of tracking me down?" she asks.

I shrug. "I had to try, at least."

She gently sets her mug on the glass-topped table between us, a curious gleam in her blue eyes. "Do you remember what you said? In that last voicemail you left me, before I finally called you back?"

I shake my head. I'd called so many dozens of artists selling work on small islands in Georgia before a post on the Not-So-Dead Celebrities message board pointed me to Little Crescent, and plenty more even once I'd homed in on the right island. They'd all denied being Margaret Ives, which I figured couldn't exactly rule them out. But she was the first to hang up as soon as the question was out of my mouth.

I hadn't called her back for a week. I'd been too afraid she'd block me right away. When I finally did, she sent my call to voicemail, and I left a short message, explaining who I was and why I wanted to talk to her.

I made myself wait three more days, and then I took one last swing: another voicemail, this one more an impassioned pitch than a question, because at that point, I was already sixty percent convinced I'd found the right person. She'd called me back nine days later and I'd almost thrown my phone out the window of the cab I was in, trying to answer it as fast as possible.

"Honestly, it's a blur," I say.

She says, "You told me you cried when you heard that Cosmo had died."

My face burns. "Did I really? God, I'm sorry. That was inappropriate."

She cracks a smile. "Inappropriate? I didn't think so. Curious? Exceptionally, seeing as how my husband had to have passed away at least thirty years before you were even born."

I set my mug aside. "Yeah, but I only found out right around my seventh birthday. My dad was a big music guy. He always used to listen to Cosmo Sinclair when we were making dinner. *Hearts on Fire* was my favorite."

"A great album," Margaret says proudly.

"When I turned seven, my parents let me have a birthday party. But my sister and I were homeschooled back then and didn't have many friends. So when my mom asked me who I wanted to invite, I said, 'Cosmo Sinclair.' And my parents, they just gave each other this look. Like, *Oh no*. They never lied to me. That was their policy. So when they made that face, it usually meant they were about to tell me bad news. So that's how I found out. And I was so sad about it."

"Sad that you'd never meet him?" Margaret says.

"Sad for *Peggy*," I say. "That was my favorite song on the album. 'Peggy All the Time.' And I don't know, I just knew it had to be true. That you couldn't write a love song like that if you hadn't found a once-in-a-lifetime love. And I didn't want her to have lost the person who gave her that."

Her gaze falls to her lap.

I wonder if I should stop, if I'm pushing too early on something too sore. But she's the one who brought it up, and if I'm going to be a witness to her story, I want her to know that I understand.

I clear my throat. "My parents were both journalists. And all they really read was nonfiction. Serious stuff, about politics and climate change and sociology. Stuff I had no interest in. But there was this one book my dad bought at a garage sale. An unauthorized biography."

Her eyes slice up to mine, and I swear I see something behind them close up, shutting me out. I understand why. But I keep going anyway: "*The Fall of the House of Ives*."

She stares at me, shoulders square, a pleasant and unconvincing smile hanging around her mouth.

"You were my dad's dream interview subject," I explain. "He mostly did political stuff, and you'd already stopped doing interviews way before he started reporting. But he loved your story, yours and Cosmo's, from his songs. And he always felt like there was so much more to it than what the press wrote about it.

"Anyway, even before I could read, I loved looking at the pictures in that biography he bought. I loved all your clothes and your shoes and your hats. You were so glamorous and my life had *no* glamour whatsoever. But it wasn't just that. You always looked . . . not just *happy*, but like you were delighted by the world. The rest of your family, they looked so serious and secretive, but you were just you. Bright and bold and full of life. Especially in the photos with your sister, and with Cosmo. And then when I got older, when I could read it . . . I *hated* that book."

A quiet laugh leaps out of her, her gaze softening. No, *glistening*. Her blue eyes have dampened, her lashes inky and dramatic.

A small laugh escapes me too. "Turns out my dad hated it too. He just didn't want to tell me and ruin it. But there was nothing to ruin. It was all conjecture and judgment and—and *recycled* tabloid headlines. There was this one line, in the chapter about your courthouse wedding, where Dove Franklin wrote that a body language expert suggested you were—"

"*Marching Cosmo to his death and he knew it*," she says quietly. "It wasn't just that they didn't believe he wanted to marry me. They also blamed me for what happened to him. My family's cursed, if you haven't heard." A shred of a heartbreaking smile flutters over her lips again.

I'd been planning to paraphrase the quote rather than lob it at her like a grenade. But hearing *her* say it outright leaves *me* feeling like my chest has been pierced. I swallow hard. "I looked at that picture, and I didn't understand how I could see something so different."

Her jaw muscles flex, and after a long beat, she says, "And what did you see?"

"I saw him trying to shield you," I say, "from everyone around you. And realizing he couldn't."

She blinks several times, her gaze dropping to her lap again.

For a moment, we're both silent. She clears her throat.

"Sorry," I say softly. "I didn't plan to start with anything quite that heavy."

"I asked," she replies, with a fragment of a shrug. "You answered. That's how interviews work, as far as I remember."

"Yes, but I'm not the one being interviewed," I remind her.

A bit of wryness seeps back into her half smile. "Oh, I don't know. I think it's only fair that I get to know you and Hayden too, if I'm going to be trotting out the family's map to all the buried bodies."

"And just to clarify," I say, "when you say 'buried bodies,' are we talking literal or metaphorical here?"

Her laugh is damp, but when she speaks, her voice is sure, clear, and bright again. "Why not both?" She leans forward over the table, where both my phone and my backup voice recorder are running, and enunciates clearly, "Let the record show that I winked." Which she does.

I lean forward too. "She did," I agree, "and then she dragged a finger across her throat like she was threatening me."

Margaret hoots out a laugh as she sits back into her chair. "So where were you thinking we'd start?"

"The beginning," I say. "I want to know what it was like to be born an Ives."

She takes another sip of tea before returning her mug to its place on the table, right between my phone and my recorder. "I'll be honest: When you told me you found me online, through those conspiracy theory websites, I figured you'd walk in here and kick off this interview with, *Margaret, did you have Cosmo cryogenically frozen to be revived at a later date?*"

"That *is* a popular one," I agree.

"So Jodi tells me," she replies.

"You never go looking?" I say. "To see what people are saying?"

She snorts. "You obviously didn't grow up in a family like mine. The trick is to try *not* to see what they're saying."

"I think it's safe to say *no one* grew up in a family like yours," I point out.

"No, I suppose not." Her eyes drift to where my bag sits at my ankles, and her head cocks, recognition writing itself across her face as she spots the book jutting out of it. "Can I see that?"

I half expect her to start tearing pages out of it and ripping them to shreds. But if that will help her feel comfortable opening up, so be it.

I pass *The Fall of the House of Ives* to her, and for several seconds, she flips through it in silence, her expression stern, until finally, a chortle leaps out of her, surprising me so badly that I jump in my chair.

She shakes her head to herself. "It's funny. My family was one of the first to figure out that it isn't *news* that sells. It's headlines. Half the time, people don't read a word past those big, splashy letters, and even if they do, the nuance isn't what they'll remember. It's the simple version that sticks. Simple and salacious, that's the winning combination."

"Clickbait," I say, "before the advent of *clicking*."

"More or less," she agrees. "That's what my family used to make themselves very rich—and like Dove Franklin says, *powerful* too. But in the end, it doesn't matter. Even if you're the one to build the monster, you're never going to be able to control it. It'll gladly eat you alive and floss with your bones, once it's finished with everyone else."

My chest squeezes as some of the crueler headlines I've read about Margaret and her family cycle through my mind. Her younger sister, Laura, had especially suffered at the hands of the press, during her preteen years when she'd put on some weight and gotten an unfortunate haircut—normal kid stuff that seemed so much worse when you juxtaposed her with her glamorous and austere family on red carpets and at ribbon cuttings and attending every other manner of highly publicized event.

Margaret, on the other hand, had been the media's darling. Until she wasn't.

"It must've been strange," I say, "growing up with all that attention on you."

She *almost* smiles. It just barely reaches the corners of her lips but goes not a millimeter further. "No one knows how 'normal' or 'strange' their own life is until they see the alternative. Life in the House of Ives was all I knew."

I must be making some kind of face, because one of her brows hooks sharply upward. "Whatever you're thinking," she says, "you don't have to worry about breaking me, Alice. I'm hard to shake."

My chest pinches. Of course she is. No one person survives everything she did *plus* years' worth of public rehashing of those sad and bizarre events without getting some grit, I'm sure.

"Noted," I say, but I don't push her to begin, even so. These interviews need to be a safe place for her. The only way to get a person's full, unfiltered story is to let them tell it to you when and how they want. The best stories are born when the words slip effortlessly from a subject's lips, rather than being painfully cranked out of them bit by bit.

She sets the book on the table, her shoulders squaring as she meets my eyes. "Okay, Alice. Let's start at the beginning."

And then she does.

The Story

THEIR VERSION: Lawrence Richard Ives made the family filthy rich. He was also a cold-blooded sociopath who may have murdered his business partner.

• • •

HER VERSION: It's not that they were *wrong* exactly. It's just that they're answering the wrong question.

Lawrence Richard Ives made the family rich. Who cares? That's not a story. It's an event.

Even the *how* isn't all that interesting. And yet countless writers over the last century have cataloged that information, again and again, like somehow it could add up to a full picture.

The what: The eighth-born son of two destitute farmers in Dillon Springs, Pennsylvania, makes a fortune prospecting out west.

The how: He spends every penny he makes on more land, more equipment, more smelting, more miners, more hotels in every soon-to-be-booming town along the trail of the so-called gold rush.

The interesting question, the interesting answer, is almost always the *why*.

That's why we read these celebrity tell-alls, isn't it? That's why we pore over cold cases. We want to understand *why* things happen. We want it all to make sense.

The reason Lawrence Richard Ives got rich wasn't because of a knack for business. It was because he was hungry. Because he was born in the harsh winter of 1830 on a failing farm, the eighth of ten children.

By adulthood, there would be only six.

The world is cruel and dangerous, and Lawrence learned this, death by death.

The worst was his younger brother, Dicky, lost in the woods one winter, taken by frostbite. Lawrence was only nine when it happened, but he felt responsible. That was how it worked in large families like his. Each sibling looked after the one who came along next.

He expected his mother and father to blame him, the way he blamed himself.

They didn't.

This was when Lawrence realized the awful truth. His parents hardly felt Dicky's loss, because they hardly knew him. Just as they hardly knew Lawrence. They were spread too thin, worked too hard. They were too *tired* to love.

The only people on this earth to whom Lawrence truly mattered—the only people who loved him as he loved them—were his younger brother and sister. And now one of them was gone, the other growing hungrier and gaunter by the day, the light seeping out of her large brown eyes, bit by precious bit.

He worried endlessly. If he let her down . . . if he lost her too, then what was the *point* of it all? All the hurt and pain that came with surviving would be for nothing if he couldn't keep her safe.

Lawrence was nineteen the first time he heard about the gold, from a young local miner named Thomas Dougherty. About places out west where you couldn't dig three feet without striking metal. About cities that were always warm, and men who'd never be hungry or cold again.

He tried to brush the stories off.

Fantasy, he told himself. A word that had no purpose in his world.

During the day, he was a pragmatist. At night, though, he dreamed.

Of gold. Of finding it in the fallow fields and the collapsing barn, and then, finally, in the sunlit creek he and Dicky used to wade through in the summers when they were small. Dicky was there too sometimes, still and forever the little boy Lawrence had failed to protect, and when he plucked a stone that glistened like honey from beneath the water, he held it out to Lawrence with an awed expression. *Look, Lawrie*, he said, *a magic rock.*

In the dreams, Lawrence wept from relief. He knew it meant that they were saved.

He awoke crushed by reality. His brother was still gone. His sister was still starving.

After a week of dreaming, he left with Thomas for California. For the next eight years, they worked on a fourteen-person crew, digging up the occasional bits of quartz.

They'd make some money, then use it to move on and reinvest in a new mine. The more money they made, the less work Thomas and Lawrence had to do. Their job, primarily, became choosing new investments, buying up land or mines, then taking the largest cut of whatever was found there. Or better yet, proving it had metal and then selling it at a vast profit. It was a gamble, but Lawrence was good at it. Every dollar he made went right back home or else into the mines, to be multiplied.

And no matter how much they made, Lawrence's hunger never abated. Instead, it grew and grew. The more he had, the more he craved. The more he accumulated, the more there was to lose, and the terror of that never let up.

Then, one day, he and Thomas visited a slice of land in Nevada, and Lawrence just *knew*, could *feel* the metal calling out to him through the rock. *Magic stone*, exactly like he'd been dreaming of.

And rather than tell Thomas, he kept it to himself.

He told Thomas he was thinking of retiring, that that plot of land they'd gone to see was worthless and he was tired of the work, of moving around, finding the crews, chasing the next lode. And he was convincing enough that Thomas left, headed back toward California to assemble a new crew on more promising terrain.

Then Lawrence bought the mine, all by himself. Weeks later, his crew struck forty-two tons of silver ore.

The first thing Lawrence bought was the local inn. Because he knew that when the news about the silver hit, there'd be dozens more men—*desperate men*—coming to try their luck and they'd need someplace to eat, sleep, and spend.

He was right. Of course he was. He himself was a desperate man. He knew how they operated.

Several weeks later, Thomas heard what happened, and Lawrence Ives made another decision that would change the course of the family's history forever.

8

"WELL, THAT'S . . . DEFINITELY the beginning," I blurt into the silence.

I figured she'd start with the year her grandfather imported snow to their Southern California home for Christmas, or talk about the caviar-eating Shetland pony she got for her third birthday. Or maybe skip all that and get right to the first time she heard Cosmo Sinclair's sexy drawling voice, and whether little cartoon hearts bloomed from her eyes in that moment.

Basically, I thought Margaret's "beginning" would've been about a hundred and fifty years later and, you know, involved *her* on some level.

But that's fine! This was interesting too! And she's leading the conversation, which was the goal.

I clear my throat while I try to figure out where to go from here. "So did your family talk about Lawrence a lot? How'd you learn all of this?"

That makes her laugh. "Never. From what I hear, my great-grandfather was a miserable man, who no one mourned. But he'd journaled obsessively. And when he died, his son—my grandfather Gerald—found his diaries in the family safe. Gerald never shared them with anyone else while he was alive. But he willed them to my sister, Laura. They were very close," she says. "He wanted her to burn them after she read them. But she couldn't bring herself to, for whatever reason. She was always more sentimental than me."

Holy shit. Speaking of mother lodes. *Journals*. From the 1800s, from the founding father of Ives Media. "Does she still have them?" As far as I knew, no one had seen or heard from Laura since well before Margaret disappeared, but because she'd never been a mainstay of the tabloids, no one was really looking for her either.

"No," Margaret answers. "I'm afraid she doesn't."

Her expression goes distant, almost watery, as if she's lost in a memory. It's the same way she looked while telling Lawrence's story—as if she were actually *there*. As if she herself had lived it, and it still made her ache.

I glance at my notes, looking for a segue, ideally toward something that doesn't make her freeze up: "That first hotel Lawrence bought—do you happen to know what it was called?"

She blinks at me for several seconds, like she's lost her place in space and time.

"Margaret?" I prompt.

"The Ebner." The word seems to stick in her throat.

Curiosity prickles at the nape of my neck. "Have you ever been? Back to visit where the family fortune began?"

"Only once," she says. "On a family trip. Just before my parents divorced, they took my sister and me to the mountains for a long weekend." Her faint smile quickly strains and she looks away. "Family finally sold it off in the seventies."

The message is clear. She doesn't want to talk more about it. Not yet.

I scribble *The Ebner* into my notebook, along with *last family trip with M's parents*, so I won't forget to revisit it once she's ready.

"Can I ask," I begin cautiously, "what made you want to tell *that* particular story?"

This time when her eyes come to mine, there's real force behind them, all that distance gone and instead a keen sharpness, like she could see right through me if she wanted, or else like she's trying to project something directly into my mind, willing me to understand.

"You wanted to know what it was like to be born into my family," she says after a beat. "Before you can understand that, you have to understand where this all began. My story, every bit of it, is tangled up with what Lawrence did."

"Do you . . . do you mean to Thomas?" I ask.

"My great-grandfather was a cold, cruel man with no qualms about taking what wasn't his," she says, that surprisingly powerful, potent gaze of hers still fixed on me, the kind of charisma that can hold a person captive.

I let the silence linger like an invitation. But uncertainty flashes across her face. Any second, she's going to retreat again, that maddening push-pull of any great interview. I make a snap decision and lean forward, stopping both recordings.

Her silvery brows lift in surprise. "Is that allowed?"

"We haven't agreed to anything yet, other than a conversation," I say. "A *monthlong conversation*, sure, but just a conversation. If you end up wanting to do the book, we can record things later. But if this is making you nervous, let's forget it for now."

You can trust me, I think at her, between every line.

She holds my gaze. Decades ago, when she was at the peak of her fame, she was so open with the press. Always smiling and waving and blowing kisses to the paparazzi, giving glib little quotes to reporters on her way down red carpets or into clubs. She's so different than those old pictures and articles made her seem, so tightly bottled into herself, with only little glimmers of wry charm and sudden blasts of emotion slipping out.

You're safe, I think at her.

Her mouth opens and closes twice before any sound comes out, and when she does speak, her voice is quieter, confessional almost.

"By the end of his life," she says, "all my great-grandfather did was ramble about three things."

Her lips knit tightly together as she carefully charts her own path forward.

"He apologized to his brother Dicky, like he was right there in the room with him. Wept about losing him like it had just happened," she says. "And he argued with Thomas Dougherty. Raged at him, really. Lawrence's son, my grandfather, wouldn't let anyone else into the room—he was so afraid of what Lawrence might say, that it might leak to the press. My family's rivalry with the Pulitzers was well underway by then—an Ives couldn't sneeze without making it in the papers."

I scribble three bullet points. Beside the first, I write *apologizing to Dicky*, and next to the second, *arguing with Thomas*. When I see Margaret watching me, I double-check: "Would you rather I didn't write this down?"

"That's my preference, yes," she admits.

I scribble out the note and set my pen aside.

She nods something like a thank-you and then goes on: "After word reached Thomas about the silver ore my great-grandfather had cheated him out of, Thomas came back into town, furious. He'd thought of Lawrence like a brother, after all that time together, and he wanted to know why he'd been betrayed.

"But Lawrence refused to even meet with him. Day after day, night after night, Thomas stood outside that tiny hotel, screaming for Lawrence to come face him. But my great-grandfather had enough money and enough men in his employ then that he could make himself inaccessible. So eventually, Thomas left. He went to the biggest newspaper he could find back in California, to tell the story of my great-grandfather's treachery. Eventually the reporter came to talk to Lawrence, and Lawrence responded by buying the paper."

My jaw drops. "The *San Francisco Daily Dispatch*?" The start of everything for Ives Media? "He bought it to protect his reputation?"

She snorts. "Oh, he didn't give a rat's ass about reputation. When he talked to the reporter, he asked how much Thomas had made off selling the story, because those were the terms Lawrence Ives thought in. When he heard the dollar amount, he knew right away that the news was one more place he could bury his money and watch it fruit.

"He started mining less, investing more. Bought a beautiful home in San Francisco and sent for his younger sister—it had always been his plan to bring her to live with him once he'd built a comfortable life. But in the years since he'd been gone, she'd grown up. She'd all but forgotten him. And worse, she'd married a Dougherty, another poor farmer. Because of what Lawrence had done to Thomas, she wanted nothing to do with her brother."

After a moment, she goes on, "At the end of his life, when he wasn't apologizing to the ghost of Dicky, Lawrence was arguing with a phantom Thomas. Blaming him for everything that happened. Telling him he deserved what he got, to die, drunk and penniless, for being stupid enough to believe that Lawrence was responsible for him. He thought anyone who relied on anyone else would pay for it, eventually. Though I've always thought the lesson was that anyone who relies on an *Ives* will only be hurt for their trouble."

I sit for a moment, absorbing that. Margaret's gaze has gone slightly cloudy, as if this thought is swirling around behind her eyes.

I clear my throat and gently nudge us back on track: "So what was the other thing?"

"Excuse me?" she says.

"You said your great-grandfather used to rant about three things," I remind her. "What was the last thing?"

A smile tugs at her lips, wispy and unconvincing. "I think we should save that for another day," she says, pushing herself up from her chair. "I'm in dire need of a nap."

"Of course," I say, as cheerfully as I can muster. "But—"

"Jodi will see you out," she says, cutting me short with a winning smile. I jam my mouth shut and nod acceptance: I've been excused.

Margaret turns and sweeps from the room.

* * *

LATER, I LIE on the sofa at the little overgrown bungalow I'm renting, ignoring my still-unpacked bags in favor of doing research. If this was an interview for a *Scratch* piece, I could've simply sent a list of questions to one of the fact-checkers to follow up on. In fact, if I get this job, it might be worth hiring someone freelance to do my legwork so I can focus on the writing and interviews themselves, but until I have someone, it's up to me.

I look back on my list of things to check out, and start with Dillon Springs, Pennsylvania.

All of this was so long ago that birth and death records weren't even being filed yet. There's no way to confirm most of what Margaret told me, since it's anecdotal, but as we move forward in history, I'm going to need to be able to verify everything.

I text a couple of freelance fact-checkers to get their availability in the coming months, then go back to reading about Dillon Springs, a tiny town that does, in fact, consider itself "the birthplace of modern American journalism," a fairly lofty claim, especially considering that Lawrence Ives never once went back to Dillon Springs *and* it was his San Francisco–born *son* who became the true media magnate of the family.

Lawrence had owned three newspapers by the time he died, but he had no involvement in how they were run day to day. His son, Gerald, Margaret's grandfather, was the one to push into the business of news.

As far as I can tell, there are no prominent Iveses still in Dillon Springs, though I'm guessing if Margaret did a DNA test, we'd be able to find a slew of cousins, given how large a family her great-grandfather was born into.

Next I search for Thomas Dougherty, but if any more of his story is out there, the first five pages of search results don't yield it. I try his name along with Dillon Springs, but still have no luck.

From there, I move on to reading about the first big mine lode, and the forty-two tons of silver, a number confirmed by multiple sources, codified into history by now, because—while, honestly, Ives made his fortune across multiple industries—this particular mine and its treasure offered the punchiest, most impressive headline.

Headline. It jump-starts something in my brain.

I open a new browser and run a search for Ives's first newspaper acquisition, rather than scouring my preinterview notes. There it is: the *San Francisco Daily Dispatch*. If Lawrence bought it out, then I'm guessing the story about Thomas Dougherty's betrayal at Lawrence's hands never ran, but I send an email to their archives department to see if they have any copies of issues from that far back that haven't crumbled into dust, just in case.

Then I start looking for information about the inn Lawrence bought, and something strange happens.

The Ebner Hotel comes up right away, exactly where I'm expecting it, in the Nevada town where the Ives fortune began.

The issue is, while the hotel *is* a historic landmark built during the gold rush, it wasn't called the Ebner until *after* the family sold it, in the 1970s. When Lawrence acquired it, it had been called the Arledge, and then in 1917, it had been renamed the Nicollet, for the duration of the Iveses' ownership of it.

So why didn't Margaret call it that? It wouldn't have been called the Ebner until . . . fortyish years after her one visit. Why would her first reaction be to call it by its current name?

It's a small, probably meaningless discrepancy, but the way her voice stuck when she said the name keeps wriggling in the back of my mind.

Maybe she *has* been back there since her family sold it off. But why wouldn't she want me to know that?

Or am I just overthinking a meaningless mistake?

I fire off a text to the group chat, and when I don't get a quick reply, I message Theo too: Can I run something by you?

Luckily, he replies quickly. What kind of thing?

Work thing, I say.

My phone starts ringing immediately.

If there's one thing Theo Bouras can't resist, it's a good mystery. Probably why he's never been quite ready to make things official with me. Mystery is not my strong suit.

"Hi," I say brightly, answering the call.

"Alicccce," he says, drawing my name out in a teasing way that makes me shiver.

"Theo," I say.

"What have you got for me this time?" he asks.

"Are you sure you're not too busy?"

"Nah," he says. "I've got you on speaker while I'm developing."

For work, his photos are all digital, but his real passion is film, so on his off days, he's usually in his home darkroom, or out shooting.

"I'm trying to figure out why a source might lie about something trivial," I say.

"And by source, do you mean *Margaret Ives*?" he teases.

"I just mean generally," I say.

"How trivial are we talking?" he asks, clearly intrigued.

"Like saying they've only been somewhere once, but maybe they've been there more than that," I say. "Maybe more recently than they said."

He hums. "Like . . . somewhere a crime has been committed, perhaps?"

I tuck my phone between my shoulder and ear and sit back down in front of my computer, searching for news stories about the Ebner and garnering nothing much of interest. "Maybe," I say. "But probably not."

He thinks again. "Maybe it was, like, a rendezvous spot. Maybe she was having an affair. Cheating on the Boy Wonder of Rock 'n' Roll before he died."

I roll my eyes. "I never said *she*."

"Fine," he relents. "Maybe *this person* was cheating on *their husband*, Cosmo Sinclair."

I take a sip of my now-cold afternoon coffee and swish it around in my mouth, like I might be able to taste the answer. Cosmo was already gone before the Nicollet Inn became the Ebner.

If Margaret's hiding a visit—or multiple visits—it's not because of an affair.

Besides, an affair might be a shocking revelation, but this is a woman who *also* wore her wedding dress to her husband's funeral, knowing full well there'd be miles of paparazzi in every direction. I'm not sure I'd buy her cheating on him, and I'm even less convinced she'd feel the need to hide it so long after the fact.

"Or I don't know," Theo says, breaking into my thoughts. "Maybe she just forgot. The woman is, like, eighty-something."

"Never said I'm talking about a woman," I remind him. "Or about an eighty-something-year-old, for that matter."

"Why not just ask her?" he says.

"Next time I talk to them," I reply, "I will. But that's not until Tuesday."

"So she's giving you a couple of days off," he says. "Interesting."

There's a distinctively flirty edge to his voice. It makes my stomach flip-flop in a not entirely pleasant way. I know what he's getting at: that I could come home and we could hook up. And that sounds pretty nice.

But a few weeks ago, when I'd sent a screenshot of one of his late-night text messages to my friends, Bianca had pointed out something that had been bothering me ever since.

Have you noticed, she wrote, that this man NEVER just asks you to hang out? He literally only ever sets you up to ask HIM to hang out.

Cillian wrote back, I've noticed. He is my enemy.

Priya chimed in, As long as you're getting what you want out of this arrangement, ignore the haters, Alice.

The thing is, I'm technically not. I would've gladly agreed to be Theo's girlfriend months ago if it was on the table. But it wasn't, and there wasn't anyone else I was interested in, so I didn't really see the point of giving him an ultimatum. So we'd continued on like this, and it was mostly fine—I really liked being with him, whenever we actually *were* together.

But I'd been paying attention since Bianca's observation. And she and Cillian were right.

Every text was what are you up to tonight, or a picture of a bottle of nice bourbon he'd gotten, or a shirtless photo he thought might be enticing but was mostly just embarrassing, no matter how good he looked in it.

The man would *not* just say, *Hey, Alice, want to come over tonight?*

And because I hadn't taken any of his bait since that fateful day in the group chat, I hadn't seen him for my last two weeks in LA before shipping out this way.

"Alice?" he says now, in my ear. "You still there?"

"Yeah, but I've actually got to go," I say. "Thanks for the help."

"Anytime," he says.

He thinks he means it, but he doesn't.

• • •

AFTER PERUSING ONLINE for a solid hour, I find a place to pass a Saturday night.

Rum Room sits tucked behind a row of scraggly trees, on the opposite side of the road from Little Croissant, though a half mile down the road.

I never would've seen it from the street, and it's not close enough to the beach to be a proper tourist spot, which is better for my purposes.

It's also only a ten-minute walk from my rental, so I leave my car behind and head over.

It looks like a small ranch home, with a wooden deck wrapped around its front half, green-and-white-striped awnings hanging over its rectangular windows. Several massive live oaks lean over the patio, multicolored Christmas lights strung haphazardly between them to illuminate the wooden tables below, all of which are full.

I walk up the ramp to the front door, past both a neon hot dog sign and a fake shark head, mounted directly to the white clapboard exterior.

The inside of the restaurant is an exercise in chintzy maximalism, every inch clad in either tropical wallpaper, tacky hot dog–related signs, or jewel-toned tile. A host dressed in black greets me with a smile and an efficient nod. "Do you have a reservation with us tonight?"

"No, sorry," I say.

"How many?" he asks.

"Just one," I say, peeking over his shoulder toward the bar. One open stool, wedged between two groups. "Can I order food if I sit there?"

"Definitely," he says. "Otherwise, we're probably running at about a thirty-minute wait."

"The bar works great for me," I tell him, and he gestures me past. I squeeze between the two parties and plop my bag on the counter. "Sorry," I tell the woman next to me when I accidentally elbow her while trying to get my jacket off.

"No prob," she says, then turns back to keep talking to her friend.

Something in my chest wilts. Maybe I should've just bitten the bullet and invited Theo to come visit me. This could be a long, lonely month. Especially if, moving forward, interviews are as short as this morning's. I do a quick scan of the room. Two more doorways jut off from this one, to a larger dining room, but this one is mostly filled with two-tops—people having a drink while they wait for a proper table.

My heart lifts a little when my gaze reaches the back corner. The one closest to the bathrooms.

Hayden's dark head is bent over a laptop, a half-eaten salad forgotten at his left elbow, and a glass of water to the right of his computer.

I leave my stuff behind and dismount my stool to go say hi.

Just like at Fish Bowl, he doesn't look up even when I'm standing right beside him, his focus singular and intense on his screen.

"Are you stalking me?" I ask.

He jumps in surprise, like he had no idea I was there. Then his gaze locks on me, and a horrified expression crosses his face. "Of course not," he says. And then, as if he needs proof: "I was here first."

"Hayden," I say. "I'm *kidding*. It's a tiny island. We're bound to keep running into each other. Relax."

He does. Visibly. But only for a second. Then, seeming to remember something, he stiffens and shuts his computer.

"I'm not here to spy on you," I promise. "I just saw you from the bar and thought it would be weird not to say hi. So, hi."

His eyes wander from me to the bar and back again. "You make friends fast."

"I'm not with them, actually," I say. "But who knows what two rum cocktails might do?"

He opens his mouth, closes it again, and nods.

The silence starts to curdle into something awkward. "Have a good night!" I say, and begin to turn.

"Alice?"

I pause, swivel back to him.

"Do you want to sit?" he asks.

I study him, trying to read his serious expression. "I can't tell if you're just being polite or if that's a real invitation."

The face he makes, I am nearly *certain*, is an actual smile, no matter how faint. "You can basically always assume that I'm not just being polite," he says.

This makes me laugh. That probably should've occurred to me sooner. It's not like he's been a paragon of manners in the last few days since we first met.

"I wouldn't want to interrupt . . ." I say.

"You're not," he insists. "I need to be done working. I need . . . a distraction."

I smile. "A *distraction*?"

He winces. "I didn't mean that to sound—"

"A distraction sounds nice," I say.

9

WHEN I GET back to his table with my jacket and bag, Hayden's put his computer away and moved his salad and water directly in front of himself. It's not until I slide into my seat that I remember the dilemma. *Our* dilemma, Hayden's and mine.

We can't sit in cramped spaces like this without a great deal of careful arranging of our legs. "Sorry," I say, my left knee bumping his and then finding itself tucked between both of his thighs, interlaced. "I think we're too tall for this booth."

"It's not your fault," he says. "I'm too tall for most booths. You should see me on an airplane."

I laugh. "I'd love to. Next time you're on one, send me a picture?"

"I don't have your number," he points out, which is not quite the same as *asking* for my number, but still sends a surprising and surprisingly pleasant *zing* down the front of my rib cage.

I could offer it to him. Normally, I probably would.

But I actually have no idea if he's *trying* to set me up to offer it. With Theo, I can always tell what he wants. There's a comfort in that.

"How'd your first day go?" I ask.

He shakes his head. "We're not talking about Margaret Ives."

"No, *you're* not talking about her." I lean forward and feel his legs tense slightly around mine. "I have no problem telling you that my first day was weird."

"You shouldn't be telling me this," he says.

"Maybe not," I allow, "but since we've both signed ironclad NDAs, I'm pretty sure you're the only person I *can* tell about this. I think she lied to me."

Hayden Anderson's face might not have the full range of emotions that I'm accustomed to, but it turns out he can definitely show surprise.

And something else, like a quick flare of understanding, before he schools his face into neutrality again.

"Hayden," I say, leaning even farther forward to peer intently into his eyes.

"Alice," he replies, a bit stiff.

"What was that face for?" I ask.

He looks away, scratching his jaw.

"Oh, come on," I say. "What if I promise not to use anything you give me?"

His eyes snap back to mine. In this warm lighting, they look almost gold. Like honey. He leans in closer too, his knee sliding in almost to my crotch in the process, the heat of him palpable against my bare thighs. "I'm not giving you anything," he says.

"But she lied to you too," I say. "Or you're at least wondering if she did."

Again, that lift in his brow and slackening of his mouth. Quickly, his features return to a scowl. "This is why I never go out with journalists."

Another flush, this one much more intense, rockets through me. Is the implication that this counts as *going out* or is he just run-of-the-mill insulting me?

He's rubbing his jaw again, his eyes distant, until the second they rebound to me, hyperfocused. He slumps back against his seat on a sigh. "There have been some..." He chooses his next words carefully. "Discrepancies I can't account for yet."

I frown. "Is she fucking with us?"

A server is walking past right then, and she slows when he lifts his chin in greeting toward her. "I think my friend wanted to order."

Friend! That's progress.

After a cursory look at the menu, I order a vegan hot dog and something called a Queen's Park Swizzle.

"Anything else for you?" the server asks Hayden, and he shakes his head.

As soon as she disappears, he faces me again, hunching forward, his forearms resting on the table. "It *is* weird. That she suddenly wants to do this. I mean, why now?"

His gaze is sharp, meaningful. It takes me a second to figure out what he's hinting at. I can tell he doesn't want to *say* it, but he's hoping I'll guess anyway. Like this is a work-around to his "no sharing our Margaret Ives stuff" policy.

What would make someone suddenly consider a tell-all memoir when they'd been virtually in hiding for three decades? I can only think of two obvious reasons.

Maybe she's dying. Or maybe...

"Memory problems?" I say.

Our server drops my drink off as she sweeps past us. I thank her and face Hayden again.

"Maybe I'm just seeing things that aren't there." He shrugs. "Ever since Len, I've been a little..." He shakes his head. "I don't know, every time I visit my parents and one of them misplaces the remote, a little part of me is asking if it's normal forgetfulness, or something else."

He shakes his head again as if to ward off the thought.

"You were really close to him," I say. "Len." It's not a question. Obviously Hayden was close to the man. He spent years with Len Stirling, with his family and friends. Of course they'd bonded. But somehow it hadn't occurred to me how painful that must have been.

To form a bond with someone on the very precipice of them slipping away. His book hadn't delved into the aftermath of Len's death. Hayden was on the page, but only in small glimpses. He was good at writing more as a porthole than a narrating character.

But now I can see the Hayden who was really there. Who knew the man he was writing about. Loved him, probably.

"I'm not sure that's what's going on here," he says suddenly, his tone distracted. "Most likely she just doesn't trust us yet."

He runs his fingertips thoughtfully over his mouth now. The motion distracts me. Hypnotizes me, really. I hadn't noticed how attractive he was before. I'm not totally sure what it is that makes him so. He's nowhere near symmetrical. His eyes are small and his mouth is wide, and his nose looks like it's been broken at least once and not properly set.

I mean, obviously his body is incredible, so when I catch myself inadvertently checking him out, *that's* not all that surprising. The way that watching his large fingers skating over his mouth affects me, however, catches me off guard.

I'm sure there's *something* biological to it. My body likes his pheromones, or my legs like the feeling of his in between them.

God, maybe I really should have invited Theo down. This is the last thing I should be spending precious brain cells on right now.

His hand falls back down to the table and our eyes connect, a feeling like a live wire touched a metal point in the center of my chest. "I'm just not sure," he says.

"Hm?" I've totally lost track of what we were talking about.

"I'm not sure why she'd invite us down here, pay us to work, and then punch holes in her own story." He shifts in his seat, our thighs grazing again.

Our server stops by to drop off my hot dog and refill Hayden's water. "You sure there's nothing else I can get you?" she asks him.

"No, thanks," he says.

She leaves us to attend to one of her other tables, and Hayden catches me staring at him. *Thinking* at him, really.

"What?" he asks, one eyebrow cocked.

"Do you only eat salad?" I ask.

His lips part, a divot forming between his eyebrows. Then his mouth presses shut again. "I try to stay in shape when I'm traveling for work. If I lose my rhythms, it's hard to get back on them once I'm home."

"So is that a yes?" I ask.

A slow tug at one side of his mouth turns into a smile, an actual, recognizable smile. "No, Alice, I don't only eat salad. The other day I actually had an amazing croissant."

"Oh my god, it was *so* good, wasn't it?" I say, right before biting into my vegan dog.

"So good," he agrees, lifting his fork to pick at his salad. "I could feel my arteries clogging, and I didn't even care."

I snort. "I think the green tea–drinking, morning running, salad-noshing wonder of the East Coast can have one croissant without having a cardiac event. Not even my sister eats like you, and she's had like fourteen heart surgeries."

His brow tightens, his smile vanishing. "Your Peace Corps sister?"

"I only have the one," I tell him.

He sets his fork back down, jaw tense. "Is she okay?"

"Yes!" I say quickly. "Sorry! I buried the lede there. She's fine. Healthy as a horse. Or, you know, a human with a healthy heart. This all happened when we were kids."

"Shit." His frown returns. "What happened?"

"It was an issue she had at birth," I say. "So she was in and out of hospitals a lot when we were small. But she's been doing really well since, like, high school. That was my whole point. You eat like a bird compared to her."

"Is she older or younger," he asks.

"Older," I say. "Three years. What about your brother? The perfect doctor one?"

His mouth twists wryly, but I wouldn't quite call it a smile. "I only have the one," he says, repeating my words back to me. "Two years older. Did I mention he was the captain of our high school football team?"

"You didn't have to," I tease. "It was implied."

He lets out a snort. It sounds like an angry bull, but I'm pretty sure it's his laugh.

"What position did you play?"

Now he outright scoffs, rolls his eyes as he sits forward again, forearms once more pressing into the table. "None."

"Basketball?" I say.

"Despite my dad's greatest wishes," he says, "no."

"Hayden," I say. "You're like six seven and pure muscle. You could be a millionaire right now."

"I don't think that's how sports work," he says. "I think you also have to have 'talent' or 'coordination.'" He puts both basketball prerequisites in half-formed finger quotes against the table. "And also I'm six three."

"Hm." I nod thoughtfully. "That's like a basketball five eight."

"Now I'm wondering," he drawls, "why *you* didn't become a mathematician."

"Well, if you'd like, I can get you my mom's phone number and the two of you can compare notes about all the more impressive jobs I *could've* had, and then I can reach out to your dad and let him know I agree you should've played basketball in high school."

"No, don't give him the satisfaction," he says. "I already know you're both right. If I could do it again, maybe I would've tried it, just to see. But at that point there was basically nothing I wanted to do *more* than the opposite of whatever he and my mom wanted me to do."

"So you didn't get along?" I ask.

His huge shoulders lift and slump again. "No, I mean, we do now. They're actually pretty great. I just wasn't a kid who did well with the kind of expectations people had for my family. It's better, now that I live somewhere else. It's not like every little thing I do reflects on them anymore."

"I get that," I say.

"You do?" he asks, the rest of his question hanging there, unsaid: *How?*

I don't talk about all this a lot, but I also get the feeling this isn't Hayden's usual conversational fare either, and it feels good, almost like he trusts me.

"My parents were kind of . . ." I search for a word that encompasses all of it. Of course there isn't one. That's the deal with people. They're always more than one thing, and a lot of times they're even a collection of contradictory traits. "They're eccentric," I say. "Super idealistic and passionate and . . . capable, I guess? Before my sister and I were born, they were actually part of this farming commune, so they knew how to do *everything*. And thanks to them, I know how to do a lot of things too."

"Such as?" he asks.

I shrug. "Darning socks. Altering clothes. Cooking. Canning fruit and veggies. Gardening. That kind of thing."

"Wow," he says. "Pretty impressive."

"Now, sure," I agree. "But when I was a kid, it was mortifying. We lived in this really small, homogenous town, and my parents were hippie journalists who literally chained themselves to trees in the seventies. Growing up, my sister and I both got bullied pretty badly, because everyone thought my parents were weird. And it didn't help that we were homeschooled until high school, because of my sister's health problems. Or that we wore homemade clothes. Or that I was seven inches taller than every other girl in my grade. Frankly, there was a lot working against us."

Another sliver of smile.

"But the thing is, none of those kids knew what was going on at home. What Audrey was dealing with. Just like I didn't know what *they* were dealing with. Most people aren't mean for no reason, you know? Stuff's going on with them too."

"Alice," he says, softly chiding. "Some people *are* just assholes."

"I know," I say. "Some. Not most."

This time, his amusement takes the form of a quiet huff.

"What?" I say.

"I just . . ." I can see the wheels turning as he considers his next words. "You might be the least cynical person I've ever met. I'm not sure I've ever known anyone like you."

I narrow my eyes. "You mean I'm naive."

"No, Alice," he replies. "If that's what I meant, then that's what I would've said."

10

"I CAN GIVE you a ride back to the hotel, if you want," Hayden offers as we leave the cool air and romantic lighting of Rum Room behind and trudge down the ramp into the sticky Georgia night. "And bring you here to get your car tomorrow, if you want."

I peel my thin jacket off and toss it over my arm. "Actually, I'm not at the hotel anymore. I found a furnished house for the month."

"Oh," he says. "Well, I can drop you off at your house then."

"That's okay," I say. "I actually walked. It's close. See?" I gesture toward the path in the back corner of the parking lot, which winds into a sparse strip of oak, pine, and palm, eventually curling behind the street on which my temporary housing sits.

Hayden stops on the pine needle–dusted earth just beyond the edge of the restaurant's front patio lights and studies the dark path, a look of consternation overtaking his face.

"It's really not far," I promise.

"I'll walk you," he says.

"You don't have to do that," I say. "I'm both tall *and* scrappy. I'll be fine."

"This isn't like New York or LA," he says.

"In that the rate of crime here is probably a very small fraction of those places," I say.

"In that there aren't people all around," he says. "If something happened..."

I hold up my hands in supplication. "I'm not trying to stop you. Just as long as you know you're not obligated."

"Again," he says, "I do very little out of obligation."

"It must be so nice to be you," I tease, bumping sideways into him as I pad toward the mouth of the trail through the trees.

"Because I'm detached and coldhearted?" he says, falling into step beside me.

It makes me think of what Cillian said about him—an *unpleasant sort*—and I feel a spike of protectiveness, followed by a small, tender ache of sympathy.

"Actually," I say, "I meant because you can always reach the top shelf."

"Good point," he deadpans. "I never stopped to consider how lucky I am."

"Speaking of that—"

"How lucky I am?"

"Your height," I clarify. "Can I ask you something?"

He stops and gives me a puzzled frown. "About my height?"

I nod.

"Okay," he allows.

"How many of your girlfriends have been under five three?"

He stares at me for a second. Longer than a second. I think I might've broken his brain. Finally, one low bark of laughter. "What? What kind of a question is that?"

I start walking again. He joins me. "It's just," I say, "uncommonly tall men seem to always date absolutely *tiny* women."

"Based on *what*?" he asks, seemingly befuddled.

"Personal observation," I say.

He shakes his head again. "I don't even know what to say right now."

"I've just been wondering," I say. "It always seemed, like, physically inconvenient to me before. But every time we're at a table together, we don't fit, so now I'm wondering if somehow evolution did it."

He squints at me, his eyes glimmering crescents beneath his stern brow. "Did *what* exactly?"

"Made tall men and short women pair up," I say. "Like if you're an exceptionally tall person, does biology just kind of nudge you toward being with someone who takes up less room?"

"For what *purpose*?" he wants to know.

I shrug. "I don't know! Maybe because you won't have to hunt as much if you're not feeding two gigantic people, or because caves are small and you've got to save room where you can?"

He eyes me sidelong. "Add scientist to that list of better jobs you've been keeping."

"Oh, trust me, that's already on my mom's list," I say. "There's a strong aura of *Why are you writing about child stars when you could be solving the climate crisis, Alice* that permeates most of our phone calls."

Once more, he stops walking. I'm used to walking and talking, but it seems like every time Hayden has something he really wants to say or ask, he has to go still first. "What about your dad?" he says now. "Is he any more understanding? About your work?"

"Um, yeah," I say, still moving, my eyes following the path of my sandals, my pink pedicure almost glowing in the dark. "He was, actually. Or, I don't know if he *understood* it, but he was super supportive. He was the more grounded of the two. Loved books and movies and all of that, whereas my mom was kind of all purpose, all the time."

Hayden's soft steps resume beside me, muffled and hollow sounding. "Did your dad . . . Is he gone?"

"Died a few years ago," I confirm. "My parents were pretty old when they had us, so it wasn't totally unexpected, but it still sucked. Sucks."

"I'm sorry," he says.

I force a slight smile in his direction. "Thanks."

"I always feel stupid saying that," he murmurs.

"I know," I agree, "but there's nothing else to say. And honestly, I would say seventy percent of my friends have pretty horrible relationships with their dads, so even if I didn't get mine as long as I wish I could have, I still feel lucky."

"You're not obligated to," he says quietly. "You can feel cheated, Alice."

I feel a surprising prickle at the back of my nose and a tender ache in my heart. Not just because I'm thinking about my dad, but because what Cillian said wings through my mind again: *An unpleasant sort.*

I could never blame Cillian for having that impression, but it bothers me to think of people out there meeting Hayden Anderson and coming away with this partial view of him.

He can be unpleasant. He can also be kind, and even funny.

He can be clueless that you are standing right next to him, but he also might notice you being harassed from the other side of the parking lot and intercede on your behalf.

"I know I can," I finally admit. "But I'd rather think of it like this. Like it only hurts this much because he was so great."

And so much reminds me of him that in a way it's like he's still here. Especially here, in the Georgian summer, interviewing a woman we'd both always been fascinated by.

Hayden nods to himself, but neither of us says anything for a while. We just hike along the path in companionable silence, our arms grazing every several steps, our skin slightly sticky.

As if reading my mind, he says, "I'll never get used to this humidity."

"I kind of love it," I say.

He looks down his shoulder at me, eyes catching the moonlight. "Of course you do."

"I bet you can't wait to get back to New York," I say.

"More or less," he agrees. We've stopped again, though I have no memory of doing it. We're facing each other, standing close, the grating chirp of the cicadas filling the night around us. In my peripheral, I spot the back of my house, beyond a slight break in the trees.

I meet his eyes again. "That's me." My voice comes out thin and quiet. I can *hear* my own regret. That I wish this walk could have gone on awhile longer.

Hayden's chin dips in acknowledgment, but he says nothing. The humidity feels Jell-O thick now, like it doesn't want me to move a muscle.

I swallow, force another smile. "Well, thank you for walking me."

"Of course," he says.

I turn toward the break in the trees, but he says my name, like it's a question, and when I look back, he takes another step toward me.

"One," he says.

I shake my head. "One what?"

The corner of his mouth tips up for just a second. "One girlfriend under five three," he says seriously.

"Oh." I'm not sure why my ears suddenly feel so hot, but they do.

"And it was like you said," he goes on.

"More room in the cave?" I say quietly.

Another slight twitch of his lips. "Physically inconvenient."

The heat spreads down my neck. It routes around my rib cage, like it's reaching toward him, like it's knitting us together.

"She couldn't get anything off the top shelf," I say.

"And horrible at basketball," he says dryly.

My nervous energy bubbles over into laughter. His smile widens. It feels like Pop Rocks are sizzling through my veins. *Oh boy, I'm in trouble.*

Even as I'm thinking it, I'm asking, "Do you want to come inside?"

Even as he's stepping closer, he's saying, "I should get home."

Our stomachs are nearly touching. I tip my chin up to meet his eyes. "Why?"

His pupils flare. "You know why."

I swallow but it does nothing to defuse the heat in my throat and chest. "Because you have a girlfriend?"

"No," he says.

"No, that's not why," I say, "or no, you don't have a girlfriend?"

"You talk a *lot*," he murmurs.

"If you've got something to say," I reply, "I'd love for you to interrupt me."

And he does, just not with words. Instead he sets one hand lightly, teasingly, against my lips.

My whole body heats from the sudden contact. From the rough feeling of his fingers, and the smell of his soap, and the awareness that, an hour ago, this same hand was sweeping against *his* mouth. I'm something *more* than hypnotized now.

I'm *entranced* by the featherlight sensation, and by the way his gaze follows the motion when his fingers skim over my bottom lip, pulling an unsteady sigh from me.

My lips part almost involuntarily, the tip of my tongue grazing one of his fingers, and his eyes flick back to mine, darker than before.

For a moment, I'm suspended. Floating in that zero-gravity moment, waiting to see if I'll fall, or if he'll catch me.

My weight shifts forward. By the time my stomach meets his, his hands are already on my jaw, his lips impatiently coaxing mine apart.

11

ONE OF HAYDEN'S hands furls around the nape of my neck, tipping my head back, and at the small sound that escapes me, his tongue sweeps over mine, a shimmer of heat going through me. My hands slide up his chest. One of his glides down to my waist, pulling me toward him, and then, when I wrap mine tight around the back of his neck, it moves to my ass, lifting me against him.

I arch up, trying to get more of him. His heat, the friction of his chest against mine, the ridge of his erection pressing into me.

I break the kiss just long enough to whisper, "Come inside."

He pushes back from me so abruptly, I stumble before catching myself.

"Fuck," he says to himself, running his hands up his face and over his hair, like he's putting himself together.

"What's wrong?" I ask, still startled and off balance.

I essentially watch the haze of lust clear from his eyes, replaced by something cold and stern. He shakes his head. "I'm sorry. I shouldn't have given you the wrong idea."

I take a half step back, a reedy laugh sneaking out of me. "And what idea is that?"

"That I was interested in something like this," he says evenly. "With you."

Heat rushes into my face, and I can't tell if it's embarrassment or anger.

To make things just a little worse, he adds, "I'm not."

"Yeah. I got that." I turn, searching for my jacket and bag, which I dropped in the fervor. I snap them up.

"*Alice*," he says, almost chiding, like *I'm* the one being ridiculous here.

I try to remind myself he's got his own stuff going on, that he's probably not *trying* to be an asshole, but when I look up, he's staring at me with those steely eyes and perfectly flat mouth of his.

"It's really not personal," he says.

Adding *with you* to the end of his statement about how this wasn't something he's interested in seems to suggest otherwise, but what do I know?

God, I couldn't have possibly misread the signals *that* badly. Could I?

"I understand," I lie, trying my hardest to smile. "I'm sorry too."

He studies me for a moment, brow knit, both of us clearly unsure what to say. It's not often that I'm rendered speechless, but I can't think of a single thing that would make this less humiliating.

"I'm not going to hook up with someone," he says, "whose dream job I'm about to take from them."

My laugh is full throated, loud, and even a little bit angry.

The *arrogance*.

"You think you already have this, don't you?" I demand. "Like I'm so insignificant I don't stand a chance."

His jaw sets. "I didn't say you were insignificant."

The rest of the sentiment, though, he has no issue with.

"Good night, Hayden," I snort, and turn on my heel to march through the trees into my bungalow's backyard, praying with every step that I never see Hayden Anderson again.

• • •

ON MONDAY MORNING, I pretend not to see Hayden at Little Croissant, picking up a green tea after—judging by the sweat dripping down him—a productive run.

On Tuesday, eager to avoid another run-in, I again get coffee from another breakfast spot in Tourist Town on my way to meet Margaret.

It's wretched—though the doughnuts are more than decent.

When I get to Margaret's house, Jodi is weeding the front garden beds. "Margaret's out back in the workshop," she tells me. "Go on back."

"Thanks, Jodi!" I chirp. Her only reply is a grunt.

I wind around the house, past the small swimming pool, to the white-clapboard-sided clubhouse just beyond it, the glass-paned French doors thrown open and Margaret visible moving around within.

The air is stiffer and hotter back here than it is out by the open ocean, and the high, unforgiving sun sends a rivulet of sweat down my neck and between my shoulder blades as I pick my way toward the small outbuilding.

From a distance, it looks like the floor inside is painted blue, but, as I get closer, I realize my mistake. It's not painted at all.

It's a massive mosaic, pieced together in glimmering shades of blue, white, green, amber. A massive mural of sea glass, arranged into a spiraling pattern of paths.

"It's a labyrinth." I look up toward the voice, shielding my eyes against the reflecting light to find Margaret in the back of the workshop. She's wearing a lilac boilersuit with its sleeves rolled up, and her silver hair is knotted into a pom-pom atop her head. She pulls a pair of protective goggles from her eyes up onto her forehead as I step inside.

"Like a maze?" I ask, glancing around the room. A series of long, scarred tables have been arranged around the outside edge of the workshop, their tops covered in tools and wire, glass and shells and driftwood. Over each of the windows, an elaborate wind chime hangs, slowly twirling, waiting for a true breeze to make them dance.

"Not quite," she says. "It's unicursal. There's only one path in and out. It's not quite the game of a maze. You can't get lost. You just walk the path, and it won't be the shortest way to get you where you're going, but you'll wind up in the center eventually. As you walk, you're supposed to meditate."

"On?" I ask.

"Whatever you want," she says.

"What do *you* meditate on?" I ask.

"Usually, what I want for lunch." Even the sparkle in her eye can't distract from the obvious dodge. Margaret Ives has an answer locked and loaded to that question—and I'm not getting it. Not yet.

I wander around the workshop, studying the things she's made and the things she's working on at the tables. It's cooler here, thanks to the shade of the roof and the ceiling fans, but not by much. The humidity holds the summer in the workshop's walls, and the open windows bring in nothing but brackishness.

I gently run my fingers through one of her wind chimes, listening to the soft clatter and tinkle. There are more mosaics on the walls, like the one on the floor, though smaller and trapped in both resin and driftwood frames. Most are abstract or arranged in geometric patterns. Like someone took a Hilma af Klint painting, shattered it, and put the pieces back together with their rough, jagged edges.

"Those don't do so hot with the tourists," Margaret says, coming to stand at my shoulder. "They mostly want turtles and palm trees."

"They're also a great tool for helping desperate journalists track you down," I remind her.

She chuckles, turning back to her tool-strewn tables. "You mind if I work while we talk?"

"Sure—are we recording today?" I traipse after her, dropping my bag on the far end of the surface and sinking onto the schoolhouse-style stool there, feeling like I'm back in art class freshman year.

She makes a gesture like, *Be my guest*, then pulls her goggles back into place. I notice then that it's not just tiny, smooth pieces of sea glass arranged in front of her, but also full bottles, aluminum cans, and, down on the floor, buckets of sand-and-grime-coated trash, things she must've found on the beach or maybe floating in the marsh.

There's a sink in the rear corner of the space, and on the countertop next to it, more bottles and cans are arranged on a drying rack as though freshly rinsed.

"Here." Margaret holds a pair of goggles out to me and I put them on, then set up my phone and recorder between us. She pulls on some purple work gloves, drapes a towel over a green beer bottle, and cracks a hammer down against it.

I try not to jump at the sound, but even muffled by the terry cloth, it's harsh.

"So where did we leave off?" Margaret asks.

"Well . . ." I flip through my notes.

Another harsh crash as the hammer comes down again. I've conducted full interviews while an interviewee was pounding away at a Peloton stationary bike class. I should be able to drown out the sounds of Margaret's work and focus.

She opens the towel to rearrange the pieces, then flops it back into place and keeps breaking them down.

I debate bringing up the Ebner Hotel of it all, right then. But if there *is* something worth poking around there, I don't want her to close off before we can get to it. This month is about building trust. "Lawrence had just bought his first newspaper. He'd gotten settled in San Francisco and sent for his sister, but she wouldn't come."

"Right, right," she says.

"But we don't have to pick up there," I say. "I'm excited to hear more about *you*, whenever you're ready."

"This is about me, Alice," she says pointedly. "I told you that."

"All right, then." I gesture for her to go on.

Three more taps of the hammer first. *Clink. Clink. Clink.* "Lawrence's sister begged him to come home and make amends, to stop his quest for *more*. Instead, he decided it was time to start a new family, one of his own. He was around forty when he met Amelia Lowe. Of the San Francisco Lowes." As she says this, she does a little eye roll, like she knows it's pretentious to describe someone this way, but it simply can't be helped.

I suppress a laugh.

"A railroad family," she explains. "AKA rich. Anyway, Amelia's father *hated* Lawrence. Hated." She notices my expression. "You're surprised."

"A bit," I admit. "Everything I read suggested it was a kind of . . . not an arranged marriage, but, you know, a *business* decision. Like things used to be back then."

She lifts her eyes to mine, a smirk lurking on her lips. "That's by design. See, Lawrence wanted to marry Amelia, and Amelia wanted out from under her domineering father. She saw an opportunity with Lawrence, but her father forbade them from seeing each other. So they eloped."

Margaret punctuates the word with a hearty whack of her hammer. "Mr. Lowe was furious of course, but by then, Lawrence had acquired four more papers. And wouldn't you know it, in the days following their elopement, each of his five papers ran its own story about the union of these two powerful families. It was sheer flattery, praising the Lowes, spreading gossip about business that *hadn't happened yet*. It forced Lowe's hand."

She opens the towel, arranges the glass, replaces the towel, swings the hammer.

"Amelia was welcomed right back into the fold, and what's more, Mr. Lowe and Lawrence went into business together. Everyone got what they wanted out of it."

"And then your grandfather Gerald was born, right?" I say. "A few years after Amelia and Lawrence got married?"

"That's right." She covers the glass with the towel again. Hits it with the hammer. "In 1875, Gerald Rupert Ives came screaming into the world." She flicks a glance my way. "He was the one who built the House of Ives as the world knows it. But I've always thought of him as the beginning of the end. The stepping stone that decided the entire path. The first domino that tipped. The one who, for better or worse, set every moment of my life into motion."

The Story

THEIR VERSION: Gerald Ives created modern journalism. He was also a failed politician, a lavish partier, and a womanizer who abandoned his family without batting an eye.

• • •

HER VERSION: Gerald Ives never spoke an ill word of his father, but he never once heard his father say a kind word about *him*.

Gerald was raised to be a businessman, and was hardly eight years old when he first realized he'd been born *in the red*. In debt. At a loss.

He came out with his father's face and an expectation he could never live up to, no matter how many tutors his parents locked him in a room with. He was supposed to do great things. That was the contract Lawrence thought he'd entered into with the universe, and thus every second Gerald *didn't*, he was failing.

He was disappointing.

He was falling short.

Things were different for his younger sister.

Eight years after Gerald was born, Georgiana "Gigi" Ives arrived, firmly *in the black*. Beautiful like her mother, quiet like her father, quick witted like both of them. And she was naturally content, which only earned her more adoration.

Gigi went where she pleased. She did as she wished. She studied painting and dance and piano, and played out in the grass with the nanny on sunny days.

And Gerald watched through the window, his tutor barking at him, "Again, again," until every math problem was solved, every Italian verb correctly conjugated, every important mining-related fact memorized and recited back.

Their house in San Francisco was large and opulent, but to him, it felt like a cage he paced, searching for weak points.

He tried—at so many points in his life, he tried—to codify what it was that made his father detest him. Or what exactly about Gigi and his mother drew out that small, soft smile on his father's lips.

Why they could drift, light as sunbeams, across the house and he would watch them go, more than approvingly, when only Gerald's rage could ever turn his father's eye.

Once, after they'd fought, Gerald had gone into an outbuilding on their property and punched a hole clean through the wall. His mother had found him there, still shaking with unspent energy even as blood dripped down the back of his hand to the cold dirt floor.

Gently, she'd touched his shoulders. "He's afraid, you know," she told him. "That's why he's so hard on you."

Gerald had nodded, and later wished he hadn't. He *didn't* know. He'd never seen any evidence at all that Lawrence Ives was afraid of anything, and even on his deathbed, Gerald would wonder what his mother had meant that day.

But instead of asking, he'd tucked away his anger, tamped it down—it did no good anyway—and did only and exactly what his father asked, until he was twenty-five and, finally, Lawrence deemed him responsible enough to join the family business.

Sort of.

He gave him a newspaper. One.

"A trial," Lawrence had said, without even meeting his son's eyes, simply scribbling his signature to make the change official.

Look at me, Gerald remembered thinking. *Just look at me, for once.*

He didn't.

One week after Gerald took charge of the *San Francisco Daily Dispatch*, he changed the motto to "Where Truth Is King."

One week after that, he cleaned house.

He and his father didn't fight about it. They didn't *talk* about it. But for the first time, Gerald knew Lawrence was watching him.

Gerald didn't understand mining. He had no natural talent for prospecting. He'd never feel the silver calling out to him from deep within the earth.

But he had something his father didn't. A fearlessness. If everything fell apart, Gerald thought, who cared? This was his chance, and he'd never get another one.

He had to keep his father's eye on him, and that meant taking big swings.

He bet everything he had on talent. He poached the best writers, the best cartoonists, the best editors from the Pulitzer family's papers and the Hearsts' presses too. He nearly doubled his new staff's pay, and with the money he had left, he bought the newest and best equipment.

Gerald Ives never spoke ill of his father.

But he ran his newspaper with a vengeance.

Lawrence had raised him to be a businessman, but his mother

had raised him to be a populist, and he took all of her ideals and fed them back to the people, for a price.

He attacked corruption. He pointed out hypocrisy.

The truth is king, he told his staff again and again, and his readers too, who began to have the sense that maybe all the other newspapers of record weren't quite *telling* the truth.

Some of his competitors folded. Others, he acquired.

He ran two of his father's papers into the ground, then bought them out from under him, and still the two men sat across the dinner table from each other in silence, Lawrence's eyes discreetly lifting off his soup to take inventory of his only son.

For the first time in Gerald's life, he was in control. He decided when and how and by whom he would be seen. What was more, he shaped the world around his readers, told them whom to rage against, what to fear.

His writers could come in late, come in drunk, not come in at all, so long as they performed their duties to his liking. Which meant even those he hadn't poached in his first wave of domination came running soon enough.

Talent was his silver. It called out to him, and he needed to possess it.

One of his writers, in particular, had a knack for penning headlines. His articles were shit, but it didn't matter, and Gerald saw that. The headline was enough.

The headline told the story, and then a person's eyes simply glazed over as they wandered down the ink-ridden page.

Who are you angry with?

What do you fear?

What do you love most in the world, and how could it be taken from you?

These were the things he drilled into his staff. The truth was king, but emotion was the truth's most valuable adviser.

Soon, San Francisco wasn't enough. Then, not even California. The true seat of power, he understood, was in New York.

Only once he had both states, both cities, unified in the press could he rest.

At the turn of the twentieth century, he crossed the country and began his second wave of domination.

The first paper he bought in New York City was a bust. The second folded too. People on the East Coast regarded him with distrust.

But once again his nose for talent did him right when he met Rosalind Goodlett. She was plain faced and petite, almost childlike in appearance, and mostly concerned herself with charity for the poor and sick.

She was also the daughter of a senator.

Yes, Gerald had fashioned himself as the purveyor of truth, but somehow that hadn't added up to *personal trust* in him. After all, his own newspapers spent the bulk of their time and space calling to the public's attention the many moral failings of the wealthiest and most powerful, and at a certain point, there was no avoiding the fact that Gerald himself had entered this stratum.

People trusted Rosalind. Perhaps because she wasn't beautiful, or because of the innocence in her eyes, or maybe it was a game whose rules she'd figured out, but in any case, Gerald watched her and he knew—*knew*—she had a rare talent.

The way Gerald saw it, though, her father was a man who'd merely gotten lucky and tripped into a position of authority.

Which made him corruptible.

Gerald didn't ask Rosalind to marry him. He showered Senator Goodlett with gifts, then suggested an alliance. When the senator arranged Gerald's marriage to Rosalind, he more or less passed Gerald Ives the key to New York.

Within three months of their wedding, he'd purchased two powerful papers in the city, filled them with *his* people, covered them with *his* fingerprints. Then he took his young wife and went back to California. He wasn't a cruel man: He didn't take her money as his own.

She gave him what he most dearly wanted; why shouldn't he let her have her own wish?

And all she really wanted, like him, was to do her work.

And yes, her work consisted primarily of *spending* money, but every penny she spent on her philanthropy came back to him in the form of goodwill. Another kind of investment, though not one his father understood or approved of. Not yet anyway.

Rosalind did not love Gerald. He knew that. But she respected him, and he respected her too, more than he could have guessed at the beginning. They became something more than husband and wife. They were partners.

He did not bed his wife for the first three years of their marriage. He waited for her to come to him. Afterward, they lay in bed and talked for hours, dreamed of everything they might someday have.

He ran one hand over her mousy blond hair, and he looked at her closely for the first time and saw that she could be beautiful. That all it took was looking long enough, close enough, and he was ashamed that he hadn't.

In 1904, they produced a son, Frederick Ives, followed by a daughter, Francine, and he was determined to be good to them, *both* of them.

It was—like his marriage, like poaching Pulitzer's people, like buying the newest printing press, like Rosalind's philanthropy—an investment.

Twice a week, Gerald took his wife and children to dine with his parents in their tasteful Victorian manse. Gigi had married an Englishman and moved to Europe, but even in his sister's absence, Gerald received no more of their father's attention.

That all went to Freddy.

Little Freddy, whom Gerald had let run wild. Who flailed in his studies. Who had plenty of his warm, good-hearted mother in him and very little Ives, except his looks.

Gerald didn't understand it—how both of his parents were all too happy to dote on his own silly, playful, unambitious son when Gerald himself still hadn't managed to glean an ounce of his father's approval.

Maybe that was why he pursued the California State Senate. If the money and business acumen weren't enough to put him in the black, then perhaps political power might.

Back then, senators were elected by state legislatures rather than popular votes, and with all the connections he'd accumulated, Gerald more or less walked into the position. In 1909, he was sworn in, and he and Rosalind began planning for an eventual ascent to the White House.

Even with the full force of the press behind him, though, when the presidential election came around, the caucus chose someone else.

Four years later, he tried again. Again, they chose someone else.

And while Gerald was still smarting from the failure, Lawrence abruptly fell ill.

Gerald rushed to be at his father's side, but even on his deathbed, Lawrence had nothing to say to his son. Instead, for several days, he raged and wept and apologized to people who weren't there. He begged a faceless specter to come home, and then finally seemed to get the answer he wanted. In 1919, at eighty-nine years old, Lawrence found his first shred of peace.

Then he closed his eyes, smiled softly, and took his last breath.

It was as if all the hunger that had lived trapped inside his body slipped out on that last exhale, then snaked its way into Gerald's lungs, where it writhed and snapped like a viper.

To Gerald, that bottomless pit of a nameless want felt less like hunger and more like rage. An anger so violent he thought it might—*would*—destroy anything it touched.

For the first time since his teenage years, he stormed into his childhood bedroom and punched the wall. Then he punched it again, and again, until the blood from his knuckles was smeared across the wallpaper.

When Rosalind came to him, he shoved his wife from the room and locked the door, letting the rage consume him. He destroyed his cherrywood dresser. He ripped the drapes from the window. He battered the bedpost until he was too tired to fight anymore, to *think* anymore, and that was a relief.

He left San Francisco a week after that. He couldn't stand to be there any longer. Couldn't stand to be seen, by his wife or his children, or to watch his mother mourn the father who'd never loved him.

He left them, all of them, and went somewhere new, unfamiliar and without ghosts. He was convinced that in Hollywood, he could sweat his fury out like a fever.

But that wasn't what happened.

His first night in town, at forty-four years old, Gerald Ives fell in love.

He sat in a lounge, sipping a martini, and he looked up at the stage and saw her, lit up like an angel. Untamable red-gold hair. Strange green eyes. A voice like a flame singeing paper.

She was no more beautiful than Rosalind, but she was *striking*. Her presence not only invited but demanded attention, and it was such a relief to give it, to feel that, instead of a bottomless pit of rage.

His want was an ocean he could drown in. Not a lack of something but an excess of it. When she finished her performance, she walked straight off the stage to his table and introduced herself.

Nina Gill had been trying to break into film with about as much luck as Gerald with national politics. Films were still silent then, and half of Nina's power was in the sound of her voice.

Unlike Gerald, or even Gerald's wife, Nina didn't hunger for wealth, power, or change. It wasn't stardom she was after.

She wanted only beauty and pleasure. And lucky for Gerald, he *was* an undeniably beautiful man, more so in middle age than he had been in his youth.

As for the pleasure piece of things, he lost himself in his pursuit of it with her. Drinking, dancing, music, sex.

All day long, every minute that she wasn't with him, he missed her. But when she fell asleep at night—before him, always—his thoughts wandered to Rosalind, which made him think about San Francisco and his old life, and the anger would rise through him again, shapeless and aimless but white hot.

This went on for months. It might've gone on much longer if Rosalind hadn't sent him word that his mother had died.

He knew as soon as he read the telegram that that was the end of it. He'd never go back to San Francisco. Again, his anger rose, but this time there was nowhere to run. So he threw himself back into work.

The First World War was two years over by then and there was talent to be found, money to be made. He needed more than to be drunk and in love. He needed to be busy, worn out.

He bought a burgeoning film studio, Royal Pictures, and put Nina under contract. When her first film came out, a comedy, he filled his newspapers with rapturous reviews of her performance, but it took two more for her star to truly rise.

As the money came back to him—it always did—he began to do something new and novel for Gerald, for *any Ives.*

He spent it. Not invested, not gambled. Spent. Vengefully.

He couldn't have the White House? Fine! He built himself a fortress on the California coast and filled it with beautiful, pleasurable things.

He covered the grounds with gardens and citrus trees, threw lavish parties most Saturday nights.

On Nina's birthday, he brought in elephants and tigers. He invited her Hollywood friends to stay for weeks on end, and they swam drunk and naked in the indoor pool together, beneath a ceiling draped in gauzy fabric.

And they fought. God, did they fight.

Rosalind had never so much as raised her voice to him.

Nina did. Every time she learned of one of his infidelities (of which there were many), she screamed at him, and whenever he suspected one of hers (likely there were none), he screamed back.

They'd fight in front of their friends, throw things at walls, storm onto the grounds and spit at each other. But it never made it to the gossip rags, because by then he owned them all.

So long as his family didn't have to read about him, about his boundless rage, then it would be as if he no longer existed.

All his fury would burn itself out, without ever touching them.

But of course that wasn't what happened. Because Nina fell sick.

12

"THE MYSTERY ILLNESS," I say. "I remember reading about that. Two years where Nina Gill couldn't work. Right as *talkies* started coming out."

"And she was in the news more than ever," Margaret agrees. "I can guess what your *Dove Franklin* had to say about all of that in his so-called book."

"Since when am I responsible for him?" I tease. "I'm not even the one who bought that book! Blame my parents. But yes, he had his theories about her time away."

She flashes me a smile over the ceaseless movement of her hands among the glass shards. "Let me guess: She couldn't hack it in the changing landscape of Hollywood. No one wanted her in the talkies and her star began to fall even faster than it had risen, leading to a two-year mental breakdown, the likes of which she never fully recovered from."

I nod. "An actress at the height of her fame, taking a two-year hiatus and then spending the majority of that in and out of hospitals around the world—a mental breakdown seemed less far fetched to me than some of his other theories."

Her hands still on her tools, and something passes across her face. "There are all kinds of reasons for a woman to want to disappear. Always have been."

"Such as?" I say gently.

Margaret peels her gloves off her small but calloused hands. "Let's walk back to the house. Jodi will certainly bring lunch here, but she won't be happy about it. She doesn't like waiting on me."

"Is she paid to?" I ask, since, still, no information about their relationship has been provided to me.

Margaret's head cocks prettily to one side. "No, I wouldn't say *that*," she settles on, as enigmatic of an answer as I would've expected from her.

I pack up my things, and we leave the workshop, the doors still ajar and unlocked, the ceiling fans still twirling.

We start down the path, in the opposite direction from which Jodi and I arrived, curving around the other side of the garden beds back toward the house. When I point this out, Margaret nods. "It's all the same path. You just stay on it, and you'll get where you're going, eventually."

"Like the labyrinth," I say, clutching my recorder, still running, in one hand and my phone in the other.

"More or less," she says. "I've thought about turning the whole thing into a mosaic, connecting it to the labyrinth. Probably don't have that many years left of my life though. That's a *lot* of work."

"So it was on purpose?" I say. "The *unicursal* path."

"I like taking away that element of decision, whenever I can."

"Why's that?" I ask.

"Because it gives me peace," she says. "Remembering my decisions don't make much of a difference in the end."

I balk, even miss a step. "You really think that?"

Another sly, nearly coquettish smile, and at eighty-seven years old, she's still pulling it off. "Think. *Hope*. Somewhere in between the two."

The path curls down to walk along the marsh, and I see a fan boat docked among the reeds. "You use that much?" I ask.

"Not much," she says. "But more often than I use the car."

"That hardly tells me anything," I point out.

"Now you're catching on," she teases.

But honestly, I'm not. When I let her talk, she'll talk. But when I want a straight answer, she's more evasive.

Which once again begs the question: What am I doing here?

"I'm curious about something," I say.

"I'd describe you as curious about *everything*," Margaret parries.

"Hazard of the trade," I say, then admit, "or more realistically, I was just born this way."

"Sounds like you're on a unicursal path of your own," she reasons.

She doesn't invite me to ask my question, but I do anyway: "Why now?"

"What do you mean?" she says innocently. I give her a look, and she laughs. "Every once in a while, you've got some bite, Alice Scott. I like that."

"Thank you. And I like when you *answer* the questions I ask."

Another laugh. "I know I look great, but I'm old. If not now, when?"

"Right," I agree. "But 'never' was an option. Something had to have convinced you to talk to me. And as great as *I* am, I don't buy that it was my rambling voicemail."

We pause at the back doors to Margaret's house. "I made a promise to someone," she says. "And then they died before I could tell them I took it back."

"You're not going to tell me who, are you?" I ask.

She smiles and opens the door. "Not today."

As we step inside, from somewhere deeper in the house, Jodi grunts, "You're back."

"Nothing gets past you, does it?" Margaret leads me through a door into a bright, powder-blue kitchen, where Jodi's slicing sandwiches into tiny triangles.

"Tuna salad?" Margaret asks, leaning over Jodi's shoulder to look at the cutting board.

"Cucumber," Jodi says, "and now that you're back, you can take over."

Margaret gives a belabored sigh, but still steps up to the task when Jodi retreats to wash her hands over the deep double sink, its overhead window looking out on the backyard.

"How long does it usually take a person to get used to this house?" I ask. "I don't understand how anything is connected. I would've thought we were at the front of the house here."

"There's no 'usually,'" Margaret says.

I frown, which makes her laugh.

"Not a facial expression I've seen you do much of," she says.

On her way out of the room, Jodi says, "No one has to get used to the house, because no one except us is ever in it."

"Ever?" I ask.

Margaret gives an unbothered shrug. "More or less."

"How do you sell your work, to the shops and galleries?" I ask.

She waves a hand. "Oh, Jodi handles all that. Not that there's much to handle. Like I said—most tourists are looking for a different sort of thing than what I do."

That certainly explains the reaction from the shopkeeper who'd finally passed along Margaret's contact information. He'd said something along the lines of, *You're welcome to it, but if Irene Mayberry is actually Margaret Ives, then I'm Elvis.*

"What about groceries?" I ask.

"Jodi," she says. "Jodi handles it all."

"And what, you just stay in this house all day?"

"I stay in the yard mostly," Margaret says. "Or out on the boat. Or in my home."

"That's got to be lonely," I say.

"Less so than you'd think," she retorts. "You get used to it, isolation. Funny thing is, I was already used to it by the time I 'disappeared.'"

"Meaning?" I ask.

"No more chitchat right now," she says. "It's nearly dinnertime, and no one needs to see the inside of my mouth while I'm eating."

• • •

ON FRIDAY, THE morning after my best session with Margaret yet, I'm picking through my notes—*and* typing up an extremely uninspiring (though blessedly short) article on new skin-care trends for *The Scratch*—when Theo texts me.

I'm shooting in Atlanta rn, he says.

Oh, nice, I write back. Who/what?

That new fashion designer Mogi, he replies. Should be a good time.

He's not giving me a ton of conversational ammo here, but I'd rather be doing anything than working right now, while sitting out on Little Croissant's patio, sweating through my sundress, so I write back anyway: Yeah, Atlanta's super cool! Let me know if you want any recs.

How far is it from where you are? he says.

I do a quick search to double-check. Not that close. Like three and a half hours by car.

Shit, he says.

A second later, a new message buzzes in. What are you up to this weekend?

Oh, nothing, just more meandering interviews that manage to avoid almost anything juicy from a story I'm *sure* is ninety percent juice.

> Nothing today, working tomorrow
> during the day, then nothing Sunday and
> Monday.

Nice, he says, adding, I prob will be done by Saturday night too.

The text just hangs there, and understanding clicks into place. He's doing what he always does: not quite asking me to ask *him* to hang out. It's annoying, how indirect he always is, but at least there's some comfort in knowing him well enough to read between the lines. Unlike the horror that unfolded between me and Hayden the other night.

I take a screenshot of the exchange and text it to my friends.

Priya is the first to reply: A girl's gotta eat, Alice.

Bianca is right behind her: Turn in your skincare piece. Also BARF.

Cillian slides in next: MY ENEMY.

I thumbs-up Bianca's text first, then write out my reply: I'm going to invite him to come down but that's where I draw the line. I will NOT be asking whether I can fly to HIM.

Tell him he can meet you there, then send him this address, Cillian says. I follow the link he's sent.

It takes me to a map of Antarctica, a little pin over something called the Pole of Inaccessibility research station.

Will do! I say, then text Theo: You're welcome to come down if you want. There's not a ton to do, but there's at least one cute bar/restaurant and a good coffee shop, and it's beautiful.

Really? Theo says.

                Yes.

  Sure, why not? I could drive down when I finish up tomorrow afternoon. Meet around seven?

Sounds good, I tell him, then turn my phone over and click back to yesterday's notes.

We covered a decent amount of ground.

Nina Gill's mystery illness. The fluctuating weight. The hair loss. The months she'd spent in the Swiss Alps while she recovered.

During their time apart, Nina had fallen in love with her doctor, and in the aftermath of her and Gerald's breakup, he finally reconnected with his sister, Gigi, whose English husband had died not long after she discovered she was pregnant.

Gerald insisted on moving Gigi and her new baby, Ruth, onto his estate, now that Nina had moved *out* and *on* with the doctor.

"Out of the blue?" I'd asked Margaret, and she'd given one of those dry, secretive smiles.

"Nothing is out of the blue, when it comes to my family," she said. "Not ever."

I could *feel* the hidden meaning beneath the words, but when I pressed her on it, she evaded me. Just kept going with her story.

For a time, Gerald had continued his management of Nina's career, even after her marriage, but the truth was, even with his media pull, the time away had changed the landscape too much for her. The reviews of her newer films were mostly concerned with the physical toll her illness had taken on her—she'd visibly aged and gained a fair bit of weight, and an outlet beyond Gerald's control had nicknamed her *the not-so ingenue*. With the emphasis on *new*.

The audiences had tired of her too. As far as they were concerned, she belonged to the silent-film era, and every time she spoke, her surprising voice convinced them she'd overstayed her welcome.

She left the business entirely in 1931, and that same year, Gerald moved his wife, Rosalind, and his now grown children down to the House of Ives, as if the last twelve years apart had never happened.

Freddy and Francine were twenty-seven and twenty-six respectively by then, both unmarried and neither excited about relocating their entire lives. But Gerald controlled all the money, and so when he said *jump*, they jumped. Thus, he; his wife; his grown children; his sister, Gigi; and her daughter, Ruth, all wound up living in the same house. If you could call the Ives estate a house, and honestly, I don't think you can. But still.

"Gerald and Rosalind never shared a room again, of course," Margaret told me. "They were cold but cordial. And it was much too late for him to fix his relationship with his own children, but his niece was just a baby, so essentially all that opulence Gerald had lavished on his mistress was turned toward baby Ruth at that point. She was the light of his life. The world had probably never seen such a spoiled child—until Laura and I came along, anyway—but she was good natured to her core. When she was small, her nickname was Little Princess, and even when Laura and I were little girls and Ruth was a young woman, we all mostly called her LP."

It wasn't a *bad* interview. It was arguably good! But I could *feel* that there was more lurking just underneath what she was saying, and she still didn't trust me enough to share it.

I'd offered multiple times to stop recording, but she'd waved off the offer.

"You can trust me," I promised her.

She parried with, "*You* can trust *me* too."

It effectively ended the discussion. If I wanted her to open up to me, I had to respect that she had her own reasons for what she chose to share and when.

Margaret refused to be rushed, and I knew that pushing would only slow us down in the long run. If I got the job, there'd be plenty of time to dig into these stories. My only real goal, these next three and a half weeks, was to earn her trust.

I just had to hope Hayden wasn't having better luck than I was.

• • •

ON SATURDAY MORNING, I'm driving through the fog to Margaret's house when she calls to cancel on me.

"Something came up," she says through my rental car's speakers when I take her call. I put on my blinker and pull off into the Little Croissant / gift shop / enclave parking lot.

"No problem at all," I assure her. "If you just need a few hours, we could meet later?"

"Not today," she says stiffly.

"Then tomorrow?" I suggest.

"Not tomorrow either," she says.

And Monday she'll be meeting with Hayden. I ignore the sinking sensation in my chest, grapple for a grip on the hope that this doesn't mean she's close to firing me, before I've even been hired.

I clear my throat. "Should we just pick things back up during our Tuesday session?" I ask, crossing all of my fingers against the steering wheel as I pull into a shady parking spot.

"If I can, yes," she says, but offers nothing else.

"Okay, well, if things change on your end, or even if you just need something, don't be afraid to reach out."

"You're a sweet girl," she says, and I swear there's a hint of regret in her voice.

She's about to fire me. Isn't she?

I swallow a lump of emotion and let my hand hover over the button to end the call. "Okay, well, take care, Margaret."

"You too, Alice," she says, and we hang up.

I sit, staring at the wheel, trying all my best pep talks on myself and, for once, getting nowhere. With a groan, I slump forward.

Something thunks next to my left ear and I sit up with a yelp, spinning toward the window.

A gap-toothed man in a bucket hat grins at me from the other side of the glass. Captain Cecil gives a hearty wave, then steps back to make room for the door as I swing it open and step out into the heat. "There she is!" he says, like I'm just the person he wanted to see.

Me, a perfect stranger he's bumped into twice.

Instantly, my mood lifts. My heart very nearly *soars*. I've found a kindred spirit in Cecil, and it makes me realize how lonely I've been since the awkwardness with Hayden last week. I should be used to the isolation of this job, but I'm not sure I ever will be.

"I was wondering when I'd run into you again," I tell him.

"And I you," he says. "I have an invitation for you."

"Oh?" I say, intrigued.

"Fish Bowl's having a little soiree tonight," he says.

"I do love a soiree," I say. "Celebrating anything in particular?"

"As a matter of fact, yes," he says. "It's an annual fete. In honor of my birthday."

"Oh, wow! Happy birthday!" I say.

He chortles. "Thank you, dear, but my birthday isn't until December. This is just *in honor* of my birthday, which happens to be Christmas. I always thought that was a raw deal, so I started throwing myself a summer bash about ten years ago and never looked back."

"Genius," I say, and his grin widens again.

"I think so," he agrees. "Anyway, small bites provided, no gifts required, and drinks at happy hour prices. Stop by if you feel so inclined."

"I will," I promise him. "Would it be all right if I brought a friend?"

"Already made a friend!" he cries. "Other than me, of course."

I laugh. "Well, no. Someone from back home. He's driving up from Atlanta later today."

"Sure, bring him along," he says. "It's a more-the-merrier situation."

"My favorite kind," I say.

"Then I'll see you sometime between seven and midnight, Ms. Scott." He tips his bucket hat at me and saunters off.

The smell of ground coffee beans beckons me, a siren call coming from Little Croissant. I grab my laptop from my back seat and head toward the robin's-egg blue coffee shop's elevated platform.

I'm out, so I might as well enjoy it, but if I can't interview Margaret, I'm at least going to do some more independent research.

I order an iced brown sugar latte at the window, then take it down to the flagstone patio.

Some deep part of my subconscious feels his presence and sends an uncanny prickle to the back of my neck in the second before my gaze sweeps over the hunched, hulking shape of Hayden Anderson.

His computer sits on the little mosaic table in front of him, but his eyes are right on me.

There's no pretending we didn't see each other.

For once, I wish I was a little less chronically polite, that I was as comfortable with a good scowl or blank stare as the man four feet in front of me.

"Hello," I say coolly.

"Hi." His reply is terse, uncomfortable. Everything about him is terse and uncomfortable, which makes me feel a *little* better about our last humiliating encounter.

Another beat. "Anyway!" I turn toward the table farthest from him. It's probably only fifteen feet away, but I think I can manage to pass five minutes there before finding an excuse to leave.

"Shouldn't you be with Margaret today?" he asks.

My shoulders rise protectively. I should brush him off, make an excuse, or flat-out not answer. That's what he would do.

Unfortunately, I'm still—at my core—me.

I'm already marching back to his table, the truth pouring out of me. "She canceled."

His face betrays nothing. It so fully betrays nothing that I'm *positive* he knows something. Which I say, as I plop down in the iron chair opposite him.

"I don't," he says.

Somehow, I can *hear* the technicality in his voice. He's telling the truth, but only just.

"So you don't know why she canceled," I say, "but you have a guess."

He lets out a sigh. "I'm not going to speculate, Alice."

"No, I know," I say. "You wouldn't possibly share any helpful information with me, even though I am the smallest and least significant threat to this job that you can possibly imagine."

His jaw clenches. "You're putting words in my mouth."

"I'm reading between the lines," I counter.

He leans forward over the table, our knees clashing under it. "Just because you've made a decision about how I feel," he growls, "doesn't make it true."

"So, what, you're *not* positive Margaret's going to hire you over me?" I ask.

"I'm reasonably certain," he replies cautiously. "Would you rather I kept that from you?"

"You're pretty keen to keep everything else from me," I say.

His frown deepens. His lips part, as if he's debating saying something. A sigh escapes him right before he caves: "I can't give this up."

I shift in my seat, my anger abating and leaving me unpleasantly vulnerable. That much I understand. That much I don't blame him for. I *expected* him to fight for this opportunity, just like I am.

"I know," I admit. "Neither can I."

He holds my gaze for one long moment. "I would like to be friends."

At my surprised laugh, his inky brows draw together.

"What's funny about that?" he wants to know.

"Don't take this the wrong way," I warn, "but you sound like a robot learning to love."

His face screws up in bafflement. "I don't know *any* way to take that."

"I just mean, you've pushed me away, kissed me, and insulted me," I say. "And now you're formally proposing friendship."

"I wouldn't describe our relationship until now like that, exactly," he says, visibly and audibly dismayed.

My head cocks to one side. "How *would* you describe it?"

His eyes train on his green tea. He pushes it farther from the ledge. "So you *don't* want to be friends."

"*You're putting words in my mouth,*" I retort.

He barely smiles. "What are you doing tonight?"

"Tonight?" I ask. "Hot date. At Fish Bowl."

"Ah. Too bad," he says.

"Were you going to ask me to hang out?" I ask.

"If you thought you could go one night without talking about Margaret Ives," he says, "then yes."

"Ah," I say. "Too bad."

"Maybe next month," he says.

"Maybe," I agree, standing. "If you can forgive me for taking your job."

13

MY LAST TEXT from Theo came in at three p.m.: Finishing up here soon.

One good thing about Theo Bouras is that he is, like me, a social creature by nature. Not only was he delighted at the thought of going to Cecil's not-birthday party, but he'd offered to meet me there, so I didn't have to wait on him.

I work until six, then take a quick shower, swipe on some mascara, and head out for the night. Downtown is *packed*, and I have to park four blocks away. As I'm doing so, my phone buzzes with a message from my mom.

I say "message," but really, it's just a link to an article about how California is going to eventually go up in flames, then break off from the rest of the country and sink to the floor of the ocean.

Ever since I first moved to LA, I've gotten a text like this a few times a year, with such regularity that at times I've wondered whether she has a calendar alert set to nudge me about my new home's impending doom.

I tried to accept it as a form of love, even if the greater implication was also that all my decisions were wrong.

Wow, that's terrible, I write back, and before I hit send, I stop short just outside of Fish Bowl, guilt creeping in.

I should be checking in with her more often, making sure she's okay. Dad would be so disappointed if he knew how little we've seen of each other since he died.

I'm in Georgia for a story, I add. And I was wondering if I could drive down to see you next weekend?

Sure, she says. Not the most emphatic of responses, but still, a weight eases off my chest.

I tuck my phone into my bag and step inside.

If Fish Bowl verged on overstimulating during my *last* visit, this time it can only be described as *visually cacophonous*. From the fishnet-covered ceiling, dozens if not hundreds of colored paper lanterns hang. Massive bouquets of tropical flowers sit atop every table, and most of the guests are dressed in bold florals to match.

The theme, if there is one, appears to be: Bright.

The place is packed, but hardly any tables are taken, everyone standing and milling instead. I pick my way over to the bartender and ask for something tropical and nonalcoholic. He comes back with a tangerine-colored concoction in a goblet, an orchid spilling out over the top of it. "Open or closed?" he asks about my tab when I hand over my credit card.

"Open's fine."

He cups a hand around his ear and leans in to hear me over the roar of both the crowd and the music.

"OPEN'S. FINE."

He goes to run the card, then slides it back over the counter as I scan for anyone I might recognize. Cecil's nowhere in sight, and the only other person I've met before, in any capacity, is Sheri, the waitress carrying a tray of some kind of cheese-puff treat around. I retreat to the booth in the corner to wait for Theo.

When I sent the address to him, he'd sent a thumbs-up back, but no other acknowledgment. I do the math in my head, trying to guess how much longer it might take him to get here.

I send him one more text: Eta?

Rather than pretending to be engrossed by my phone, I opt to set it aside and try to look approachable. This mainly consists of gazing hopefully around the room for anyone not already engaged in conversation whom I could make small talk with.

I would've been more careful what I wished for—if I'd thought for even one second that there was a chance Hayden might be here. Again.

He's the stillest thing in the room, which makes him stand out. His height, even sitting, and his stark black-and-white wardrobe don't help either.

He's at a table on the far side of the restaurant, and I become acutely aware that I've taken *his* go-to spot, in the corner, near the bathrooms.

He lifts his water glass in greeting. I lift my ridiculous mocktail back. Then he unfurls from his seat and stalks toward me.

"Twice in one day," I say.

"It's a small island," he says.

"Still," I say. "An incredible coincidence."

"Can I sit?" he asks.

I glance toward the door.

"Your hot date," he says. "Right."

"He's running late," I say, just a hair defensive.

"I can keep you company," he offers. "If you'd like."

His voice is low, even, warm—a surprisingly *inviting* combination. I glance at the time on my phone again, finishing off the calculation that spotting Hayden had interrupted. "For a minute," I say. "He won't be much longer."

His chin dips once and he slides into the booth, across from me. "So are you here tonight by coincidence or have you also met Cecil?"

I crack a smile. "Cecil invited me. And I was feeling *pretty special* for that, until ten seconds ago."

"Oh, you should still feel special," Hayden assures me. "He only invited me because he decided—based on nothing, I should add—that I'm doing a write-up on this place."

I laugh. "No, that's pretty much why I'm here too."

"Maybe," he allows, "but was he smiling when he invited you?"

"I have yet to see that man *not* smiling," I say.

"And that, Scott, is where our experiences with Cecil diverge."

I shift in my seat, suppressing a laugh. Even when I want to be cold with him, I can't. Maybe I should just give it up. Accept that, as is typical for me, I like and even respect someone regardless of whether they like or respect me. "Then why'd you come?" I ask him.

He stares at me for a beat. "I felt bad."

"Honestly, I doubt Cecil would have noticed if either of us didn't show up," I say, "especially since he doesn't even seem to *be* here."

He gives one firm shake of his head. "Not about that. About the other night."

Oh, god. A burn begins at the tips of my ears, spreading toward my face.

At the top of the list of things I want in this moment: to pretend the kiss never happened.

My phone starts ringing on the table between us, Theo's name flashing on-screen. Once again, the universe is coming through for me. I flash Hayden my sunniest smile. "My date." I tip my head toward my phone and answer the call, turning sideways on the bench. "Theo?"

"Alice, hi." Whatever he says next gets lost in the noise.

"Hold on a second," I tell him. "I have to go outside. I can't hear you."

I excuse myself from Hayden with a *one minute* gesture and head out to the street. "You still there?"

"I'm sorry, Alice," he says.

"Sorry?" As I say it, something sinks in my chest.

"The photo shoot ran long," he says.

"That's fine," I promise him. "How far away are you?"

He sighs. "I haven't left yet."

"Oh." I turn back to the window, inadvertently meeting Hayden's eyes. The embarrassment and disappointment bubble over then in the form of stinging tears. I face the street again, urging my voice into steadiness. "So what are you thinking?"

"I just bit off more than I can chew," he says. "It would've been fun to meet up, but my flight's tomorrow night, so at this point, I feel like I should probably just chill here. The drive wouldn't be worth it, I don't think."

I stop myself, right in the nick of time, from suggesting he change his flight to leave from here. Surely this has already occurred to him. He travels as much as I do. He knows how all of this works.

It's not worth it to him. That's the end of the conversation. And it's not a surprise, but after the last few days of emotional highs and lows, it hits me harder than it should.

"I understand," I tell him. "We'll just catch up later."

"I knew you'd get it," he says. "You're the best, Alice."

I smile but can't quite will myself to thank him for the compliment. I clear my throat. "Get home safe."

"Enjoy the rest of your stay," he tells me. "See you back in LA."

"Yep!" I cheep. He says bye and clicks off. For a second I just stand there, phone still pressed to my ear, debating what to do.

I can't face Hayden right now. It was bad enough being rejected by him, mid–make out. Now I've bragged about a date that isn't happening.

But my purse is still inside, sitting at the table with him.

Get your bag, go home, and get back to work, I tell myself. It will be fine. A nice night in might be exactly what I need. I can text my friends and do some more research, or else settle in with some key lime pie and reality TV.

All that stands in my way is walking through that door and snatching my purse.

I can do it. I steel myself, drop my phone to my side, and march back in.

Hayden's brow shoots upward at something in my expression as I approach. "Everything okay?" he asks.

"Fine," I say, grabbing the strap of my bag. "Something just came up, so I've got to head out."

"Like an emergency?"

"Sort of." I avoid eye contact while I stuff my phone into my bag. "Enjoy your night."

I hear him call my name at my back, but with the party in full swing, I figure I have plausible deniability there. I don't turn around.

I just flee down the dark street.

I've made it two blocks toward my car when I hear him shout my name again.

Shit.

"I have to go," I call back, not slowing my pace. It doesn't matter. He's too tall; he's got the advantage. He catches up to me right as I'm turning down the narrow, empty side street where I left my car parked between two palm trees.

"What happened?" he asks. "Are you okay?"

Something in me snaps. I whirl back around on him. "Are you *trying* to embarrass me, Hayden?"

Shock splashes across his face. "What?"

I stalk toward him. "It wasn't enough for you to kiss me—and let's be clear here, *you* kissed *me*—shut me down, and insult my ability. You had to show up here tonight, to what? Ruin my date? Or—did you not even believe I *had* a date? Well, guess what! You win! I don't! He's not coming after all! He, like you, changed his mind at the last second. I guess I have that effect on a certain kind of man. So if you're done chasing me down the street to get a good look at my humiliation, I'd love to go home right now and pretend this night—this whole last week—never happened."

I spin toward my car.

He grabs my arm.

My gaze snaps from his loose grip up to his face, hovering over me and torqued in frustration.

I wait for him to say something, or to let go. One second. Two. Three. It's like we're both frozen there.

"I thought you invited me," he blurts.

"What?"

He huffs, eyes dropping to our feet before rebounding to my face. "I thought you were kidding. About the date."

I stare at him, utterly shocked.

"*Not* because I don't believe you could get a date," he goes on gruffly. "Just because we've only been here a week and a half, and almost everyone who lives on this island is a retiree."

I'm still staring, blinking at him, mouth open, like a goldfish who accidentally plopped out of her fish tank.

"So I thought when you said . . ." He grimaces. "*You* don't have anything to be embarrassed about here, Alice. I know I'm the one who kissed you. I know I'm the one who shut it down."

I still haven't regained control of my voice. Or my limbs. His hand softens on my elbow, and I do everything I can not to lean into the touch, to find comfort there.

"There's something I have to tell you," he says, shaking his head.

I finally manage a small "Okay."

Once more, his dark gaze sweeps toward the gap between our feet. "She asked for me."

Our eyes connect. "What do you mean?"

"I didn't track Margaret Ives down," he says. "You're the only one who found her."

I sway slightly on the spot.

"*She* found *me*," he says. "She reached out to my agent. I guess she read *Our Friend Len*, and she asked if I'd be open to doing some meetings to see whether I'd be a good fit to write her biography."

My legs wobble. Hayden's grip on me tightens slightly as I lean back, slowing my fall as I slump against the side of my car. He steps in close, balancing me for a second before his hands uncertainly release me.

"So she's already chosen," I half whisper.

"No," he says quietly, but when I meet his eyes, he looks down. "I don't know. Maybe."

Now I'm the one to study our feet, both of mine in between both of his. "You could've told me sooner."

He sighs. "I felt bad. You did all the work of finding her, and then I just showed up."

"Why did she even have me come down here?" I ask, shaking my head. Tears well in my eyes. A snort of laughter escapes me when I realize. "Long day," I say, wiping at the damp spots in my tear trough.

With a frown, Hayden touches the side of my face, a gentle slide of his palm and then a sweep of his thumb over the top of my cheek, collecting the moisture. "You wouldn't be here if she wasn't still open to working with you."

"Yeah," I say half-heartedly. He's right though. He has to be. There has to be a reason I'm here. "Or maybe it's all some kind of game to her. Maybe she's just using me to try and get your best work or something."

"I don't know," he admits. "But I started with an advantage. It didn't feel right, kissing you, when you didn't know the full story."

I look up into his eyes. "That's why?"

His hand curves softly around my ear. "That's why."

Delicate warmth unfurls through my belly. "No girlfriend?"

"No girlfriend," he says. "And your date?"

"Real," I say. "But not a boyfriend."

I straighten away from the car, the movement pressing me against him. "This still wouldn't work, Alice." His voice rumbles through my stomach and my hip, where his free hand has settled.

"What wouldn't?" I ask.

His eyes track the rise and fall of my breath. "We're still competing for the same job."

"So I'm competition again?" I tease.

His hand flexes at my waist, and I'm pulled snug against him, where I can feel every hard line of him. "You were always competition."

"I'm going to kiss you, Hayden," I say, almost a warning.

But I don't get the chance. His mouth is already on mine, one of his hands snaking into my hair, his other sliding down my backside as I arch hungrily into him. I'm pinned against the car, gasping into his mouth, my thigh lifted up along his hip on this abandoned street. His long fingers curl into my skin. His hand slides higher, pushing my skirt up along my thigh, moving closer and closer to where I want him. He brushes along the damp lace of my underwear and swears against the side of my throat. "You never wear pants," he murmurs, his thumb tracing down me. "It makes it hard to think."

"You *always* wear pants," I manage to breathe out. "I'm worried you'll have heatstroke."

His laugh is gravelly at my ear, the sound sending as much of a thrill through me as his careful touch. I move against him, and he slides his hand down me more fully. A jumble of voices and footsteps approach us from around the corner, and he steps back abruptly, smoothing my skirt down my thighs again.

"You can come over, if you want," I say thickly.

"Stop inviting me," he says.

"Why?" I ask.

"Because eventually I'm going to say yes," he replies.

"That's the general idea," I say.

"I'm obviously attracted to you," he says.

"Obviously," I agree.

"This can't go well, Alice," he says.

"Which part?" I ask, doubtful. There's at least one thing I'm very nearly *certain* could go well.

"We both want this job too much," he says. "Even more than we might want . . ."

"You're worried I'll get too attached," I guess.

"I'm worried about the work," he says. "Neither of us can afford to be pulling punches here. If either of us doesn't give this our all, we'll regret it. And then we'll resent each other for it. And I don't know if I can handle being the one person on the planet Alice Scott doesn't like."

"Oh, I'm sure you could," I tell him.

His smile—wide enough to reveal teeth—dazzles me for a moment. I want to climb inside of it.

The group that came from around the corner staggers tipsily

past. When they've moved off, he steps in close again, our waists connecting, the infinitesimal amount of pressure flooding me with want. "Maybe some other time," he says, the rest of the sentence hanging in the air, unspoken. "After all of this."

"Maybe," I agree.

"Would you be able to forgive me?" he asks, looking up at me through his lashes.

Of course I wouldn't hold it against him if he got the job, but would I be able to handle the way his presence would remind me of my failure?

"Would *you*?" I ask him, rather than answering.

He frowns, and I can see it in his face. For all of our differences, we're both proud. This spark between us is fun and surprising right now. In three more weeks, it could settle into something bitter.

"Okay." My nod feels strangely final, like a handshake agreement: *May the best writer win, and may it be enough to make up for the orgasms we forsake.*

He steps back from the curb, and I straighten, pulling my keys free from the outside pocket of my bag.

He gives me the same kind of nod. "Get home safe."

The formality of it makes my heart twinge. "You too." I turn and round my car, unlocking it.

"Alice?" he calls over the top of it.

"Hmm?"

"She lies to me too," he says. "For whatever it's worth, Margaret Ives isn't telling me the truth."

14

ON MONDAY, I'M working over dinner at Rum Room when I find something strange.

I'm prepping for tomorrow's interview with Margaret, to continue her grandfather's story after his affair with the actress Nina Gill ended, and I come across a news item, in *Vanity Fair*, covering the opulent 1949 wedding of Gerald's niece, Ruth Allen. *The little princess* he'd raised more devotedly than his own children.

Ruth was twenty-one years old when she married the actor turned decorated World War II pilot turned talent manager James Oller, and their wedding was the event of the summer.

Starlets, politicians, famous artists of all stripes descended on the grounds of the House of Ives to celebrate the union. Margaret and her sister, Laura, eleven and eight years old at the time, acted as flower girls for their first cousin once removed, wearing crowns of vibrant yellow sunflowers to match Ruth's bouquet.

Even Nina Gill, accompanied by her husband, had attended, sitting on the same expansive lawn as Gerald for the first time since their affair ended twenty-two years earlier.

The wedding festivities lasted three days, and were completely devoid of photography, which made every society journalist covering the affair that much more committed to making the reader feel as though she were *there*.

It's effective. I've read four articles about the wedding back-to-back, my food going cold on the table at Rum Room, when I hit on the thing that jolts me back to the present.

To *my* reality.

It's a line that contains Ruth's middle name. Not *legal* middle name—a quick search tells me she doesn't have one, officially. But apparently, among close family, her full name was Ruth Nicollet Ives Allen.

A sizzle of recognition goes down my spine. *Where do I know that name from?*

It only takes a second to hit me. I scroll back through my notes, double-checking.

The very first inn that Lawrence Richard Ives purchased, to capitalize on other prospectors once he'd struck silver ore. Margaret had called it the Ebner. When Lawrence had first bought it, it was called the Arledge. And then, for a chunk of time in between that, just like I thought: the Nicollet. Same spelling and everything.

Coincidence? Or is Nicollet a family name?

But if it is, it makes even *less* sense that Margaret referred to the hotel by its current name. Nicollet should've been burned into her brain.

I do a quick search of "Nicollet" paired with "Lawrence Ives," and the results are scant. The only thing of note is the website for the current-day Ebner, whose "History" page proudly declares its former ownership by the famed family, where it also lists its previous monikers.

I shake my head. Most likely, Margaret read something years ago about the Nicollet's new name, and simply called it by its latest name because that was what came to mind. And maybe Nicollet *is* a family name, but not one she's familiar with.

It's a far more likely explanation than the one my brain keeps circling: that Margaret Ives doesn't want me looking closely at that hotel, even as she pretends to bare the Ives family's history and soul.

What Hayden said keeps replaying in my mind.

Margaret Ives isn't telling me the truth.

I shovel some now-cold lobster mac into my mouth and pull up the email address for the Ebner Hotel.

* * *

ON TUESDAY, WE'RE sitting out back in Adirondack chairs, sipping more of Jodi's incredible mint lemonade, and I decide to take a big swing.

"What's significant about the name Nicollet?" I ask.

Margaret's glass clinks against her teeth. Rather than follow through with her sip, she returns the glass to the arm of her chair.

"What do you mean?" she says. Her tone is so innocent that, if not for that flicker of surprise in her reaction, I'd be sure I'd read too much into nothing.

"The Ebner Hotel," I say. "It was called the Nicollet, for a long stretch of time when your family owned it. And Ruth Ives Allen's unofficial middle name was Nicollet."

Her head cocks, like she's trying to anticipate where this is going.

"I'm curious why you'd call the inn by its new name," I explain. "Have you been there recently?" I disregard the fact that she's already told me she hasn't. If she wants to give me new information now, I don't want to call her a liar for withholding it earlier.

She considers for a beat, her eye contact unyielding. Then she sighs. "I suppose you'll find out now, one way or another."

"Probably," I agree. "But remember: I've signed a nondisclosure.

I'm not going to force you to publicly share anything you don't want to. Whatever you tell me, it doesn't have to go beyond this room."

Her eyes narrow. Then, slowly, she leans forward and stops both of my recorders. "This includes the boy."

"What boy?" I ask.

"I have *two* NDAs," she says. "So whatever I tell you, you can't take it to him. You understand that, don't you?"

The word *boy* is so wrong that it takes me thirty seconds to track her train of thought. "Are we talking about Hayden here?"

She nods. "You've known I was here for months, and no one else has tracked me down, which makes me think I can trust you. But him, I'm not so sure of. I'm still figuring him out."

I'm surprised by the swell of protectiveness in my gut. "You can trust him too. He won't break your confidence."

One of her silvery brows curves. It tugs on her lips, pulling her mouth into a sly smile. "Oh? So you're campaigning for *him* to get the job now?"

"Definitely not," I say quickly. "I want this. And I'll do a great job. I know that. I just . . . You can trust him, that's all."

"I'll take that under advisement," she says. "But still, my point remains. You're about to be the first person outside of my immediate family to hear something, and I don't want it going any further just yet."

I set my pen down. "I swear."

She gathers herself for a second. "My grandfather Gerald was the one to rename the inn. In 1919."

"The year your great-grandfather Lawrence died," I point out—I noticed the correlation while I was on the Arledge/Nicollet/Ebner's History web page.

Margaret nods. "I told you that in those final days of Lawrence's life, he was raving to his former business partner and apologizing to his little brother. But there was one more thing he kept saying." A look of resolve steals over her, her shoulders relaxing as if whatever she's just decided to share has given her some measure of relief. "Nicollet."

I've read it dozens of times in the last couple of days, but still the way she says it, almost reverentially, sends goose bumps prickling down my arms. "Who was that?"

"The one it was all for." The corner of her mouth twitches into a smile, small and fleeting. "That's what Lawrence told her. *Nicollet, this was all for you. Tell me to come home, and I'll leave all of this behind.* Gerald had never even heard his father say the name before. And he only found out who Nicollet was after Lawrence died, when Gerald read his father's journals."

A *lover*, I think at first, but then it dawns on me. "His sister."

She nods confirmation. "In my family, that's what the name came to represent: the person you'd do anything for. The only one who could make you give it all up. That's why they gave Ruth that middle name."

My chest pinches. "That's beautiful." I mean it. But it doesn't answer the question. "Why didn't you just . . . tell me about that?"

She studies me, another small smile unfurling over her lips. "And here I thought you'd already figured it out."

I hadn't, evidently, but there's nothing like a challenge to get your brain turning, and as soon as she says it, my mind turns into a prime-time police procedural's serial killer board, pinning details and suspects together with little bits of red string. Ruth's mother, Gigi Ives Allen, wasn't in the room with her father when he died. She wasn't even in the country, until well after her father died. Only Gerald was there, at their father Lawrence's bedside, to hear his ranting about Dicky and Thomas and Nicollet. Only Gerald had read their father's diaries.

Then he'd fled the rest of his family, shortly after Lawrence's death. He'd met Nina in Los Angeles, and they'd passed nearly a decade together, before her mystery illness took her overseas and she married someone else.

Right around the time Ruth Ives Allen was born.

"She wasn't Gigi's daughter," I blurt, before I'm even sure of it.

Margaret doesn't look scandalized or even surprised by the theory. If anything, she looks a little satisfied, slightly . . . *smirky*. "I knew you'd get there," she says approvingly.

"Nina's mystery illness," I say. "The time spent in the Alps . . . it was a pregnancy?"

"Nine months would've been too suspicious," Margaret explains. "They had to drag it out. And publicize it, when they were able. Staged hospital visits, complete with photographs, in those first few months of the pregnancy, and then again right after the birth, which happened overseas. When Gigi's husband died, Gerald and Nina saw an opportunity to bring their daughter home without a scandal."

"But their affair was an open secret," I point out. "I mean, even Dove Franklin knew about it."

"Yes, but back then having an affair was one thing. Maybe *everyone* wasn't doing it, but loads of people in Gerald and Nina's circles were. Not to mention all the showmances of the era. But Gerald was raised Catholic and was never going to subject Rosalind to a divorce. And even if he *had* been willing, the timeline wouldn't have borne out, and Ruth would've been the one to suffer. Nina didn't want that for her daughter, and neither did Gerald. So they split up. She married someone else. He raised their daughter as his niece, and they were only ever in the same room again the week Ruth got married. He gave up the woman he loved to be the father he should've been the first time around, and Nina . . ." Margaret's voice settles into a flat, matter-of-fact tone. "Well, she gave up everything."

The words seem to echo around us. It takes me close to a minute to muster a reply. "Did . . . did Ruth know?"

Margaret's gaze falls. "No. You remember what happened, in the end, to Ruth Allen and her husband."

My heart clenches. I can picture the headlines and the black-and-white photographs so clearly, their small plane mangled on a jetty south of San Francisco. "It was a tragedy."

Margaret's throat bobs. "I always thought the worst part was, she was so much more than that. She was smart and wickedly funny, and so kind she'd stop to help a caterpillar onto a branch before the gardener cut our lawns. More than anyone I know, she lived her short life in raging color, and all she's remembered for is what she *didn't* get to do."

"Maybe by strangers," I say. "But not by the people who knew her. And someday, everyone who reads your story will have the chance to know the real Ruth. The truth."

A sad smile passes over Margaret's lips. "Maybe." She takes a long sip of lemonade, then sets it back in its ring of condensation and looks at me, shielding her face against the sun. "A few years after Ruth's wedding, Nina Gill came to Gerald and begged him to finally tell their daughter the truth. Nina was sick. *Actually* sick. Lung cancer. In the fifties, the prognosis for that wasn't so hot. Somehow, she managed to get Gerald to agree. But they never got the chance. The weekend of my sixteenth birthday, LP—*Ruth*," she corrects herself, "and James were flying down to the House of Ives, and their plane malfunctioned on takeoff."

Margaret clears her throat. "Hard not to feel like it was the truth that killed her. Like even the universe had bought Gerald's lie, but once it figured out that Ruth Allen was well and truly Ruth Ives, her happiness couldn't be allowed to continue."

I swallow, emotion tightening my windpipe. "Do you believe that? That your family is cursed?"

"No, honey." The flash of a smile doesn't reach her once-sparkling blue eyes. "My family *is* the curse."

An alarm goes off on her phone then, cracking the moment in half. "Ah," she says, eyeing the screen. "Time for my massage."

I clear my throat, emerging from the dark cloud of her story and reacclimating to this reality: a day full of sunshine, the smell of salt water and grass and pine, a world in which massages and mint lemonade are at your fingertips instead of loss and sorrow.

"I thought you didn't leave the property," I say.

"I don't, usually," she says.

"So Jodi knows Shiatsu?" I guess.

She cackles at this. "Good lord, it wouldn't surprise me, but no. We have a routine. A gal comes to the house. I'm already lying on my stomach by the time she gets here."

"And that works? She's never seen your face?" I say, my skepticism only mounting.

Her narrow shoulders lift. "Maybe a glimpse or two across the years, but she's young. I doubt she'd have any idea who I was. Doubt anyone would. The world's moved on."

"That's not true," I say. For all Margaret knows, this massage therapist is "Linda," who emailed me the tip about Margaret's life down here. A tip whose origins Margaret insisted she had no guess at, when I first tracked her down. I'm about to suggest as much when Margaret pushes herself up onto her feet.

"It *is* true," she says, adamant. "The world moved on. Just like I hoped it would."

• • •

ON WEDNESDAY MORNING, I step out into the thick mist and immediately kick something sitting on the walkway.

A cup of iced coffee—now toppled onto its side and leaking onto the stone—beside a paper bag. I crouch to pick them up, heart floating upward at the chocolate croissant inside the bag *and* the word scribbled on the outside of the coffee cup.

Friends?

I carry my bounty with me to the driveway and head toward downtown.

The gallery that carries Margaret's wind chimes and mosaics sits between a seafood shack and an ice cream shop, one block from the water, and because this is a world of retirees and vacationers, it hardly matters that it's late morning on a weekday.

The shop is crowded with women in sun hats, men in sandals, and teenagers either glued to their phones or surreptitiously checking each other out.

I fight a smile as I pass a couple of sunburnt ladies excitedly cooing over a "darling little turtle mosaic"—not one of Margaret's, of course.

But there is a large rectangular one framed in the dead center of the back wall, a spiral of pale blues, the shades so similar that you can't quite see the pattern until you squint. And when I do, it's like one of those old Magic Eyes, a clear path coming into focus.

Unicursal, with one way in and out.

I find it strange that someone like Margaret, who comes from a family so thoroughly ensconced in history and culture, would be drawn to this idea, that no matter what you do, you'll end up in the same place.

It would be much easier for me to imagine her strangely specific upbringing shaping her into the kind of person who fancies herself the master of her own fate.

Then again, maybe suffering the kind of loss she has makes a person *need* to yield some control. To stop asking *What could I have done differently?* and just accept that this is the path she's on.

One that started with a man who tried to control the world with money, and then one who tried to control it with the written word, and eventually led to her and Cosmo Sinclair in a doomed car chase.

Maybe it's a kind of comfort to her, to believe she was never the one in the driver's seat.

Even that day. Even when she lost the love of her life in a stupid, preventable accident.

"This one's underappreciated."

I jump at the voice just over my shoulder and turn to find the shopkeeper smiling up at me, her curly hair held back from her freckled face with a neon-green headband to reveal large wooden hoop earrings.

"Is it for sale?" I ask her.

"Technically," she says. "But I can't bring myself to drop the price any lower. I love it too much. So it will probably live here for the rest of its days."

"How much?" I ask.

"Twenty-three hundred," she says.

I try not to flinch, which makes her crack a smile.

"Yep, that's about the usual reaction I get," she says. "It's not exactly the kind of thing you buy as a vacation memento. But I thought someone would at least want it for their vacation home down here." She leans toward me conspiratorially. "You interested?"

"Currently I don't even have a wall big enough for this," I say, "let alone the money to buy it. Who's the artist?"

"Her name's Irene Mayberry," she says. "A local. A gruff sort, not very chatty, but she's a true artist."

"Not to be a plebeian," I say, "but how exactly can you tell?"

She screws up her mouth as she thinks. "I think what it is . . . is that just from looking at it, you can tell she had a reason for making it. I mean, aside from making it to sell, you know? A lot of the people

I work with, I'd consider artisans. They're great at their craft and they make things they love, and that they know my customers will love. And that's extremely valuable.

"But there's another way of making things too. Irene's stuff . . . every time I look at it, I can't help but feel like she was trying to *find* something. Or maybe get somewhere. Like she was bushwhacking through a very dense forest because something she just *had* to know lay on the other side."

She flashes a knowing smile. "Or who knows? Maybe she's a total charlatan, and I'm an easy mark. Either way, I like it."

"Me too," I say honestly. "Do you have any smaller ones? Or . . . more specifically, *cheaper* ones."

She chuckles and jerks her head toward the opposite wall. "I might have just the thing."

I follow her to a much smaller mosaic, no larger than five inches by five inches, the slivers of glass so small they must've been pieced together with tweezers and a magnifying glass, and—unlike every other piece I've seen of Margaret's—composed of amber, red, translucent gold, a tiny tight spiral that almost looks like a galaxy.

"Two hundred and fifty," the shopkeeper says.

Then I see the tiny penciled title at the bottom right corner, just inside the frame. Beside Margaret's assumed initials, her own in reverse, in her own handwriting: *Nicollet.*

"I'll take it," I say.

15

NORMALLY I DON'T have trouble sleeping, but Thursday arrives, for me, well before the sun rises, and no matter how many times I turn over beneath the top sheet, the bed feels too warm, and I can't drift back off.

Around four thirty, I finally flick on the bedside lamp, the buttery glow hitting the tiny framed mosaic sitting just beneath it.

Nicollet. The one you'd give it all up for.

But what does that mean for Margaret? Twenty years ago, she walked out of her life and became a different person. *Why?*

What the shopkeeper-cum-gallerist said comes back to me: *She was trying to* find *something. Or maybe get somewhere.*

Voice croaky with sleep, I whisper, "What are you trying to find?"

I slide out of bed and get dressed.

• • •

THE HOTEL IS back in the other direction from Little Croissant, but I've got plenty of time to kill before I'm set to meet with Margaret, so

I drive through the wee hours of the gray morning with my windows down, the sea air cycloning through the car.

It's a good day, I think.

I'd wondered if Hayden had also relocated from the hotel, but when I pull into the quiet parking lot, I spot his car right away.

After parking, I lean into the back seat and dig through my backpack until I find a Sharpie, then pluck the green tea from the cup holder, poised to write on its damp side.

I debate for a second which missive to leave for him and settle on jotting down my phone number. That seems like a decisive reply to the question he left on mine: *Friends?*

I run it up to his door and make it back to the car before six a.m. A full two hours before I need to be at Margaret's.

"Now what?" I say aloud.

The sound of the waves crashing against the shore behind the hotel answers me.

I've been so absorbed in the Margaret of it all that I actually haven't been down to the beach since my first couple of days here—and that was at the *peak* of the afternoon, when the tourists nearly outweighed the sand.

Now I leave my stuff in the car, roll the windows up, and take the wooden walkway between the Grande Lucia and the next resort over, through the dunes and down toward the water. A sign warns of venomous snakes in the dune grass, and I find myself treating the walkway like a tightrope, sticking to the very center, just in case.

The tall pockets of wispy grass dwindle as I get closer to the water, and then drop away entirely, the platform ramping downward toward open beach.

At the end of the walkway, I slip my sandals off and step into the sand. It's surprisingly cool between my toes, though the air is already dense with humidity. The first glow of the rising sun is peeking over the gray-green waves, seagulls cutting stark silhouettes overhead as they squawk across the sky.

A silver-haired woman in a wind suit is my only company, trawling along the lip of the tide with a metal detector. I perch atop a long, thick piece of bone-white driftwood, enjoying the stillness and the quiet, trying and failing to take a few phone pictures that might come close to capturing the feeling of energy and possibility that emanates from all around: the beach, the water, the sky.

On my phone, it's a blur of blue-black pixels.

The most beautiful things never hold up on a screen.

That, I think, is why I became a writer instead of a photographer. I'd had a phase, back when we were kids and Audrey was still sick. For the first couple of years that I was aware, really aware, of what she was dealing with—and of the very real possibility that we could lose her—I remember spending all my time worrying. And then one year, for Christmas, my parents gave me a camera.

And instead of useless worrying, I began instead to catalog her. To stockpile every happy memory for later. Like if I had enough pictures of her, of our whole family, then I'd be able to reconstruct her if I had to. Or maybe I'd capture enough of her soul to keep her here.

Except I was bad at it. Terrible. So to supplement my visual log, I began to journal too. I stopped worrying so much, channeled all my frustration and helplessness into *documenting*. And whenever I was scared, I'd go back to my favorite entries and reread what I'd written, and I'd feel like I really was there.

All the emotions and sensations of the moment would rise, an echo, or a kind of time travel. With writing, you could always add more. More, more, more until you got to the heart of a thing, and after that, you could chip away the excess.

With photography, you had to get it right the first time. I didn't have the patience for that. Or the faith in myself, if I'm being honest. I liked the security of revision.

She was trying to find *something. Or maybe get somewhere,* I think again.

It's not dissimilar to why I started writing, or why I still do it. Not just the pursuit of some clinical truth, but the need to understand a person, make sense of what's at their very core, closest to their heart.

To present that, clearly, truthfully, and to preserve it.

Across the water, the sun inches higher. Brilliant gold ripples toward me, bouncing across the choppy surface of the waves.

Then red, orange, white, pink. If the cool, moody tones of morning represent promise and potential, then these are that of hope, of a dream being realized.

The colors, it occurs to me, of the tiny mosaic on the side table in my rented bedroom.

• • •

"I SUPPOSE WE should back up," Margaret shouts over her shoulder at me.

She *has* to shout to be heard over the roar of the airboat as she guides it through the murky reeds behind her property. She's letting me record today, but transcribing the recording later is going to be a nightmare with all this ambient sound, and I suspect that dousing ourselves in bug repellent before we boarded was also a fool's errand, because the mosquitoes seem to be taking our precautions as a challenge rather than a deterrent. I've slapped four off me within the first ten minutes.

"It might be easier if we stopped for a while," I shout.

"What?" Margaret shouts, proving my point.

"It might be easier if—" She cuts the propeller, and the sounds of the marsh swell to replace it. Dropping my voice to a more reasonable volume, I say, "Could we just drift for a little bit while we talk?"

"We'll get eaten alive," she says.

"Just for a little bit," I say.

She adjusts her sun hat and sprays some more repellent on her arms.

"Do you take the boat out often?" I ask.

"Fairly often," she says. "I find some of the best trash here."

She hefts a net up from the base of the boat. "Bottles, plates, mugs, you name it. It's my favorite spot to scavenge."

"What about the beach?" I say. "Do you go there often?"

"We don't have much of an offseason," she says. "So occasionally, sure, but mostly I just let Jodi bring me back whatever she finds there."

"Does *she* go often?" I ask, more out of personal curiosity than anything.

"Loads," she says.

I think about my new mosaic, *Nicollet*, and how much the sunrise over the water reminded me of it. I guess sunrise over a beach is just one more thing Margaret gave up. The question is why.

"So now that we've talked about your great-grandfather and your grandfather, I was thinking we could talk about your dad," I say. "Frederick Ives was born in . . ." I glance through my notes.

"In 1904," she supplies, a second before I find the same number in my barely legible handwriting. "And his sister, Francine, was born the next year. And like I told you earlier, my grandfather was initially determined to give his children the freedom and ease that his own strict childhood had lacked. They more or less ran wild as kids, and then Gerald abandoned them for Hollywood when they were teenagers."

"Right." It's going to be tricky to keep all of this straight. The book will need a family tree up front, with dates, for easy reference. "So, Frederick is 1904, Francine is 1905, and then Ruth Allen is born in secret in..." I check my notes. "Nineteen twenty-eight or twenty-nine?"

"I'm not sure which," Margaret confirms. "They flubbed her birthday by a few months, I'm sure, just to make the lies more convincing."

"And then they all end up living together. Gerald; his wife, Rosalind; and his sister, Gigi. Gigi's adopted daughter, Ruth—who's actually Gerald and Nina's biological daughter—plus Gerald's older children, Francine and Frederick, your father, who are... twenty-six and twenty-seven at that point?"

"Sounds about right," she agrees.

"So before the whole family reunited, what were Francine and Frederick up to in San Francisco?" I ask.

"Still running wild. Their mother spent most of her time invested in various philanthropic efforts—this was during the Great Depression after all—but neither her son nor daughter had much interest in work of any kind, so they'd become known eccentrics, spending their estranged father's money like it was a contest. Francine was obsessed with showing dogs and horses—at one point, she owned over twenty dogs and fifty horses."

"Dear lord," I say. "If I could whistle, I would."

Margaret chuckles at this. "She had a dozen trainers on retainer but was also constantly firing and replacing them. She also, if my father is to be believed—which is a rather large *if*—treated them like a stable of lovers. She was constantly 'falling in love,' hiring the objects of her eye, then falling out of love and eventually firing them or driving them to quit."

"Yikes," I say. "That sounds like..."

"A lawsuit waiting to happen?" She snorts a laugh, then unscrews the cap on the bottle of water at her feet, taking a long glug. The sun is high, and I've become drenched through in sweat without noticing it happening.

I open my bottle too and chug, then swipe the sweat from my eyes. "And your father, he was . . . ?"

"Gambling, mostly," she says. "His . . . *idiosyncrasies* were more about what he'd bet with."

This, I've read about. "Physical labor instead of money, right?"

Her chin dips, her mouth tight with distaste. "Money was of so little consequence to him that I guess losing or winning it didn't provide much of a thrill. He preferred to play with *humiliation* on the line. He once had the third-wealthiest man in San Francisco mucking out his sister Francine's overly bloated stables for a week. And he found himself on the other end of those situations plenty too."

"How did your father get people to agree to these kinds of terms?" I ask.

"Honey, you haven't been around many exorbitantly wealthy people, have you?" she says.

"I've interviewed a lot of actors and singers," I disagree.

"That's different," she says. "That's *fast money*. Money a person *finds*. The people who are born with it, they're different."

"You were born with it," I point out.

"That's how I know!" she says. "Remember, I was married to Cosmo Sinclair. I knew someone like your usual interview subject. Cosmo's family had nothing. He never got used to the money or the attention. He was afraid that either he'd burn through the former, or the latter would burn through him. More like Lawrence." Another one of her sad smiles, the kind that still makes her eyes seem flinty. "Cosmo missed it, the life he couldn't go back to. All the time. But I couldn't miss it, because I could barely imagine it."

Hearing her talk about him makes me feel like there's a hook in my heart, and I'm eager to be reeled in, to hear more about their love and their life together.

"I was a news story the moment I was born," she goes on. "From before my first breath, there were two distinct Margaret Iveses. There was *me*, and then there was the other one, the one who belonged to the public. Who got written about. Who people loved at times and hated at others, and no matter where I stood with the public, I understood that it wasn't *really* me.

"It was just a character the press made up. For Cosmo, he was splintered. His fame came on hard and fast, and once he got tangled up with me, it only got worse.

"Every bad thing that every perfect stranger said about him mattered. Because he wasn't used to discounting it. He was *used to* people's opinions of him having been formed by . . . well, *him*. His actions and intentions, their personal experience with him.

"It was killing him long before the accident." She peers across the marsh, losing herself in the haze of memory.

I want to reach out and touch her hand, comfort her, be a friend to her. But I'm not, not yet. And I can't be one more person projecting my knowledge of the iconic Tabloid Princess into belief that I actually truly know her.

So instead I let her sit, take her time, hoping she knows it *belongs to her*. That I don't consider it *mine*, just because of who she is.

She blinks, facing me again. "Anyway, it wasn't hard for my father to talk men of absurd wealth into absurd bets. He enjoyed his ridiculous life in San Francisco, and his sister, Francine, did too, right up until the moment Gerald sent for them. Neither had any interest in joining their father in Los Angeles, but not a single penny they'd been spending was truly theirs, so in the end, they had no choice.

"At first, my father and my aunt Francine tried to resume their previous lifestyles, but Gerald was down to business then. He decided it was time for his kids to get serious too, or risk being cut off. He wanted Francine to get married and my father to learn the family business.

"The irony was, Aunt Francine had decided she didn't ever *want* to get married. She felt so strongly about it that she decided her best bet was to try to earn a place in the family business instead. Whereas the only thing my father felt strongly about was doing as little work as humanly possible.

"Dad thought he could skate by if he started working at the film studio, so Gerald set him up there, and Francine took over a failing ladies' magazine. There had been women journalists there for years, but she was the first female coeditor in chief, then editor in chief when the coeditor quit. Years later, she told me she knew in her heart that when her father gave her that journal, the point was to scare her into marriage. Instead she worked hard to learn the business, and she turned it around. She had something my father lacked."

I ask, "And what was that?"

"Desperation," she says. "My father didn't find his until later."

The Story

THEIR VERSION: Frederick Ives was a jealous man.

· · ·

HER VERSION: Frederick Ives was a jealous man.

As a boy, he was jealous of his schoolmates. Of their grades, of their success in sports. Of their teachers' affection for them, and sometimes even of the ire they could inspire.

At home, he was jealous every time his sister, Francine, took the seat at the head of the dinner table, and when he started arriving early so he could have it, he was jealous of how casually late she'd stroll in, still covered in mud from the stables, how unbothered she seemed by their mother's disapproval.

When he was twenty, a girl who'd spent weeks batting her eyelashes at him got engaged to another man, and though he had no intention of marrying her, he was jealous then too.

At twenty-seven, when his long-absent father forced him to relocate to the castle he'd built on the coast, Freddy was jealous of his half-orphaned cousin Ruth.

Of the delight she seemed to cause her uncle Gerald, and the careful structure to her life, which neither of Freddy's parents had ever bothered to give *Freddy* as a boy.

He was born with enough money to buy almost anything, and so all he ever wanted was the things he couldn't.

He was jealous too when Francine found something new to want, in the form of success at *Hearth & Home Journal*, and when she strong-armed the business back into the black, proving herself as their father's true heir.

He tried to *want* Royal Pictures. To want the sleek, wood-paneled corner office he'd been given for no good reason—and frankly spent many afternoons napping in. He tried to want the secretary, Shelley, he'd been assigned and then promptly began sleeping with.

About twice a week, she informed him of a new meeting set by his father, and he quickly learned that these were the negotiations for contracts Gerald didn't actually care about securing.

He brushed off actors, writers, and directors onto his son with regularity. And just as Gerald hoped, Freddy bungled those talks time and again with his total lack of knowledge about the business.

Even though he knew this was the role he was set to fulfill, it made Freddy feel incompetent, and he didn't like feeling incompetent. Lazy? Sure. Incompetent? No. It was a matter of control.

He was asleep at his desk, face plastered to a stack of unread scripts (on which he'd been supposed to write notes last week), when Doris Bernhardt stormed into his office one day in 1935.

"So this is what I'm worth?" she demanded, marching right up to him. "I make him a pretty penny, and he shunts me off to the deadbeat son?"

Freddy's secretary came rushing in next, slowed down by her kitten heels, and never had he seen such a stark contrast between two women. Shelley was dainty, bird boned with auburn hair and lush lips that matched her lush hips. She wore a long skirt that swished with every step she took and had a habit of toying with the necklace she wore around her delicate throat.

Doris Bernhardt was tall, angular, with thin lips and narrow hips. She wore flat shoes and wide-legged trousers, and not a lick of makeup that he could see. She had to be nearly thirty years old, but he doubted she would've had *leading lady* potential even if she were younger.

"Mr. Ives," Shelley said, oozing apology, "I tried to tell Ms. Bernhardt—"

Ms. Bernhardt rolled her eyes. "Oh, yes, she told me all about how *busy* you are this morning. She insisted I come back next week for my scheduled meeting, but I had a feeling you'd be able to squeeze me in between some of your other *important* appointments."

Shelley gaped at him, helpless. He became aware, abruptly, that if he didn't take control, he was automatically ceding it to Bernhardt.

"Thank you, Shelley," he said. "I'm happy to speak with Ms. Bernhardt. Hold my calls."

He never really got calls, but it felt like the right thing to say, like it might give him back a fraction of his power, which suddenly seemed absolutely essential.

Shelley wavered.

"Goodbye, Shelley," he said coolly, and she finally retreated.

He waited a second, just stared Bernhardt down. She stared right back, jaw set.

"Would you care to sit?" he asked.

She snorted, then slowly walked behind his desk and took *his* chair. He fought a smile. Rather than sitting across from her, in one of the slightly lower chairs positioned there, he rounded the desk too and leaned against it, arms crossed. "So what would you care to speak to the deadbeat son about?"

"Nothing," she said. "I *wish* to speak to Gerald Ives about a new contract."

"What about it exactly?" he asked, because he of course had not yet *read* the new contract being proposed to her, and did not in fact even know who she was.

"Well, for one thing," she said, "I'd like to know why I'm being offered *less* money, for a *longer* term, when I've already been benched for the last six months. Is he *trying* to send me running to Universal?"

Of course he was. But for some reason, Freddy wasn't supposed to admit this. "You know," he said instead, "it's not uncommon for actresses around your age to see fewer opportunities in this business."

"*Actresses my age?*" she spat at him, lunging to her feet.

"I don't mean any offense," he said. "But you've got to be realistic here."

She tipped her head back on a throaty laugh before leveling her fiery gaze on him. "I've got to be realistic?" she repeated. "*I've* got to be realistic? Yes, of course *I've* got to be realistic! I'm one of two female directors this studio has ever worked with. I'm acutely aware of my reliance upon realism at all times, whereas someone like you—someone raised in a castle and handed a job he doesn't do, in an industry he knows nothing about—need never trouble himself with anything so mundane as *realism!*"

"You're a *director?*" he said.

The question triggered her derisive snorting instinct.

"You're a *woman,*" he reminded her.

"Yes, I believe my speech touched on that," she said.

"Have you directed anything I've seen?" he asked.

Her face went red with anger. "I should hope so, given your position at Royal Pictures."

She named three of her films. One he'd never heard of. Two he'd seen, and of those two, one was a smash hit. "Why would he be trying to get rid of you?" he asked.

Most of the time, he understood his father's decisions.

Ms. Bernhardt snorted again and waved down her length with a flourish.

"Because of your dreadful wardrobe?" Freddy said, flummoxed, and he saw the first flash of what Doris Bernhardt looked like when she was smiling.

Like a cat with three canaries lined up in its jaw, little yellow feathers sticking out in a row. He couldn't look away, could barely stand to blink and miss a second of that expression.

"I don't have much sway here, Ms. Bernhardt," he said.

"Bernie," she interjected.

"Bernie," he said. "As you pointed out, I do very little and know even less about this industry, and as for my father—well, he may have built a castle, but I assure you I wasn't raised anywhere near either *it* or *him*. But you're right that offering you less money is insulting, after what you've brought in. I'd be insulted too. Which *might* be the point. But if I had to guess—and of course I do—it has less to do with willfully insulting you and more to do with taking a gamble that you *won't* walk, because you *can't*. Because Universal and MGM won't want you. *He* found you. *He* gave you your chance and cultivated your talent, and now he thinks he can get you for cheaper than you're worth, because, very likely, he can."

With another angry huff, she threw out her arms. "So it doesn't matter that I've proven myself again and again in this business?"

He arched an eyebrow at her. "Judging by what I've heard from the many women I've come to know in the business, this is the industry standard. It's . . . *realistic*."

She collapsed back into the chair, a look of exhaustion sweeping over her, and though she was tall and angular, she looked delicate then. He both wanted to comfort her *and* suspected she would sock him in the jaw for his trouble.

He cleared his throat. "I will ask him though. I'll plead your case."

Her gaze narrowed warily. "Why?"

With total honesty, he answered, "Because I want your next movie. I want it here, at Royal Pictures."

She surveyed him for a long moment, then rose from the chair. "Thank you for your time," she said, not with deference but not with sarcasm either. "But I won't be renewing my contract with Royal."

She turned and walked from the room, and Freddy felt that loss, that emptiness, that *moroseness* he sometimes awoke to in the morning, multiplied tenfold.

He wanted something. He wanted something he couldn't name, and so couldn't reach out and take.

After that, he was a goner.

16

"MY MOTHER," MARGARET says, "was a magnificent woman."

"Everything I've ever read about her agrees," I say quietly, matching Margaret's volume, trying not to jerk her from the memory fogging over her eyes. I want her to linger. We've finally reached the people who shaped her most, and I want to stay here.

"My father loved her," she says. "Dearly. It's important that you know that."

I nod, my pen going motionless in my hand.

"Because so much of the news was about their divorce," she says. "And what they wrote about him was true. He loved her, but he didn't treat her like he loved her. At the time, I couldn't make sense of this, but now I understand it perfectly."

"Could you explain it to me then?" I press.

"He didn't love himself," she says simply. "I know how trite that sounds. Even hearing it come out of my mouth, a part of me is thinking, *Margaret, get a grip. He was a weak, jealous man.* But then I remember the early days, and it breaks apart that easy, clean-cut story. He adored her. He adored all of us. You know they spoke on the phone every single day until she died?"

"I'd heard that, yes," I say. "But I didn't know if it was true."

"They were best friends," she says. "That's how it started, and that's what they got back to. Eventually."

"Well, not how it *started*," I point out. "You did just tell me she tore him a new one the first time they met."

Her lips part on a grin. "That was his favorite story to tell. She'd chime in with, *I thought he was a real prick*."

"So what changed then?" I ask.

"Well, she got her MGM contract, for one thing. And when word got out, he sent her a huge bouquet. Which she didn't care for. She hated seeing cut flowers, made her sad. I never see them without thinking of her, which makes the way *I* feel about them more complicated, I suppose. Sad, then a little happy, then sad again."

"I get that," I say.

She gives me an odd look. "Do you?"

"I think so."

She waits for me to go on, so I do: "My sister and I had this cartoon we always watched when we were kids. *The Busy World of Richard Scarry*. We basically only ever watched it while she was too sick to do anything else. So every time I see anything to do with it, that's what I think of. And maybe it's different, because she's okay now, but the memories attached to it . . . I don't know. They're complicated."

"Everything's complicated. Everything. Once you start paying attention. My father loved my mother, and he was a shitty husband. He was a horrible father for a couple of years there right before they split up, but he was a wonderful one for the rest of his life after that. And honestly, even saying those words—*shitty*, *horrible*, *wonderful*—how can that come anywhere close to conveying everything I mean?"

"You don't have to whittle it down like that," I say. "You can take as long as you want, Margaret."

"But people stop listening," she says. "They want the sound bite. They want the headline. That's what my family built, and now we don't get to stop it from coming for us."

"You're a human," I say. "The machine can try to compress you into something two dimensional, digestible, but that's not *you*. And we're not here to service the machine."

"Don't you get it?" she says. "It won't matter. If we do this book, I go back to being their paper doll. They'll splash the most salacious tidbits across the top of a . . . what do you call it? A listicle! And the audience will pass their judgments on all these people, who are just characters to them, but are real to me. On Cosmo. On my mother and father. On . . ." She trails off, choked up.

My chest cramps. I can't help it: I'm already crossing the boat, taking her hand as I sit. "I'm so sorry," I say. "And I won't pretend you're not right. The listicles will exist. The headlines will be salacious. But your story will be out there too. The whole thing. You just have to figure out if one is worth the other."

She raises her eyes to me. "See?" she says. "Nothing's ever simple."

I squeeze her hands. "We can be done for today, if you need."

"No." She pulls her fingers out from between mine. "Not yet. I want to tell you about them. My parents."

I feel myself smiling, feeling both proud of her for opening up and proud of myself for slowly starting to earn her trust. "I'd love to hear all of it. But . . . maybe we *should* go somewhere less buggy?"

She chortles. "Now, that's good thinking." She starts the boat's fan back up and steers us back the way we came. Something about her posture seems lighter, her shoulders relaxed so that her neck looks long and stately.

It makes me happy, to think that even if this is hard for her, and she's uncertain about what we're doing here, it's unburdening her in some way. To be seen.

To be known again, after years of hiding.

• • •

I'M SITTING CROSS-LEGGED on the living room rug, a hot mug of decaf at my knee, when the first text from an unknown number with a New York area code buzzes in.

Hello.

Nothing else. Just *hello*. I smile to myself. If I'd been offered a million dollars to guess what Hayden Anderson's first text to me would be, I'm reasonably sure I'd be a millionaire now.

Hello! I write back.

Who is this, he says.

I snort. Wow, okay. Six weeks of fiery passion and you've already forgotten me????

Sorry. I have the wrong number, he says.

I take a sip of coffee, then swipe a throw pillow off the couch and flop back onto it. Isn't this Hayden?

He starts typing right away, but it takes forever for his reply to come through. I'm really sorry, but I have no idea who this is.

YOU texted ME, I remind him. Another long pause for typing. I'm just kidding. It's me.

I send a follow-up: Alice.

And then another.

Scott.

He writes back, From The Scratch?

From the tiny island you're currently on, I say.

Oh THAT Alice, he replies, playing along. Then adds, You really had me scared for a minute. I was looking back through my calendar for a six-week stretch of "fiery passion."

I laugh aloud, flip onto my stomach, and push my laptop out of sight. I was typing my notes out from the rest of today's session, and riveting as it was, I'll have all day tomorrow to finish that up. How far back did you go?

> Six months, but I only stopped because that's when I got this phone. What are you up to?

Not working, I say. What about you?

Also not working, he says.

A good night for it, I write back.

Would you want to do something? he says.

He sends me a pinned location for another twenty-four-hour diner, in Savannah. Only if you think you can stand not talking about Margaret for a few hours.

A few hours? How many courses are we having? I ask.

Didn't mean to be presumptuous, he says.

I'm kidding, Hayden, I say. I'll be there in half an hour.

Great, he says.

● ● ●

HE IS, OF course, at the back corner booth of the Atomic Café, looking too sharp and clean for his colorfully shabby surroundings.

He rises to greet me as I approach, which feels like an exceptionally old-fashioned way of doing things, so I go in for a hug.

Immediately, I regret this, because he palpably *startles* at the gesture, but just as quickly, he relaxes, looping his arms around my back. "Good to see you," he says, his voice a rumble through my bones. He smells like almond, like amaretto drizzled over sponge cake, sweet without being cloying.

"You smell like dessert," I tell him as we pull apart.

He visibly balks, frowning to himself, as he slides back onto his bench. "It's Dr. Bronner's."

"Wow," I say. "Utilitarian yet delicious."

His facial expression softens on a laugh. It occurs to me that somehow, he thought *you smell like dessert* was a complaint, and not, as I personally suspect, a subconscious and involuntary come-on. "Got you coffee," he says, pushing one of the mugs on the table toward me.

Our knees bump. We rearrange so that we're sitting diagonally across from each other, rather than straight on. We're not touching, but somehow I can still feel him. He has a presence like that, a magnetic field he carries with him always, but mostly tries to play off as a *force field*, a barrier to entry rather than an invitation.

"Thanks." I take the coffee mug between my hands, the heat pleasantly juxtaposing the overzealous roar of the air-conditioning. I gesture toward his glass. "I'm concerned that your green tea is brown."

"My green tea," he says, "is sweet tea. Because the Atomic Café doesn't 'have it in that color.' At least that's what the server said."

"Did she say it as a full sentence at least," I ask, "or did she jump right into the middle?"

"Full sentence," he says. "That's one point for them, but Ray's Diner is still winning."

I take a sip of coffee, and I must make a face, because he says, "Okay, that's one more point deducted right there, clearly."

I look around at the neon-turquoise and pink light that lines the windows on the outside of the building, and the matching booths inside, the little jukeboxes at every table and the atomic age wallpaper slightly curling away from the interior walls. "It's got good ambience though," I say. "Why *aren't* we at Ray's?"

"I like to try as many diners as I can when I'm in a new place," he says. "Compare them and find the best."

"Ah. Of course."

"Of course?" he says.

I shrug. "The journalist in you."

"The Midwesterner in me," he counters. "Always looking for the best deal."

I hold up the wide rectangular menu. "Six ninety-nine for a steak, eggs, and toast. You can't beat that."

"I mean, you could, but you'd probably end up hospitalized," he says.

The server comes by and takes our order. I go with the two-egg breakfast, and Hayden does the egg white omelet.

"I'm actually surprised you eat at places like this," I say.

His brows pinch together. "Why?"

"Because even the doorknobs here are buttered," I reply, "and you seem to be an exceptionally healthy eater."

"Bad habit," he says.

"*Good* habit, if my doctor is to be believed," I argue.

"I just mean, I was raised that way," he says. "Obsessively so. My mom used to be really health anxious, and she was that way with my brother and me when we were little. Just . . . really cautious."

"Oh." Now it's my chance to frown. "I'm sorry. I wasn't trying to be critical. I just noticed—"

"No, I know," he says. "It's fine. Promise."

After a beat, I say, "So I should probably stop leaving you big-ass croissants."

He smiles at me. It's kind of a rusty expression, but it still makes my heart flutter victoriously. "No," he assures me. "Just so long as you're not offended if I give some of them to Margaret."

I faux gasp. "Uh-oh, Hayden. Looks like someone has to put a quarter in the M-word jar."

He rolls his eyes. "I'm not talking about *work*," he says. "I just acknowledged her existence. That's not breaking any rules."

"Maybe none of *yours*," I say.

A smirk pulls at his wide mouth. "Okay, fine." He digs around in his jeans pocket and puts a handful of coins on the table.

"Not going to ask why you actually have quarters on hand," I say, sliding two toward me. "Just going to assume you and *whoever you currently work for* are spending a lot of time at arcades."

"That's your prerogative," he says.

I slip the quarters into the tabletop jukebox and flip until I find a winner. No one else in the place seems to be queuing up songs, because as soon as the fifties rockabilly number playing over the speakers ends, "Say You Will (Be Mine)" by Cosmo Sinclair starts playing.

"Oh, come on," he says on a huff of laughter. "How is *this* not breaking a rule?"

"What are you talking about?" I say. "This song is a classic."

"And you know who he wrote this for?" he asks.

I grin and slide my forearms across the table until they meet his. "No, who?"

He studies me as he works out his next play. I don't back down either, holding his gaze fast.

The challenge building between us is starting to tip over into something else, a heat in his eyes, a pull in the center of my chest.

"Here you folks go." The server plops our plates down beside us. *Really* plops them. Like probably gets them no closer than three inches from the tabletop before letting go. We jolt apart and take a beat to study our respective plates before tucking in.

"What do you think?" I ask him after a couple of bites.

"Should've gone with the six-dollar steak," he says.

I choke on a laugh, lean forward, and drop my voice. "Yeah, I'd say this round goes to Ray's."

He picks up his cup of sweet tea. "To Ray."

I straighten up and tap my mug against it. "To Ray," I say, "and to whoever inspired this song, because it's absolutely undeniable."

"To her too," he says with a nod.

17

WE WANDER THE quaint streets of Savannah, past old stone buildings and Greek revival homes with porches stacked up three levels, live oaks sweeping low and draped in Spanish moss. It's late, but we're not alone. Pockets of revelers spill out of a redbrick bar on the corner, and a woman on the steps of a brownstone across the street smokes a cigarette while talking on the phone, the humidity muffling their voices, nature's soundproofing.

"It's almost like New York," Hayden says. "Parts of it anyway."

"Rich parts," I say.

"True," he muses.

"Do you think you'll stay there forever?" I ask.

He blows out a breath. "I don't know. I like it. A lot. But I grew up with a yard. With woods behind my house. If I had kids, I'd want that for them, I think."

"Do you want to have kids?" I ask.

"Sometimes," he says. "When I'm feeling optimistic."

I bump sideways into him, the skin of our arms sticking slightly from the heat. "Does that happen often?"

He looks down his shoulder at me with a slight smirk. "Not often, no."

"So the rest of the time," I say, "when you're not feeling optimistic, what do you think?"

"The rest of the time . . ." Another long exhale, his eyes straight ahead as we go back to ambling down the block. "The rest of the time, I think, what if the polar ice caps keep melting? What if medical care keeps getting more expensive, and social security runs out, and housing prices keep rising while minimum wage doesn't, and what if they resent me for bringing them into all of this?

"What if they just hate *me*? Not because of the state of the world, but just because they hate me. Or what if they're sick? What if they join a cult, and I can't convince them to come home? What if they *start* a cult? What if they get into some heinous shit, and I can't love them anymore—or worse, I keep loving them even though I can't change anything?

"What if there's another world war? Or what if . . . what if everything else goes right, but at the end of my life, they're sitting in hospice with me . . ." His voice thickens uncharacteristically, wavering just the slightest bit. "And there are things they wish they could say to me, or hear from me, but I don't remember who I am, let alone who they are. What if they have to care for me, for *years*, after I've stopped calling them by their nicknames or telling them I love them?"

I stop walking, a cold weight pressing against my chest, and he does too, but he doesn't face me.

"I wasn't sure I wanted to do another book," he says finally, his voice a rattle. "It's hard, spending years with a person. Especially someone at the tail end of life. The same thing I love about this job is what I hate about it."

"What's that?"

"It feels like you've lived their whole life with them," he says. "And I just can't help but think, we're not supposed to know how it all ends, this early. It's too much of a burden."

I slide my hand into his, his fingers rigid at first, then relaxing into my grip. "Is that all?" I say softly.

His eyes drop on a smile, then climb back to mine. "Yep, that's it."

I squeeze his hand, tight enough that I can feel his pulse, or maybe it's just mine, amplified by the contact, the pressure, the heat. "Maybe," I say slowly, "it's a burden, but it's also a gift.

"Life is so complicated. And I think it's human nature to try to untangle those complications. We want everything to make sense. And that's okay. It's a worthy pursuit. But back when my sister wasn't well, when every day felt uncertain . . ." I search for the words.

His forehead creases, his tone so hopeful it nearly breaks my heart. "You understood how much each one was worth?"

"I understood what really mattered," I offer. "I understood my priorities. I understood what, in this life, was nonnegotiable for me. A lot of people don't find that out until it's too late. They wait to say things, and they don't get the chance. So collecting other people's stories, learning from their mistakes, it *is* a gift too. You are who you are right now in part because of what you did for Len and his family. You can't control any of that other stuff you worry about, but you can control what *you* do."

He gazes down at me, his expression vulnerable, his usually severe features somehow diffused in the streetlight. "I don't know anyone like you," he says.

"I don't know anyone like you," I tell him.

"I'm serious," he says, voice hushed.

"So am I," I reply.

He lifts our interlaced fingers between us, studying them with a divot between his brows. After a long pause, he lifts my hand higher, pressing his lips against the back of it. It's such a tender gesture, so careful and light, but it makes my heart speed and my throat tighten.

When his eyes rise to mine, it feels like the world has tilted just slightly on its axis.

Like this is the first time I've ever felt the full weight of his gaze, and I can hardly breathe, and I want to say something or do something, but I'm not sure what I *can* say, *can* do, where the delicate invisible boundary between us lies.

So I do what he did. I bring his hand up to my lips, my eyes falling closed as I press a kiss to his skin, smell his almond soap, and taste the salt of his sweat on the tip of my tongue. I feel his forehead bow to press against my shoulder, his free hand coming up to gently cradle the back of my neck as we stand there together on the walk, in a puddle of light.

When I open my eyes and let go of his hand, he snakes it around my waist too, crushing me to his chest, my cheek to his collarbone, my arms winding tight around his hips: a hug that's more than a hug, that stretches out indefinitely, our breathing heavy and our bodies hot everywhere they're touching.

I think we must have both decided the same thing—that nothing else can happen between us—and I think that just makes both of us all the less willing to stop. I feel him growing hard, and an ache begins between my thighs, my nipples peaking against his chest. He lets out a soft hum against my ear, one of his hands running a trail up and down my spine as he buries his mouth softly in my neck, not a kiss, just an incidental touch of his parted lips to my skin.

Just his breath there, on that sensitive place between my throat and my shoulder, is enough to unspool something deep in me. I arch a little, and he squeezes me tighter, molds me to him.

I let my hands climb into his hair, twist my face into *his* neck the way he did to *mine*, taking every bit of him he'll allow.

He touched my hair, so I touch his; he dragged his mouth along my throat, so I let mine trail over his.

He tries to pull me closer again, as if there's any room at all left between us. There's not, other than the one unbreachable divide: the job.

And I can't help myself any longer. I take just a little more. The smallest bit. A flick of my tongue against his skin, and he groans into me, my body shivering with the sound. The ache in me deepens. I tell myself not to roll my hips against his, but it happens anyway, and his breath hisses at my neck, his hands clenching. "I have to stop," he murmurs roughly.

"We're not doing anything," I whimper back. He grinds against me. Just for a second, but it's enough to send sparks all through my body, flickers of color across my vision, a harsh gasp between my lips.

He grips my hips, pushing me slowly away from him, almost like we're peeling apart, like there's resistance there, trying to keep us close, the memory of that friction still hanging around me like an afterglow.

Stone-cold sober and he looks almost as drunk as I feel, his eyes abyss-dark and face fraught with unspent tension. "Can I walk you back to your car?" he says softly.

I nod, still too unsteady to speak.

Nothing happened, I'll remind myself later while I'm lying awake, eyes turned up to the stucco ceiling. *It was just a hug.*

My body will tell a very different story. *Yours, mine, and the truth.*

• • •

I SPEND FRIDAY morning back down on the beach, watching the sunrise and then wading into the water and floating on my back. Afterward I send pictures to the group text between Mom, Audrey, and

Dad's old number. Someday, I know, it will be reassigned to someone new and we'll have to take him off the chat, but so far none of us has.

Audrey probably because she's too busy to care about that kind of thing, but Mom's a little bit more of a mystery. As much as she and Dad loved each other, I still would've assumed her no-nonsense attitude would preclude anything so sentimental as keeping her late husband on a text thread.

Then again, it's just as likely that she doesn't know how to remove it and can't be bothered to start a new chain. She and Audrey are similar that way—not Luddites, exactly, but far from tech savvy.

I send them some shots of the sunrise earlier and the water now, the tourists teeming across the sand with babies in floppy sun hats and raucous preteens carting foam boogie boards behind them.

Not a bad office for the day, I say.

Mom chimes in quickly: lol. She's at least savvy enough to use abbreviations that have been around for multiple decades, I'll give her that.

She follows it up with another message: Must be nice.

I don't think she means it as a dig. It feels like one.

Audrey replies with a selfie of her and a local farmer planting fruit trees in a community garden. Please take a nice long dip in my honor! Audrey writes.

We should come here on your next trip home, I say, and she writes that she'd love that. Then Mom asks how the garden is going, and the conversation moves on, and in a way it's a relief, to not have to worry that Mom's disappointment in me might bubble up any further, spill over from unsaid to said.

Audrey talks about work. Mom talks about her chickens. They both look forward to Christmas, the next time Audrey will be in Georgia for a few weeks, and I sit on my towel, the sand warming beneath it, and miss my father and the world when he was still in it.

When this conversation would have at least one other person who was, as Mom used to lovingly call him, *fanciful*. The beach pictures would have almost certainly elicited a reference to a song about nature's beauty, maybe even a Cosmo Sinclair original, or else a shot of our composting outhouse with a caption about it being *his* office, most days. Potty humor, dad jokes, old music, and deep laughter. Those are the holes he left behind in our family unit.

The texts peter off, and I fish my notebook out of my bag, popping in my earbuds and queuing up the rest of yesterday's recording. I'll want to transcribe *everything* later, but for now, I just want to let Margaret's story wash over me again, see what jumps out, and jot down time stamps.

This interview felt so different. Before, she'd been recounting her family's oral history. Now we've reached the part where—as she put it—all of the characters were real to her. People she loved, people she'd fought with, people she'd lost.

She started with her father and mother's friendship.

Freddy Ives had sent Doris "Bernie" Bernhardt a bouquet to celebrate her new contract with MGM, and they hadn't spoken again until her first MGM film released.

He'd gone to see it, opening night. Sat by himself in the fourth row, dead center, at Grauman's Chinese Theatre. The following Monday she'd walked into her office to find another bouquet and a card.

Realism be damned. You're going places.

X

F. Ives

She called Freddy to thank him—though she pretended to think his name was Fives, and he went along with it. They wound up on the phone for an hour and a half, mostly talking about the film, but a little about other things too. He updated her on Royal Pictures interoffice drama—who was sleeping with whom; who had found out about it; which A-list actor had most recently shown up to set, still wasted from the night before, and thrown up on a camera while it was filming.

She was surprised by his sense of humor, and when she told him as much, he became uncommonly serious. "You shouldn't be," he told her. "I was born into a life where I needn't take anything seriously if I don't want to."

"But don't you *want* to?" she asked, and then *he* had a turn at being surprised, because he found he did.

He took her seriously. He took her work seriously. By then, he'd seen all of her pictures a number of times, mostly from a position of curiosity: Now that he *knew* they'd been directed by a woman, would he be able to *tell*? Was it different?

He hadn't come to a concrete conclusion, other than this: Every time he watched one of her films, he noticed something new.

And this made him better at his job, if only marginally.

The next week, he called her again. The same A-list star had knocked over a full wall in the studio while filming. "Most of his pay is going to his insurance by now," he said.

They laughed about it together, but it wasn't entirely funny. Bernie had been let go after over-performing. This man was knocking down walls and still under contract. He was the face, the reason people went to the movies. In Royal Pictures' estimation, they needed him, whereas Bernie needed *them*.

Realism.

Freddy knew this, felt it in the long pause after their laughter died down, and wanted to say something about it but couldn't seem to find the right words. So instead, he asked her if she'd like to go for a walk sometime, and she said yes, and it became a tradition.

A weekly walk.

He dated other women. She dated not at all.

They had hardly even touched, when finally, after eleven months of weekly walks and triweekly phone calls, he had stopped abruptly with an idea, a bolt of lightning, looked her in the eye, and said, "Bernie, I think we should get married."

And she'd laughed because it was ridiculous, but eventually she realized he was serious.

"Why?" she said.

"Because you're my favorite person in the world," he said. "And talking to you three times a week isn't enough. At least for me. So would you consider it?"

And she said, "Don't you want to kiss me first?"

He said, "Of course I do, but I thought I'd better see whether you were amenable to the idea first, or you might slap me."

She told him she would have. And then she stepped forward, set her hands on his face, and kissed him.

It wasn't fireworks, according to either of them. It was more like slipping into a warm bath. They were engaged for a few months, with no real rush to the altar, until Bernie missed a period and it became obvious it was time to scramble.

The ceremony was small, just a few friends and family, all of them shocked the union had made it to the finish line. The derelict playboy and the shrewd lady director.

They made no sense to anyone except themselves, and later—once Bernie had gotten to know her a bit better—to Freddy's sister, Francine. But it worked. Bernie moved into Freddy's wing of the House of Ives. She attended his mother's charity auctions, and she joined their awkward thrice-weekly family dinners. She played in the family's expansive orange groves with her husband's seven-year-old cousin,

Ruth, and even came around to calling her LP, the Little Princess, like only family members did.

In 1938, their daughter came, screaming like a banshee, into the world—as was the Ives tradition—at a hospital whose entire upper floor had been cleared for the family.

They named her Margaret Grace Ives, after Bernie's late mother, and by the time they left the hospital, *Photoplay* had already published her name. Normally, the fan magazine only concerned itself with *actors*, but Freddy was handsome and charismatic, and Bernie was something of a novelty, so they'd reached a certain level of celebrity, which their daughter inherited, along with everything else that came with being an Ives.

For the first two months of Margaret's life, her father rarely left her or her mother's side, but eventually he had to get back to work.

Bernie missed directing, missed being at the studio every single day. But she also missed her daughter every time she fell asleep. She wondered how she would survive having her soul split like that. She knew for certain she could never be fully contented again as long as she lived. Half of her would always be elsewhere.

Three years later, Laura Rose Ives was born, and she was Margaret's polar opposite.

As a newborn, Margaret would wail and cry every time she wanted anything, and so she and Bernie quickly developed an unspoken language. At four months old, before Margaret could crawl, she was already trying to figure out how to stand up.

Laura was a quiet little blob. Watchful, curious, but not demanding. Margaret had her mother's sandy hair and her father's tan skin, whereas Laura had her father's thick black waves and her mother's creamy complexion.

As the girls grew, Laura was cautious, careful, a little shadow trailing down the long marble halls after her reckless older sister.

Bernie worried about her. She worried about both of them, for different reasons.

She waited until Margaret turned five and Laura was two before broaching the subject of going back to work, late one night as she and Freddy lay curled together beneath the deep blue and gold canopy of their bed, their reading lamps still on. He asked if she was sure. "Won't you miss them?"

"Of course I will," she said. "Don't you?"

And that settled it. He knew he couldn't keep her cooped up there, half of her nurtured while the other went bone dry.

It took several months for her to get a new contract. Freddy, of course, wanted her to come back to Royal, but she'd wound up at Universal instead. At first, they met for walks twice a week, but she was making up for lost time, which meant working more, working harder.

That was when the fighting between Margaret's parents had begun. It was also where we left off for the day.

The recording ends and I pull my earbuds out, set my phone and notebook aside, watching a young family building a sandcastle just out of reach of the tide, digging a moat all around it so that when the water finally does rise, it won't knock the whole thing over.

I mean, probably it will, but at least they'll know they tried.

Once, years ago, when I was in college and taking an entry-level writing class, I "interviewed" my dad as part of an assignment.

He told me about growing up in Oklahoma, and about seeing the ocean for the first time when he moved out to California, where he and my mother had met when they were just out of college.

I wish I'd recorded that whole conversation. I didn't. But I took notes, and I wrote the paper, and a couple of things stuck in my memory, clear and sharp.

When he saw the ocean for the first time, he said it terrified him. Made him dizzy and almost nauseated, and just truly, deeply *afraid*. That anything could be that big. That powerful. That natural and uncontrollable, something society couldn't take credit for and could never fully tame either. He told me he'd only ever felt that way two other times in his life.

"When your sister was born," he said, "and then you."

"Gee, thanks, Dad. That's great to hear," I replied, and he grinned. He was a grinner, like me.

"You're supposed to be learning to write nonfiction, right? I've got to tell you the truth. Those were the three times in my life I felt true wonder. And it was so much to take in, it felt like my body might spiderweb with cracks. Honestly. And then I was happy too, if I didn't mention that."

"You sure didn't," I said.

"I was getting to it," he joked. "But it wasn't the first feeling. The first feeling was *Holy shit, this is a whole person. How is that even possible?*"

He didn't swear a lot, because Mom didn't like swearing, but sometimes, when it was the two of us, he'd throw in a good *shit* or *hell*, for emphasis.

Why didn't I record him? I think again, with a deep pulse of pain.

And just as fast, I feel a breeze ripple over my back, and it's hard not to believe—or maybe just hope—that maybe I didn't need to record it.

That maybe he's here, his atoms redistributed, the ashes we sprinkled in the river near our house now mixed with the sand all around me, his love permanent and intractable as ever.

Love isn't something you can cup in your hands, and I have to believe that means it's something that can't ever be lost.

I grab my phone again and open a text thread I've let sit empty for two years now. The one with just Dad's number.

I want to say the perfect thing, in this missive to no one, but even with all the time in the world, I can't find the words. The closest I get is a two-word message.

> Thank you.

Right after I send it, my phone vibrates, and I almost choke on my tongue.

But—perhaps obviously—it's not my dad texting me back.

It's a *one*-word message, and for some reason, it really does feel like the perfect message.

Hello, Hayden writes.

Hello, I write back.

> What are you doing tonight?

18

OLD MO'S SUGAR House is a hit from the beginning.

For one thing, the entire exterior is painted in three separate shades of *frosting pink*. It's a little grungy from the passing of time, but still looks like the setting of my childhood dreams. It's the same kind of fare as Ray's or the Atomic Café, and the same kind of no-nonsense service.

If you were out of touch enough to ask for a latte here, I'm *sure* you'd be the proud recipient of a nice *bless your heart* from the staff.

When our server drops off our dangerously hot plates, I catch Hayden's gaze traveling straight past his steel-cut oatmeal to my gravy-doused biscuits and short stack of pancakes.

"You look like a wistful war bride right now," I tease him, "watching at the window for your baby to come home."

"What?" He looks up abruptly, blinking clear of his biscuit haze.

"Would you like a bite?" I offer.

"No," he says, "that's okay."

"Are you sure?" I ask. "I really don't mind." I push the bowl of biscuits toward him.

"Maybe just a bite," he says, and retrieves his silverware, neatly cutting a small hunk from one of the biscuits, swooping it over his plate, and popping it between his lips.

His eyes go glassy. He makes a little hum in his throat. I lean forward and scoop the rest of the biscuit he cut into onto his plate. "Wow," he says finally.

"Good?" I ask.

"Very," he says.

"You know what I bet would make it better?" I ask.

"What?"

"Pink food coloring," I say, sawing into my pancakes.

He snorts. "I don't think that has a taste."

"Maybe not, but it would have an *impact*. I'd *feel* the pink."

He grins crookedly, and my heart leaps. "You'd feel it? What does pink *feel* like?"

I think for a moment. "I think it's, like, the giddy part of a sunrise."

"The giddy part of a sunrise," he repeats.

"Yeah, you know how sunrise mostly just makes you feel like . . . awed, or moved? Like it feels profound?"

"No," he says.

"Well, for me it does," I say. "But there's a moment when everything's just all pink. Pink-lemonade pink. And it feels almost silly. Like the sky is playing. It's a color that I'm shocked can be in nature. But since it can be, I really see no reason why it couldn't also be in biscuits."

He laughs, shakes his head to himself as he stuffs another bite of biscuit into his mouth.

"What?" I say.

"I've never once thought the sky seemed like it was playing."

I shrug and sip on my coffee. "You think I'm being ridiculous," I say, half statement, half question.

"I think you live in a world that's more interesting than the one most people live in," he says, and just as my heart starts to sink with disappointment, with a kind of loneliness, he adds, "and I wish I could live in it too."

I feel myself beaming. "I'll take you sometime."

"I'd like that," he says.

• • •

AFTER BREAKFAST-FOR-DINNER, IT'S clear neither of us wants to go home yet, but it's just as clear that neither of us is going to suggest going back to my house. We can be friendly, if not merely professional, as long as we're somewhere public.

We walk for a while around Old Mo's, but there's nothing cute or quaint here—we're trapped back in an industrial complex much newer than the diner. When we get to our cars, I say, "I know what we should do now," and his expression is so dubious, I can only assume he's bracing himself for a pitch that we chug a vat of pink food dye and have sex in his car.

I step away from him, toward my own rental parked two spots over. "Follow me," I call, unlocking the car.

He doesn't ask any questions, just nods.

I remember the day he hesitated to shake my hand at Margaret's house, and the change from then to now makes me go so warm I have to blast the air-conditioning on the ride over.

• • •

HAYDEN FOLLOWS ME through the dark, up the wooden platform through the grassy dunes to the beach proper.

"Are you sick of the beach by now?" I ask, given that we're only a half block from the Grande Lucia here.

"I haven't really been," he says. "I'm not a huge beach person."

I slant a look at him. "It's hard to be a *beach person* when you're not a *shorts person*."

"Good poi—*fuck! Shit!*" He lurches sideways on the platform, grabbing me bodily and hauling me against the railing.

"What! What!" I yelp, eyes skittering around the path ahead of us. A tail slithers over the side of the walkway, disappearing into the dunes.

"It's just a little snake," I say, trying to be soothing.

"I *hate* snakes," he says.

"I thought you grew up playing in the woods," I say.

"I did," he says, "and every time we came across a snake, I had to completely disassociate and pretend it wasn't happening so the kids I was hanging out with wouldn't find out."

I start forward again, and his arms come around my waist, pulling me back toward him. "It's fine," I say, wiggling out of his grip. "It's gone."

"It might just be waiting to strike right over the edge," he says.

"It's not," I tell him.

"How could you possibly know that," he says.

"I know," I insist. "Can't you disassociate and pretend that didn't just happen?"

He shakes his head. "It won't work. I'm not afraid of humiliating myself in front of you."

I feign offense.

"I just mean, I can't imagine you making fun of me for it."

A smile uncurls over my lips. "Well, I'm willing to try, if that helps."

"Your heart won't be in it," he says. "It won't work."

"Well, we're almost to the water," I point out. "Let's just run."

"You're wearing a skirt," he says.

I'm sure I have a full-blown Cheshire cat grin now. "Are you worried for my virtue here?"

"I'm worried for your ankles," he clarifies. "I don't want you getting bitten."

"I won't get bitten," I promise, and start forward again.

"No, no, no." He hurries after me, bending and sweeping me off my feet and into his arms.

My yelp of surprise becomes a breathless laugh as he essentially runs past where the snake disappeared, as close to the opposite railing as possible, then moves back to the dead center of the walkway. I try to tell him he can put me down, that he doesn't have to do this, but I'm laughing too hard.

As we reach the beach, he slows, the grass and any hidden reptiles now in the rearview.

"I can't believe you risked your ankles for me," I tease, the moon glowing behind Hayden's head.

"I'm wearing pants," he reminds me.

"I wouldn't have blamed *you* if I'd gotten bitten," I say.

"*I* would've blamed me." He comes to a stop and bends a little to pour me back onto my feet. His forearm brushes up my thighs in an electrically charged way, slipping under my skirt in the process and leaving me shivering and weak-kneed by the time my feet meet sand.

"Sorry," he says thickly, reaching out to pull my skirt back into place, and the light tug of his hands on the fabric doesn't have the cooling effect I'd guess he's hoping for. Instead we wind up standing chest to chest, the dark humming around us, like we're two tuning forks vibrating in resonance.

I start to panic, because the more this happens—the more we find ourselves acting like something other than friends—the less likely that I think it is he'll keep *being* my friend, and even though it's only been a couple of weeks, I would miss him.

"Should we go down to the water?" I ask, a little too loudly, and turn on my heel to start trekking that way without even checking that he's following.

He is, of course, and with his long strides, he comes even with me almost instantly.

We stop just before we reach the edge of the ocean and sit, our legs stretched out across the sand, eyes on the dark horizon.

"What's your life like?" I say. "Back in New York."

He looks over at me. "What do you mean?"

"I just only know you in this bubble," I say. "It's kind of strange."

He thinks for a minute. "Well, I work a lot." His eyes flick back to mine. "As I'm sure you do."

I nod.

"I'm busy all the time," he says.

"Do you like it?" I ask.

His head cocks to one side, his lips parting. "I like being busy with work," he says. "But sometimes the pace gets to me. Or maybe it doesn't, but then I come someplace like this and . . ." He holds an arm out toward the ocean.

"It's nice, right?" I say.

"I used to think I'd get so bored if I lived anywhere else," he says. "Which is weird because I actually loved growing up in the middle of nowhere. Other than the whole mayor's-family-under-the-microscope thing."

"Me too," I say. "I mean, small towns definitely have their drawbacks. Especially when it comes to gossip. But I love the pace here."

"And LA?" he says.

"I love it there too," I say. "I mean, the food's great, and it's sunny every single day, and I've got a good group of friends there."

"Did you always want to end up there?" he asks.

"I did," I admit. "I started writing to deal with the stuff going on with Audrey, and then, unrelated, I was always obsessed with Hollywood. I *loved* magazines, but my parents would never spend money on them, so I'd literally just sit in an aisle of the grocery store and read about clothes and beauty trends and celebrities. My mom was always so annoyed when she found me. She'd have been waiting for me at the checkout for a while, and I'd still have to go put the magazines back."

"Well, at least you were polite enough to reshelve," he says diplomatically.

"Oh, you've *got* to reshelve," I agree. "What about you? Was New York your dream?"

"I didn't really have a dream," he says. "If anything, I think I assumed I'd be a mechanic, because my best friend's dad was one, so we were constantly working on his shitty VW van. But my parents really, really pushed college, and then I got into Purdue, which was a shock, because I only really did well in school the last two years. And then I got into writing my freshman year and stuck with it. Got an internship in Chicago after graduation, and that turned into a staff writer job.

"I didn't really plan on ever leaving, but a better job came up in New York, and I'd just gone through a breakup, so I figured it might be good to get away for a while. My best friend from college lives there too, so that's been nice. Watching him get married and have a kid."

I beam at him. "Are you Uncle Hayden?"

"Of course not," he says sternly, "I'm Uncle Nayda."

I let my head settle against his shoulder as the laugh ripples through me. "Oh, excuse me," I say. "I should have guessed."

His chin tips down and he smiles, his mouth so close to mine, his eyes soft. After just a second too long, he says, "Do you ever come to New York?"

"A few times a year," I say. "What about you? Are you ever in LA?"

"Not often," he says.

I nod. We go on staring into each other's eyes until it feels like I *can't* any longer, not without brushing my mouth up over his full bottom lip, tasting him, feeling the heat of his tongue.

I pull away and lie back, staring at the sky and waiting to catch my breath. "What happened with your ex?" I ask, and *this* is a far more successful dousing of the mounting ember between us.

His brow rumples as he gazes over his shoulder toward me.

"The one in Chicago," I say. "Before you went to New York."

"Ah." He turns back toward the water. "Piper."

"Piper," I accidentally repeat aloud, and hope he can't hear the mix of desperate curiosity and (hopefully subtle) jealousy in my voice. "What happened with her?"

He clears his throat and takes a beat before answering. "We worked together. I mean, we were already dating before she started working there. Since college. But we'd been working together for two years when we applied for the same promotion."

"Oh, shit," I say. "Did you *know*?"

He looks back, a completely unconvincing smile on his lips. The expression, though small, makes him look a little feral. "It was my idea. I was applying, but I thought she might as well too. And then I got it, and things fell apart between us really fast. So I found a different job, quit that one, thinking they'd promote her instead and we could . . . I don't know, go back to how things were. But instead they promoted someone else, who had started there four months before her, and everything got worse."

"I'm so sorry," I say. "That sounds *horrible*."

"It was years ago now," he says. "But honestly, it was the last serious relationship I was in."

"Really?" I say.

His head cocks to the left. "I find it hard to believe that's surprising."

"Well, it's even harder picturing you *casually* dating," I say.

"I don't, much," he says. "Just feels like work."

"Do you get lonely?" I meant it in the most innocent way possible, but as soon as it sneaks out, I *tingle* with embarrassment.

But he just studies me seriously, like it's a perfectly normal thing to ask someone you very clearly want to sleep with. "Sometimes I . . ." He hesitates.

"You can tell me," I say, almost a whisper.

His jaw muscles leap. "Sometimes I just miss *this*. Being close to someone. Being touched. Not just sex, I mean."

The tingle on my skin turns inward, my *veins* whirring eagerly now. I pat the sand beside me meaningfully. He doesn't move for so long that I've already accepted he's not going to join me by the time he finally does lie back, his long body rigid and hyperaware. Slowly, watching his face for a reaction, for any sign that it's too much, I shift closer to him, rest my head in the divot just inside his shoulder. I set one hand on his chest, and it expands with a deep breath, the muscles down his flank seeming to relax between us.

He sets one hand over mine, dwarfing it, and even though we'd already been touching so many places, incidentally, this purposeful contact makes me pleasantly shiver. His eyes flutter closed, his dark lashes kissing the tops of his cheeks.

"I love this," he rasps after a second, in a rush, like the thought went straight from his brain to his lips, and judging from the way he tenses as soon as he's said it, I think that might be exactly what happened.

"I do too," I whisper back, and this soothes him. I let myself wiggle closer, his other arm snaking under my back to curl around me. I move a little, restless, and he squeezes my hand under his as he shifts too, turning onto his side, our arms and limbs rearranging until I'm on mine too, the medium spoon to his big one.

I can feel his heartbeat against my shoulder blade, and now his hand is draped over my stomach, lightly atop one of my own. I take a deep breath just for the excuse to feel more of the wall of him behind me. "*I love this*," I admit, nestling back into him.

"Me too," he whispers right beneath my ear.

He's hard against my back, and I will myself not to move around too much, but it's an effort. I feel antsy, exhilarated. His next warm breath makes me bow, and his hand folds over the top of mine, not touching me himself but touching me all the same.

He moves my hand up higher, brings it fully over my chest with a groan into my ear. I push myself back against him, and he skims higher, reaching the neckline of my shirt, letting me pull it down myself, his warm breath feathering down to dance along my bare skin. His hand tightens around mine, gripping me without gripping me. I press back, trying to find the friction between us, and he takes the opportunity to guide my hand lower, pulling the neckline down until my left breast is exposed to the moonlight. "*God*, Alice," he hisses. "We'd be so good together."

I whimper as he sets my hand where he wants it, catches my nipples between my own fingers. "I want to," I whisper.

"Not now," he says. "If you still want to, after all of this . . ." He trails off as his lips brush the side of my throat, not quite kissing, just teasing.

He drags my hand down my center, all the way to my skirt. I squirm at the pressure between my thighs, but he keeps moving until he reaches the hem and then guides my hand beneath the fabric, settling my palm against myself. I grind myself back against him, and he gently cups me over my hand.

He swears, thrusts behind me, and the sensation shoots through my bloodstream like firecrackers. "We were just supposed to touch," he murmurs.

"Then touch me, Hayden," I say.

His hand releases from mine and slides up over my chest, tight, kneading. I bite down on a cry as he pushes the fabric down again, and I arch back, desperate for his mouth to touch my bare skin. Instead he buries it safely in my hair, and does what I asked.

Touches me. Drags a thumb roughly over my nipple, then catches it between his pointer and middle fingers on a groan. I turn hungrily toward him, reach for his belt. He catches my wrist, stilling me. "I'm touching you, remember?" he says, gently removing my hand from the buckle. He sets it on the side of his neck, then slips *his* hand between my thighs.

I gasp at the smooth glide of his fingers over me, my legs parting. His eyes watch me drunkenly, and as I move myself against him, he swallows hard, gravels, "You're so wet."

"I know," I whisper.

He buries his face in my neck again, a frustrated groan vibrating through him as he slides his hand down the inside of my thigh, as if with great effort. "What are you doing tomorrow night?" he says finally.

Surprise pulls a shallow, breathy laugh out of me. "Why?"

"Because I think we should go out," he says. "Somewhere with a lot of people, and very bright lights."

I'd personally rather be somewhere warm, dark, cozy, and private. "I can't."

He stills for a second, then nods, his expression seeming to *zip up*, going from raw and intimate to cool and almost businesslike, despite the very *un*businesslike position we're lying in. "Of course," he says, as if he expected this, as if *he's* the one who crossed the line when it was, as always, me.

"No, Hayden!" I grab his hand and pull it in between us. "I mean, I *can't*. I'm going down to see my mom tomorrow."

"Oh." His brows flinch upward in surprise, then slowly settle into a furrow. "Is that stressful for you?"

"No, not really," I say. It's only partly a lie. *Partly* in that it is *definitely* stressful, but it's also nice and fun and everything else, at intervals.

"It'll be lonely here without you," he says matter-of-factly, and I try not to melt into the sand, where the goop of my former body would never be entirely recovered.

"You could come with me," I say. At the way he startles, I hurry to add, "Not like *come meet my mom*. Just, like, she's always happy to have guests. And her house isn't exceptionally *bright*, but it's *not* private because *she's* there, plus a bunch of chickens, and—never mind. Just an idea."

"Wouldn't that be weird?" he asks, gaze narrowing. "I mean, how would we explain what . . ." He trails off, apparently unwilling to say the mortifying phrase *what we are* or the equally damning *what's going on between us*.

But I meant what I said: "My mom's an amazing host, actually. It's one of her passions. I've brought home a lot of friends over the years. She'd love to have you."

He thinks it over.

"No pressure." I sit up, a more respectable distance between us. "Just if you wanted to get out of town."

He does the same, still silent, face serious and eyes watchful on the waves.

My cheeks start burning.

"I don't want you to invite me to be polite," he says suddenly.

My gaze snaps toward him. "I'm not," I promise. "And I *really* don't want you to say yes to be polite."

"You forget," he says, "I never do anything to be polite."

At my laugh, he reaches out and gently touches my lips, light and fleeting. "I'd love to go."

I beam back at him. "Good."

And then, quickly, almost like he didn't mean to at all, Hayden leans forward and kisses my cheek. "I'll walk you back to your car," he says, starting to stand.

"You mean you'll *carry* me," I tease. "I hear there are snakes around here."

19

MARGARET ANSWERS HER own door on Saturday morning, and I'm so caught off guard that for three seconds after she greets me, I just stare.

"Where's Jodi?" I finally ask when I step inside and slip my shoes off.

"Day off," Margaret says shortly, and leads me down the hallway. "Too hot to be outside today. Mind if we sit in the living room?"

"Works for me," I tell her.

We stop by the kitchen first, and she shakes a box of colorful frozen macarons onto a plate. "Coffee? Tea?"

"Coffee," I say. "But I can get it myself."

She waves me toward the pot, and I pour myself a mug and find the sugar in a jar beneath the cupboard. "You want one?" I ask.

"Already got mine waiting in there," she tells me, and I follow her back to the room where we first met. It's so hot out today that the air-conditioning can't keep up. The air feels stiff and damp. Even for me, it's a bit much.

Just not enough to keep me from drinking hot coffee.

I must wince when I taste it, because Margaret laughs. "All right, all right, I don't usually make the coffee."

"It's not that bad," I say.

I try another gulp. My reaction makes her start laughing again, and it's contagious. As I rein my giggles in, I set my mug aside and take out my recorder. "So today's the day."

"What day is that?" Her silver brows leap upward, but there's something in her expression that tells me it's an act. That she's actually just as excited for today's interview as I am.

"The day it becomes *your* story," I say, hitting the button to start recording and setting the device on the table between us.

She flicks a hand over her shoulder, an unconvincing *pishposh*. "I told you: It's all my story. When you come from a family like mine, you're a part of a whole, like one square in a quilt. Anytime you try to pull in a particular direction, there are hundreds of other squares to resist. To pull you back."

"I get that," I say. "But today, try to ignore those squares. I want to know what it was like to be you."

She smiles wide. "For a time," she says, "it was pure magic."

The Story

THEIR VERSION: What it must be like to be raised in a castle!

• • •

HER VERSION: What's it like to be raised in a castle?

What's it like to have everything you want before you've asked for it?

What's it like to have your food plated by a chef when you're still a toddler?

What's it like to have the Ringling Bros. and Barnum & Bailey Circus perform at your fifth birthday?

To have snow blown in on the hill behind your house in time for Christmas, and to spend all summer wandering through your private orange groves and playing hide-and-seek in the hedge maze, or the chapel, or the slew of Greek follies? To grow up with horses and dogs, swans and zebras and peacocks all wandering past your window, bonded enough to you to eat straight from your hand?

What's it like to break your arm sliding down a grand staircase's banister and take your family's helicopter to the hospital? To live inside a ten-foot stone wall, so far from your front door that anything beyond it might as well be a different world?

What's it like when your father loves your mother madly? When he fills the breakfast room—because there is a room just for breakfast—with daisies—potted, not cut—on her birthday, and she rolls her eyes but laughs too, because she doesn't have an ounce of his whimsy, but she understands the hundreds of ways her husband tries, again and again, to say something along the lines of *I love you*?

When they were younger—Margaret and her sister, Laura—life came in flickers of yellow gold. Warmth, that's what she remembers. Laughter. Her mother blowing raspberries on her stomach. Her father trying, and failing, to make daisy chains for his girls to wear. Her cousin Ruth braiding her hair, her aunt Francine taking her horseback riding. Strolling with Great-Aunt Gigi down the perfume aisles in the glossy department stores along Seventh Street. Grandmother Rosalind reading to her in the library, Margaret sitting in her lap and toying with the string of pearls that lay against Rosalind's cashmere sweater, while her grandfather Gerald smoked an overpriced cigar over by the window.

She remembers kissing her parents good night before they left for premieres, balls, galas, and loving the smell of her mother's soap, the oh-so-rare appearance of a muted mauve paint on her lips. She remembers sneaking out of bed to meet Laura in the tent strung up in their playroom—because there was a room just for playing—and staying up all night, giggling and whispering, and shining flashlights on their picture books.

There's one day in particular she remembers best. A Sunday in late summer, before the heat had broken, when she spent the whole day with her parents and her sister in the ornately tiled outdoor pool—not to be confused with the indoor pool. She remembers practicing diving with her mother. She remembers her father tossing her up, up, up, then catching her right before she crashed against the surface.

And holding her little sister's hand, running as fast as they could from the edge of the pool, convinced that if only they were fast enough, worked hard enough, they could sail right across the surface of the water without sinking.

She still thinks about this day a lot, as a kind of *before* picture. The last golden day.

After that, the world turned blue. As if when she dove under the surface of the water, the cool tones had washed across her eyes and never left.

After that, Margaret's memories are different. Fights—sometimes screamed, and other times whispered. Slammed doors. Bits of jagged blue sentences, sneaking through doors and walls.

—Do you even care that you're a mother? Do you even love them—

—out again until all hours, so you can do whatever you want, but I should be here—

—not the person I married, not even close—

—if you hate your life so much, why are you even still—

She remembers her grandmother Rosalind introducing her and Laura to their new nanny, and feeling so sure it was all a punishment, if she could only figure out for what, what she had done wrong. She was always getting herself into trouble, in the form of scraped knees, muddy tracks across rugs, and broken vases. It could have been anything.

She remembers quiet meals at the dinner table—one of the tables was exclusively for dinner—with the whole family, and then one day the small table moved into the playroom, and all her and her sister's meals taken there, apart from the others.

She'd go days, sometimes, without seeing her parents, and worse still, somehow, were the nights they came in one at a time to say their good nights, looking tired or angry or pained.

What is it like when all of your clothes were made to fit your body, your shoes resoled without your asking, your hairdresser waiting for you on the veranda once a month? What is it like to cry when your favorite swan dies, and to have your grandfather look you in the eye and say, "Your father was supposed to have a son. Who's going to look after all of this when I'm gone?"

What's it like to roller-skate in the ballroom with your sister, or to read a book about a pony and wake up the next morning to find one wearing a big velvet bow in the marble foyer, and to love it, to love it so much you name it after the swan you lost, and tell yourself that maybe, somehow, it *is* the swan, come back from beyond the grave to care for you, because while everyone around you *takes care* of you, you aren't really sure that any of them *care about* you?

When you fall and scrape your knee, there's a mad rush for gauze and rubbing alcohol, but when you weep over the delicate broken neck of a bird, you're given a lollipop.

When you want something you have no idea how to ask for, and no clue whether it even exists.

What do you do when you live in a world that was built around you, and so you find yourself trapped, like one sentence in a myth, one brick in a wall? When you're built into the fabric of a place and that place was built to keep everyone out?

What's it like to feel yourself alone in the world?

20

"THEY DID THEIR best," Margaret says. "The truth is, I think all my mother ever really wanted was to make her art. And I think all my father ever wanted was to be my mother's husband. When either of them felt like those things were being challenged... well, they never really learned to compromise. Not until they split up."

"I've read some old articles," I say. "About the divorce."

She winces, and I can guess why. The tabloids—and Dove Franklin—had all positioned Bernie Ives as an uptight nag who'd never been worthy of the rich, charming, handsome Freddy Ives.

"I remember my grandmother Rosalind trying to convince them to stay married," she says. "She loved my mother, and she knew the world would be unkind to her. Or... less kind than it already was. But my parents weren't ever invested in controlling the narrative the way my grandparents had been. And besides that, as long as I've been alive, there was a strict rule against any tabloids in the house. Laura and I were young and secluded enough not to be exposed to the worst of it, but I *would* occasionally hear Rosalind talking about it with my aunt Francine and great-aunt Gigi.

"She convinced my parents to take us up to the mountains, to stay at . . ." She considers for a second, like the name is just barely evading her. "The Nicollet. One last long weekend, to remind them what they were giving up."

"How'd it go?" I ask.

"It was bliss," she says. "And then we got home, and the next morning, they sat us down in Laura's room and told us Mom was moving out. Years later, she told me she wanted to leave while she still loved him. For us. I think it broke her heart to do it though. I'm not sure she ever got over it. Even after she remarried."

I stay quiet, half expecting her to clam up again, but she doesn't.

"You know, my mother was ahead of her time. The kind of woman who wanted to have it all," she says. "She knew she deserved it too. But the problem is, once you love someone, you *can't* have it all anymore. Love comes with sacrifice. That's how it works. Lawrence left his little sister in Dillon Springs thinking he could help her, and instead he never saw her again. Gerald loved Nina, but he had to give her up to take care of Ruth. Rosalind loved Gerald, but she had to accept his secret as her own, had to believe the story until it was true."

"You mean about Ruth?" I ask. "You think your grandmother knew the truth? That Ruth was her husband's daughter, not Gigi's?"

Margaret nods. "She never said, but I'm sure of it. She loved her family too much to cause a scandal by bringing it up, and besides that, I think she came to genuinely love Ruth. Everyone who ever met her did. She had a *spark*.

"Anyway, my parents' divorce was highly publicized, and it didn't help that my father's reaction to losing the love of his life was to throw himself back into public womanizing with a vengeance."

The Playboy and the Shrew Part Ways, I remember one article declaring.

"We barely saw our mother that first year they were divorced, but we saw even less of him. It was an incredibly lonely time."

"When did things thaw out between them?" I ask. "*How*, after all that?"

"My mother had a movie release," Margaret says simply. "And my father hadn't missed a single one since they'd met. So he went, by himself, the same way he had done years earlier. He couldn't keep being her husband, but he couldn't *stop* being her fan."

I feel myself smile even as my chest aches for her.

She shakes her head as if dispelling a cloud of dust. "Anyway, he sent her potted daisies the next day. She called him. They had one short, civil conversation, but a couple of weeks later, something funny happened—I don't remember what, though I'm sure she told me at some point—and she wanted to tell him. So she called him. Soon they were talking every day, going on walks every once in a while.

"She started coming by for dinners occasionally. We had her over for Christmas. Eventually we were happy again, even if things were never the same."

"You were fifteen when she married Roy?" I say, checking my notes.

"That's right," she says. "And Dad married Linda a year later, but they split up when I was twenty-one."

"And after that," I say, trying to sound as even and nonjudgmental as possible.

"Carol for about . . . six years?" she says. "Does that sound right?"

"It does," I agree. "Were you close with either of them?"

"Close enough," she says. "It was a big house, and it wasn't uncommon for Great-Aunt Gigi's latest beau to be hanging around too. We'd see everyone for dinners, but if anything, Dad's wives after Mom were like . . . like distant cousins. We knew each other, but we didn't spend much time together."

"And Roy?" I ask.

"We loved Roy," she says. "Laura and I both. He was a good man. And he let us be a family. He did what our father couldn't."

"And what was that?" I ask.

Her narrow shoulders hitch upward. "He shared her." She pauses for a long moment, and I watch her weigh her next words, deciding whether she can trust me with them.

I don't rush forward to comfort or to cajole. The next couple of weeks are likely going to feel a lot harder for her than the first two, and as eager as I am to prove myself, I can't force her to be ready.

"Roy and my mother were married for thirty years, you know," she says.

"I do," I confirm. "Until he died."

"Afterward . . ." She pauses again, still unsure.

I reach forward and turn off the recorder, stopping the one on my phone as well.

"She loved him," she says, a sideways lurch in the conversation, or perhaps a detour that will lead us to the same place. "She loved him, and he loved us, and I think she appreciated him every day of their life together. Dad went first, from liver failure, and then a few years after that, Roy died from heart disease. Mom had him buried in the family cemetery, because Roy was family."

Her lips quiver. "After his funeral, after everyone had left but Mom and me, she went over to my dad's headstone, and she started weeping. You know, she'd held it together all that time. She was never an easy crack, my mother. But she lost it, slumped down at his headstone and coiled her arms around it. And she said something I won't ever forget. Something I still hear, in her voice if I try, like I'm replaying it on film.

"Why couldn't it have been you? Why couldn't you be who you were supposed to be?"

Shivers crawl down my arms, and my chest feels too small for my beating heart. "What do you make of that?"

"I don't make anything of it," she murmurs. "I know exactly what she meant." She sets her mug down. "He was the love of her life, and he let the world make him too small for her.

"The world Freddy Ives lived in was built around him. There wasn't room for her."

I swallow a knot. "What do you think he should have done?"

She turns the full force of those shining blue eyes on me. "For the one you love? Anything. You unmake the world and build a new one. You do *anything* to give them what they need."

• • •

"YOU'RE STRANGELY QUIET," Hayden says.

"Hm?" I look up from the road, nearly startling at the sight of him hunched in the passenger seat of my slightly too-small rental car.

"Are you regretting this?" he asks. "It's not too late to turn around."

"No," I say. "*No.* That's not what this is about."

On my next glance, I see his skepticism.

"It's about... *work*," I say, as vaguely and innocuously as possible.

His features tighten and he turns his gaze forward again. "Ah."

"Sorry," I say. "I know we can't talk about it."

There's a long silence before he says, "We can't talk about *her*. But we can talk about you. If there's a way to do that, without..." He trails off, but I know what he's saying.

The problem is, I'm not sure there *is* a way to separate the two: what Margaret's saying and how I'm feeling. It's all braided tightly together.

The thing that's gripping me right now, the part of Margaret's and my last conversation that I can't shake, isn't just her sadness, her melancholy, her air of loneliness, or even the way the poised, confident octogenarian had become almost childlike in front of me, but the fact that, for the first time, I felt sure she was telling me the truth.

The *whole* truth, not a modified version with select bits and pieces tweaked or dodged.

It's interesting, how this part of her family's history—the part most firmly planted in her point of view—is also the most honest.

It's nearly the opposite of what that famous quote suggests. There might be three versions of any story, but does that mean that *hers* is any less true?

Maybe truth is less about a compromise of conflicting viewpoints and more about an integration of them. The thought discomfits me. I've always wanted to make my interview subjects feel seen and heard, but there's also been a comfort in believing I'm nothing more than a conduit, a funnel, for the truth to pour through, a sieve catching and dispelling any unnecessary bits.

It changes things, to think that maybe *everything* is necessary. Maybe truth can't be whittled out of a pile of research but instead has to be built from all of it, no spare pieces left behind, absolutely nothing discarded.

And if that's the case, how can I possibly succeed—at this job, or any other?

From the passenger seat, Hayden sighs and scrubs a hand over his face. "I wish I could help you."

"I'm okay, really," I promise him. "I guess I'm just . . . do you ever doubt the job?"

One inky eyebrow curves up. "Doubt the job? How so?"

I shake my head. "I don't know. Forget I said anything."

There's a long pause, no sound but the highway whirring under our tires as the sun beats down on the glass and the kudzu-covered trees whip past us on either side of the road.

"I haven't seen you like this before," he says with a small, tight frown.

"What? Mopey?" I say. "It doesn't happen much."

"Is it because you're going to see your mother?" he asks.

My stomach clenches and relaxes. "I don't know," I admit. "Maybe." It hadn't occurred to me, but it feels true.

When I'm with my mom and sister, no matter how many times I promise myself I'll handle things differently, I always catch myself sliding into the defensive when it comes to my job. Trying to legitimize it in their eyes.

"It's not like she's rude about my work," I clarify. "She really isn't. It's more just . . . what she doesn't say."

"That she's proud of you?" he guesses.

My cheeks flame. "I'm thirty-three. Why do I care?"

"Everyone cares," he says.

I give him a look.

"Fine," he says. "The vast majority of people care."

"When do you think you stop?" I ask. "When you're forty? When they die?" I shoot him a teasing look. "When you win a Pulitzer?"

He scoffs quietly. "No, not then. Because then, suddenly, they're *incredibly* proud, but they're proud of the accomplishment, not of the work. So you feel like you have to keep *accomplishing* instead of just *creating*. It affirms the idea that the value in what you do is how people react to it, and not just in the making of it. I've written stuff I'm really proud of that hardly anyone read. I've written stuff I'm proud of that no one *liked*. That doesn't mean it didn't deserve to be written."

Now I'm genuinely smiling, my mood lifting almost instantly. "That's a nice thought."

His huge shoulders lift in a shrug. "It's true. How many of your favorite shows got canceled? How many of the best albums barely sold when they came out? I mean, *It's a Wonderful Life* was a box office flop in its time. If everyone who worked on that movie had known, could see how things were going to pan out in the short term, would they have even bothered to make it? And then the world would've lost out on something beautiful. Just because something doesn't make money or win awards doesn't mean it doesn't have value. Or doesn't deserve to exist. The job is alchemy. You take a hunk of rock and you try to turn it into gold, and the gold isn't even really the point."

"Right, because the goal is immortality," I joke.

"It's permanence," he says. "Not, like, having your name on the side of a fucking airplane or skyscraper, or some shit like that. But bringing something intangible into the world that can live on without you. Something bigger than the person who made it. And even then, the goal is secondary to the process. The process is for *us*. It changes us in ways that can't be measured. At least, that's what I've always thought."

My grin is getting bigger by the second.

"What?" he says, an edge of *oh, here we go* to his voice.

"Nothing," I say. "I just . . . didn't expect you to be so . . ."

"Whimsical?" he says, reticent.

"Optimistic," I correct him.

His brow furrows, his expression somewhat dour, but I'm not falling for it anymore. Below that stony face and beneath that *equally* stony chest, there's a soft, thrumming, hopeful heart.

He clears his throat. "Are you sure your mom's okay with me coming?"

"She's excited," I tell him.

It's a classic example of the slippery nature of truth: Did my mother *say* she was excited when I told her I was bringing a friend?

No, she absolutely did not.

She said, and this is a direct quote, *Okay.*

But is she excited?

Certainly. There are two places my mother is most alive, most herself. The first is in her garden, with mud up to her shins and Dad's hideous wide-brimmed hat atop her head, the chin strap tight and her cheeks red from digging.

The other place is more of a *state of being*. When she's caring for visitors, when she can be a good steward of her little plot of land, she's happy.

"Excited," Hayden repeats to himself. "Not sure I can live up to that."

"Just eat whatever she puts in front of you, and she'll be happy," I say. "And offer to help with the dishes."

His knee jogs up and down, his jaw stern as he gazes out the window.

"Are you . . . nervous?" I ask.

"I don't know," he says, then, "No. Should I be?"

"Definitely not," I say. "She's easy."

Another example of the amorphous nature of the truth: She really *is* easy. Simultaneously, there are knots in my stomach.

Hayden nods but doesn't say anything else.

I turn on the radio and Gladys Knight and the Pips' "Midnight Train to Georgia" fills the car.

• • •

THE SUN IS setting by the time we pull into the long driveway to the single-story home where I grew up.

I try, as always, to see it how an outsider must, and as always, I fail.

This place is just home to me, the same way the opulent House of Ives was to Margaret.

There's a chicken coop built out of repurposed boards and plywood, and at least one kitchen cupboard Dad had found years ago on a neighbor's curb after a renovation, and a little fenced-in area surrounding it for the birds to wander as they so choose. There's a shed that's similarly haphazard in appearance and, I know, sturdy in construction.

Along the edge of the property on our right, a split-rail fence, repaired piecemeal as needed, runs through overgrown grass, a couple of blue rain barrels gathered together in a row, while to our left, garden beds in various states of growth spread out, a thicket of peach trees beyond the shed, the coop, the huge compost bins, and the outhouse Audrey and I helped Dad build around his and Mom's prized possession (slash the bane of our adolescent existence): the composting toilet.

The house itself appears to slightly lean, but that's only because of the strange grade of the ground. The paint on the shutters is peeling off in chunks, but the roof is fairly new, covered in solar panels.

"Wow," Hayden says. An impressed *wow*, I think, and not a mortified one.

I can't help but feel like he just passed a test, albeit one I hadn't meant to set up.

As we rumble closer, I see Mom unfold from where she was crouched in the garden. Just as I predicted, Dad's green khaki hat sits snug against her head, the chin strap all the way tightened, her worn-out and too-large overalls stuffed into her wellies and her bare arms disappearing at the elbow into her thick green gloves.

She waves one arm over her head as I pull up, squinting against the light.

"Oh," Hayden says beside me. "She's . . ."

I save him the trouble of finishing the sentence. "Beautiful, yeah." I shoot him a teasing look as I put the car in park. "Don't act so surprised, or I might finally start taking things personally."

"It's not like that," he says.

"I know," I promise, but the truth—the *other* version of it—is that I'm feeling a little raw and vulnerable.

My mom raised Audrey and me not to care about appearances. She and Dad never talked about how we looked. And I know why she did it—and for my sister, I think it even worked—but the truth is, without makeup and hair dye and nice clothes, my mom has always been stunningly pretty. And my sister looks just like her: big green eyes, gold hair, little pointed chin, petite with curves.

I've always taken more after Dad. Tall, lanky, with only the faintest strawberry undertone to my generally mousy hair.

Maybe it's easier to say looks don't matter when you look like Hollywood's version of a hardworking, outdoorsy woman with a heart of gold.

Mom peels her gloves off as she comes toward us, and I unlock the doors and get out.

"How was the trip?" she asks, giving me a firm hug and one quick pat on the back before pulling away and wiping sweat from her brow with the back of her wrist.

"Great!" I pop open the back door to grab my bag, while Hayden does the same on the other side of the car. "This is my friend Hayden."

Mom flashes a naturally perfect, if slightly yellowed, smile across the top of the car. "Nice to meet you," she says, then adds simply, "Angela."

"Nice to meet you too." Hayden hoists his duffel out of the back seat and comes around to shake her hand.

"Oh, we're huggers," she says, bypassing the hand and going straight for the kill, the same kind of firm grip and single hit between his shoulder blades, over before it even began.

"Thanks so much for having me," he says as they separate.

"Oh, it's nothing." She flicks the glove in her hand. "I'm still not used to cooking for one, honestly, so this is better. Come on in, and Alice will get you settled while I clean myself up."

"What are you working on?" I ask as we follow her to the front door.

"Well, mostly the strawberries and peaches, of course," she says.

"What about the beans and peas?" I ask. "Are they ready yet?"

She nods. "Yep, and the cucumbers this year are incredible. I mean, you wouldn't believe! Well, you *will* believe. Figured we'd have them in a salad tonight."

She kicks open the squeaky screen door—the door behind it is *never* shut—and steps aside to let us pass.

Inside, Mom and I kick off our shoes, and Hayden follows our lead. Luckily, he's not any more of a *sandals* person than he is a shorts person, so he's wearing socks, which I didn't think to warn him is a bit of a necessity in our house.

Even though we're a no-shoes-inside family, when you spend as much time outside as Angela Scott, the dirt finds its way into the old floorboards. I watch him scan the entryway: the tidy rows of boots, clogs, and sandals coated in varying degrees of dried mud, the reusable grocery bags and totes dangling from the hooks drilled into the wall over them, the pencil marks where Dad documented Audrey's and my growth spurts on the doorjamb on the left, which leads into a dining room that's long been treated more as an *extended pantry*.

"You want to show Hayden to his room?" Mom asks me, draping her gloves across the mouth of a bucket sitting in the corner.

"Sure," I say. "I'll meet you in the kitchen after you shower?"

"Sounds like a plan." She leans in and plants a firm kiss on my forehead. "Glad you're here, kid," she says.

"Me too," I say. The truth, and not the truth.

Then she pats my shoulder and ambles down the hall toward her bedroom. When I face Hayden again, he's leaning in to study the

Polaroid pinned to the wall beside the front door. Mom and Dad, back in the seventies, standing in front of a newer and less rambling version of this house, their arms wrapped around each other, both proudly beaming, the day they moved in.

Hayden feels my eyes and looks over to me. "You lived here all your life."

"I did, yeah," I say.

"You must miss it," he says.

"Sometimes," I admit. "Come on, I'll show you where you're staying."

21

THE UNTRAINED EYE might think this is a guest room. Or that, even if it *was* Audrey's room at one time, it's long since been emptied out and converted to the sparse little office with the fold-down Murphy bed that Hayden and I are standing before.

The untrained eye would be wrong.

This is exactly what Audrey's room looked like even when we were in high school. A desk. A dresser. A filing cabinet. A bed that pushes up to the wall to make room for anything other than sitting on the bed.

Hayden catches me smiling. "What?"

"You just," I begin, "don't fit here."

He frowns at this. "I grew up somewhere pretty rural, remember?"

"No, I mean, you literally don't fit," I explain. "You make this room seem comically small. Or, I don't know, maybe it makes you look cartoonishly large."

"Oh." He cracks a faint smile too, looks up—not very far—to the ceiling, and then lets his gaze sweep around the room before settling on me again. In my chest, it feels like a latch clicking into place when our eyes meet.

"Are you used to having tiny guests?" he asks.

"This was Audrey's room," I explain. "She's always been a minimalist."

"What about you?" he asks.

"Oh, I'm across the hall," I say. "Want to see?"

"Of course," he says, following me over to it. It's just as small, but nowhere near as sparse. I used to love it, but now it makes me feel vaguely panicky how full I packed the walls with photos, magazine clippings, notes my sister and I had written back and forth between classes, games of MASH we'd played on notebook paper, trying to predict our futures and pairing ourselves up with our crushes du jour.

Like Audrey's bed, mine is covered in a quilt Mom made from repurposed fabric, but unlike the light, breezy colors Audrey had selected, mine is a disgusting blend of neons. "This poor quilt," I say. "A victim of 2001 trends, like so many of us."

"I've never seen anything like it," he agrees.

"Oh, there's a reason for that," I say, walking over and pointing to one of the magazine pages pinned to the wall. An old Limited Too catalog, an advertisement for their room decor, wherein everything is sparkly, inflatable, or covered in highlighter-green and pink fur. "*This* is what I wanted." I wave toward the quilt, devolving into laughter. "And this is my poor mother trying to humor me."

"Looking at it is giving me a migraine," he says, dead serious.

I chortle, flip the top back to expose the other side: a sensible light purple with tiny white flowers—Mom trying to ensure maximum usage, beyond the length of time it would take me to get sick of the other side.

"What's this?" Hayden asks, picking up a leatherbound book that rests atop one of the stacks of books that line the top of my old bookshelf. On the front, embossed, is *The Scotts: A History.*

"A present from my sister, when we were in college," I say, going to stand beside him as he flips it open. "It's just this service that will bind a story for you. I had all of these old photographs and journal entries from when we were kids, so . . ."

He flips slowly through the first couple of pages, gets to an old shot I took of Audrey crouched atop the compost toilet—fully dressed, not *using* it—the day we helped Dad build it. She's wearing his wide-brimmed hat and making a funny face.

"Wow," he says. "An outhouse."

"Oh, yes," I say. "This is our family's opus."

"So I see," he deadpans, turning the page. There *I* am, out of focus, because Audrey took this one (thus it's one of the very few shots of me in the book), lying on my back in a garden bed, spread out like a starfish in denim overalls like the ones Mom was wearing earlier, a mini bouquet of purple and orange wildflowers tucked behind my ear. I look beatific, under the sun. I can *feel* the humidity of that day on my skin, smell the grass baking, and catch the subtle buzz of the bumblebees bobbing around.

Behind me, crouched in front of the garden bed with his back to us as he digs, Dad is visible, just his lower half. Seeing it jogs something loose: the sound of Cosmo Sinclair's signature vibrato crackling out from the old boom box Dad used while he worked, that velvety smooth voice singing about a woman who moved around with the light of the sun inside her, making everything better, warmer, brighter.

"You look so happy," Hayden says, snapping me back to the present.

"I was." I pass the book to him. "I am."

"Mind if I borrow this after dinner?" Hayden asks. Then, teasing: "Might like to do some light reading."

"Oh, that's not light," I say as he sets the book on the shelf. "This is a dense, academic doorstop. You're going to want to take notes, have little colorful paper tabs to mark the sections you want to come back to. Actually, now that I think of it, there should be some highlighters in Audrey's de—"

He pulls me into a hug abruptly, like he couldn't resist, his face nestling into my shoulder. My stomach swoops up into my throat, trilling like a hummingbird. I loop my arms around his neck and lean back to peek into his face when he lifts it. "Were you trying to shut me up again?"

"No," he says, shaking his head once. No other explanation, and if there was one, I'm fairly confident he'd give it, which means that he just wanted to do that. Which thrills me, makes me feel weightless and jittery, like that first second of a roller-coaster drop.

I can't remember the last time I had a crush like this, not one that merely aches, the way I'd felt about Theo the first few months, that painful yet addictive feeling of wanting something that is being very intentionally withheld from you.

This is the other kind. The dopamine hit of *proof*, evidence, facts that add up to the knowledge that maybe the person whose very presence excites you is also excited by *your* presence. That *I think he likes me back* feeling.

Still, I can't resist the impulse to double-check: "You regret coming yet?"

I'm expecting something jokey or deadpan. Instead, he just says again, simply, "No." I let my arms tighten. His hands move to loosely circle my wrists.

It's strange, how being here has instantly changed the boundaries between us, made everything feel more relaxed. Not just *natural* but *inevitable*.

"How would you feel about a walk?" I ask.

"Good," he says.

We drop our stuff and go outside into the fading light, meandering down the driveway. At the corner of the country road the house sits on, his hand finds mine. We lace our fingers together and keep walking, kicking up dust, churning up sweat.

From the outside, we probably look picturesque and peaceful. Inside, my heart feels like it's riding along the top of a very active geyser.

That's the first time it occurs to me: I'm falling in love with him.

Maybe it should scare me.

It doesn't. I never want it to stop.

● ● ●

IN THE CROWDED little kitchen, Mom drops a bundle of still-dirt-smeared carrots on the counter for me to chop, then goes to fill a pot with water. While she pops it on the stove, I connect to Dad's old Bluetooth speaker and start up a playlist. Cosmo Sinclair's "Say You Will (Be Mine)" croons out between us.

In my peripheral, I catch her twitch in surprise.

It strikes me that Dad was the one to put on their cooking soundtrack, largely because Mom always enters a kind of cooking trance that renders conversation with her nearly impossible. For all I know, she's been cooking in silence these last two years.

The thought makes me sad. Wordlessly, she fishes a canister of noodles from the pantry and shakes some into the boiling pot.

"How can I help?" Hayden's voice rolls over me as he steps into the room, freshly showered and dressed in a worn Purdue sweatshirt and black sweats. He looks so clean and cozy that suddenly I want nothing more than to nestle up in him, the human equivalent of a comfy bed after a long day.

My face must betray this, because he's looking at me like *What am I missing?*

"You can help Alice peel the carrots, if you want," Mom says over her shoulder.

I hand him the peeler and grab a knife from the block before rinsing the carrots. He peels, and I cut them on the diagonal, tossing them in a bowl with some oil and salt before spreading them out on a pan to roast.

If he's bothered by the lack of conversation, he doesn't show it, which is good, because I learned to cook at my mother's hip and thus never developed a talent for talking *while* working.

With the carrots roasting, I put Hayden on salad-prep duty, rinsing and chopping Mom's freshly collected cucumbers, tomatoes, and onions, while I massage the kale with some oil and smoked salt. Mom makes her Alfredo sauce from scratch, and when the timer goes off, I pull the carrots out, stir them around the pan, drizzle them with some honey and spices, and pop them back in for a few more minutes.

I'm so immersed in the process that it takes me a while to realize Mom is humming along to the music, another one of Cosmo's love songs on the playlist, "Peggy All the Time."

My chest twinges at the sound. Dad used to sing this as *Angie all the time.*

> *When I close my eyes at night,*
> *Every time I'm down and out,*
> *If the sky is blue and bright,*
> *I'll tell you what I'm thinkin' 'bout.*
> *It's Angie all the time.*
> *Angie all over my mind.*

Tears unexpectedly spring to my eyes. Not just for my mom, but for the woman Cosmo Sinclair wrote the ballad for.

For Margaret Ives, and the part of her story that broke an entire generation's heart.

"Hey," Hayden says, so quietly his voice is more of an *impression* than a sound, tucked beneath the music. "You okay?"

When I let myself dream,
Or it all comes crashing down,
If it all turns out all right,
And at every pretty little sound,
It's Peggy, Peggy on my mind.
Peggy all the time.

"Onions," I say, the first outright lie I've ever told him, and he knows it. I lift the cutting board and swipe his neatly sliced veggies into the salad bowl with the kale.

"Soup's on, kids," Mom calls from the stove. "Grab some forks and plates. It's serve yourself around here, Hayden. Hope you don't mind."

"Not at all," he says. "That's perfect for me."

His eyes connect with mine, and the moment of melancholy slips past, the kernel of something warm and giddy swelling in its place at the word *perfect*.

I'm not sure why. It's not like he said *I'm* perfect. But all those little zaps of excitement must be melting my brain a little.

Hayden on my mind, I think.

Again, I wonder if the thought should terrify me. But there's no room for terror. There's just warm golden light, the smell of freshly cracked pepper and almond soap, the soft pop of a cork Mom's pulling from a bottle of cabernet, and a pair of pale brown eyes set into a thoughtful expression I can't believe I *ever* mistook for a glower.

Perfect for me.

• • •

"I'M SERIOUS!" MOM says. "I hated him."

"You did not *hate* him," I argue with her over my own laughter.

"I did!" she says, turning to Hayden, who's fighting a smile. "I'm serious. First impressions are so meaningless. I hated him." She throws her hands up, then grabs her glass and takes another swig.

"Just to be clear," I tell Hayden, "I've heard this story ninety thousand times—"

She rolls her eyes. "You're exaggerating, my girl."

"—at ninety thousand different dinner tables," I go on, "and she's never once said she *hated* my father at first. She's always said she barely noticed him."

"That's because I didn't want to hurt his feelings," she says. "Now he's gone, and I can admit I was *not impressed*."

"Mom!" I cry, laughing a little from the shock of it. She so rarely talks about him, let alone acknowledges the humongous hole in this world where he should be.

"I had bad taste, and I didn't see what a gem he was," she says. "I just thought he was so . . ." She scrunches up her face as she finishes. "*Silly*."

I snort into my glass, narrowly avoiding inhaling wine straight into my lungs. "Okay, that tracks," I admit. My dad *could* be silly. My mom, though she has her own sense of humor, is *not*.

"What did you think was silly about him?" Hayden asks.

She gives an exaggerated eye roll and pushes her empty plate back from the edge of the table. "God, what *didn't* I think was silly? I mean, we were living in a farming commune. Most of us took ourselves very seriously, you know? Alan was ridiculous. He was *always* singing, for one thing, and he couldn't carry a tune to save his life.

Beyond that, he was terrible at remembering lyrics, so most of what he sang was nonsense anyway."

"And what did he think about you?" Hayden asks, leaning in, engaged, naturally curious like any good interviewer should be.

I catch myself beaming, waiting for the familiar beats.

Her exuberance softens into a calm smile, her fingers resting at the base of her glass's stem. "Oh, he says he did all of that singing and everything to try to get my attention," she says. "But seeing as how he kept doing it until his dying day, I'm pretty confident all he really meant was, he thought I was pretty."

Here is where Dad would chime in, and so I do. "Beautiful. Smart. Hardworking. With great taste in books."

"He'd just graduated from journalism school," she says, "and I was taking a year off after undergrad, trying to figure out what to do. He'd see me reading in our downtime, so that was how he first struck up a conversation with me. Honestly, I thought he was so silly, it hadn't occurred to me how much we'd have in common."

The corners of her mouth tighten, her smile tilting toward woeful, and she says something I haven't heard before, something new to the story: "He had this joy in him, this softness, and it took me a long time to realize that didn't make him dumb. In fact, he was a hell of a lot smarter than me."

She's never been touchy, and so I've never been particularly touchy with her, but in that moment, for some reason—maybe it's the wine, or the music, or Hayden's comforting stone-steady presence—I reach out and touch her forearm.

Her smile tenses up a little, unconvincing, and she pats the back of my hand before pulling away to stand. "Dessert?" she says, moving the conversation on, and my heart flags in my chest.

"Sounds great," I say, but it comes out thin.

22

"I SHOULD'VE KNOWN you'd be out here," I say, crossing the garden to the stone bench where Hayden sits beneath the starlight.

"Couldn't sleep?" he asks.

I lower myself beside him. "I'm so far off this schedule. Early to bed, early to rise—not really my thing."

"And I'm just *early to rise*," he says. In the distance, a barn owl hoots.

"Have you always been bad at sleeping?" I ask.

"Always," he says.

"What is it?" I ask. "Afraid of the dark?"

The way he glances at me, I can tell he's gauging whether I'm teasing him. I'm not.

"No, not that." He leans back, scanning the sky. "You know what I think it really is?"

"What?" I ask.

"I think I don't like people looking at me," he says.

"Oh." I turn my gaze purposefully forward, across the dark garden, toward the lone lit bulb beside the door to the house.

"Not like that." He nudges my thigh with his, his eyes sweeping back to my face. "Not you."

"Oh." A pleasant warmth vibrates through me.

"I think . . ." He begins again. "I think as a kid, I felt so much pressure. To act a certain way, be seen how my dad needed his sons to be seen. And I was bad at it. Clumsy. Rude. All day long, I think I sort of felt like I was flexing every muscle in my body, or something. And then nighttime would roll around, and my family would be asleep—the whole world would be asleep, and . . ." He cocks his head to one side, his eyes sparking when they catch mine. "I started sneaking out when I was like ten."

"And what exactly was there for a ten-year-old to do in the middle of the night in rural Indiana?" I ask, letting myself lean against him, my head tipping to rest on his shoulder.

He laughs a little, one soft rasp, and presses a kiss to the crown of my head that makes me feel volcanic, like lava is coursing down me. "Nothing," he says. "Nothing at all. I'd just walk around our neighborhood, listening to music on a Walkman my mom gave me, and absolutely everyone would be asleep, or at least inside with the lights off. And I just remember feeling . . . light. No one was looking at me." He seems a little bashful as he says, "I've always felt most myself when I'm alone."

It reminds me of something Margaret would say, of things she *has* said, and I wish I could tell him that. But I can't, not without breaking our most important rule.

"You want me to leave you to your alone time?" I ask instead, and hurry to add, "I won't take it personally, I promise."

"Nah," he says. "This is better." He rearranges his arm across the back of the bench, and I move closer, his head resting against mine. "Does your mom know? What you're working on?"

"I didn't break the NDA," I assure him.

"No, it's not—that's not why I was asking," he says. The same owl hoots in the distance. "She hasn't asked you about it. About work. Why you're here."

I shift uncomfortably. "I already told you. She doesn't care about most of the things I write about."

"But she cares about you," he says. "That much is obvious."

Is it? I almost ask. But I know he's right. Mom's love has always been an action, rather than words. Making that hideous quilt, teaching me how to bake my favorite peach cobbler and my favorite cast-iron cornbread casserole, and serving one or the other every time I come home. "I think . . ." I'm not sure how to say this. I feel *guilty* saying it, because I think it would break her heart to hear, even if it's true. "I think she loves me because I'm her daughter. But I've never felt sure she loves me because I'm *me*. Does that make sense?"

He pulls away and ducks his head to peer into my eyes, his expression torqued. "I'm sure that's not true," he says quietly.

"Maybe it doesn't matter," I say. "Maybe the fact that she *does* love me is all that does."

She made me who I am, in so many ways—not just the skills she passed on, but the *strength*. When we were all scared shitless about Audrey's health, Mom was as steady as a metronome, day in and day out, working our land, making our meals, providing what we needed, driving my sister to and from doctors' appointments, and helping Dad homeschool us. She taught me to think of life not just in terms of how many executioner's blades were poised over our proverbial necks at any given time but in terms of how we could use our time before that ax fell, or didn't. And a lot of the time it didn't.

Keep working, keep moving, keep hoping.

He wraps his arms more tightly around me, pulls me in against his side, and tucks my head beneath his chin. I take a deep inhale of his almond soap and feel my chest loosen. My eyes flutter closed, his even breathing soothing me.

When I next open them, the sky is deep purple, the chickens just starting to move around, clucking in their enclosure. I pry myself away from Hayden and he stirs awake, his eyes slitting open on a sleepy smile.

"Hey," I croak.

"Hey," he croaks back.

"Did my snoring keep you up?" I ask.

He runs a hand over his face, wiping the sleep from himself. "Weirdly, no."

We smile at each other a beat, a silent acknowledgment of how strange this all is, and—at least for me—how strangely normal it feels.

"We're going to be covered in mosquito bites," I say.

"Not me," he teases scratchily, "I'm wearing *pants*."

"Well, your arms have double the surface area of mine, so things will probably shake out pretty evenly." I fight off a yawn. "Want some tea?"

"Tea sounds good." He groans a little as he unfolds himself from the bench, giving me a hand to pull me upright and straight into a hug I wish I could wear like an almond-scented coat, morning, noon, and night. "I think my neck is stuck at an angle," he murmurs against the side of mine.

I reach up and knead the tight muscles there, and the way his groan travels through me makes every little hair on my arms and legs stand up, like they're reaching toward him.

Behind us, the door creaks open, and we lurch apart, but Mom hardly looks our way as she trudges toward the coop, a basket over her arm. "Anyone want to help me collect the eggs?" she calls to us, the mist seeming to nibble away at her voice like thousands of tiny fish pouncing on a piece of bread.

I look to Hayden. "Tea can wait," he tells me.

"Yep," I shout back to Mom as we start toward the coop.

• • •

SLEPT WITH HAYDEN, I type to the group text, and when a flurry of !!! And WHAT and tell me everything chimes in from Cillian, Bianca, and Priya respectively, I send a clarifying follow-up: As in, we fell asleep on a stone bench outside my mom's house.

Priya replies with an unimpressed ellipsis.

Cillian writes, I still can't believe you took him to your mama's house. I'VE never even been there.

I have, Bianca brags. Best spoon bread of my life. I dream about it sometimes.

RUDE, Cillian says.

Next time you're in GA, let me know, I tell him. It's an open invitation. I promise.

Let's back up to you sleeping on a stone bench with a (hot) man, like you're not two grown adults, Priya says.

They're at her PARENTS' HOUSE, Pri, Bianca says. What do you WANT them to do?

Priya sends through a winky face.

How are you guys? I ask. I miss you all.

Pretty good, Cillian says. Except my editor is breathing down my ass about this profile on the team making the new E.T. miniseries.

I have never and I will never breathe "down your ass," Bianca says. The piece needs work.

Can you guys handle this privately, Priya says. I come here for the goss, not to feel like I'm at work.

I can literally see the top of your head poking out of your cubicle from here, Cillian says.

Wait you're at the office today?!? Priya says, and then the messages go silent, probably as they reconvene in real life, at the water cooler or office Nespresso.

I go back into the kitchen to wash the rest of the breakfast dishes, then join Mom in the garden. I'd assumed Hayden was still out on his run, but he's actually back, drenched in sweat, and working by her side.

"Hey," I call, trudging up. "Could you use another set of hands?"

"Actually, I was about to shower," Hayden says, pushing himself up and handing the spare gardening gloves over.

"Lunch in about two hours?" Mom asks, without looking at either of us.

Hayden's eyes and mine connect. He gives me a small nod.

"Sure," I say. "And then we should head out."

Mom nods, still digging with a trowel, focus buried in the dirt. "Nice kid," she says after a minute.

I ignore the flip-flop my stomach does and take up my post beside her. "He's great. Really good writer too."

She sneaks a glance at me, then goes back to digging.

Is she picking up on my crush, or is it something else? I've brought lots of friends here over the years, but never a boyfriend or love interest of any kind.

In fact, imagining Theo here in my childhood home makes me feel like I'm three seconds from breaking into hives.

I'd always been too afraid she'd disapprove. If she knew about my dynamic with Theo, I'm sure she *would*. And that would bother me in a way that her disapproval of Hayden, I'm fairly sure, wouldn't.

I'm still trying to figure out why when she says, "I read his book."

I feel, instantly, like I might burst with pride. But I'd be lying if I didn't say there was a fair bit of jealousy mixed in there. "It's amazing, isn't it?"

"I liked it very much." That's high praise coming from her. "You want the hat?" she asks, pulling the drawstring loose under her chin. "You're going to get fried out here."

"I'm wearing sunscreen," I promise her, but she ignores me and pops the wide brim over my face.

After another minute or two of silence, she says, "He showed me that story you wrote. About the child star. Bella whatever?"

I sit back on my heels, absorbing the shock. "Oh."

Still digging, still focused earthward, she says, "Your writing's come a long way."

I know—in my heart of hearts—she means this as a compliment. It still feels couched in an insult. "Thanks," I say.

"You've always been talented," she goes on, the pressure easing from me, only to push down again when she adds, "You could be doing anything."

I don't want to fight with her—that's the last thing Dad would want—but I suddenly feel too thorny and raw to accept any subtle digs about my career without snapping.

It's not just about me, I remind myself. My mom's got her own stuff she's dealing with. I take the hat back off and hand it to her, determined to maintain a breezy smile. "I'm going to see if the shower's free yet," I say.

She nods once, without meeting my eyes. I stand and go inside.

• • •

AFTER LUNCH, WE pack the car and say our goodbyes. "Feel free to come back anytime," Mom says, to both of us, and I know she means it.

In lieu of hugs, she gives us a stack of leftovers in Tupperware, and walks us partway to the car, lingering at the point where the walkway spills into driveway.

"Safe travels," she calls from there, like she can't come any farther, and waves over her head.

"Thanks," we call back in unison as we climb inside. "Love you," I add through the rolled-down window.

"You too," she says, and then we're pulling away.

It's strange, how no place on earth feels like home to me like this house shrinking in the distance, and yet, every time I'm there, I can't help but feel it's too tight around me, like a sweater that shrunk, or the house in *Alice in Wonderland* that Alice ends up wearing like a dress after she eats the magic cake.

"You okay?" Hayden asks from the passenger seat as we reach the intersection of the driveway and the road.

For once, I'm not in the mood to talk. "I'm good," I say, pulling onto the road.

He nods, but after a few seconds, clears his throat and says, "You can talk about it, Alice."

"I'm good," I repeat.

In my peripheral, he shakes his head. "You're not good. You're upset."

"What am I upset about?" I say.

He gives a frustrated laugh but doesn't answer right away.

"What?" I press.

"Your mom," he says. "You're angry with her."

My face warms. "Why are you acting like you're mad at *me* now?"

"*I'm not trying to—* I just don't understand why you won't say something."

"About *what*?" I ask, my own irritation mounting to match his.

"About how she just made you feel." He throws his hands up like it should be obvious. "About how she doesn't ask you about your job or your life, and when it comes up, she can't wait to move on. About how it hurts you that she doesn't read your stuff, and how when you reach for her, she *literally* pulls away. And instead of telling her you're angry with her, you're just bottling it up and pretending it's fine. Even with me. Even when I can see it's not fine."

"Stop," I murmur.

"I just don't understand why you won't admit you're—"

"*Stop*," I say, louder than I mean to, but not steady. Shaky, trembling, overwhelmed. "I'm sorry you think it's some moral failing that I choose to focus on the good things in life, but not everyone sees things like you. Not everyone *wants* to just—just go through life like a steamroller."

"This isn't about me," he says quietly.

"It is about you." My grip tightens on the steering wheel. My eyes burn. "I'm sorry you felt like you had to be the perfect, happy little mayor's son, who had to hide all of his feelings—"

"That's *not* what this is," he snaps back.

"But that's not me," I go on. "I'm okay with my life. I'm happy with it. I don't know why you need me to be angry with her, but—"

"Because you're *lying to yourself*," he says. "You're pretending the whole world is rainbows and butterflies, like I can't see what's right in front of my face. You're a *journalist*. You're smarter than that."

Now the anger surges through me. Not at my mother. At him, and at myself for bringing him here with me, for putting myself in this situation to be seen in a way I've never wanted to be, by someone who, by nature, doesn't leave well enough alone.

"You're right!" I cry. "I *am* smarter than this. I should've known better than to take a man I barely know to my home. But I guess it's like you said: I was just lying to myself, pretending you were someone else."

The car falls silent.

I'm shaking, my breath shallow, and hot from my forehead to my toes. I try to talk the anger back into its tunnel deep inside me. I keep myself from looking over at him, from imagining the hurt or frustration that might be on his face. *I'm fine.* Everything's fine.

I just need to get back to Little Crescent.

To finish this audition.

To get this job, and write this book, and everything will be okay, like it always is.

I turn on the radio, and Diamond Rio's "Meet in the Middle" plays, the irony nearly as thick as the tension.

We don't say another word for the rest of the drive.

By the time we pull up to the Grande Lucia, night has begun to descend, and the ice between us is no closer to thawing. I half expect Hayden to invite me in for a minute, but one glance at his steely face tells me that's not going to happen.

It's probably for the best. For once, I don't really have the energy to socialize.

I need to be alone, to refocus on the job, to figure out how to handle these last two weeks of interviews.

He averts his gaze as he unlocks the passenger door and gets out. He pulls his bag from the back seat, pausing for a beat. "Goodbye, Alice."

He swings the door shut and heads for the stairs without a glance back.

It's only once he's out of sight that I realize: He said *goodbye*, not *good night*.

• • •

"YOU DON'T SEEM quite like your usual overly chipper self today," Margaret says.

We're sitting across from each other at the table in her workshop on Tuesday morning, each of us polishing off our own latte from Little Croissant, while she arranges shards of sea glass into a rough pattern in front of her.

"I'll be okay," I say with a reassuring smile.

Her forehead lifts skeptically. "This process not going how you hoped?"

"It's not that," I say quickly. "It's just family stuff."

She sets down the two pieces of green glass she was arranging. "You can talk about it, if you'd like."

I laugh a little. "No, that's okay. We should get back to you."

"He's the same way, you know," she says.

"What? Who?"

"Hayden," she says. "Hates talking about himself."

I stuff down a laugh. "You're trying to make him talk about himself?" Despite his and my fight, I'm still charmed picturing it: this feisty woman trying to trick her staid interviewer into dishing about himself.

She gives a small shrug. "It only seems fair. I'm airing out all my dirty laundry—"

At the not-quite-believing look I give her, she changes course: "Fine, *a lot* of my dirty laundry. The least he could do is let down his guard a bit. But that boy is basically an animated suit of armor, as far as I can tell."

"I think he's just private," I say, surprised by my defensiveness. "I think you can understand that."

"Have you two spent much time together?" she asks.

My eyes dart to the recorder, aware that everything I say will be captured. It's one thing to make *myself* vulnerable with her, but it's another to drag Hayden into it. Even if he and I aren't on the best terms right now. I settle on, "A little, yeah."

"And what do you think?" she says bluntly.

"About?" I ask.

"Hayden," she says. "Do you still think I can trust him? You think there's a warm, beating heart under all that ice?"

The flicker of memories that licks across my mind is tawdry. I pray I'm not flushing. And even as the hurt and irritation of our last conversation push up through those *other* flashes, the truth is, I mean it when I say, "You can trust him."

At the return of her suspicious eyebrow tilt, I add, "He's got his reasons for being guarded, but he's always honest. You can trust him."

I trust him. There's no talking myself out of it. I just do.

That's why what he said bothered me so much. Because if he's saying it, I can't shake the idea that there might be some truth to it.

Margaret looks at me for a long moment and then, quite suddenly, drops her eyes and hands back to the glass shards. "So," she says. "Where did we leave off last time?"

The Story

THEIR VERSION: Margaret Ives loved the camera.

• • •

HER VERSION: The camera loved Margaret Ives, and she didn't mind one bit. Laura was the great beauty of the two of them, but whereas the younger Ives sister was shy and bookish, Margaret was expressive, talkative, curious.

Being raised in the Ives bubble had made Laura cautious and timid about the world, whereas Margaret was voracious for it. She wanted to try everything, go everywhere, meet everyone. Even as a very little girl, she'd strike up conversations with perfect strangers, smile and wave to anyone who looked their way, while Laura hid her face against their mother's trouser-clad leg.

But then their parents split, and Bernie wasn't there for Laura to hide behind anymore. *That* was when Margaret discovered her superpower.

Getting attention. She loved the way it made her feel when she could make someone smile or laugh, like the whole world was opening up to her. But even negative attention was better than none, because so long as people were watching her, they'd leave her sister alone.

When Laura wore drab neutrals, Margaret adorned herself in burning red.

When Laura got a dreadful haircut after an incident with chewing gum, Margaret bought a ludicrous hat and refused to take it off for weeks.

When Laura tripped in front of everyone at a gala in the blue ballroom—not to be confused with the green or gold ballrooms—Margaret knocked over an entire champagne tower, whooping with laughter as she slipped in the spill, then bowing to the resulting applause when she'd clambered back to her feet.

When Laura gained weight and the society pages took notice—discussing her body like a stage play in need of a review—Margaret started a small fire in the bathroom at her all-girls school and got kicked out.

Her stoic, intimidating grandfather hadn't looked at her for two weeks of family dinners after that, which made her feel like she needed to not just escape the House of Ives but also potentially crawl out of her own skin. But still, it was worth it.

She drew the eye everywhere she went, sometimes by accident, but often by design. People were going to talk about her family anyway—why not be the one to make them laugh?

It had worked for her favorite cousin, Ruth, and now she was an actress on a beloved sitcom and married to the love of her life.

It more or less worked for Margaret too, until she turned sixteen.

In 1954, the night before Margaret's birthday, Ruth and her husband, James, planned to take their small plane down the California coast. There was going to be a celebration at the House of Ives, and Ruth wouldn't have dreamed of missing the chance to dote on

Margaret, the little girl who'd once trailed her around the orange groves like an eager puppy. They'd always had a special friendship. Ruth made Margaret feel as though it was okay to be her, in all her fantastic brightness.

But on takeoff, the engine of James's plane experienced trouble. They crashed.

James Oller was a decorated World War II veteran, and Ruth was a rising comedienne, irresistible in her television role as the gorgeous, accidentally hilarious ingenue next door.

It seemed the whole country had mourned them together. Aside from Ruth's own father, who'd grieved her death the same way he'd celebrated her birth: in private.

Margaret had been devastated. It had changed her. It had changed her grandfather too. Before that, Gerald was a domineering presence in the House of Ives. The kind of man you might not like and yet *still* caught yourself jumping through hoops to please.

After Ruth's death, he'd shrunk.

It was like turning on a light in your bedroom and realizing the terrifying shadows in the corner had just been a jacket hung on a peg all along.

Without her dear cousin's affection or her grandfather's harsh eye, Margaret felt as though a shackle connecting her to the House of Ives had been cut.

Laura's reaction was different. The more Margaret pulled away from the family, the nearer her meek younger sister drew. She saw a wound in her grandfather that no one else did, or else no one was willing to admit they'd noticed.

It made sense: Laura was always more comfortable being face-to-face with pain, more at ease with the bluer shades of life. Whereas Margaret spent every second of every day trying to get back to the golden magic of her childhood, when life was one endless possibility.

Not long after Ruth's death, Gerald suffered a stroke that left him mostly blind. For months after leaving the hospital, he spent his days shut away in his rooms in the east wing. Then Laura began to visit him, to read to him. And after a while, he left his rooms and started passing his days in the library.

She'd bring his cigars there, cut and light one for him, arrange his ashtray so that he could easily find it on the windowsill, and then she'd take the overstuffed armchair opposite him and read for hours, stopping only to light a new cigar whenever he asked.

He had nurses at first, but over time, Laura took over his care entirely. She earned his trust, collected his secrets, while her sister, Margaret, was out on the town, being photographed at every boutique, restaurant, and nightclub of the time.

Margaret never wanted to go back to her life of being wrapped in tissue paper, on a shelf in the House of Ives. She wanted a *big* life.

She dated movie stars and did some modeling. She traveled to France, Spain, Monaco. She danced with Rock Hudson and drank under the exotic birds of Ciro's with Frank Sinatra and Marilyn Monroe. Once, she broke a heel on her way out of Mocambo, and paparazzi captured shots of her being carried to her car, head thrown back in laughter, by a doorman who'd later sold the broken heel for a pretty penny.

She was not graceful, poised, demure, or reserved. She was silly, irreverent, and clumsy, and the press adored her for it. The Tabloid Princess, they called her.

She attended her mother's movie premieres, often with one of the film's leads, and was once photographed on the back of James Dean's motorcycle, clutching a wedding veil to her head and laughing as they peeled away from the curb.

They were only seen together one other time after that, the night after which she was spotted at dinner with another up-and-comer.

This earned her a new nickname: Two-Date Peggy.

The truth was, she hadn't been on even *one* date with James Dean. The wedding veil was a gag, a wrap gift that Bernie had jokingly given him when they finished filming *A Western Wind Blows*.

Margaret had been visiting her mother when she bumped into Jimmy and mentioned that she'd always wanted to ride a motorcycle. He'd volunteered to make her day, and she'd popped the veil onto her head, hiking her skirt up and swinging one leg over the motorcycle's seat behind him.

She didn't worry about what the press would say. Her whole life outside of the House of Ives had been carefully observed, but at least it was *hers*.

She was an expert at chitchat, at having a bit of fun, and doing so fought back the loneliness of her life at home without any real risk.

The more they wrote about her exploits, the less gravity any of it seemed to have to her. Laura was different.

The more fascinated the paparazzi became with Margaret, the more salacious their gossip, the less Laura was willing to leave the house. She withered, she wandered, she read to her grandfather and recorded his own stories. She listened to the radio and argued with him about the merit of the newly popular rock 'n' roll. She pushed his wheelchair on walks through the grounds, and described the sunset to him, and while she insisted to Margaret that she was perfectly happy with her life, Margaret worried.

She worried endlessly about her softhearted younger sister. Their grandfather's health was declining fast, and while she didn't know that she'd ever understand her sister's friendship with him, Margaret was terrified about what would happen to Laura once he was gone. When, someday, their parents were gone too.

Margaret begged Laura to go out with her, to meet people their age. To attend dinners, to appear at fundraisers and visit art museums and take drives down to the beach—or join her on boats with the handsome men and beautiful starlets she befriended!

But the inevitable attention terrified Laura. "I don't *want* to be photographed," she'd say. "I don't want to be seen."

Margaret would sometimes go to visit her mother at work, or walk past her father's mahogany office at home, and catch the tail end of a murmured phone call between her parents.

They'd take turns in the two distinct roles of worrier and consoler. They'd promise each other that their younger daughter would be all right. They'd agree not to push her.

And then Cosmo Sinclair came to town.

The Boy Wonder of Rock 'n' Roll.

At least that was the nickname he'd had two years earlier, before a *different* singer usurped him as King.

Now the tabloids—the same ones calling Margaret Two-Date Peggy—had dubbed him the Poor Man's Elvis.

But neither of these titles were what interested Margaret. His music didn't really interest her either, from what she'd heard at that point.

The only thing that interested her about Cosmo Sinclair was her younger sister's total adoration of him, and the fact that he'd be performing at the Pan Pacific Auditorium soon.

She had an idea. It ballooned into an obsession. That snowballed into a plan.

One night.

She would sneak her sister out of the house for one perfect night.

That was all it would take to change their lives forever.

23

"WHERE'S JODI?" I ask Margaret as she's walking me back through her house to the front door at the end of our session.

"Taking some much-needed time off." She gives me a dry look. "Apparently, I'm something of a pill."

"Hard to swallow, but ultimately good for your health?" I ask.

She laughs, grabs my arm affectionately as we reach the door, and she pulls it open. "Now, you're prepared for the storm, aren't you?"

"The storm?" I step out under yet another late-afternoon scorcher of a Georgia day, but note that while we were inside, the cirrus clouds that were hanging along the horizon have been replaced by great dark masses, the wind ripping through the front garden, making everything shiver.

"News is tracking it," she says. "Should get to us tomorrow, and it's not a hurricane yet, but . . . you know how these things are."

"June through November," I agree, scanning the sky one more time.

"I guess you forgot what it's like when it rains, out in Hollywood," she teases me.

I smile. "I did, actually."

"Well, you're welcome to come hunker down here, if you want," she says. "We've got a guy coming to cover the windows and everything tomorrow. You'd better make sure there's a plan at your place."

"I'll check with the rental management company," I promise, and then she sends me on my way.

I haven't heard from Hayden since we got back into town, and as I park at the grocery store and head inside, I debate texting him.

The winds have already amped up further since I left Margaret's, the rain finally starting to hit. The grocery store is not only *packed* but thoroughly picked over. I grab a jug of water, some candles and batteries, and the kinds of snacks that won't require a refrigerator or a microwave, just in case.

When I get back to the house, someone from the rental company—a middle-aged man with a chest-length brown beard—is there, in an anorak, swinging his toolbox into the bed of his pickup. "Tried to call you," he shouts over the pouring rain as I run with my grocery bags toward him.

"Sorry," I shout back.

"Got you all situated." He jerks his chin toward the plywood he's fixed over the bungalow's windows.

"Thank you so much!" I shout back.

"You should be good here," he says. "Not supposed to turn into a hurricane, just a big storm."

"Got it." I nod, shivering in the cold as the rain pounds against my skin, plastering my clothes to me.

"I'll let you get inside," he says, and I thank him again as he gets in his truck, then run the rest of the way to the front door and let myself in.

The house is dark with all its windows blacked out, and for the first time since I got here, I'm *cold*. I peel off my shirt and throw on the first sweatshirt I come across, then run around the house flicking on lamps, stopping by the bathroom to wring my hair out over the tub.

Afterward, I change into dry sweatpants and clean, dry socks and unload the groceries.

I find the emergency lanterns in the linen closet and check the batteries, replacing the ones that are dead, and I arrange the pillar candles in the bathroom, living room, and kitchen, just in case, with lighters or matches by each of them.

It's been years since I've been caught in a storm like this, and I'm trying to run through the checklist I *used* to know by heart, as a kid.

I double-check that the fire extinguisher is under the kitchen sink, and I find a first aid kit in the bathroom, then gather my passport and driver's license and put them by the door—all things that seemed overkill to me when I was a teenager, given how many storms we'd weathered without any real danger or damage.

But that was back then, when I had parents to watch out for me, and a house that was an hour from the coast. This is different.

My stomach growls miserably, and I decide to make myself a veggie burger while I've still got electricity. After I've eaten, I debate taking a shower before deciding the thunder has already moved too close. I settle instead for the world's fastest face washing, then smooth some retinol and moisturizer over my cheeks and forehead before going back to the living room.

I flop down on the couch and turn on the TV, then realize I must've left my phone in the other room when I changed. I pad back to the bedroom and grab it off the foot of the bed, only to find the screen dark and unresponsive.

Shit. No wonder the maintenance guy couldn't get a hold of me.

I yank my charger from the wall and take it back into the living room with me, plugging my phone in right beside the couch.

On TV, *The Real Housewives of Miami* is playing, the volume nearly all the way down. The house rumbles as a pocket of thunder draws nearer, and the wind howls against the plywood-covered windows.

My phone finally has enough power to turn on, and messages start buzzing in, one after another, along with a couple of voicemails. When I see a text from Margaret, I tap it open immediately.

At that precise second, there's a loud *cheep* sound from the kitchen, and the power goes out, plunging me into dark.

I only manage to read You're still welcome to come here, if you'd feel safe before my phone shuts off.

I'm abruptly reminded of what I missed from the storm-prep checklist: *Charge your devices while you still can.*

I fumble through the dark to the nearest lantern and click it on, bathing the room in pale light, then using it to make my way around the space, lighting the pillar candles. Without the low drone of the TV, the wind's shriek seems louder, more intimidating.

I need to be judicious with my computer battery since my phone's dead, but I figure now might not be the worst time to double-check that the storm hasn't been upgraded to a hurricane. I dig my laptop out of the bag by the front door, then fling myself onto the couch, only to realize my mistake. *Another* mistake.

Without electricity, there's no internet.

You're worrying for nothing, I tell myself. It's just a storm. I've been through hundreds. I just need something to distract myself with.

Work usually does the trick. I can read through my notes by candlelight, brainstorm a little bit.

I pad back to grab my notebook from my bag, and right as I'm nearing the door, something slams into it from the outside, making me jump and yelp. Two more swift thumps follow the first, and then two more.

Almost like...

Is someone *knocking*?

I run over to it and push my eye against the peephole to find a tall, darkly dressed figure hunched against the sideways sheet of rain, his fist thwacking at the door.

I swing it open, and the wind and precipitation gust inside, pushing Hayden forward.

"What are you doing?" I yell over the onslaught.

His eyes are wild, his drenched hair tucked behind his ears, and his clothes absolutely sopping.

"I'm sorry," he says, and in this context, I'm so confused that all I can do is shout back, "*What?*"

"*I'm sorry!*" he yells.

I shake my head and explain what I *really* meant when I said *what*: "What the fuck were you thinking coming out in this?" I grab his jacket as I step back into the house, pulling him with me. It takes both of us to get the door shut and latched, and then I round on him again.

"You could've been killed!" I rage.

"You weren't answering your phone!" he says. "Margaret couldn't get a hold of you either. What was I supposed to do?"

I stare at him for a second, his face torqued, rivulets racing down the sharp planes of his face, joining the absolute pool at our feet. A couple of weeks ago, I would've mistaken the furrow in his brow for cold irritation, but now it couldn't be more obvious to me.

He was scared. He was worried for me. The same way that, on Sunday night in the car, he'd been worried for me. Not just annoyed, not judging me for how I handle things with my mom, but *worried*.

And I don't know what to say to any of it, so I just pitch myself at him. I fling my arms around him, pressing up onto my tiptoes, and within a second or two, his arms come around me too, and we just hold on to each other, the rainwater from his clothes and skin seeping through my second change of clothes of the day.

I don't care. He's shivering in my arms, his left hand wrapped around his right wrist at the small of my back. "I'm sorry," he murmurs again, against my temple.

"Me too." I shake my head as I tear myself away from him. The flicker of the nearest candles catches the edge of his jaw, but otherwise, his face is caught in the dark. "You were right."

"No, you were," he says. "There's stuff I should explain."

"Let me find you dry clothes first," I say, pulling him deeper into the house. He waits in the living room while I duck into the bedroom with the lantern. I find my biggest T-shirt and pair of sweatpants, along with a pair of socks I *think* Theo must've left at my apartment ages ago, because they're definitely not a women's size 9. They are, however, the most comfortable socks I've ever worn.

"There are towels in the bathroom," I tell him when I emerge. I tuck the stack of clothes into his elbow and hand him the lantern, but he doesn't move right away.

Instead he stares at me, the bottom halves of our faces monstrously lit by the lantern, and his somehow just as beautiful as ever.

Then he takes the back of my neck in his free hand and kisses me, deeply, slowly, hungrily, and it's been too long since his mouth was last against mine, but even then, it wasn't like this.

It was feverish and desperate, like we were both trying to get as far as we could before reality set in and we had to stop.

Now it's *thorough*, a deep stroke of his tongue into my mouth, a purposeful slide of it over mine. Not an accidental release of pent-up lust but an intentional exploration, of each other's topography, of what feels good, of the sound he makes when I bite his lip, and the way my spine curves inward when he traces mine with the tip of his tongue.

My bones seem to melt, every muscle softening into him, his hair slick between my fingertips and the chill of his skin waking up every nerve from my collarbone to my thighs.

And then it's over, with one last sweet brush of his lips on mine and a quick tightening of his hand before he releases it and walks into the bathroom.

I stand there not only *thrumming* but also trying and failing to wipe the ridiculous smile from my face.

24

JUST WHEN I think I might be able to get the toothy grin under control, the bathroom door swings back open and Hayden steps out in my clothes. I dissolve into giggles, and his white smile flashes in the dark as he stalks toward me.

"I'm glad this amuses you," he says.

The shirt fits him all right, but the pants are capri length and *tight*. He looks completely absurd, and also incredibly sexy.

"Who knew you were hiding all of that behind those fancy full-length pants of yours," I tease as he comes closer, lantern swinging in his hand.

"Is this punishment?" he deadpans. "Is it my penance for not calling sooner?"

"Don't think of it as your punishment," I say. "Think of it as my *reward*."

Another flicker of smile, or something very like it. I reach for him and he lets me pull him toward me, ring my arms around his waist, and look up into his face.

He brushes my wet bangs from my eyes, tucking my hair behind my ear. "Why didn't you answer?"

"My phone died," I say. "I would've. I promise."

He lowers the lantern onto the coffee table beside us and cups my face in his hands, kissing me again, once. "I'm so sorry."

"Hayden, no," I say, but before I can go on, he tugs me toward the couch.

"I want to tell you something," he says.

"Okay..." Is this where he confesses something terrible? That he actually *does* have a girlfriend? Or that somehow this has all been to sabotage me?

My usually overactive imagination refuses to bite. I really do trust him. Still, that doesn't totally eliminate the worry growing in my belly at his heady silence.

He runs a hand over his mouth as he considers his word choice. "No one knows this," he begins.

"You don't have to tell me anything you don't want to," I insist, reaching for his hand.

He knots his long fingers through mine. "I told you that when I was a kid I felt like I had to be perfect. But there's more to it than that."

"Like what?" I ask.

He blows out a long breath and blinks hard a few times, like he's working himself up to something. "It wasn't just me. My mom...she had pretty severe depression and anxiety, when we were younger. I guess my dad knew, but no one else really did. And when I was in high school..." He trails off, coughs. "It got really bad, really suddenly. Or I don't know, maybe she just suddenly stopped hiding it from us. She almost overdosed, and she had to go get inpatient treatment for a while. My dad was in the middle of a campaign and...she asked us to lie about it. Pretend she went to help her parents for a couple of months."

"*What?*" I crawl across the small gap on the couch, lifting his other hand into mine, his fingers still chilled from the cold rain. "Hayden, I'm so sorry."

"I understood why she didn't want strangers knowing," he says. "If it had gotten out, it honestly would've been big news in my hometown, and it *wouldn't* have been treated sensitively. But the thing that bothered me was that . . . until then, I had no idea what she was dealing with. She always acted . . . fine."

I lift his hands to my lips, breathing warmth into them. "That's not your fault," I tell him. "You can't tell what's going on with a person just by looking at them."

"I know," he says. "But I always felt like . . . if she weren't trying to be so perfect all the time, if she didn't *need* to look so happy . . . maybe we would've known before it got that bad. Pretending everything's fine only works for so long. And I don't know. It freaks me out a little, that I could . . . that I could feel like this, about someone who's good at pretending to be fine. That I could miss it, if you're actually not. It was about me. Like you said."

His words crack something open in me. I climb into his lap, winding my arms around his neck. "I'm sorry," I say. "That all makes sense."

His arms curl around my back, holding me to him. "I was rude," he says. "I'm sorry."

I touch his jaw, angle his face toward mine. "One of us is going to have to stop this, or we'll be apologizing all night."

He kisses me again, this time a little faster, rougher. He pulls back to rest his forehead against mine. "I'm sorry," he whispers, teasing, and I laugh into him, kiss him again, soft and tender this time. His hand rises to cradle the back of my head. Both of mine skate up his jaw. I pitch my weight forward into my knees, on either side of his hips, and shift myself into him, letting the kiss deepen.

He reaches for the bottom of my sweatshirt, and I draw back to let him lift it up my torso and over my head. He drops it on the floor, whispering something under his breath when he realizes I wasn't wearing anything under it. He lets his large hands skim up from the base of my bare stomach to my chest, and I hold my breath, anticipating the moment his palms will cup me, scared they won't.

My head tips back on a sigh at the light contact when they finally do, chills erupting from the waistband of my pants up to the crown of my head. He leans in slowly, kisses one side of my collarbone, then the other. "Yours too," I whisper scratchily, and his eyes tilt up to mine in the dark.

I reach for the hem of the shirt I loaned him, and he straightens, letting me slowly slide it up him, the heels of my hands tracing his warm skin as they go. My thighs go hot and liquid at the texture of his skin.

He lifts his arms and lets me push the shirt over his head, leaving his chest bare in the mix of soft candlelight and the lantern's harsh glow. "I wish I could see you better," I whisper, letting my hands rove down him now that the shirt's out of the way.

"Me too." His voice is low and hoarse. Gingerly, he pulls me back to him, our bodies melding together. The low sound that moves through him makes my blood vessels start singing. The pressure between my thighs builds into an ache. I roll myself against him, and he returns the favor, a white-hot streak of pleasure searing through me at the firm feeling of his chest pushing into mine. His hands climb down beneath my ass, angling me where he wants me. I roll my hips against him again, the friction pulling a small, breathy sound from me. He wraps me around him as he kisses the side of my neck, lets his mouth move lower.

"What about your rules?" I say hazily. "Aren't we breaking them?"

"Bending," he says roughly. "Not breaking." He takes my nipple into his mouth, and I almost start crying. I slide my hand into his way-too-tight sweatpants, and to my incredible relief, he lets me. "God, Alice," he groans against my chest, his teeth scraping over me again. "It's not enough."

I move myself against him harder, but he's right: It's not nearly enough. I want to taste him. I tell him as much and wind up on my back on the couch, him crawling down me, yanking my sweatpants down my hips as I buck up from the couch. His hands squeeze my bare thighs, and I writhe toward him as he presses his parted lips to the inside of one leg. He licks me once through my underwear, then sits back to pull my pants the rest of the way off, settling himself between my thighs. For a few seconds, we're mindless with hunger, my thighs wrapped around his hips, our mouths colliding, his hands clutching every bare part of me and mine scratching down the wide expanse of his back.

"These pants are about to rip," he half laughs into my mouth.

"Then take them off," I suggest.

Instead he kisses his way down my body, lets his mouth chart a slow, purposeful path along the edge of my underwear, before finally dipping his tongue under the fabric. I press up into him, and he slides the waistband down, bringing his mouth back to me as soon as he can. My hands twist into his hair, my lungs struggling over each breath as the flat of his tongue presses against me, and colors blaze against the backs of my eyelids at the slow, sure movement of his mouth. His grip on my thighs is firm but gentle, careful, like I'm not only delicate but valuable, and it feels as if something inside me is overflowing.

I want to say his name, to tell him how good this feels, how good *he is*, how much I missed him in the last two days, and how easy it would be to love him, if he'd let me, but I can barely breathe as the pleasure mounts, and with it so much affection for him that it couldn't possibly fit in my body.

And then it all peaks, breaks, and I cry out raggedly, waves of sensation rolling over and through me, dragging me under like a riptide I would gladly give myself over to.

He crawls up me as the final shock waves are settling, kisses me deep, our hands wound into each other's hair, our skin slick with sweat between us, his heart hammering a million miles per minute against my ribs.

"I want you," I whisper into his ear, wrapping my thighs around him as he shivers against me.

He slides off me, onto his side, his arms pulling me tight to him. "If you still feel that way in a week and a half," he says, his voice rough, splintering from restraint.

"I will," I insist, touching his sweat-dampened face. I can barely see his features in the dark, just a splash of light in the corner of one eye.

"You don't know that," he says, tenderly running his fingertips over one side of my jaw.

"What do you think is going to happen?" I ask.

Under his breath, nearly a whisper, he says, "I think if I get this job, you're going to break my fucking heart."

Tears sting my eyes, and my breath catches. "No," I say softly, trying to pull him back to me, kissing his left cheek, then his right, then his forehead. "Hayden, no."

"You can't know," he says softly, almost pleading. "This is a bad position to be in, Alice."

"I don't know," I tease quietly. "It was working out all right for me."

His face remains serious. "I know you think you'll be fine, no matter what happens," he grates out. "But I need you to be sure. I don't want to do this and have you hate me in two weeks."

"I won't," I whisper, kissing the corner of his mouth again. He lets out a slow exhale, his eyes closing and hand cupping the back of my head, relaxing a little but not completely.

I can tell he doesn't believe me.

He clears the gravel from his throat. "Maybe I should just drop out."

I snap up onto my elbow. "Absolutely not," I say. "I'd never forgive you if you did that."

He blinks up at me, runs a hand up over the back of my arm. "Okay, okay," he says quietly. "Then what do we do? Because we have less than two weeks until one of us goes home, and there's no winning for me here. If I get the job, you're not going to want anything to do with me—"

"That's not true," I cut in.

"And if I don't, then I'm going back to New York, and you're here, and it doesn't matter anyway. So what are we doing here?"

"I don't know," I admit.

He laugh-groans, slings one hand over his eyes. I pry it away from them, kiss the center of his palm, and he nestles closer. "I don't understand what's happening."

"We'll figure it out," I tell him.

"No, I mean..." He huffs. "I mean, we barely know each other. And I feel like—like... I don't know."

"Tell me." I take his face between my hands. He sets his over them.

"All I ever want is to be around you," he says raspingly. "It's not just sex. I mean, I do want to have sex with you."

My limbs warm at the suggestion, but he continues. "But that's only a part of it. This is different. It's . . ." He looks at me, hopeful or maybe expectant, like he thinks I might have the words that are evading him.

I don't. I'm so overcome that the closest I can get is a threadbare "I know."

He smooths my hair away from my eyes again, kisses my temple so gently I could cry, and then his stomach gurgles, volcanically loud, and I descend into laughter. "Hungry?"

"A little," he admits. "I was in a hurry to get here, before the storm got worse."

"Come on." I sit up, grabbing my sweatshirt at the sudden rush of cold air that hits me from all sides. "I'll make you a snack."

25

HAYDEN AND I sit in a nest of blankets on the living room floor, eating our peanut butter and banana sandwiches, the candles glowing in a line on the mantel and TV stand.

"I haven't had one of these since I was a kid," he tells me between bites.

"I'm not sure I've ever had one," I confess. I just happened to grab the ingredients in my last-minute grocery run.

"Do you think that eating these is a betrayal of Margaret?" he asks, and I try to subdue my surprise that he's mentioned her.

"Why would it be?" I ask.

"Peanut butter banana," he says. "That was Elvis's thing, right? Not Cosmo's."

"True," I allow, "but I don't think Cosmo Sinclair had a famous sandwich of choice. And aside from that, I doubt they were ever enemies. I think the media just loved to speculate about that." My eyes cut back to him. "Unless she's told you otherwise?"

He gives me a sly, slightly disapproving look.

"Oh, come on," I say, lightly shoving his shoulder. "You're the one who brought her up."

He sets his sandwich down on the plate beside his knee, keeping his eyes on it as he chews. "So now that we've been here longer, does anything about this job seem . . . weird to you?"

"How so?" I ask.

He drinks some water before meeting my eyes. "I don't know how to explain it."

I remember what she said—that he was basically *an animated suit of armor*—and debate telling him, but that seems like crossing a line, different than talking generally about our time together.

"I think it's a little strange that she's making us audition like this, but she's not very trusting, and I can understand why."

"It's not that, exactly," he says, shaking his head, lips parting like the words are right there and he hopes they might spill out. "I guess I feel like she's testing me. And I'm not sure how, or why. And maybe it really is just about choosing which one of us she'd rather work with, but I don't know."

"Well, in a week and a half, maybe we'll know," I say.

"Maybe," he agrees, clearly unconvinced. "I meant what I said. I don't have to do this. I can find a different book."

I push my own plate aside and scoot forward against him, his arms wrapping tight around me. "I meant what I said too," I say. "We're in this situation because of *her*. Let's let *her* choose how it ends."

"If you change your mind," he says.

I rest my head on his shoulder. "I won't."

He holds me a little more tightly, burrows his mouth against the crown of my head.

• • •

I STIR AWAKE on the couch to the sound of birds, but the room is mostly dark. It takes me a minute to remember why.

The storm.

The plywood window coverings.

Hayden.

There's a soft clink in the kitchen, and I blink away the sleep in my eyes to see Hayden putting a mug in the dishwasher. On the table beside the couch, the lamp has turned on at some point, the electricity evidently restored.

Hayden catches me watching him. "Hey," he whispers.

It feels like my *heart* is splitting open in a smile. "Hey." Despite his size, his footsteps are nearly silent as he crosses back toward me. "Leaving?" I murmur.

"Storm's over, so my interview's back on." He crouches in front of me, his hand palming the entire right side of my head, like the basketball player he never was. "Go back to sleep."

He leans forward and kisses me once on the lips, my eyes drooping shut, like if I can't *see* him leave, maybe it won't happen.

I listen as he approaches the front door, then give in, slitting one eye open as he turns back, his hand on the knob. "See you tonight?" he asks.

"I'll have to check my schedule," I joke. "Don't want to forget anyone's half birthday party."

"No, never," he agrees.

"Tonight," I say.

He opens the door, and another beautiful day of Georgia sunshine pours in around him.

He looks like an angel. I mumble something along those lines and then close my eyes and let sleep pull me down into itself.

● ● ●

WHEN I NEXT wake up, with a crick in my neck and sweat coating my skin, light is spearing into the room. I sit up, bleary eyed, and nearly scream when someone appears in the window directly across from me.

It's just the bearded maintenance guy from the rental company, prying the plywood off the windows. He gives me a cheery wave, and when I return it, he flashes me a thumbs-up.

For some reason, I return that too. Then he goes back to his work, his whistle mostly muted by the glass between us.

I gather the blankets off the couch and carry them back into the bedroom, my stomach flipping at the smell of almond caught in the sheets. Last night we'd drifted off together on the couch, and twice we'd woken up already moving together in our sleep, then kissed and touched each other until we were shaking with need, only to eventually, against all odds, fall asleep again.

Or I did anyway. Hopefully Hayden did, or his full day of interviewing will be grueling.

I toss the blankets back onto the bed and grab a change of clothes before heading into the bathroom for a shower.

Afterward, hair combed and sunscreen on, I make a cup of coffee and take it out front. The maintenance guy has left, and out on the driveway, two trash barrels are stuffed with fallen branches and debris from the storm, including one of the bungalow's shutters, which looks like it ripped off and broke in half at some point in the chaos.

Otherwise, you'd never know there was a storm at all.

When I go back inside, I remember to plug in my phone, which is now thoroughly dead. The second it turns on, I'm barraged with all the calls and messages I missed last night.

There are the ones I knew to expect—Margaret and Hayden each trying to get a hold of me, Hayden in an increasingly panicked fashion.

The ones I could've guessed I'd get—my friends' group chat devolving into an argument about a true-crime docuseries that Priya, Bianca, and Cillian all had vastly different opinions on.

And then there are the messages that surprise me.

Theo, at some point yesterday, wrote to say I'm really sad our visit didn't pan out. Miss chilling with you. And when I didn't leap to reply to that, he followed up with Might actually be heading back to ATL soon. You still in that area? I leave that one alone. Regardless of what does or doesn't happen with Hayden, I'm finally done making Theo's plans *for* him.

And then the last, and most worrying, surprise.

Four voicemails from Mom.

Three messages.

> Call me.
>
> Why aren't you answering your phone?
>
> Please call me, Alice.

The panic is immediate. The heat, then cold, that flushes through me is intense. I'm instantly sweating, afraid I'm going to be sick, despite the fact that my throat feels impossibly tight.

My first thought, like so many times before this, is a deep, desperate *Audrey!*

I dial Mom, and it rings out, all the way to her voicemail. I hang up and try again, wishing I could pace, but tethered in place beside the electrical outlet, all the restless energy inside me trapped.

The line clicks halfway through the third ring. "Oh, thank *god*," she says.

"What happened?" I get out between chattering teeth. "Is she okay?"

"What? Who?" Mom says.

"Audrey," I blurt.

"Why wouldn't your sister be okay?" Mom sounds very nearly offended by the idea.

That alone is enough to interrupt the anxiety circuiting through my body. I slump onto the arm of the couch, my shoulders slackening and a headache starting up, as if the sudden burst and then abrupt dissipation of cortisol has put me in a state of withdrawal.

Why wouldn't your sister be okay? What a strange question to ask, after all those years when her very existence wasn't a sure thing, let alone her *okayness*.

I shut my eyes tight and massage the bridge of my nose. "What did you need?" I ask.

"Why weren't you answering your phone?" Mom asks with her signature bluntness, entirely avoiding *my* question.

"I let it die by accident," I say. "And then the power went out."

There's a silence on the other end.

"Hello?" I prompt.

"So you're still in Georgia?" she says.

"Yeah, for now," I say, noncommittal. "What did you need, Mom?"

"Nothing, nothing." She sounds distracted if not disinterested.

My gut twists. "You sent me a few texts and left some messages. I thought there was an emergency."

"Well, good thing there wasn't," she says lightly. "Seeing as how I had no way to get a hold of you."

I grimace, move my fingers up to the spot right between my brows, and draw little circles there, trying to ease the tension. "Sorry. But I'm here now. What's up?"

"Nothing," she says. "I just saw we had a big storm coming in, and realized I didn't even know where you are."

There's a serrated edge to her voice, almost like she's mad at me. But it's not like I was keeping my location from her. I told her I was on a work trip a couple of hours away from her, and she didn't ask for any more information.

"I'm up on Little Crescent," I tell her now.

There's another long pause before she says, "You guys get hit pretty bad up there?"

"Not too bad, no," I say. "Lost some branches, but the power's already back on, and the house I'm staying in didn't take too much damage."

"Good, good," she says, distracted again.

"What about you?" I ask. "Any issues?"

"Oh, no, nothing major," she says. "You know how it is. We're far enough in from the coast to miss the worst of it. Heard there was some flash flooding, but we were fine."

That *we* lodges itself into my heart like a tiny arrow.

I'm not sure if the *we* in question is her and my dad, or if it's her and the chickens, and I'm not sure which of those possibilities would break my heart less.

I clear my throat. "Good."

"And your friend? Hayden? He's all right?"

"He's good," I assure her. "I saw him this morning. He's fine."

The truth, just not the whole truth.

"Well, good," she says, like we've settled something. "Then I'll let you go."

"Okay, well, thanks for calling," I say, uncertain what exactly just happened.

This is how it is sometimes between the two of us, like we each speak a different language and so have to do our best muddling through rough translations in a *third* language, one that's native to neither of us.

"Yeah," she says, then adds, a little more softly but still almost chiding, "Charge your phone, kid."

"I will," I promise.

She hangs up without a goodbye.

• • •

AT OUR NEXT session, we board the boat prepared. For one thing, I'm wearing a pair of loose linen pants and a light button-up, so my limbs are covered. For another, before we came down to the dock, Margaret doused our hands and feet in some kind of homemade concoction that Jodi swears by.

"She still on vacation?" I ask as we're climbing into the boat, and Margaret blinks at me for a moment before averting her gaze and settling herself on the seat beside the fan.

"Yep," she says. "You know how it is. Sometimes you just need a break."

I try to give her a reassuring smile, but she's not looking at me, already focused on starting up the fan. I take my position on the seat nearest to her, and we motor away from the dock, into the reeds, the thick air billowing over my hair and skin like thousands of tiny fingers.

We can't really talk until we get to "The Spot" she's keen to show me—not over the roar of the fan—and in the interim, I find my mind wandering back to Hayden.

After he finished with Margaret yesterday, we went to dinner at Rum Room, sat on opposite sides of his favorite booth, picking away at our work while eating veggie dogs and fries, our legs tangled together beneath the table.

Every time I got up to use the bathroom and had to walk past his side of the booth, he snapped his laptop shut, as if the temptation of seeing his screen might be too much for me to bear.

I started making a game of it, getting up and walking past him every few minutes. Finally, after four trips to the bathroom in twenty minutes, he left his laptop open, and in my surprise, my eyes actually *did* go straight to the screen.

In ludicrously large font, on an otherwise blank page of a Microsoft Word document, he'd written, *Having fun?*

At my snort of laughter, he turned sideways on the bench and hauled me down into his lap, a public display of affection that surprised and delighted me.

Made me feel like he was claiming me as *his*, like he was openly *mine*.

After that very long working dinner, he drove me home, walked me to the door, and kissed me slowly, roughly against it until we were both out of breath.

He didn't stay over, and I understood why. He looked so tired a light breeze could probably have knocked him over, and it had occurred to me, way too belatedly, that the fiveish inches of height he had on me had probably made our night together smooshed on the couch all the more brutal for him. Plus there was my snoring.

I doubted that spending the night in my bed would've been any more restful.

So we said good night, and then he texted me from his hotel room, can't stop thinking about you, and I lay awake a solid hour anyway, regretting not dragging him inside when I had the chance.

The boat's fan cuts, and Margaret tosses a speculative gaze my way. "What's got *you* smiling like that?"

"You know me," I say. "I'm always smiling."

"Not like that," she says, digging a net out of the bottom of the boat and passing it to me. "That's a *secret* smile." She waves an arm toward the shore. "See that little outcropping there?"

We've stopped at a bend in the creek, and a sandy gap in the dense curtains of live oak along the shore reveals the charred remains of a campfire and a couple of wooden crates I'd guess someone's been using as makeshift chairs.

"Yeah."

Margaret pulls another net out of the bottom of the boat and swings this one over into the water. "*That* is where the teenagers come to drink."

"And?" I must be making *some* kind of face, because she rolls her eyes, as if to chastise me.

"And they litter," she says. "A lot. You can't see it here, but there's a road back that way through the trees, and Jodi says the cops patrol around here because they know kids like to come here to get in trouble." She sweeps her net through the water in a slow, graceful arc.

She pulls it up, and the water gushes down through the net, leaving behind two green glass bottles. "And either these kids hate the planet, or else when they see the headlights, they throw their shit out here. Maybe it's both—what do I know?"

"Bummer," I say.

"There we go," Margaret replies. "There's a frown. I'm much more familiar with that expression. It's comforting even. We'll make a cynic out of you yet."

"Good luck," I say, dropping my net into the water on the other side of the boat. While I'm swooshing it around, she opens up a trash bag and dumps her bounty into it. Under the surface, I catch something too. A little whoop of excitement escapes me.

"Reel her in," Margaret orders, and I lift the net upward, water pouring through it to reveal . . . a neon-green rubber clog. A Croc, or an off-brand version of the same thing.

"I hope no one's missing this," I say.

"I guarantee they're not," Margaret replies, and opens another trash bag. "Here." She thrusts it toward me. "For all the trash we *can't* use."

I drop the shoe into it. "So should we get started?"

She sighs, like the thought exhausts her, and I wonder for the millionth time why she agreed to this, if she's genuinely still considering my original proposition or if she's already checked out. "How are you feeling? About the interview process?"

"I've been dreading today."

"Really? Why?" I ask.

"Because," she says with a small shrug, "we're coming up on all my greatest mistakes."

I frown. Is *that* how she'd categorize it? Her epic, highly documented love story?

"Guess we might as well get to it," she says. "But keep working while we talk. There's plenty more shit in the creek."

"I'm not sure that's how the saying goes," I say.

"Should be, though, shouldn't it?"

The Story

THEIR VERSION: In 1958, as Gerald Ives lay dying, his granddaughters were out drinking and dancing until the sun came up.

• • •

HER VERSION: One perfect night. That was what Margaret needed to give Laura to shake her out of her isolation, to bring her out of the gilded tomb that was the House of Ives and into the land of the living.

It started with the head gardener. Daniel lived on the Ives property, but he had a truck, and it wasn't uncommon for him to make deliveries and pickups from nurseries between the glimmering coast, where the House of Ives sat perched, and downtown Los Angeles.

Leaving with Margaret's usual car and driver was out of the question. That thing had become a press magnet, and while ordinarily she figured the cameras would find her no matter what so she might as well cut to the chase and pose, she knew that sort of attention would send Laura skittering home, more determined than ever to hide from life.

So Margaret's driver, Darrin, was out. Daniel the gardener was in.

"He'll take us off property in the back of his truck," she told her sister. "We'll wear disguises and everything, like we're spies."

Laura was hesitant, but when wasn't she these days?

"Gerald isn't doing well," she said, because the girls had been raised to call their grandfather by his first name rather than a more affectionate nickname. "I don't know about leaving him alone."

"He won't be alone," Margaret said, which was true, because there were *always* people in the house, even if primarily those people were staff.

"He doesn't like anyone else, really," Laura pointed out.

"And they don't like him either," Margaret said. "A match made in heaven."

At that, Laura gave a begrudging laugh. It made Margaret's heart leap with hope. "We'll ask Mom to come sit with him for a while. He likes Mom." An exaggeration, but only slightly.

Gerald had disapproved of his son's marriage, but disapproved far more of his divorce, and in the years since, he'd adamantly refused to learn any of Freddy's partners' names *and* showed a clear preference for Bernie over his son during family dinners.

"One night," Margaret whispered eagerly, clasping Laura's hands in hers.

She saw the moment she won her sister over. She had a knack for that sort of thing—reading people. In her mind, she was already celebrating before Laura ever said the breathless, exhilarated words, "I wonder what he's like in person."

He of course being Cosmo Sinclair, whose concert they'd be attending.

Margaret fought a powerful urge to roll her eyes. She'd had plenty of gentlemen friends over the years, had plenty of fun with them even, but she knew Cosmo Sinclair's type.

Preening, self-important, and with enough sparkle to hide the fact that his skull was more or less a wind tunnel. But that didn't matter. Cosmo was a means to an end, and that means had just done its job.

She got the wigs from her mother's studio, and as for the clothes they'd wear, she'd asked the housekeeper to buy them each a dress straight off the rack at Bullock's. Something pink for Laura, because it would bring out the glow in her cheeks, and something drab for Margaret, because anything too colorful or glamorous might too clearly read *Peggy Ives*, rather than *anonymous concertgoer*.

On the night of the concert, the two lay in the bed of Daniel's truck with a scratchy wool blanket pulled over them, and they rumbled off the property, right past the row of not-so-patiently-waiting photographers who'd started gathering outside their tall iron gates.

A friend of his, handsomely paid for his discretion, met the girls on the side of a road and drove them toward Pan Pacific. Not *to*. *Toward*. It felt like overkill to Margaret, treating themselves like Audrey Hepburn's Princess Ann in *Roman Holiday*, but the subterfuge was both a fun game and a way to make Laura feel more comfortable. Maybe, she thought, this could even become a tradition of theirs.

Daniel's friend dropped them at a burger joint, and Laura hovered close to Margaret's shoulder, intimidated rather than comforted by the excess of rowdy young people eating and socializing at the counter.

"It's too crowded," Laura whimpered. "Someone will recognize us."

"Why would they?" Margaret said. "We've never been anywhere like this in our lives."

They ate their burgers and drank their sodas in a corner booth. Laura was quiet and watchful at first, but when Margaret bumped her ankle to her sister's and said, "What do you think Cosmo is doing right now?" Laura gave a meek smile.

"Oh, that's right," Margaret said. "I'm sure he's pomading his hair right up until showtime."

And this earned a real belly laugh from Laura. "I know, you think he's ridiculous."

"Of course I do," Margaret allowed. "But most men are. Look at our father."

Laura gave her an amused yet reproachful look, but she didn't disagree. After a second, she said, "Roy's not ridiculous."

"No, no he's not," Margaret agreed of their stepfather. "But then, Roy's not the sort of man they let up on a stage with a microphone."

Laura tittered. "Can you imagine?"

"I can, and it's a tragedy, Laura." The picture of their mother's even-keeled and soft-spoken husband wailing on a guitar, a lock of Cosmo-style hair falling across his forehead, made them both howl with laughter. "More than that, picture Mom watching him from the audience."

It was too easy to imagine the highly practical Doris Bernhardt observing the spectacle, horrified.

When Laura's laughter finally settled and she wiped the tears from her eyes, she said thoughtfully, *"Although . . .* I suppose Dad's always been a bit of a showman. And she loved him once, didn't she?"

It made Margaret's heart ache, to realize her sister didn't have those precious memories from the early years that meant so much to Margaret herself. That she couldn't recall the day she'd first toddled across the grass and Freddy, Bernie, and Margaret cheered on the smallest of their band.

They'd eaten ice cream sundaes, down in one of the kitchens, to celebrate, the girls sitting up on the long oak prep table.

"Not that she doesn't love him now," Laura added. "I only mean, they were *in* love, weren't they?"

"I think so, yes," Margaret said. "And if they weren't, they were still happy."

The truth was, Margaret wasn't sure she knew precisely what love was. Sometimes she lay awake late at night, thinking about the word until it came apart like little bits of alphabet soup, the letters drifting off in opposite directions and the meaning lost somewhere in the gaps.

She knew she felt an almost feral protectiveness of her sister.

She knew she admired her mother, thought her quite possibly the loveliest woman in the world, though she'd heard and read enough to know the world at large didn't agree with this assessment.

And she knew that though she no longer felt *close* to her father—not deeply known by or deeply knowledgeable of him—she'd felt a kind of peace every time she'd sat opposite him in the drawing room, playing chess while the fire popped and crackled in the grate.

She knew what it was to have fun drinking and dancing with a man, and that occasionally there was a fair amount of pleasure to be had doing *other things* with one, but love . . .

She didn't know what it was, and she couldn't imagine being *in* it, the way people described.

And the joy of having two parents who were not only ludicrously wealthy but also extremely eccentric was that no one in her family minded much whether she fell in love and got married or not. Look at Aunt Francine—she was fifty-three years old and had never been married, and then there was Great-Aunt Gigi, who at seventy-five had never bothered to remarry after her first husband's death, instead spending most weekends during Margaret's youth either *at* the ballet or entertaining some attractive male ballet dancer or another in her rooms at the house.

And Bernie had certainly never pushed either of her daughters toward matrimony. If anything, Margaret had occasionally felt as though her mother hoped Margaret might fall in love with filmmaking the way Bernie herself had, but even *that* romance evaded her.

She and Laura finished their burgers and shakes in a thoughtful quiet, then walked down the street to hail a cab. As long as they'd lived, they'd had a dedicated driver, and lifting her hand as she stepped off the curb triggered a delicious thrill in Margaret's chest.

She felt, for the first time in a long time, the distinct possibility of *getting it wrong*. Of trying something new in a world that wouldn't bend for you. In the back seat of the cab, the sisters grinned at each other and clasped each other's hands tightly, and Margaret knew Laura felt it too.

It made her feel *young* again. She wasn't a socialite. Wasn't the Tabloid Princess. She was one of two giggly sisters playing make-believe, or hatching a prank on their good-spirited father, like the time they'd filled his shoes with eggs and hidden around the corner to watch the moment he stuffed his foot into the leather.

They made it to the Pan Pacific without a hitch and joined the mass of people pouring toward the recently opened doors of the green-and-white building. Laura tensed again, but the thrill in Margaret's chest only renewed.

Had she *ever* waited in line before? Not that this was a *line*, per se. It was more like a thousand different lines, all colliding and dividing in every direction, as the crowd jostled forward.

Margaret could sense Laura's nerves, but she thought she could feel her excitement too.

The Ives sisters might possibly have been the richest people in that room of thousands, but they were far from the most famous, the private boxes packed with movie stars and professional ballplayers, other singers.

And no one seemed interested in craning their necks to catch a glimpse of anyone other than the one person they'd come to see.

Even Margaret got caught up in the energy of the crowd. The whole first half of the show was dedicated to a series of opening acts, and while the audience didn't seem *interested*, she noted the way the entire crowd kept their eyes bouncing between the stage and the wings.

She caught herself doing the same, watching for Cosmo, wondering how he could ever live up to the myth and legend.

How would thousands of people not leave here tonight disappointed?

She couldn't imagine it ending any other way.

Every time one of the openers asked some variation of the question "Who here's excited about seeing Mr. Cosmo Sinclair?" the audience response rivaled the roar of a jet engine. The floor trembled.

When the last group had played and left the stage, the lights dimmed, as they had between each of the acts, and then the dim melted into outright jet-black darkness.

The screaming of the audience started up again. This time, it didn't sound so much like excitement as sheer desperation, as if the need had grown too much to bear. A joy that verged on *terror*.

Her whole body erupted into goose pimples.

And then a fierce white light flared out, and a coyly smirking man in all black came into focus at a microphone dead center of the stage.

Margaret had never heard anything like the overwhelming screech of the thousands of people in that room. She realized Laura was screaming too, her eyes saucer wide, one splayed hand pressed over her lips but doing nothing to stop the sound. Margaret let herself join in.

Laughing and screaming and laughing some more. She felt as if they'd all been caught in the same riptide. Like her emotions didn't belong to her, but she didn't mind. It was *fun*, to feel so much.

Behind Cosmo, the band started to play, and she marveled that she hadn't noticed them, when *they* were dressed in vibrant red satin, whereas *he* was little more than a shadow in his black suit.

She and her sister hung on to each other.

He opened his mouth and the first note came out. For a split second, it was as if the audience had been turned off, just the flip of a switch, to let his low clear voice ring out, and then the screaming was back, ratcheted up.

Margaret could barely hear a word of that song, or the next. It hardly mattered. She was swept away in the magic, the charisma of the man at the center of it.

Entranced.

The opening ballad melted into a raucous, playful number, his careful restraint giving way to a frenzy of movement. At one point, he ran down the length of the stage, still singing, then stopped, tossed the microphone up, caught it behind him, and whipped it back to his lips to pick up singing like nothing had happened.

Margaret waited for the energy in the room to wane. It didn't.

Every time Laura looked at Margaret, her eyes alight, her wig slightly askew and cheeks flushed, one or both of them burst out laughing. They danced ferociously, sweat blooming under the synthetic fibers of their department store dresses. Margaret had brought a flask in her bag, and to her utter shock, Laura took her up on a few gulps when she held it out in offering.

Once, when Cosmo did a particularly salacious swirl of his hips, Margaret leaned over and shouted against Laura's ear, "ROY," and that alone was enough to set them off again. She couldn't hear her little sister's laughter over all that noise, but she could *feel* it in her chest. Like an animal rousing from hibernation.

How long had it been since she'd seen such reckless joy on Laura's face? Had she *ever*?

Laura leaned in, arms around her sister's sweaty neck, and kissed the side of her face. "THANK YOU," she shouted, and suddenly, Margaret thought she might cry. Not those little leaking drips that came with laughter either.

She thought she might crack open and sob, but she couldn't let herself, so she just danced, hand in hand with her little sister, screaming and laughing and passing the flask between them as the best night of her entire life unfolded around her.

Eight songs in, Cosmo finally played the song everyone had been waiting for. His biggest hit yet. "A Girl Back Home."

Margaret had never seen anything like the fever that spread through the room as he danced and thrashed and yelped the song:

> *Ain't got no girl*
> *back home*
> *No place in this world*
> *to call my own*
> *But darling*
> *For tonight*
> *Maybe we don't*
> *have to be alone.*

He slid forward on his knees, right to the edge of the stage, and those first few rows erupted, gushing up toward him like a volcanic blast, their arms outstretched to him. Somehow, the screaming amped up further. Laura and Margaret pushed up on tiptoe, trying to get a look at what was happening.

Cosmo had taken one girl's hand and was holding it in his while he sang. He lifted it and rubbed it against his cheek, and suddenly, all down the length of the stage, people were trying to climb up to him.

In an instant, the energy in the room changed. There was a swell in the crowd behind them, like a typhoon moving from back to front, bodies pushing in tighter, people clamoring to get closer to him.

Laura was knocked off balance, her shriek disappearing into the wall of sound. Margaret tried to move sideways to catch her sister by the arm, but there were already people moving between them, trying to shove their way closer to the stage.

Anxiety knotted up her throat as she tried to push through. Instead she was caught in the stampede, half carried deeper into the writhing throng. She screamed her sister's name as the tide of bodies pushed her farther from where she'd been. An errant elbow connected with her eye, and pain flared through her head, her vision blurring behind tears, all sense of balance lost to the dark.

She had to fight just to stay upright as the crowd jostled her back and forth, and real panic filled her up when she realized how easy it would be to be crushed underfoot.

She blinked away the tears in her left eye. Her right was already swelling. She reached up to her temple, and her hand came away with blood.

Screaming for Laura, again and again, she tried to fight her way back toward where they'd been standing, but she was turned around now, had traveled so far. The band had stopped playing, police were moving in from the outside edges of the room, but the chaos wasn't dying down.

She saw a flash of pink fabric in between the tightly packed bodies and struggled toward it, still screaming her sister's name. She pushed. She shoved. Some people pushed back. Her wig was yanked off.

She didn't care. None of it mattered.

The only thing that mattered was getting to that flash of pink before anything bad happened.

She didn't yet know that something already had.

Hands clamped down on her arms and she struggled uselessly against the firm grip until she realized it was yanking her toward the side of the room, the man bulky enough to cut a path through the pandemonium.

And then—there she was!

Laura, slumped against the wall, clutching the sides of her nose, her wig crooked and blood dribbled down her collar, cheeks stained with tears. Margaret's heart plummeted into her stomach. She shook off her attacker and ran toward her sister. "Are you okay?" she asked, clutching her sister's cheeks.

"I'm fine, I'm fine," she croaked, but it was clearly a lie.

"Ms. Ives," someone shouted behind her, and she whirled back to face the man who'd hauled her over here. A security guard. And beside him, Darrin, the Ives family's driver.

"What are you doing here?" she demanded.

"We need to get you both outside, Ms. Ives," he said with a terse politeness, reaching for her arm. She shook him off and went back to fretting over her sister.

"Let me see," she said, pulling on Laura's wrists to remove her hands from her face, taking in the swollen bloody mass of her nose, and then, more disconcertingly, the teary blankness of her eyes. Did she have a concussion? Why did she look like that?

"Ms. Ives," Darrin said, more forcefully this time. "We have to go *now*."

She looked between her sister and him desperately. She wanted so badly to say, *No, we're not going, we're staying here, in this perfect night*. But the perfect night had blasted apart in a millisecond, turned into an outright brawl all around them.

She gave Darrin a nod, and he guided Laura from the wall, in against his side, with a grim look as he and the security guard rushed them toward a discreet side door.

But on a night like that, there was no such thing as discreet.

As soon as they stepped out into the night, the flashes of cameras popped all around them, voices shouting over one another, trying to get answers about what was happening inside, why people were fleeing while, simultaneously, police were streaming in.

The security guard, who'd surely been generously compensated for his cooperation, tried to fend them off as Darrin led the sisters to his car, but Laura was in such a daze that she lifted her head and blinked sorrowfully right as a flash went off. In a rage, Margaret stormed toward the man, demanding the film, going so far as to reach for his camera when he refused.

Next thing she knew, there were a dozen more flashes going off in her face, and Darrin's arms were dragging her back to the car, stuffing her inside with her sister. Her purse had gone flying at some point, but Darrin threw that in after her before slamming the door shut. The flask was gone—she prayed she'd dropped it inside, not during the scrape with the photographer.

Only once they were driving away did it all really hit her.

"How did you find us?" she asked Darrin. He didn't answer, merely kept his eyes on the dark road ahead of them. "Did Daniel tell you?"

Beside her, Laura, who'd been hanging her head in shame, looked up, that startled blankness still splashed across her face. "Laur? What is it?"

Her eyes shifted from the rearview mirror to Margaret guiltily. She swallowed. "I told Gerald."

"You told Gerald . . . ?" It didn't sink in right away. When it did, she didn't get a chance to chastise Laura.

"He wouldn't have just sent for us like that unless it was important,"

Laura insisted. "I know he wouldn't." She looked toward the mirror again as if for backup.

Darrin kept his gaze astutely forward. Something new came over Laura's face. It went slack, her mouth opening. "Darrin?" she said in a small, strained voice.

He didn't meet her eyes. Dread gathered in Margaret's stomach now. "*Darrin?*" Laura said more sharply.

"Yes, Ms. Ives?" he replied.

"What's happened?" Margaret asked. Beside her, Laura began to weep, even before the words left Darrin's mouth.

"I'm sorry, miss," he said. "Your grandfather doesn't have long."

"I shouldn't have gone," Laura wheezed jaggedly. "I knew I shouldn't have gone." A sob scraped out of her, and Margaret pulled her in close, careful not to bump her bleeding face as she broke down fully in Margaret's lap.

The world whirred furiously past the car windows, but still, the drive seemed to last forever.

They pulled up to the front of the house as the team of doctors was leaving.

For some inane reason, Margaret took that as a good sign—trouble averted, pain schooled into submission by the iron grip of the Ives patriarch. Laura knew better.

She collapsed in the driveway at the sight of those white coats descending the steps.

Margaret sank down in the gravel beside her, holding her sister as she trembled.

Twenty minutes. That was how long he had been dead already. Margaret's first thought had been a selfish one: *She'll never forgive me.*

But she was wrong. That very night, her younger sister had slept beside her in her bed—or not slept, rather, but cried and hiccuped and cried some more—while Margaret stroked her hair and tried to think of soothing words that wouldn't be outright lies.

It will be okay didn't feel right. Neither did *he's in a better place now*, because who was she kidding? She had no idea if that was true.

Instead, she murmured "I'm here," over and over again, like a prayer, until Laura's breathing finally evened out into the rhythm of sleep, just before sunrise.

The headlines were horrible. She shouldn't have gone looking, and ordinarily she *wouldn't* have, but since this was about Laura, she felt it was her duty.

Socialite Sisters Cavort at Cosmo's "Rock 'n' Brawl" as Grandfather Dies, one rag proclaimed, beside a picture of the scene that had unfolded outside the arena, between her and the photographer who'd taken Laura's picture.

One spot of luck was that, in Margaret's efforts to take the man's camera, *she'd* become the shiny object at which all the others pointed their lenses, her face hideous in her fury, her hair slicked to her head so that it could fit beneath her wig, and her left eye nearly swollen shut.

Another spot of luck: She and Laura were just *one* story after a night full of them. Most of the news Margaret pored over with her morning tea was more concerned with the melee of the concert and the "sheer depravity" of Cosmo's performance, which supposedly brought it on.

The low, guttural singing. The wild dancing. And the moment he'd touched one concertgoer's hand to his cheek, which she'd seen every paper describe in its own wildly different way, including one confident assertion that he'd *licked* the woman's palm.

On the one hand, there was a comfort in seeing the media criticizing someone other than her or her sister. On the other, now that she'd escaped last night's trance, the scales had abruptly fallen from her eyes concerning Cosmo Sinclair.

She felt furious with him for his part in how everything had gone. One concerned clergyman had been quoted in an article calling him a *pied piper, leading young ladies to their doom*, and while ordinarily this would've struck her as ridiculous, now she thought that uptight puritan might've been onto something.

She'd been stewing on this when Briggs, their butler, came into the breakfast room to inform her that she had a visitor.

"I don't have anything on my calendar," she told him.

"I know, ma'am," Briggs replied.

"Then why did they let someone through the gate?"

Briggs's face went red. "I'm not sure he knew what else to do. Mr. Sinclair was adamant."

"Mr. Sin—" She dropped off, backtracked while she asked herself the question, *He couldn't possibly mean* that *Sinclair, could he?*

By the tiny dip of Briggs's chin, yes, yes, he did mean *that* Mr. Sinclair.

She didn't remember standing, but she was standing nonetheless. "What does he want?"

"I'm not sure, ma'am," Briggs said.

She wavered for a moment, unsure what the best course of action would be. Then she remembered Laura sleeping up in her bed and had a thought.

"Show him to the library," she told Briggs. "We'll be down shortly."

Only several minutes later, as she sat on the edge of her bed, Laura—whose nose had been reset by a doctor last night and looked all the worse for it today—drew her legs up to her chest, wound her arms around them, and said, "I'm not going down there."

"Oh, come on, Laur," Margaret said. "You look *fine*. Much better than *me*." She waved a hand at her black eye, but Laura shook her head and lay back down.

"It's not about that," she said. "I just—I don't want to see Cosmo

Sinclair. I don't want to think about him. I don't even want to listen to him anymore. For the rest of my life, that song will make me sick to my stomach. All he'll ever remind me of now is the night I lost my dearest friend."

Oh, how that made her chest keen.

There had been a time when Margaret had been Laura's best friend, but that didn't sting nearly so bad as the rest, the fact that her younger sister was now almost totally alone.

"Oh, sweetie," she cooed, smoothing one hand over Laura's head.

"Just get rid of him, will you?" Laura said quietly.

"Of course."

And Margaret went downstairs to do just that.

26

HAYDEN PARKS AT my house on Thursday night after work, and we take the trail through the trees back to Rum Room with our laptop bags slung over our shoulders.

"Does it ever bother you?" I ask. "Not being able to talk about what you're working on?"

Creases form at the insides of his brows. "Yeah," he admits. "More lately."

"Really? Why?" I say. "She finally getting to the good stuff?"

He gives me a look.

"I'm just kidding. This isn't a trap."

"I know." He slips his hand through mine, our knuckles locking together. After a minute, he says, "Almost everything she tells me, I find myself imagining her telling you."

"So competitive," I tease, bumping sideways into him.

"I just wonder how you'd react," he replies. "What you'd say. How you'd write it." After a beat, he adds, "I think about your Bella Girardi profile, and realize you're probably getting entirely different stuff than I am. Asking different questions."

"I don't know." I shrug. "I'm not really asking questions. I'm mostly just letting her talk."

He gives me a strange look.

"What?" I ask.

He shakes his head, the grooves in his forehead smoothing out. "I just think we're having different experiences."

"How so?" I ask.

"In a week," he says, "I'll tell you."

"A *week*?" I cry. "That's two days *before* she's going to choose one of us. Aren't you worried I'll scoop you?"

"Fine," he says, "a week and two days. We give her our pitches, and then I'll tell you everything I legally can." He stops walking, withdrawing his hand from mine only to offer me a handshake.

"You want me to say the same thing?" I ask.

"That's up to you," he says.

"I can *really* talk," I remind him. "If I try to recap everything, you'll get sick of me before I'm halfway through."

He grabs my hand, yanks me into him, and kisses me there in the middle of the dark path.

"That's a pretty good strategy," I whisper happily. At the ridge that forms in his forehead, I specify, "For when I'm talking too much."

"I'm not trying to shut you up, Alice," he says. "It's just that somehow, almost everything you say makes me want to kiss you."

I laugh, but my heart is whirring like a helicopter attempting liftoff. I lace my hands against the back of his neck and grin up at him like the lovestruck fool I'm quickly becoming. His own expression remains serious, and I just *know* he's thinking about next week, the week after, the week after that, an entire indefinite future with us on opposite sides of the country.

Despite learning early on the merits of being *present*, of focusing only on the moment you're in rather than dreading all the ones that might follow, my grasp on this nearly perfect moment slips a little too.

"Come on." I start back down the path. "Let's go eat."

Rum Room is packed, but the patio is entirely empty, so the host inside at the stand tells us to take whichever picnic table we want.

We choose one at the back edge, where we'll be more or less tucked out of sight, and set up our computers opposite each other. I know I should be working on my proposal, but I'm having trouble concentrating.

Stay in the moment, Alice, I chide myself. *Worry about tomorrow when it gets here.*

Easier said than done.

"Let's do something fun this weekend." I bat my laptop screen down for a better view of him.

His left eyebrow curves upward. "Such as?"

"I don't know," I say. "But we have Sunday off. Let's do something."

Some unspoken word balances on his bottom lip.

"What?" I press.

"I just . . ." He considers carefully. "I wondered if you'd try to see your mom again."

Oh. Right. I think it over. "Next weekend." Then I'll either have good news to share with her, or be done holding my breath and able to tell her I wrapped up my work here and am heading back to California.

He nods, eyes back on his screen, but *again*, there's something he's not saying.

"Hayden."

"It's none of my business," he replies.

I frown. "Don't say that. I want you in my business. I'm *inviting* you into my business."

His smile is half formed and far from long lasting. He's still tiptoeing.

"I promise," I add.

"I guess I still don't understand why you don't want to tell her how you feel." He hurries to tack on, "I *want* to understand. But I don't."

Now that I'm feeling less defensive, this line of questioning feels less like an attack. "I am who I am," I explain. "I like the things I like. I'm good at the things I'm good at. And my mom—she's *her*. Telling her that it hurts my feelings that she's not interested in my work won't change how she actually feels. She'll just act different. And I don't need that. I don't *want* her to pretend to think what I do has value. That would feel so much worse to me."

He nods, tight lipped, but I can tell it's an *I understand*, not an *I agree*.

"So that's it," I say.

"Got it." Under the table, his hand grazes over my knee. I think he means it to be calming, affectionate. But it sets me on fire.

I seriously doubt I'm making it another full week without having him. Something possesses me to blurt out as much, and his hand tenses on my thigh, his eyes darkening. I shift forward to the very edge of the bench, his hand crawling higher along my skin, heat pulsing through me to the rhythm of the crickets' song.

Around the corner from us, the screen door bangs open, and Hayden's fingers retreat abruptly, right in time for a cute twentysomething server with a topknot and Converse tennis shoes to bound out.

"Hey, y'all!" she says brightly, pulling her notepad from her black half apron. "My name's Tru. What can I get started for ya?"

Hayden clears his throat. "Ice water."

"I might need something a little stiffer," I say, genuinely not *aiming* for a euphemism, but by his sudden cough, I know that's how it's received.

I turn a guileless smile up to Tru. "Actually, we might need a minute," I say, because clearly neither of us is quite fit for public consumption just yet.

"Sure thing," she says. "I'll be back in five."

Five minutes, I tell myself, should be enough to make my body stop throbbing.

• • •

AFTER DINNER, WE don't even make it inside the rental before we're kissing, slipping hands beneath each other's shirts, whispering into each other's skin and mouths and hair. We pause long enough to fumble the lock open and stumble inside.

"We're not going to have sex," he tells me while his tongue is in the notch above my collarbone.

"We're not?" I say, somewhere between alarm and complete disbelief.

He shakes his head and pushes me toward the surface nearest the front door—the kitchen counter. "Not tonight." He scrapes my shirt up over me and tosses it aside before lifting me onto the counter.

"If you change your mind," I say, reaching for him now, "let me know." I throw his shirt over his shoulder, and then, as he's moving in between my thighs, I set a hand to the middle of his warm chest, holding him off. "Let me see you first."

His face screws up, and my heart clenches with the realization that he's *shy* about his body. "You're beautiful," I tell him earnestly.

His gaze lifts, the hard lines of his face cast in sharp relief. This time when he steps in close, I reach for his waist and pull him nearer, our stomachs kissing as he eases me to the edge of the counter. His hands trail up the sides of my neck, then back down my chest, cupping me through my bra as our lips melt together and draw apart, our breath mingling.

I slip one hand into his waistband, and he groans as my fingers curl around him. The sound drags down my spine like a fingernail, and I arch into him. One of his hands smooths around my back, makes its way up to the clasp of my bra while the other brushes my skirt up my thighs and gently slides under me, the heel of his palm pressing into me.

I cry out, my free hand gripping the back of his neck, seeking something firm and steadying as I move myself against him.

My bra vanishes. His mouth connects with skin. Our breathing frays, our pulses racing as we chase the sensations mounting everywhere we're connected. My chest aches with the need for more pressure, and I pitch myself forward, his mouth drawing me deeper. I gasp his name.

He pushes me back, the same way I did, one hand in the center of my chest, his splayed fingers nearly spanning the width of my rib cage.

He looks at me hungrily, eyes dark as the Atlantic beneath a new moon.

"Have you changed your mind yet?" I ask between breaths.

In answer, he pulls me by the hips off the counter, turns me so that my back presses into the cold steel of the refrigerator, and thrusts his knee between my thighs, his mouth descending on my throat and his palms raking up my body.

"Is that a yes?" I whisper. His hands pin themselves against my hips as he kneels on the tile in front of me, one hand bunching my skirt as the other tugs my underwear down.

He leans in, his breath warm and eyes tilted up to watch my reaction as he presses his mouth to me.

I forget all about the question. I forget all about *every* question that's been haunting me. I forget my name. I forget how to control my body or the words rasping from my throat.

I forget everything that isn't Hayden, isn't this moment.

• • •

WE DRINK DECAF. We eat the chess pie I got from the grocery store's bakery the other day. (Okay, mostly I eat it, but he has a couple of bites.) We try to work on our separate book proposals from our separate couches, and when that fails, try to play a game of Scrabble, and when that fails, we end up making out on the couch. And though mentally I really am trying to stop at making out, I find myself climbing down him, undoing his fly, drawing him into my mouth. His hand is gentle against the back of my head, the sounds emanating from him making my toes curl and thighs twinge all over again.

"God, Alice," he gravels out. "I love this."

I pull back. "Me too."

His eyes flick down to me, heavy lidded, lust drunk. "You don't have to say that."

"I mean it," I insist.

Even through the haze over his face, I catch a glimmer of skepticism.

It occurs to me then that in my effort to be positive, optimistic, and understanding, I might've made myself into an unreliable narrator of sorts, someone who can't easily be trusted not to sugarcoat things.

A strange realization to have in this specific moment, but I guess wisdom doesn't have to choose when to foist itself on a person.

"I promise," I whisper, his expression melting into something more raw, more vulnerable than before, his hand featherlight in my hair. "I love touching you. I love kissing you. I love hanging out with you. I love this."

He reaches for my face, draws me up the length of his body to kiss me sweetly, and I oblige, kiss him back until we're both writhing, until I can't bear going any longer without making him come. When I crawl back down him, his hips lift, letting me draw him into my mouth again. Bring him to the edge. Break him open, the same way he breaks me open. The sound he makes is something I know I'll play back to myself later tonight while I'm lying awake, aching for more of him.

His whole body.

His whole heart, a little voice adds. I push it aside.

Stay in the present.

When we've finished, when he's drifted back into himself and pulled me up to lie against his chest, I murmur, "Tell me something no one knows about you," and he's quiet and still for so long I start to wonder if I've crossed a line.

Then he tips his chin down to his clavicle to meet my eyes and says simply, "I'm in love with you."

I feel my lips part. Once I've absorbed it, I rush to reply, but he very lightly sets his fingertips against my mouth. "I don't want you to say anything now," he murmurs.

"Anything at all?" I whisper.

The corners of his mouth twitch. "Anything about that. Not until after."

I nod agreement, even as it feels like the words are climbing up my windpipe. "After."

He kisses me once. "Should we watch something?"

I blink back the rising tears and reach toward the coffee table for the remote. *Almost Famous* is on. I don't hear a word of it. My mind is an endless loop of *I'm in love with you too*.

After more than three decades on this planet, all it took was a few weeks and the right person to entirely rearrange my composition.

27

ON FRIDAY, I take a nature trail that runs along the creek. I think of it as a run to clear my head, but since I stopped at Little Croissant beforehand and am also incredibly unathletic, it's really more of a mosey or an amble.

A productive one though.

I decide to pitch structuring the book like a call-and-response. The rumors in the gossip rags of the time, followed by Margaret's confirmation or rebuttal.

When I've finished the walk, I drive over to the enclave and wander the colorful gift shops, picking out small presents for Bianca, Cillian, and Priya—tiny hand-painted wooden turtles—along with a postcard to send Audrey, since anything larger than that will just be something she has to find a way to store or send home.

Afterward, I cross the drive to get an iced decaf and take up my post in the garden patio beneath Little Croissant's raised platform. Other than a couple in yoga gear and a teenage Bible study, I have the place to myself and a fully charged laptop.

I'm more focused than I've been all week. The hours fly by, and it's nearly four p.m. when a jolly "Well, hey there, stranger!" jolts me out of work mode.

I blink against the sunlight until a gap-toothed smile resolves in front of me, along with a bulbous nose and a bucket hat.

"Cecil! Hi!" I rise to hug him on instinct, despite having absolutely never hugged this man before.

He takes it in stride, hugs me back like we're the oldest friends in the world. "How you been? Missed you at my half birthday."

"Oh, sorry about that." I drop into my seat and wave for him to join me.

He does. "No, no worries. Honestly, I hear I had a bit too much to drink and did the Macarena on the bar, so it's probably for the best you weren't there."

"Now you're *really* making me wish I'd stayed."

His wispy brows flick up. "So you stopped by?"

"Yeah, we were there for a while, but then something came up."

"We?"

My cheeks heat. "Oh, my friend Hayden. I guess you met him?"

He snaps his fingers. "The other writer!"

"Right," I say.

"So he missed the bar-top dancing too?" he asks hopefully.

I laugh. "He did. Although I think anyone reading about that would only be *more* excited about Little Crescent."

"Oh, no." He waves a hand. "Not the four p.m. dinner crowd. Most of them know better. I'm lucky I made it through the night without breaking my new hip. Now tell me, Alice: How are *you* finding our little island?"

"It's great," I say honestly.

"You did okay with the storm?" he says.

"That sprinkle the other night?" I say.

He guffaws, slapping the table as he lumbers to his feet. "Knew I liked you. Hey, if you see your friend Hayden, tell him I found that picture we were talking about."

"Picture?" I say.

"An old photograph," Cecil says. "He and I got to talking, and I told him about how I used to have hair down to my waist in the seventies. He wanted to see the proof." He stops and laughs gruffly to himself. "I'm sure he was just humoring an old man, but..."

I'm torn between trying to get more information and feeling like that's somehow *cheating* in this strange competition Hayden and I have found ourselves in.

Because if I know anything about him, he's *not* just humoring Cecil. He doesn't do that. Which means he had a real reason for asking to see this picture. Or else he didn't ask at all and Cecil just volunteered it, another distinct possibility, though with how direct Hayden tends to be, I'm really not convinced that's what's going on.

I tamp my curiosity down. "I'll tell him," I promise, and Cecil raps his knuckles on the table before turning and strolling away.

• • •

HAYDEN LOWERS HIS fork from his mouth, the bite of diner hash browns still dangling from it. "A picture?" he asks.

"That's what he said."

One side of his mouth inches up. "And you just let that go, did you?"

I fold my arms atop the sticky table. "Actually, I did. It felt like cheating."

He sits back, dabbing his mouth with a napkin. "I don't want you to do your job any differently because of me."

"It's fine," I say. "It's a lead *you* chased down."

"I never said it was a lead," he points out.

"Is it?" I try to arch my brow at him.

A quiet grunt of laughter escapes him. "You're bad at that."

"Well, I can't be perfect at everything, I guess," I say wistfully.

He sits forward again, his hands settling over my kneecaps under the table. "You could've asked him."

"What if I ask you instead?" I say.

His head tips, and he draws in a breath between his parted lips.

"Never mind!" I say.

"Ask to see the picture," he says intently, then adds, "It might not mean anything to you. It might not mean anything, period. But I'll tell you why I wanted to see it. After."

Not *after you see it*, I know, but *after we know how this ends*.

I stretch one hand out over the table, another handshake agreement in a series of them.

His hand eclipses mine, and I pull it across the table to press a kiss to the back of it, the only way I can keep myself from blurting *I love you*. The tender expression that dawns across his severe features makes me think he heard the words all the same.

* * *

ON SATURDAY MORNING, on my way out the door, I run back inside and dig through the stack of junk by the front door until I find Captain Cecil's card.

I fire off a quick text, and then I head over to Margaret's.

Since Hayden's and my arrival, she has apparently let her regular exercise fall to the wayside, which is how she convinced me that today's interview should largely be conducted from her swimming pool.

I wish I'd packed a sensible one-piece, but being me, I've only brought a skimpy hot sauce–red bikini. The least professional swimwear, arguably, but we'll make do. I sit on the edge of the sun-drenched pool, my legs in the water, and set up my recording devices beside me.

At the far end of the pool, she shrugs off her robe and tosses it onto a lounger to reveal a canary-yellow tankini, and I'm instantly less self-conscious about my own sartorial choices.

"I love your suit," I call to her as she descends the steps, clinging to the metal handrail.

"Right back atcha!" she says. "I tend to trust people who love color. Shows good judgment, don't you think?"

I can't tell if that's a compliment to me, a jab toward Hayden, both, or neither. Stranger, I can't tell which I want it to be.

It's a *good thing* if she trusts me. I *want* this job. But if she's implying that Hayden in his understated, monochromatic wardrobe isn't trustworthy, then I'm having a hard time not being a little offended.

Shit. Maybe he's been right all along. Maybe this is all stickier than I realize.

It's just one more week. Either way, things will be settled very soon.

I grab my notebook and pen and stack them on my thighs as Margaret begins wading back and forth, arms akimbo. "So," I say, clearing my throat, "we'd just gotten to—"

"Cosmo," she interrupts, still sloshing back and forth. "We'd finally gotten to Cosmo."

The Story

THEIR VERSION: For Cosmo Sinclair and Margaret Grace Ives, it was love at first sight.

　　　　●　　●　　●

HER VERSION: She hated him. She blamed him. She didn't care whether it was fair or not. She went down to the library with the intention of eviscerating him. She threw open both doors, for dramatic purposes, and stormed into the room like a heat-seeking missile.

He'd been looking at one of the many shelves of Gerald's unread books, and when he turned toward the sound, his quiet smile was disarming.

She stumbled, just for a second, before resuming her march.

"Hello, ma'am," he said. "I'm Cosmo."

The Southern lilt of his voice surprised her. She'd heard the accent in his stage chatter, of course, but much of it had been buried beneath thousands of screaming voices, and what she *had* heard, she'd assumed was a put-on. An exaggeration.

It wasn't.

"I know who you are," she said. Then: "Why are you here?"

"I came to apologize," he replied. At that point, she noticed the small bouquet hanging from his hand: a bundle of white lily of the valley, knotted with twine.

"Apologize?" she repeated, befuddled.

He came toward her, his slick shoes clicking on the floorboards, and presented the bouquet, almost sheepishly.

Everything about him was a bit sheepish, actually. What could have passed for cool aloofness from a distance struck her now as shyness.

"I saw the paper this morning," he said, letting the bouquet hover between them. "Felt awful about what happened to you and your sister, and everyone else. Things got out of hand."

"Oh, I see." She forced her shoulders away from her ears. "You're here to kiss the ring."

His brows pinched. "Ma'am?"

"You can relax. Our family's papers won't have any vendetta against you," she assured him, though personally, she couldn't say the same. She wasn't angry enough to try to tank his career, just angry enough to be rude.

He shifted between his feet, the bouquet falling back down to his side. He seemed uncomfortable in his body, as if he'd grown too quickly, in stature or frame or both, and wasn't quite sure how to move through the world. He looked younger than he had onstage too, so young that she couldn't help but ask, in that seemingly random moment, "How old are you?"

If he was surprised or offended that she—someone fan enough to attend the concert—didn't already know, he didn't show it. Laura probably knew his exact birth date, his associated birthstone, what kind of car he drove, and what his dog was called. Not that Laura cared anymore.

"Twenty-three, ma'am," he said.

Only three years older than her. It made his performance the night before all the more shocking. How could he look so at home on a stage in front of thousands, thrusting his hips and screaming his heart out, but become such a quiet, mild-tempered boy in this room with only her?

"I was raised never to ask a lady her age," he said, the tiny smile on his full lips surprising her.

"I'm twenty," she volunteered, for god only knows what reason.

He stepped a little closer. "Did you enjoy the show?" he asked in that hypnotic murmur. "Before all that hubbub, I mean."

His dark eyes shone with an eagerness that surprised her, as if the answer mattered very much. She wanted to lie, but she wasn't a liar.

She settled on an obfuscation. "I'd never seen anything like it."

His smile twitched across his lips but faded quickly. He reached toward her, and she flinched for just a second before she realized he was merely brushing his fingers lightly along the edge of her bruised eye, a frown deepening the grooves in his forehead. His eyes flicked back to hers. "Will you come again tonight?" he said quietly.

Her stomach flipped nonsensically as their sudden eye contact jolted her back into reality. "What?"

"To the last concert," he said. "Police will be there this time. Can't promise it will be a good show, but it'll be a safer one at least."

"Oh." She looked away, and his calloused fingertips fell from her face. "I'm not sure."

"Your sister too, of course," he volunteered. "We can bring y'all backstage, where no one can see you. You can watch from the wings."

Her heart soared, only to crash when she remembered what Laura had told her upstairs—was that really only minutes ago? It felt like days, weeks. In a way she couldn't understand and certainly couldn't have expressed, Margaret felt as if the story of her life had been written onto a piece of paper she'd only just now realized had been folded in half.

Now it was open, a full second half of a page appearing abruptly, with a sharp crease dividing this new chapter from what came before.

Laura's words dropped through her like a cold stone—*all he'll ever remind me of now is the night I lost my dearest friend*—settling in the pit of her stomach.

"Laura won't be able to make it," she said.

"But you?" The way his eyebrows pitched up in the middle, tenting hopefully, made something in her stomach feel like it was unraveling.

"Fine," she said.

A smile broke across his face, bright as dawn, and he lifted the bouquet toward her again.

This time she took it.

He won her over that night. Truthfully, that was all it had taken. He'd come off that stage, drenched in sweat, and caught up in the thrill of it all, when he strode purposefully toward her, she'd pitched herself into his arms, intending only to hug him, to praise the performance. But as soon as his strong arms came around her and his heat and scent hit her, it was as if she'd hopped universes. Moved parallel into one where the plan had always been to kiss him, just as his had always been to kiss her.

His band made a couple of little hoots and whistles, but the sound of the audience still cheering out in the dark amphitheater ate away at their teasing, and even if it hadn't, she likely wouldn't have registered it. She'd stopped registering anything but him. When he drew back, his fingers falling from her jaw, he took her hand and pulled her through the narrow backstage hallway, all the way to his dressing room.

"I don't do this," she said as, together, they pushed the door shut behind them.

"I do," he said.

"Fine," she said, "I do too."

Because of that, she thought she was safe. Insulated. This would be one more wild night, a private story that would belong just to her, in a life that she largely lived as a worldwide broadcast.

It couldn't be more than that, if for no other reason than she refused to subject Laura to Cosmo's presence.

So it was just one night.

And in the morning, when he sent her dozens of bouquets, each one a different flower, with a note that read *Didn't know what you liked. —C*, she told herself that was just an addendum to the night itself.

Laura continued her grieving. Gerald had left her his father's old journals, and all day long most days, she sat in his favorite chair, reeking of his cigar smoke, and read about the past, closing herself off from the future.

Margaret continued her life out on the town once her bruises had healed, and while some astute members of the press noted that the spark seemed to have left Peggy Ives's eyes, this change was always attributed to the recent loss of the "beloved patriarch of the Ives family."

Margaret passed as much time as she could with her sister, but all Laura really did, aside from read, was sleep, with the aid of the pills the family doctor obligingly prescribed.

Once the coverage of Gerald's death had dissipated and the news cycle hit its first lull, the pictures from the so-called Rock 'n' Brawl made a renewed appearance in the papers. Margaret knew this because she'd become obsessed with tracking them since that night. But she never brought the papers home. For once she was grateful that Laura was housebound, protected from the unkind things people were writing about her.

Still, one night, Margaret had walked past another of her father's secretive phone calls and heard him whispering, "Laura's not like you, Bernie. She's not tough. She can't handle this kind of scrutiny," and the shame filled her up from her feet to her head.

Three months passed since her night with Cosmo.

Occasionally he sent Margaret letters from his home in Nashville. Letters might've been an overstatement. They were more like notes, short missives about things that had reminded him of her, or mentions of vague plans to be back in Los Angeles, well-wishes for her and her sister. He always included Laura, which cracked Margaret's heart a bit deeper every time.

She kept every letter.

She replied to none of them.

Gradually, Laura emerged from those first stages of mourning. She'd finished reading the journals and moved on to new territory. Books about physics, biology, philosophy, religion. Sometimes, she could be coaxed outside to read on a blanket alongside Margaret, with the makings of a tea party spread between them.

Margaret kept waiting to stop missing the man she'd spent one night with. But when the letters stopped coming, she felt like a melon that had had its insides scooped out. She ached. She was . . . lonely, like she hadn't been since Ruth died, and before that, in those dark days when her parents' anger with and mistrust of each other had been so great that there was no room for anything else, even in a castle as large as theirs.

Three more months of silence went by. Margaret read about

Cosmo turning twenty-four years old, about the raging, star-studded party thrown at Chateau Marmont, and thought she might break in half at learning he'd been so close to her.

It terrified her. That one person could have so great a pull on her. That she could feel so much. That she could miss a person she didn't know. She wondered if something was wrong with her.

Laura had become obsessed with a young, controversial psychologist whose book she'd read. She'd excitedly spout some of his nonsensical theories at Margaret, one being that people were always the source of their own pain.

There was no logical reason Margaret should've felt this kind of loss at being disconnected from a total stranger like Cosmo Sinclair, which for the first—and, frankly, only—time made her think Dr. David Ryan Atwood might not be completely full of shit.

But time moved on and she thought of Cosmo less and less, until finally she stopped thinking of him at all.

In 1962, four years after Margaret's grandfather's death, one of Bernie's films was nominated for an Academy Award. Margaret's stepfather, Roy, never liked attending awards shows, so sometimes Freddy would step in to escort his ex-wife, but that year Bernie took Margaret as her date.

Margaret wore a silver gown, her hair piled glamorously atop her head, while Bernie wore simple black, as was her approach *every* time she found herself in a situation where a dress was more appropriate than her usual slacks.

Margaret felt more like herself that night than she had in a long time. It was promising. She and Laura would recover from the last four years, and things would go back to normal. That page would be refolded along its crease, and she would continue wandering through her sumptuous, extravagant, *fun* life.

She talked, she flirted, she drank, she laughed. She and her mother rolled their eyes at the inane stage banter and roared their applause for their favorite films, actors, writers of the year. Or Bernie did, and Margaret followed her lead, happy to bask in the glow of her lovely mother.

She felt filled back up by the time the night was over. She even decided to stop by the Board of Governors Ball, the after-party that had started up a few years ago. Their driver took her to the doors of the venue, and she kissed her mother—who'd decided to head home—good night, then stepped out into the line of paparazzi fire, smiling prettily. She paused to pose for several who called out her name. Just ahead were Paul Newman and Joanne Woodward, who wore a beaded gown and long white gloves. They chatted with Margaret for a moment before heading inside.

When she moved to follow them, her hem had been snagged underfoot by whoever'd stepped out from the latest car to arrive.

She turned, her reflexive apology whizzing back down her throat before it ever reached her lips.

"Hello," Cosmo said, his dark eyes glimmering, his mouth quirked in that funny, almost-sheepish, heartbreakingly sexy smile of his.

The smile that launched a thousand teenage tears, and plenty of shrieks of excitement around them now, even from a crowd of seasoned celebrity journalists.

The flashes went off all around her, like distant stars exploding, imploding—significant, sure, but not to her, not then.

She was barely aware of the actress on Cosmo's arm, an ingenue who'd been nominated for Best Supporting Actress earlier that night and lost out to *West Side Story*'s brilliant Rita Moreno.

Cosmo didn't seem too aware of his date either, his eyes glued to Margaret, his smile just for her.

His date, for her part, was relatively unbothered, waving and posing for the cameras in a ruby-red Dior.

The next day those pictures would be everywhere.

Two-Date Peggy and Two-Timing Cosmo? one headline asked.

Stars Collide at Governors Ball, another article's caption began.

There were dozens more, but only one felt right to her. One, she thought, was true.

Cosmo Sinclair Spots Margaret Ives and the World Stops.

28

WHEN I GET out of the shower Saturday night, my phone is still lit up on the counter with a new text from Cecil.

I'd told him I was curious to see the photo of him in his "hippie days" too, and he sent a grainy phone picture of the old film photograph.

I wrap my hair in a towel, another around my body, and then open the message to get a better look, balancing on the edge of the baby-pink tub.

Nothing especially jumps out to me from the image. He's sitting on a boulder in front of some pine trees, smiling and waving. He's much thinner and less wrinkled, but the biggest difference between the Cecil of then and the one I've met is exactly what he prepared me for.

His long blond hair hangs past his shoulders, gleaming in the light, a thick blond mustache slightly covering his smile.

Is there something kind of familiar about him, or am I just staring so hard I'm willing myself into a sense of déjà vu?

I forward the picture to Hayden but don't ask any questions.

I'll figure out why this picture matters on my own, or I'll wait until this game is over, but I'm *not* going to let him hand me any information.

In the bedroom, I pull on my pajamas.

Hayden and I decided to do our own things tonight, largely because we both could use the time to catch up on work, and we made plans to explore more of Savannah tomorrow.

I only have one week to push as far into Margaret's story as I can *and* piece together a proposal and writing sample, and I'm going to need every spare second.

But first, I drop the picture of Cecil into a reverse image search. Nothing noticeably useful turns up, and when I add the surname from his card—Cecil Wainwright—I still find nothing of consequence.

Then again, it's not like I know what I'm looking for. I close out of the window, tie my hair into a stubby little ponytail, and pick up transcribing Margaret's story from earlier.

The Story

THEIR VERSION: Cosmo Sinclair and Margaret Ives's relationship caused a rift in the Ives family that would never be completely repaired.

• • •

HER VERSION: He came to see her the morning after the Academy Awards. When Briggs told her, Margaret was giddy; she was terrified. She was hopeful; she was miserable.

She changed her clothes three times—the last outfit being the one she'd already had on before Cosmo Sinclair showed up at her door—and went down to meet him.

But the library was empty. She traipsed back into the hall and heard voices from the breakfast room. She went toward them, unsure what to expect, and found herself quickly at the doorway, looking in on a scene that squeezed her heart ferociously.

"There you are," Laura said, smiling with a mug of tea in hand. "I was just keeping Cosmo here company."

Cosmo here had lurched to his feet, his forehead canted slightly down and mouth in that funny little shy smile of his that turned her inside out.

Laura stood too. "It was lovely to meet you," she told Cosmo. "Now, if you don't mind, I'm in the middle of a good book."

"The pleasure was all mine, ma'am," he said, his drawl irresistible. Laura grasped Margaret's elbow on her way from the room, and she took it as the sign it was: *It's okay.*

She knew. Somehow, Laura knew. Margaret had no idea how, but there wasn't much room for guilt or shame over her secret right then. Cosmo had taken a slow, hesitant step toward her, his hands stuffed into his back pockets, chin still tucked to take her in, accommodating for their height difference.

Suddenly, his closeness felt like too much. It overpowered her. Stole her breath.

"Would you like to go for a walk, Mr. Sinclair?" she said, more formally than she'd intended.

His smile split open. "I'd like that very much. And you can call me Cosmo."

"Cosmo," she said, so quietly she was surprised he could hear it. But she knew he did, because his smile grew.

They walked through the orange grove, and while that was sizable, it wasn't enough. They wandered through the other rows of fruit trees, and then circled the tennis courts. They wandered past the Roman-inspired outdoor pool, and down to one of the lakes. They ambled through the rose garden, the greenhouses, the chapel, the various follies.

At one point they'd wound up at the very edge of the land, where they could look down over the cliffs to the water below, watch it sparkle under the sunset—because the sun was *setting* by then.

"Would you like to go to dinner with me?" he asked, and she would. She would like to go to dinner, dessert, bed, breakfast, lunch, and dinner again with him.

But she wanted to speak with Laura first.

"Tomorrow?" she asked.

"Tomorrow," he agreed.

When he'd left, she found Laura in her bedroom. For once she was writing at her desk, instead of reading. She smiled as Margaret approached.

"So the rumors are true." Laura looked tired, and she'd lost a lot of weight since Gerald's passing, but *her smile*—her smile made Margaret believe that maybe, someday, everything would be okay again.

Playing along, Margaret rolled her eyes and flopped herself dramatically backward onto Laura's grandiose, hand-carved bed. "And what rumors would those be?"

"You're in *love*," Laura sang at her, then, on a giggle, "with *Cosmo Sinclair*."

"Says who?" Margaret rolled over and propped herself up on her forearms.

"David," she replied.

"David? Who's David?" Margaret sat up the rest of the way.

"My friend David," Laura said. "Dr. David Ryan Atwood."

"*Dr. David?*" Margaret said. What she thought was, *That quack?* "Since when are you *friends* with him?"

"Since I wrote to him five months ago, and he wrote back." She set her pen aside. "We've been corresponding. And talking on the telephone, sometimes." She added, "I had to hear about what happened at the Governors Ball from *him*."

"Nothing happened at the Governors Ball," Margaret said.

"I spoke with David earlier. He told me all about it."

Margaret felt a pinch of guilt. "I won't see him again."

"*Peggy*." Laura stood and came toward her, dropping onto the side of the bed and taking her older sister's hands in her own. "You can't watch me every second of every day."

"Who says I'm doing that?" She'd meant it rhetorically, but from the odd look that passed over Laura's face, Margaret realized there was a literal answer. "Dr. David?" she guessed.

Laura squeezed her hands. "You need to live your life. Go out and fall in love. Or travel, or do whatever else it is you're *not* doing while you're sitting here with me."

Margaret's throat twisted, her voice splintering. "I don't know how to be without you."

"You won't," Laura promised. "You won't ever be without me. There will just be a little more . . . space. It's a good thing."

"What will you do?" Margaret asked.

"What I always do," Laura said. "I'll read and I'll write and I'll go for long, marvelous walks."

Her smile dazzled Margaret. It made her feel like an ember in her chest had been gusted into a raging flame. It made her feel braver. She hugged her sister and didn't let go for a long time.

The next night, Cosmo picked her up for dinner. He drove them himself in a nondescript black car rather than his dark blue Ferrari Spyder, and he wore a chauffeur's cap as a half-assed disguise. Margaret had dressed for dinner out, somewhere they'd be seen and photographed, but instead he took her to the house he was renting, and they walked down to a dark stretch of private beach with a picnic basket, a blanket, and a six-pack of beer he'd gotten from his trunk.

They ate, they drank, they laughed. They took off their clothes and ran into the dark waves, and afterward made slow, patient love on the blanket.

"What is it about you?" he'd asked quietly, reverently, pushing her wet hair away from her face as they lay together afterward.

"I don't know," she murmured back. "Could it be my family's millions?"

"I'd marry you, Peggy Ives, if all you had to your name was a gunnysack and a can of corn."

"Are you proposing to me, Cosmo?" she teased him, but his face remained serious.

"Sure," he said. "Why not?"

She laughed in disbelief, swatted his chest. "You're not serious."

"I am," he said. "Marry me."

"No," she said.

"Why not?" he asked.

"Because I don't know you," she said.

"What do you want to know?" he returned. "I'll tell you anything, and then we can get married."

"That's not how this works," she said.

"Honey, there's never been a me or a you before," he replied. "This works however we say it works."

"*I say* that two people should know each other's middle names at least," she joked.

"Andrew," he said. "What's yours?"

She couldn't resist him. Not that innocent, eager expression of his, not the twang in his voice, not the smell of him all around her or the heat of his arm draped over her waist, or the lock of hair damp against his forehead. "Grace."

"That's beautiful," he told her. "Maybe we'll name our baby that. Grace."

At that, she absolutely howled with laughter, but the joke was on her. They spent every day together for the rest of his time in Los Angeles—two and a half weeks—and, at the end of it, when he asked her to marry him again, it wasn't really a question. They both already knew the answer.

The press had taken to tailing Margaret and Cosmo ever since the morning after that first date, when he'd gone to drive her home early, only to discover cameras waiting outside the gates. Every time they went anywhere after that, a crowd of reporters and fans alike seemed to find them, so they agreed to spend three days apart, a kind of distraction before they married at the courthouse. A faux breakup.

He told only his security guard and his manager—who tried to talk him out of it, of course—and Margaret told only her sister.

She and Laura had a miniature bachelorette party of sorts, staying up late eating snacks and candy and listening to records (not Cosmo's though; Laura wasn't there yet), then sleeping together in the tent in their playroom like they had so many nights when they were girls.

They woke before the rest of the house and crept out to meet the black car idling in the driveway, Cosmo Sinclair sitting behind the steering wheel in his chauffeur's hat again, a disguise that would fool no one at this point.

A gaggle of paparazzi were waiting at the bottom of the House of Ives's drive. A swarm of cars followed them to the courthouse like a marital parade.

Margaret was glad to have ridden with Laura in the back seat, where she could hold her sister's hand tight as her anxiety mounted. Again and again, she whispered her gratitude for Laura being willing to do this, and all that Laura could really muster was a tense smile and nod.

"It will just take a minute," Cosmo promised her, his eyes darting to the rearview mirror, his smile soft and reassuring.

It was more like ten minutes, in the end. As soon as the courthouse came into view, Margaret forgot, however briefly, to worry about her sister.

She felt only joy, rightness, and some amount of shock that the universe would grant her something so beautiful and precious as this without her having done anything to earn it.

Then again, maybe love was always a gift. The only thing that couldn't be bought or sold or bartered for.

Cosmo opened the door for the girls and, with a calming smile, gestured for the cameramen to step back so he could hand Laura onto the sidewalk. He ran her up the steps and dropped her inside with the nearest security guard, then came back for Margaret.

When she stepped out onto the walk, she might as well have been floating.

She didn't mind the attention. She didn't care whether no one or everyone watched what happened next. She hardly noticed the crowd swelling around her on all sides, jockeying forward, shouting, grabbing.

Cosmo's warm hand took hers, and he tucked her against his side, physically blocking them from getting too close. She'd never felt so safe in her life.

They were in and out of there fast. One of the other waiting brides was so awestruck at Cosmo's presence that she'd handed over her bouquet to him, her mouth gaping open. He'd thanked her earnestly and passed the flowers to his new wife, and then they left through the back door to get in a waiting car Cosmo had hired, their luggage ready and in the trunk. He'd send someone for the other car later. Now he was eager to get back to Nashville to wrap up some business so he and his wife could take their honeymoon.

Margaret tried to convince Laura to join them for either or both portions of the trip, but she'd wanted to get home to her books and her letters with Dr. David. So the driver took Cosmo and Margaret to their waiting plane, where they each hugged Laura tight on the tarmac and said their tearful goodbyes.

"I'll see you soon," Margaret promised. "A month at the longest."

"See you when I see you," Laura said, kissing each of her sister's cheeks, the wind from the engines billowing her hair across her face.

It was a month exactly before the newlyweds came back to Los Angeles.

They'd spent two weeks in Tennessee, during which Cosmo had canceled, delayed, or cut short every business dealing he had, aside from one hometown show, during which Margaret had watched from the wings, then made love to him in the dressing room like that first time. After that, they'd gone to Italy, a small town where they'd expected to find some privacy. Only the members of Cosmo's team closest to them knew the exact details, and still they'd been swarmed by international press from the moment they touched down.

The Poor Man's Elvis was rebranded as the Rich Man's Elvis, a joke about his heiress wife. She didn't care. She didn't care either when they were dubbed "the Closest Thing Americans Have to Royalty."

They'd been relentlessly followed and relentlessly *observed*. They tried more disguises. They tried scheduling reservations at multiple restaurants and going elsewhere. They tried assumed names. They tried firing the suspected sources of the leaks, but a new one always sprang up. Every time the paparazzi captured a shot of Cosmo looking hunted or glowering, the headlines asked, *Trouble in Paradise?*

When they stayed in for days on end, tabloids ran stories about *Peggy's rules*, and the *short leash* on which Margaret kept the *famous former Casanova*.

The highs and lows of their public perception bothered Cosmo. While they'd been in Rome, his manager had told him about an article back home that lined up Margaret with the other women Cosmo had been (loosely) attached to, rating her face, her body, her talent, and her money against the others'.

It was the first time she'd seen him truly angry. He'd flung a coffeepot at the wall in his rage and paced like a caged, helpless animal.

"It's all right," she promised, crawling to the edge of their bed and pushing up onto her knees to touch each side of his face. "I'm used to it."

"That doesn't make it right," he said.

"No," she agreed. "But we can't change the whole world with our love, Cosmo."

He circled her wrists with his hands. "I should be able to protect you. I should be able to protect your sister, and anyone else you care about. If I can't do that, then what's all of this for?"

Cosmo had grown up without money, so he knew the value of a dollar. While he liked to *spend*—especially when it came to her or his parents back in Dennis, Tennessee—she'd also learned that his anxiety about money ran much deeper than his love for it.

Not having it had been the greater strain, no doubt about it, but he wasn't *at ease* with having it either.

"I don't need you to protect me," she whispered, kissing him slowly. "I just need you to love me."

And he did. Every minute of every day of that first month.

She'd gotten two letters from Laura since they'd been gone, but both had come in those first two weeks, when they were at Cosmo's Nashville estate.

She was eager to see her sister, to prove that this hadn't been a mistake, that the universe had given her permission to love and be loved deeply by both of them.

That she wasn't being greedy, and she wouldn't be punished for it.

But Laura wasn't home, Briggs informed Margaret as soon as she and Cosmo had set foot in the vast marble entryway of the House of Ives. "What do you mean?" she asked. "Is she out on the grounds?"

Briggs cleared his throat, his eyes switching between Cosmo and her as if to indicate this was a delicate matter. He might've been Margaret's husband, but Cosmo wasn't and would never be an Ives.

"Briggs," she said. "Tell me where my sister is."

The butler cleared his throat again, his face going beet red with embarrassment. "Miss Laura is getting treatment in New Mexico at the moment."

"*Treatment?*" Her heart pattered through her chest, a loose pinball zigzagging against her rib cage. "Is she sick?"

"Did something happen?" Cosmo pressed, one hand settling comfortably at the small of Margaret's back.

"It is my understanding," Briggs said diplomatically, "that Dr. Atwood is assisting your sister with—"

"Atwood?" she interrupted. "The psychologist?"

"Yes, Ms. Ives," Briggs said. "Miss Laura is at his 'center' for the next several months."

She spun toward the library, the nearest phone. "Did she leave a number?" she shouted without looking over her shoulder.

She'd made it all the way to the phone when Briggs finally caught up with her. "There are no phones on the property, ma'am," he said. "But she left an address if you'd like to write."

"We can go there," Cosmo told her. "Right now, if you want. Bring her home."

Briggs took an audible breath, and she looked to him, waiting for whatever he was going to say. "She left you a letter in your room, I believe. She told me that would explain everything."

Margaret and Cosmo set off together, barreling through the

castle. The ivory envelope sat in the middle of Margaret's bed. She tore it open, shaking out the paper within.

>Dear Margaret,
>
>I am sorry not to give you more advance notice, but I have gone to New Mexico to work with Dr. David. Already, through our correspondence, I have made tremendous leaps in improving my well-being. For the first time in a long time, if not ever, my mind feels clear. This space, I must confess, has been a significant part of my growth. I have been caught so long in the shadow of our family's name, and it has allowed me to ignore the truth of who I really am.
>   For my continued self-improvement, I kindly ask you to respect my wishes and grant me the space I require from you and the rest of our family. For the time being, please do not contact me. When I have completed Dr. David's program, I will return to you the very best version of your sister. Until then, know all my thoughts and love are with you, Mom, Dad, and Roy.
>
>Yours always,
>Laura

Contrary to what Briggs had said, Margaret thought, this explained nothing.

29

HAYDEN AND I wander the long, manicured paths of the old Bonaventure Cemetery, iced tea and coffee in hand, sun warming the tops of our heads. I've been here one other time, and it's as beautiful as I remember, a gorgeous interplay of light and shadow cast by the hundreds of old trees dripping in Spanish moss.

"I've always liked cemeteries," Hayden admits.

"Really?" I say. "What about them?"

"I guess just the permanence," he says. At my look, he adds, "Not the bodies. I know those don't last. Even the headstones wear down. But the idea of there being one place where you can find the people who came before you. And where you go back to them."

He misses a step as we crest a hill and come into view of an active funeral, a group of people in black gathered around a grave with their heads bowed.

Anguish splashes across his face.

"You okay?" I ask.

He glances down, pupils flaring at the sight of me, and takes my hand, tangling our fingers. "Sorry. The last time I was at one of those, it was for Len."

I lean over to kiss his shoulder. "There's nothing to apologize for."

As we start walking, he studies me sidelong. "Was your last one for your dad?"

I nod, keep my eyes ahead. "It was kind of weird. He'd been a journalist when he was younger, and tons of people he'd worked with or written about came."

"That's sweet," Hayden says.

"It was," I agree. "But I would've liked something a little more private, I guess."

"That makes sense."

I think about Cosmo and Margaret running up the courthouse steps, half the world watching, and still those pictures feel intimate. I wish, for the hundredth time, that I could talk to Dad about it. About everything I spent the night transcribing and fact-checking. So far, I haven't stumbled on any other lies or half-truths, not since we talked about Nicollet, but I can't help feeling like Margaret's still keeping major secrets, and wonder if Hayden's having the same experience.

She and I have only three sessions left, and some of the very worst things to befall the Ives family are coming up.

The situation with Dr. David. The arrests. The court case. The accident.

I have no idea how Margaret has managed to move through life so isolated, carrying all of this on her shoulders, when I'm only three weeks into cataloging it and wishing desperately to share it with Hayden.

As if reading my mind, he stops walking and pulls me into an embrace, tucking me against his sun-warmed body, his chin resting atop my head. And even though we're not talking about it, it *does* feel like some of the load shifts onto his shoulders.

"Did you see the picture," he says.

I pull back to peer up into his face. It takes a beat for his meaning to set in. "I did. But I don't know what it means."

He nods curtly, his eyes narrow and mouth tense.

"Why?" I ask.

"Because you need to," he says, "before you agree to take this job."

"So now I'm the one getting the job?" I say.

"You won me over," he murmurs. "I have to assume you've won Margaret over too."

"Yeah, but I'm not *sleeping* with Margaret," I say.

"You're not sleeping with me either," he says.

"*Yet*," I say. "And whose fault is that?"

He laughs, kisses me once, and then starts walking again, tugging me along by our linked hands. "A cemetery was a good idea."

"Bright and crowded," I say. "Or crowded enough, anyway."

Back at my house after, we make dinner. Green tomato pie, fried okra, buttermilk biscuits—two-thirds of which he's never had, and certainly never made.

"Your parents didn't teach you how to cook at all?" I ask as we're slicing tomatoes side by side.

He shakes his head. "My mom did all the cooking, and she had a weird thing about other people being in the kitchen while she was working."

"And was that *weird thing* 'Mom guilt'?" I ask.

"Maybe a little," he allows. "But also she told me the kitchen was 'her church,' which was confusing since she and Dad *also* dragged us to First Presbyterian every single week."

I laugh, go check on the biscuits. They could use a few more minutes.

"I think," he says, "what she meant was, the kitchen was her *nighttime*."

"Her nighttime?" I come back to stand beside him, his large hands still slowly, carefully slicing the plump tomatoes we grabbed from a farmers' market in Savannah.

"Like how I used to wander, after everyone went to sleep," he says. "Looking back, I think she liked the privacy and the control." He pauses for a beat. "I know my parents love each other, but I don't think she was well suited to be a politician's wife. No matter how small time."

"What do you think she was meant for then?" I say, curious.

His shoulders lift. "I don't know. When she was a teenager, she wanted to be a singer. But she had stage fright. Ended up on a stage anyway though."

I think of the labyrinth on Margaret's property, the path that winds all through her workshop. *Unicursal.* One beginning, one end. Or, depending how you look at it, no beginning and no end—just a journey.

"Do you think we have free will?" I ask.

He lets out a verifiable bark of laughter that lights me up from the inside. "You," he says, "surprise me more than anyone I've ever met."

"So I take that as a yes?" I say. "To free will?"

He sets his knife aside. "Without researching it?"

"Such a journalistic response." I fight a smile. "Gut instinct, yes or no."

"I think . . ." He raises his eyes to the ceiling, then settles them on my face. "I think there's so much out of our control. Almost everything about how our lives go. But I think deciding that we're all just on a track, that we never really had any say over our own decisions— it feels like the kind of thing someone with a lot of regrets would need to be true. Maybe I need something different to be true."

"Like what?" I ask.

"That we don't have to end up with regrets," he says. "That if we really care about something, we can decide to hold on to it."

"I prefer that version of the world," I say, smiling up at him. His arms ring my waist, his nose scraping along mine.

"You do?"

I nod, the movement gliding our lips briefly across each other.

"It's yours," he offers.

I laugh. "Oh? I can have the world?"

"Mine," he says, "yeah. You can have mine."

• • •

"THAT FIRST YEAR of marriage was the best and worst that I'd lived thus far," Margaret tells me. We're side by side in her garden, the sky gray and overcast but the heat thicker than ever. My body feels like a swamp, my bangs plastered to my forehead as I dig out yet another bundle of weeds from the flower bed in front of me, my recording devices face up on the grass between us.

"At first, I tried to honor Laura's request," she goes on, still digging, huffing from the effort. "I waited a full month to write to her, and I waited a full month after that for a reply that never came before writing again. Didn't hear anything back, of course. Sometimes I was furious, other times I was devastated. Mostly I was worried. My parents had tried contacting her too. Mom got one reply, asking for more space. Laura said something about how every time we crossed the boundary, it set her healing journey back and made it so she'd have to be away longer."

"Did you know what she meant by 'healing journey'?" I ask.

"Not at all!" she says. "I was reading 'Dr. David's' books trying to make sense of things, but it honestly sounded like a whole lot of nothing. He used big words, sentences so long you'd lose track of where they'd started, and everything was so vague. The main thing was, he thought the world was dying. He thought humanity had crossed a threshold and there was no coming back without drastic measures. Even when my sister had been back in the Ives bubble, she'd wrestled with anxiety, and the apocalyptic slant of his teachings spoke to her."

"Is that what you think drew her to David Ryan Atwood? Existential dread?"

She sits back on her heels, wiping a bead of sweat from her forehead. "That *and* loneliness. She'd lost our grandfather, and our parents were busy, and I—I wasn't as present as I could've been."

"She told you to go out with Cosmo," I remind her.

"I know, I know," she says. "And I could *never* regret that. Believe me. But the thing is, some people aren't meant to be aimless. I was okay with just . . . just *living*, whatever that looked like, before I met Cosmo. And after that, I was mostly okay with just loving him, being loved by him. Laura was so smart. She should've been in a graduate program, or doing surgery, maybe, I don't know. Working for NASA! But having everything at her fingertips, every single door open to her, I think it made it hard for her to find any kind of purpose. I think she was taken in by that man because he *saw* her. And so few people did.

"I read some of his first letters to her, you know? Way later. He told her she was brilliant, which was true. He told her she could help heal the world, which mattered to her. And he told her she was suffocating inside our family, inside her life, and that wasn't wrong either. The problem is, he told her all that stuff for a reason."

"To manipulate her?" I ask.

She nods somberly, freeing another weed with long, tangly roots.

"She was brilliant, and compassionate, and stifled," Margaret says. "But she was also from one of the richest and most powerful families. We didn't know until later that she'd been sending him money for weeks before he convinced her to come out to his 'center.' She probably funded the whole thing, honestly."

"Did you keep writing to her? After your mom got the letter?" I say.

"I was too scared to," she says. "She made it sound like there was a set amount of time she'd need to be away from me, and I was only making that window grow every time I reached out. So I tried just being patient. After about five more months, my parents, Cosmo, and I decided to hire a private detective. He went out to New Mexico for a couple of weeks, and he came back with all these big black-and-white photographs. And there she was. My sister, with Dr. David and another woman, who looked a few years older than her."

"How did she look?" I ask.

Something flashes across her face, dark and lightning fast, akin to shame. "She'd lost more weight. Now that I know how things ended up, I realize I should've paid more attention to that. But at the time... The thing is, she was smiling." She looks at me dead on, her pale blue eyes filling with tears, even now, sixty years after the fact.

She blinks them away and goes back to digging. "Laughing. Smiling. She looked happy. Sometimes she was holding his hand. I remember one where her hair was blowing out behind her as they walked down the street with all these bags of produce. In every single picture, she looked happy. It was a relief. And a dagger to my heart.

"After that, I promised myself I wouldn't write to her anymore. Or I guess I still *wrote*, but I didn't mail the letters. Every time I had something I wanted to say to her—which was all the time—I'd write it down and tuck it into a drawer. Pretty soon I had dozens, hundreds maybe, stored all over my family's home, and Cosmo's place in Nashville, and our house in Beverly Hills.

"Just seeing her happy like that . . . it gave me a lot of mileage. Sometimes I was happy too, almost unbearably happy, for weeks at a time. And then something would happen, and I'd think of my sister, remember I no longer had her, and I'd barely be able to drag myself out of bed."

"I'm sorry," I say. "That's terrible."

"Cosmo had to go back on tour, and I started out with him, but I hated it. Really hated it. I loved traveling with my husband, but it was hard sharing him like that. It got lonely. Half the time all I could think was, *I wonder if Laura's written back yet.* So finally, I went home."

"Then what?" I say.

"The press noticed," she says with a wry smile. "Every day it was something different. Articles suggesting we were splitting up. Photographs of him and every beautiful woman he so much as spoke to while we were apart, along with plenty of implications that *speaking* was the least of what he was doing.

"The worst part is, I wasn't sure. I didn't ask, because I didn't want to find out anything that could ruin our marriage, and I sure as hell didn't want him to lie. I knew he loved me, and I focused on that. He'd call me every single day, sometimes twice, and a couple of times, I flew in to surprise him at shows. He was always thrilled. If there *were* other women waiting in his dressing room, they were always gone by the time he and I got back there.

"Sometimes we'd talk about having kids, but the first time we had a pregnancy scare . . . I'd never felt that kind of terror. I couldn't have even told you why. Cosmo was great about comforting me. I more or less sobbed for six hours, until my period started, and once the relief set in, we had a fight.

"We almost never fought. It just wasn't a part of our relationship, for good or bad. I never felt like we needed to agree on things, and he never pushed me to do anything I didn't want to. But he was upset by my reaction, that I wasn't sure if I wanted children."

She shoots me a meaningful glance. "Probably would've been a more important question to ask before we got married than 'What's your middle name?'"

"What would you have said?" I say. "If he'd asked that?"

She blew out a breath. "I would've said *I don't know*. Because I didn't. And after that fight, I felt even less sure. In a moment of weakness, I wrote another letter to my sister, and this time I sent it. I told her everything she'd missed. I told her about the baby that didn't exist, and how conflicted I felt about bringing anyone new into this world. I even tried to butter her up by asking if Dr. David had any wisdom on the matter. She didn't reply, of course, but after that letter, I felt like I found some peace with the situation. It never got easier being without her, but I got used to how it felt to carry that pain with me. I learned to put it on a shelf and live my life.

"We threw parties and hosted lavish dinners. We went to galas and award ceremonies and charity fundraisers. We fought and made up, fucked and made love. And he wrote me ballads so sweet that the first note could make your heart break."

A bittersweet smile sweeps across her face, even as her eyes stay trained on the garden bed. "On Sundays, when we were in Los Angeles, we had family dinners with my parents and Roy at the house, and whenever my dad was in one of his *divorced phases*, Cosmo and I would stay there for weeks at a time. My grandmother had passed away, and my great-aunt Gigi had moved to Paris, so he needed the company.

"We packed a whole life into those short years together. Cosmo's schedule had slowed down since the Beatles set foot in America, in February of 1964, but the paparazzi seemed keener than ever to catch him doing something scandalous or me doing something horrible. We did our best to shut it out, but I could see how it grated on him, the way his world had shrunk so hard and fast. Writers who'd fawned over him five years earlier were mocking him now. 'The Boy Wonder of Rock 'n' Roll' was looking older by the minute.

"The more time went on, the less we talked about Laura. It was too painful, and Dad, as he got older, leaned more into his anger. Probably easier that way. To rage against how she'd turned her back on us instead of mourning that she was out of reach."

"And your mother?" I ask.

"Eventually she admitted to me that she'd kept that private investigator," she says. "Dad wouldn't fund it anymore. He was too hurt and angry. So she couldn't get as many check-ins as she would've liked, but every six months or so, she'd get a new envelope of pictures delivered to her. And then one Sunday night, after dinner, my father set his silverware down and stood up and said, 'Bernie, Margaret, I need to speak with you in the drawing room.' A family meeting."

"Roy and Cosmo weren't included," I note.

"Dad had always welcomed Cosmo into the family, and to a lesser extent Roy," she says. "So I knew this had to be something delicate. We went into the library while Roy and Cosmo had dessert. I remember there was a fire roaring in there, even though it was the dead of summer in California. But that was Dad. He had his routines.

"He had us sit down then and blurted it out, without any kind of preamble. He just said it: 'We're being extorted.'

"Mom nearly fell out of her chair. 'By whom?' I remember her asking. 'For what?' But something about the look on my father's face broadcast the answer loud and clear to me. I just knew. Then he pulled the letter out of his dinner jacket and handed it to us.

"The funny thing is—well, not *funny*, but you know, *peculiar*—is that I didn't even care about what Dad had said once I saw that handwriting. All that mattered to me was that Laura was okay. That she was finally writing to us."

The Story

THEIR VERSION: Laura Ives was the right hand of the high control group the People's Moment for Metaphysical Healing. Laura Ives was just another victim of David Ryan Atwood. Laura Ives was a sucker. Laura Ives was a mastermind. She was a villain; she was a fool.

• • •

HER VERSION: When she was small, Laura loved zebras. The family had had some, for a time. They'd gotten them because her grandfather's mistress made a crack about wanting one. They'd gotten rid of them when Laura was eleven and her heart couldn't take seeing them in captivity anymore.

Freddy had granted his younger daughter's wish immediately. He wasn't attached to the zebras. He wasn't attached to much in his father's mansion on the coast. For some reason, he just continued doing things the way Gerald always had.

Freddy's anger was like his father's too, flaring up whenever control over his life slipped out of his grasp. Freddy may have never stormed out on his family the way his father had, but he'd let his jealousy and shame destroy his marriage all the same.

He didn't understand how it worked—why he couldn't stop himself from driving off the people he loved most in the world, how he always ended up right back here, in this big, empty castle.

He never said any of this aloud. Not to anyone. He wouldn't have known how to begin, or when to say it. But Margaret wasn't the only person writing letters that were never sent.

Years later, after he died, she'd read them. Most, heartbreakingly, were to her mother. But many were for Laura and for her.

The night he told Bernie and Margaret about the extortion, about the four million Laura was demanding in order to keep her grandfather's secrets, he was strangely calm. As if all that anger, covering up the pain and regret, had calcified into something stable rather than explosive. Steel. A blade.

They argued for a while about what to do. Bernie cried—a startling rarity, and just as startling was the way Margaret's father wrapped her mother in his arms, soothing her. It had been so long since she'd seen them touch each other like that. They were a true family in that moment, which only made Laura's absence more pronounced.

The problem with determining what to do was, none of them *knew* Gerald Ives's secrets or how much they were worth. Only Laura did. Bernie was inclined to give her the money on the chance Laura might actually need it, that it might soften her stance concerning the family. Freddy was inclined to refuse. "She won't be able to prove anything she says," he reasoned, "and if we pay them once, they'll keep asking for more."

"Then we give them more," Margaret said. "Who cares? If it brings Laura back . . ."

"How would it bring her back?" Freddy said. Rhetorically, Margaret figured, but she had an answer ready.

"We'll give it to her," she said. "But only to *her*. In person."

Bernie straightened up at that.

"There's no reason to think she'll agree to that," Freddy reasoned. "Those weren't her terms."

"Then we negotiate new ones," Margaret insisted. "We have to try."

It took five days to set the plans, all orchestrated over quick phone calls made from public telephones by a woman who *wasn't* Laura and gave them no name. All the usual stipulations you saw in the movies were made: no police, come alone, tell no one, no funny business.

The calls came straight to the Ives family home, fielded by Freddy at all hours of the day and night. But after the meeting was set, the three of them agreed it should be Margaret who went. She told Cosmo she was going to see her sister but didn't dare give him the details, beyond that Laura had agreed to meet.

Any more information than that and they would've found themselves in their second real fight. A fight without any purpose, since nothing Cosmo could possibly say would change Margaret's mind about this.

Darrin drove her to the diner, out in Palm Springs, with strict instructions to leave her there for exactly two hours. Whomever Freddy had spoken to on the phone was adamant that no one else from the Ives family—or representing it—could be present, or the deal was off, and whatever information Laura had would be released. Not that that mattered to Margaret, but it was important that Dr. David and whoever else *believe* it did, or she doubted she'd ever see her sister again.

The diner was grubby and mostly empty. The air inside was stiff and thick with cigarette smoke. Margaret took a seat with her back to the corner, where she'd have a clear view of the front door. A man in drab gray clothes sat in the corner exactly opposite her, and she couldn't tell whether he was watching her or not, but she decided it was wise to treat him as if he were, just in case.

The bells over the door rang three times, two customers coming and one going, before Laura finally walked in, and at first, Margaret's eyes grazed right over her the same way they had the strangers.

It took her several seconds after Laura made eye contact to recognize the emaciated woman in the sagging brown dress as her sister.

Her hair looked lank, her face pale and sickly. Worst of all, when she saw Margaret, something like *fear* flared through her eyes.

Fear.

She was *afraid*. Of her *sister*.

Margaret thought she might throw up. She willed herself to smile. Laura began walking toward her. She seemed to float almost. She lowered herself into the booth, and with a frail, rattling voice said, "Dad was supposed to come."

Margaret's heart split open. She'd had a plan. She'd meant to get answers. To talk sense into her sister, but all of that went out the window when she saw her. She noticed the man in the corner again, definitely watching them. They wouldn't have much time.

She dropped her own gaze to the tar-thick coffee she'd been nursing since she got there. Her voice broke as she murmured, "Tell me what you need, to get out."

When she chanced a glance up, that same fear had coalesced in her sister's peaked face. "I'm not leaving," she whispered.

"Do you want to?" Margaret asked, to no response. Laura's eyes were downcast, her hands trembling against the edge of the table. "Tell me what you need," Margaret said again, more slowly.

Her eyes darted sideways, paranoia wafting off her. But was it really paranoia if there *was* something to be afraid of? She whispered, "He'll never let me go."

"Tell me," Margaret said once more, low, quiet.

"He won't let me," Laura replied. "He says I belong to him."

An unprecedented rage knifed through Margaret. "And you think he loves you more than I do?" she hissed. "You think he'd do more to hurt you than I'd do to protect you?" She leaned forward, eager, trying to school her face into something like calm, willing the man in the corner to give them just another minute. "You *can't* think that," she whispered fiercely. "I know you, and you know me. I'll win. If it's him versus me, I'll win. I won't let him take you. I'm yours, and you're mine, and he can't have you."

Laura stared back at her, tears glossing over her eyes. Back in the corner, the man in gray coughed, and Laura blinked the emotion away, her face going blank.

So blank that the moment would haunt Margaret's dreams for the rest of her life, the moment she truly believed her sister had slipped away from her.

Then coolly, dispassionately, Laura said, "3488 Gates Road. September first. Eleven a.m."

That was all. The man in the corner had risen and tossed some bills on the table. At the sound of his boots approaching, Laura went rigid.

Margaret pulled the suitcase out from under the table and set it between them. The man appeared right at Laura's shoulder and reached for the suitcase before she could.

Margaret didn't recognize him. He was younger than Dr. David, with a buzzed head. She thought she spotted a gun under his jacket, but it might've been her imagination.

He slid the suitcase off the table and said calmly, "Go wait in the bathroom for ten minutes. If you come out before then, we'll know."

"And then what?" Margaret asked.

He looked from her to Laura with a smile that chilled Margaret's core. She nodded and stood, excusing herself to the tiny, dumpy bathroom in the back of the too-hot diner. She hadn't worn a watch, and there was no clock in the restroom. So she counted. Sixty seconds for a minute, ten times. And then, because she wasn't sure she'd counted correctly, she did it all again.

She went back to her table, finished her coffee, and waited for Darrin to loop back for her.

With the information Laura had given them, Freddy went to the police. The police took them to the FBI. The address was an old warehouse. They had no idea what they'd find there, or if Laura would have led them on a wild-goose chase, but the Ives family had enough power and money to be taken seriously.

There were so many ways it could go wrong. Laura could've lied. Laura could've told the truth, then admitted as much to whoever was controlling her. Laura could've gotten it wrong. She could've gotten it right, and whatever was meant to happen at 3488 Gates Road had been postponed or moved up, or canceled entirely.

Even if they found evidence of criminal activity, there was no guarantee they'd have enough to prosecute David. But none of that mattered as much as getting Laura away from him.

This was a means to do that.

At eleven a.m. on September 1, the FBI raided a warehouse registered to a man named Bill Jones. They arrived several minutes after a large shipment of illegally obtained guns.

Three members of the People's Moment were killed, along with one agent, in the cross fire that followed. Each of those people had a name. Each of them had loved ones they'd cut themselves off from, fear and anger and pain that the world would never know about.

They'd be mentioned in articles for months afterward, written about in books for years longer. But Laura—Laura would be at the center of everything.

She wasn't there to receive the shipment. She was back at the center, on the other side of town, with David and three other women he considered his wives.

Federal agents swarmed them too. But David and the women barricaded themselves in a bathroom. It took seven hours to get them out.

There was nothing illicit, in that room or on the center's grounds. Dr. David's name wasn't associated with the warehouse full of weapons and schematics, and in-depth plans for the assassination of several high-ranking government officials.

With Laura's testimony, it wouldn't matter. She could connect all the dots. The problem was, she was a wreck when they found her. Underweight, sleep deprived, strung out on a mix of stimulants and depressants.

"He kept Laura Ives and several other women in a highly suggestible state," a doctor would testify after David's lawyers tried to pin everything on Laura.

If Margaret thought Laura's state at the diner was bad, it was nothing compared to Laura in the aftermath of the raid.

She jumped easily, barely slept, got sick when she tried to eat—David had had her on a diet of mostly liquids and fruit, juices and sugary sodas he called her "medicine." They were supposed to cleanse her of something or another. She suffered from terrible nightmares and she didn't trust doctors, though logically she now *knew* David Ryan Atwood wasn't a real doctor.

Her mind was at war with itself. She didn't know what was real and what wasn't. He'd distorted her view of reality so thoroughly that she didn't trust her instincts.

For the first few weeks, she'd stayed back at the family home, rereading Lawrence's old journals again, their familiarity a balm to her. Most nights, Margaret and Cosmo stayed in the next room over, but when they couldn't, Bernie and Roy took their place.

Margaret wanted nothing but to hold her sister close and promise everything would be all right, but Laura had spent the last several years being told that her family was watching her, controlling her, and she still flinched when Margaret reached for her.

Margaret would pace the halls at night, listening to Laura whimpering through her bedroom door, until Cosmo woke up to find his wife missing and went to her. Sometimes they'd sit in the hall together until she drifted off in his lap.

The press was unending, right up until the trial and well beyond it. Laura's already destroyed self-esteem only got worse.

She felt stupid, she felt worthless. She felt angry, she felt hopeless. She felt trapped.

It was Cosmo's idea to bring Laura with them to Nashville, where the glare of the spotlight wouldn't be quite so harsh. Margaret had never loved him more than in that moment.

"Are you sure?" she asked him as they lay in her old bedroom together late one night.

He smoothed her hair away from her face and tipped his head up so he could kiss hers where it lay on his chest. "Your heart's broken without her, Peggy," he said, "and mine can't be whole until yours is."

The three of them left two days later, Bernie, Roy, and Freddy seeing them off at the airport with pained hugs and sturdy handshakes.

Margaret knew her parents' own hearts must be breaking to let Laura go again, but they did what they thought was best for her, and she'd never loved *them* more either.

When they got to the Nashville house, Margaret grabbed her bag and ran ahead to Laura's room to set things up. The tent from their childhood playroom was only half strung up by the time Laura and Cosmo made it upstairs, but seeing it half draped over Margaret's head, Laura let out a laugh that thawed something that had been frozen over in Margaret's heart for years.

"So you can sleep somewhere a little . . . cozier," she explained, because Laura had been sleeping in her own closet until then, the only place she felt safe in the House of Ives.

"Thank you." Laura reached out to take Margaret's hand, and she smiled. It was brief, and it was beautiful.

It took time. Months. But it started to feel as if they were making their way out of the woods. As if the sun were slowly rising after an interminable night.

Laura even began to see a doctor friend of Cosmo's regularly. Very, very gradually, she began to trust him.

She wasn't *well*, but she was better, and Margaret could be okay with that.

Cosmo toured, for *older* crowds and less money. Margaret stayed home with her sister. The media had largely stopped searching for weak points in their marriage, and instead devoted itself fully to questioning whether Cosmo had lost all of his bite and his talent when he signed a deal with the devil that was the Ives family—or if he'd just aged out of rock music.

The reviews for his new album were worse than biting—they were middling. Nothing about him scandalized the American public anymore. They were simply tired of him.

"I don't understand how they could go from loving me to hating me when I haven't changed one bit," he said one night, and Margaret's heart sank as she tried, from her own vast experience, to explain it.

"Because they never loved you," she said. "And they don't hate you now either. They don't know you, Cosmo."

It didn't make sense to him. He'd always been so thoroughly a part of the world that he saw these people—the writers, the photographers, the anchors, the reviewers—as peers, *acquaintances.*

It had felt good to him to believe that they loved him, and it tore him up to feel now that they hated him. You couldn't buy into one side without making room for the other.

"Just focus on us," Margaret said. "The people who know you. Who love you. Who see your heart."

He promised to try his best.

Laura's new doctor came every few weeks, usually on a Tuesday, to check in on how she'd been sleeping and eating, whether her anxiety had improved at all. But on one of these Tuesdays, after a week of exhaustion and nausea, Margaret asked him to examine her as well.

As she described her symptoms, he looked on, (badly) fighting a smile. When she'd finished, he asked a question that would change her life forever: "Any chance you're pregnant?"

This time—with Laura in her bedroom down the hall and Cosmo down on the patio sipping iced tea with his manager—Margaret felt only joy at the possibility.

So much joy.

A bright flame that burned so hot it chased away the blue that had coated her world all those years ago, as if all along it had been nothing but a flimsy shadow.

There was so much to be afraid of, so much to make a person hurt, but right then, with the people she loved most in the world safe and close, all she could see was the brilliant light.

She *hoped*.

For the first time in a long time, she hoped. And that was everything.

30

ON TUESDAY NIGHT, I fill in my notes from my session in the garden with Margaret, adding details from my outside research as I go.

Back in the sixties, when all of this happened, no one knew for sure what Laura had given the authorities to earn her own legal protections. Most people took it for granted that, after the group's arrest, she'd flipped and agreed to be a witness for the prosecution, a deal offered to her only because of her family's wealth and power.

I'd never read anywhere about the extortion, or the tense diner meeting. I wonder now why the lid had been kept so tightly shut on that. If it was the preference of the government or if the Iveses themselves had pushed to keep Laura's role in the raid a secret.

Based on everything Margaret's told me, the trial was hard on Laura. Even in the quick and loose courtroom sketches, she looks terrified. It wouldn't surprise me if she was too afraid of retribution to allow David Atwood to find out she'd done *more* than turn on him. She'd set him up.

I flip between web browsers until I get back to an old article from the *New York Times*. Front page. In the grainy photograph to the right of the article, Laura walks with her head down out of the courtroom, surrounded by lawyers and bodyguards. Several paces behind her, I spot *half* of a face I didn't notice before. A man in a three-piece suit, with oversized glasses, turning to speak with someone else in the crowd. He's only partially visible, but it's enough to send a *zing* down my backbone.

I *recognize* him.

From more than one place. I click back to the browser where I was analyzing courtroom sketches. I scroll down, checking my hunch.

There, just like I thought.

A loosely scrawled cartoon version of the man in the suit. Round face, a gap between his teeth. The associated documents describe him as *Dr. Cecil Willoughby, testifying on the medical state of Laura Ives during her involvement in the People's Moment Plot.*

I'm shaking with adrenaline as I pull out my phone from my sleep-shorts pocket and flip to the picture Cecil Wainwright texted me.

I zoom in, close enough to get his long hair out of the frame.

Round face. A gap-toothed smile. The same man.

I feel almost dizzy as *another* wave of déjà vu hits me. Because I'm fairly certain this isn't the only time I've seen Dr. Willoughby in the news.

In a new window, I pull up the infamous press conference video, the one filmed outside the hospital two hours after the accident, announcing the death of Cosmo Sinclair.

There he is again, clad in a white coat, his hair short and slicked neatly down.

Dr. Cecil Willoughby.

Captain Cecil Wainwright.

The guy who owns Fish Bowl. The one who throws himself yearly not-birthday parties and never leaves home without a bucket hat.

The one who's been *incredibly interested* in the presence of not one but *two* writers on Little Crescent Island.

With shaking hands, I text Hayden: Holy shit.

I know, he says. I'm coming over.

• • •

I SCOOP COFFEE into a fresh filter. "What does this mean?"

"I still don't know," Hayden replies, leaning against the counter. He braces his hands on it, on either side of his hips, and a tiny sliver of his stomach shows when his shirt rides up.

I pull myself back to the task at hand. "I mean, it's too big of a coincidence, right?" I fill the pot at the sink. "There's no way this doctor *and* Margaret end up in the same place, both using different names, and don't know about each other." He opens his mouth to respond, but I get there first: "If you don't want to talk about this—"

"I do," he says. "Anything I say, you'd get to anyway. It's faster if we just do this together."

I nod, chest warming at the thought, and pour the water into the coffee maker's tank, then drop the pot on the warmer and hit BREW. "I mean, theoretically, is it *possible* she doesn't know he's here? Or vice versa?"

"Sure," Hayden says. "Anything's possible. But it still feels like we're being *played* here somehow, and I can't figure out *how* or *why*."

I frown. "Same." I want to trust Margaret—I mean, I keep asking her to trust *me*, so I should be giving her the benefit of the doubt—but something's strange about this. "She's never mentioned Cecil to me. I mean, she talked about the doctor who testified at the Atwood trial, but she didn't use his name, and she's definitely never suggested she has *friends* on the island. As far as I know, it's just her and Jodi, in that house, all day, every day. And lately Jodi hasn't even been there."

"Same for me," he says.

We fall into silence while the coffee burbles. Then I pour each of us a mug. "Have you asked her about it?" I say. "About him, I mean?"

Hayden shakes his head and sets his mug on the counter. "I didn't want to press her if there's some explanation that she's working up to. But like I said, something's been off about this job since the beginning."

His head cocks, his lips parting.

"Just to say it again," I chime in, "there's no pressure to tell me anything."

"No, it's not that," he says. "It's just... you know when someone's lying to you, right? Or when they *think* they're telling you the truth, but there's more to it?"

"Sometimes, yeah." And then after a second of thought: "A lot of times."

"It's just that feeling. All day, every day. Even when she's telling me things that are *verifiably true*. And for someone who's gone so far out of her way to concoct this whole ridiculous scenario," he says, "she's weirdly reticent actually talking about herself."

"She's *quiet* during your sessions?" I say, shocked.

He snorts. "No. Never quiet. Just... evasive. She's fine to talk about books and movies and recipes and the fucking weather, but she's so guarded about the rest. Sometimes she cancels last minute even though, ostensibly, she doesn't go anywhere."

An idea clangs through me, something we already visited once long ago. "Maybe she really is sick. Maybe Cecil's here because he's a doctor, someone she trusts. And he's taking care of her." When I'd *asked* her *why now*, the only answer she'd given me was *If not now, when?*

"Why keep that from us though?" Hayden asks. "It's not uncommon for people to decide to do things like this right at the end of their lives. I mean, three-quarters of every meeting I've taken since I wrote about Len is with some aging celebrity who sees the end coming and wants a chance to tell their story. We've signed NDAs. If she's sick, why not tell us?"

"Because people aren't always logical or practical," I say. I think back to being a teenager, to Audrey and me finally going to public school, all of her surgeries safely ensconced in the past.

We could've shut up some of the bullies if they knew what my sister had been through—*why* we'd been homeschooled and isolated up to that point. But Audrey was adamant no one know. "Would you mind if I ask her outright?"

"What, if she's sick?" Hayden says.

I shake my head. "About Cecil."

He grimaces. "It's up to you, but . . ."

"But?"

He sighs, rakes a hand through his dark hair. "I don't know. It's possible she won't take it well. We're so close to the end of this. If you want this job—"

"I want this job because I want to tell her story," I say. "But if she can't be honest with us, there *is* no job."

"Okay." He nods. "So we ask her."

"We ask her," I agree.

I hold my hand out as if to shake on it, as if it's a deal. As soon as he clasps it, though, I yank him close, wind my arms around his neck, and kiss him. His hands slide back along the counter on either side of me, his chest pressing into mine as he deepens the kiss.

"You taste like coffee," I whisper.

"So do you," he says.

"Yes, but I *always* taste like coffee," I point out.

He slides my shorts down. "Maybe I wanted to taste like you." He kneels in front of me, work forgotten, everything forgotten except that thing that we're not saying. That we love each other. That when he looks right at me, the world stops turning.

• • •

ON WEDNESDAY NIGHT, I meet Hayden at his hotel room at the Grande Lucia.

He opens the door before I've even knocked. On the table just inside sit a pizza box and a salad from the place right behind Little Croissant.

There's a heaviness in the air, and I know we can both feel it: the hotel walls closing in on us, the sand pouring through the hourglass, the back half of the book thinning with every turned page. His balcony drapes are drawn to one side, the door open and the ocean beyond painted purple, pink, and blue by the setting sun. Even this feels like a reminder that our days, our hours left together in this bubble, are numbered.

Hayden snatches the remote and turns off the muted TV before facing me, our hands linking together. He kisses my forehead once, then draws back to gaze at me through the half-light of the bedside lamp. "Do you want to know what she said about Cecil?" he asks me.

My gut clenches. I know he'd tell me, and I'm dying to hear, but with how little time we have left and how many rules we've already broken, this feels like a line I can avoid crossing.

I'll ask her myself tomorrow.

"Tonight, I want it to just be us." No thinking about the job, or about our lives on opposite sides of the country, or how heartbroken I might be come Saturday night.

"Just us," he agrees softly, lifting my hands to kiss the tips of my fingers. When our lips next meet, every ounce of my restraint cracks. I reach for the buttons on his shirt. He slips mine over my head and lifts me against him, my thighs wrapping around his bare waist, his heart and mine pounding in sync. He carries me to his bed and we tumble onto it, the rest of our outer layers coming off as we bury ourselves in the blankets, the soft smell of almond everywhere and still not enough. I press my nose against his neck and inhale, his low laugh vibrating through me.

He skims my underwear down my legs, leaving trails of goose bumps behind, and I push his briefs down too. We tangle together, a knot of heat and electricity. "Is this okay?" I whisper, my hands on his jaw, his on my hip bones as he settles his weight on top of me.

"It's just us tonight," he whispers.

My heart thrills, but I still ask, "Is that a yes?"

He kisses me more deeply as his hand wanders over to his wallet on the bedside table. "Yes," he says, pulling a condom out and kissing me once more before sitting back on his heels.

"Thank god," I breathe, watching him work the condom on. I pull him back to me hungrily, my whole body tightening in anticipation of the moment he presses against me, then relaxing to make room for him as he pushes into me with a rough groan.

"Oh, god," I cry out, a little *too* loud, but I've never been great at playing it cool, and it feels so good to finally have him. He shivers over me, holding still until I urge him closer, gradually taking more of him, little sparks flying across the corners of my vision from the sensation. He bucks his hips once, a test, and I cry out again.

"You okay?" he asks, cupping my jaw in one hand.

"I'm amazing," I breathe.

"You are," he replies. My laugh is cut short when he moves again. The pleasure whites everything else out. I arch up under him, and his hands scrape down to my thighs, gripping hard as he thrusts into me. "I want you on top of me," he says.

We roll together until I am. I sit up on my knees, then slowly lower myself onto him, my eyes falling closed at the hot slide of our bodies together. He folds me over him, kissing me deep, his tongue stroking into me as I lift myself slowly and sink back down.

"God, Alice." He grips my waist, hard enough that his nails will likely leave marks but still not hard enough. No part of him could ever be deep enough in my heart or body to satisfy me.

I grind myself against him; knot my hands into his dark, overgrown hair; bite down on the side of his neck to keep from crying when he grabs my ass and pulls me even harder against him. He catches my breast in his mouth, and everything in me tightens. I sit back, gasping for breath before I come undone.

"Sit up," I tell him, pulling on his shoulder, and he does, his back pressed to the headboard. I shuffle closer, his hands gently guiding me onto him in this new position.

"Alice," he hisses against my throat as I move with him, slowly now, almost delirious. A small noise rises in my throat, a *hm?* that turns into something more like a purr.

"I can't get enough of you," he whispers, his lips moving in a light, teasing pattern along my neck. "I thought I'd been in love before, but this is different."

"I know," I whisper back, still moving in that languid rise and fall, the need in me mounting with every glide, my voice thin and breathless. "I feel like you're mine. Like you're mine in a way no one else ever has been."

"I want you to be mine," he murmurs, gripping me harder. We move faster.

I try to tell him *I am*, to explain to him that all the things we don't know about each other, all the time we haven't spent together, couldn't possibly weigh more than this feeling in my bones, the joy of being close to him.

But I can't. The feeling swells within me, too big for words.

We flip over again, him stretched out on top of me, one of his hands holding both of my wrists above my head.

"I love you," he tells me again, and I try to say it back, but the only thing I can get out is his name, again and again, like I'm begging him for something. Begging for *him*.

And then his name breaks into a wordless cry as I bow up under him, the waves of sensation pummeling me, his hiss of my name my only tether through the dark wash of pleasure.

He breaks too, and I tighten my thighs around him, holding him to me as we crest. I have no idea if it goes on for seconds or for hours, that feeling. But finally it draws back, and he slides clear of me and drops beside me onto the bed, pulling me into a curl against his sweat-slicked body.

We lay there, catching our breath in a heap, the blankets kicked off and his arm a loose coil around me, so long that we start to drift off.

"Will you stay?" he murmurs sleepily.

"We haven't even eaten dinner," I tease. "You can't kick me out yet."

"Tonight, I mean," he says.

"If you want me to," I say.

"I want you to," he says. "I always want you here."

"Here?" I sit up and straddle him again. "Or here?"

He smiles. "There's good for me." He pulls me back down to him.

Dinner will have to wait.

31

EARLY IN THE morning, I stop by the house for a hot shower and a change of clothes. With my hair still wet, I swing by Little Croissant and grab coffee for both myself and Margaret, along with a couple of pistachio croissants.

Am I trying to butter Margaret up? Maybe. But I'm also buttering myself up. I'm going to need a lot of sugar and caffeine to get through today.

I'm not just tired; I'm *anxious*. To ask Margaret about Cecil, and about how asking might affect my chances of landing the job.

I stifle another yawn as I park in front of her house, and my phone vibrates in the cup holder.

> Out on the patio, come on through.

I let myself through the unlocked front door and wind through the house to the sliding back doors. Margaret sits at one of her little garden tables under an open umbrella, with a heavily creased novel balanced face down on the arm of her chair.

"Brought you something." I set her croissant and coffee in front of her.

"Oh, you're an angel," she says.

"Hardly." I sit in the chair across from hers. "It's just our last real session before the pitch, so I figured we'd better celebrate while we have the chance." One of her eyebrows goes up. "I mean, I'm either going to be on a plane back to California *or* we're going to be *really* getting down to business."

"And what have these last few weeks been?" she says, looking suddenly as exhausted as I feel. "Easy peasy?"

I take a long sip of coffee. "An overview. Next I'd take what we've done so far and divide it into categories, then dig deeper into everything, one category at a time."

"You'll have time to sell me on all this later, you know," she reminds me.

"I'm not selling you on it," I say. "If anything, I guess I'm warning you. If this has been hard for you already . . ."

"Then it's only going to get harder," she guesses.

"There will be things you don't want to talk about," I say. "Things that might be important for the rest of the book. If you pull one loose thread out, sometimes things unravel."

She eyes me over the lip of her coffee. "You let me worry about that."

"Of course," I say. "Just trying to be transparent."

Over her shoulder, in the kitchen window, I see a flash of movement. "Is someone here?"

"Jodi," she says.

"She's back?" I say, surprised.

"Until I piss her off again, I suppose," she says.

All my unanswered questions bubble to the surface. "You know, you've never told me what your relationship to Jodi is."

She stares at me, unblinking, almost a challenge.

I can't help it: I laugh. "Is it a secret?"

"It's part of the story," she says. "Which we may or may not get to, depending how today goes."

"We'll get to it," I promise, shifting to the edge of my seat as a breeze lifts my hair off my neck, the smell of my sunscreen drifting toward my nose. "But first I wanted to ask you about something else."

She sighs, like this notion fatigues her, but she waves a hand, gesturing for me to go on.

"Do you know anyone else on the island?"

Her head tilts. "What do you mean?"

I shake my head. "Just what I said. Do you know anyone here, other than Jodi?"

"Well, there's the gal who does my massages," she answers.

"Right," I say. "Other than Jodi and her."

She opens her mouth, a smile blooming on her lips, and I just *know* where this is going.

"And me and Hayden," I add.

She presses her lips closed. "Where is this coming from?"

"You're not going to answer the question?" I say, intrigued by her evasiveness.

"Are you going to answer mine?" she throws back.

"Cecil," I say. "Wainwright. Or Cecil Willoughby."

The look of shock that flares across her face quickly hardens into something like irritation, maybe even anger. "You know, you're not the first person to bring him up to me this week. Strange coincidence."

When I don't reply immediately, she goes on, "Do I need to remind you that you've signed an NDA?"

I balk. What exactly is she implying here? That Hayden and I have been sharing information, or that she's angry enough about it that she might sue me?

"Hayden found a lead," I say. "I stumbled on his lead and chased it down myself." He didn't tell me anything, really. And even if he did, I'm not sure why it should matter so much.

This is why she brought us here, isn't it? To tell her story. Cecil's a part of that.

After a second, Margaret's expression melts back into exhaustion. "I suppose I should've known you'd find him."

Actually, I can't help but feel like *Cecil* found *me*.

I think back to the email that brought me here. The address—LindaTakesBackHerLifeAt53—didn't seem particularly Cecil-ish, but maybe that was intentional. Maybe he's the person who brought me here.

But if so, why?

The mystery of it makes me feel like there's electricity firing all through my body, usually dormant synapses searching for connections I've missed. It's like being a treasure hunter, this part of a job. It's addictive, really.

"What is your old family doctor doing here with you, Margaret?" I ask.

She stares back, face steely.

"Are you . . ." I swallow hard. "Are you sick?"

Her brows just barely jump. "No. No more than the average old lady who spent her life smoking cigarettes and drinking martinis."

"Then what's going on?" I ask.

"Get out your tape recorder," she says. "I'll tell you the rest of the story."

The Story

THEIR VERSION: America's "Royal Baby" on the way?

• • •

HER VERSION: Margaret wasn't pregnant.

The symptoms she'd been experiencing, the weight gain, it had all been a coincidence. No sooner had they learned this than the tabloids noticed her physical change and started to speculate on whether the Tabloid Princess had "let herself go" or if she was expecting an heir to the Ives-Sinclair dynasty. If soon she'd be promoted to *queen*.

It was crushing. Not just because now she could imagine nothing so wonderful as having a baby with Cosmo, but because it opened her eyes to what that would mean, for all of them.

Just the *suggestion* of fatherhood briefly shot Cosmo right back to a pedestal, to public adoration. Margaret even seemed forgiven for her connection to the nastiness that unfolded around David Ryan Atwood.

But none of it was real. And now Cosmo knew that too. The love of strangers was mercurial. You did nothing to earn it and so *could* do nothing to prevent it from vanishing, or souring into hatred.

They tried their best to shut it out and focus on their future, on the baby they were both dreaming of. But every time they left the house, they were swarmed, people blocking the front of their car, cameras pressed right up to every window. Every week, their security team would catch someone digging through their trash, in search of something worthy of print. They started keeping their drapes shut tight all day long, their windows and doors bolted. They spoke in murmurs, as if ears were pressed against the walls.

It was as if, one night, Margaret and Cosmo entered their Nashville home from one world, and in the morning, they emerged into an entirely different one, where everything and everyone was a threat.

Deep down, she knew *she* was the one who'd changed: She kept thinking about what it would be like to carry a baby through this crowd, to see him written about by strangers, as if they knew him, as if he belonged to them.

She no longer saw Laura's panic from the point of view of an outside observer. She *felt* it, and she agreed when her sister's doctor suggested Laura spend some time away, where she could be anonymous, be *herself*, while they waited for the media frenzy to die down.

Margaret's father offered a long-forgotten family chalet in Switzerland to his younger daughter, the very same place where their grandfather had once taken his mistress Nina Gill to deliver their daughter in secret.

"I've always wanted to see Switzerland," Laura said when Margaret told her, and with a long, tearful hug between the sisters, it was settled.

Margaret had expected Laura's anxieties, her trauma, to keep her from allowing a doctor to chaperone her to Europe and help her settle in, but the two of them had grown so close, more like friends really, and she trusted him. Just as importantly, Margaret trusted him.

So they left. The sisters wrote to each other daily, almost as if they were just sending each other diary entries.

I hate this, Margaret once wrote. *I worry about you when you're far away.*

The response she received read, *I will never be far from you. Even from the far side of the world, my heart is with you and I feel yours with me. But it's time you save your worries for your baby.*

Margaret still wasn't pregnant, but when Laura said it, Margaret felt like her heart might burst with love for this nonexistent person.

The longer they tried for a pregnancy, the more she ached for a child.

For the first time, she and Cosmo fought regularly. Margaret was more anxious than usual, so she didn't sleep well. And Cosmo was restless. He'd never been in one place so long. He'd go out without her when he couldn't make Margaret go with him, but then get angry about paparazzi invading his space, which only ever escalated things.

All Margaret ever really wanted to do was stay home, but he thought that was "letting them win."

"We're allowed to exist outside of this house, Peggy," he told her once.

"It's not about whether we're allowed," she tried to reason with him. "Why bother if we're just going to be miserable?"

The fight went out of him and all that was left in his face was sorrow. "We can't do this," he whispered hoarsely.

"Cosmo . . . what are you—"

"A baby," he rasped. "We can't bring a child into this. Our baby deserves to run around on playgrounds and climb trees and make friends and do all the things kids do."

Her heart broke, and at the same time, she was relieved. Because she had known it too, had been too afraid to say it, had been waiting for it to hit him.

And now it had.

What a child would deserve and what the world was were two very different things.

He began to cry first. He was an emotional man, but she'd never seen him sob like that, so unguarded. She drew him into her arms and held him as he cried, his forehead bowed and pressed into the side of her neck.

"We'll get through this," she promised him in whispers, running her hands through his pale hair. *Our love can be enough*, she thought but didn't say, as if that might jinx it.

The accident happened on a Tuesday.

Margaret would never forget that.

The day had started normally, but around noon, a wave of nausea sent Margaret running to the bathroom. An hour later, she felt a sudden pain in her abdomen. Twenty minutes after that, she developed a fever, and the pain worsened to the point that she couldn't stand. She crumpled to the floor, clutching her stomach, and screamed for Cosmo.

He came running and, at the sight of her curled up on the rug, dropped to his knees beside her, trying to find the source of her agony.

"Call a doctor," she hissed, and he tried to, but their trusted physician, the one who'd once escorted Laura to Europe, wasn't home. He was on a shift at the hospital. So Cosmo scooped Margaret up, already shouting orders toward their driver, and carried her downstairs. Out front, he loaded her into the back seat and slid in after her, holding her gingerly as they flew down the driveway.

The driver almost mowed down several of the journalists waiting at the bottom of the hill before they dove out of his way. They careened onto the road toward the hospital, but they weren't alone.

Several cars shot out from the shoulder to chase them.

Margaret was crying. Cosmo was promising her everything would be okay, but he wasn't fooling anyone. He was terrified; he was furious.

Cars pulled up on either side of them, cameras dangling out windows. They were approaching a yellow light.

The driver floored it, the other cars keeping pace.

At the very last second, the one on their left slammed its brakes and skidded to a stop as Cosmo's car sailed straight through the intersection.

One-third of the way.

Half.

Two-thirds.

And then the truck barreled into them, and everything went dark.

32

"I WOKE UP in an ambulance," Margaret says. "But it was a short trip. We were only two blocks from the hospital when it happened."

Her voice barely wavers. I wonder how many thousands of times she's played out this monologue in her head, maybe even practiced saying it aloud. I've read hundreds of accounts myself, but hearing it from her lips is different. Excruciating. I've known where all of this was heading from the beginning, but the closer I've gotten to Margaret, the more I've dreaded today.

"I kept trying to ask for Cosmo," she rasps. "No one would tell me where he was.

"They got me into the ER, but I was more or less fine. Scraped and bruised, but that's it. I remember begging them to call Laura. For some reason, I was sure she could fix everything. I don't know why.

"Dr. Willoughby met me there," she says. "Cecil had become a close friend of ours since he testified at the People's Moment trial. He was the only one Cosmo trusted to take me to when he found me that day, in pain.

"He told me Cosmo was in surgery. He had a collapsed lung and swelling on his brain. All I had was a case of appendicitis. That was what had caused the fever and the pain. They put me under for the operation, and when I woke up . . ." Finally, a crack in her voice. "My parents were in the hospital room, and Cecil was too, but . . ."

Her eyes glaze over. She looks distant. Less like she's deep in the memory and more like she's holding it back, behind a pane of glass, where it can't hurt her.

"My husband was already gone." Her watery eyes cut to me. "He was the love of my life and all we had was four years. My parents couldn't bear to tell me. So Cecil did."

"What about Laura?" I can barely get the words out.

"She wasn't there." Her voice wobbles, a mix of anger and heartbreak. "My sister didn't come."

The silence extends between us for several seconds, then she swallows hard and says, "She was too afraid. To be back in the thick of everything. And I couldn't forgive her for it. So we stopped speaking."

"For how long?"

She swallows but doesn't answer.

Tears prick my eyes. In a whisper, I ask, "Do you regret it?"

She laughs harshly. "Of course I fucking regret it. I regret all of it. I regret almost every decision I ever made in my life and how they all got me here. And I'm still angry with her too. But even when I was a ball of rage, I never stopped hoping . . . I hoped . . ." She shuts her eyes, one tear loosing from her dark lashes to curve down her cheek. "I hoped she was happy."

She takes a moment to pull herself together, like she has so many times before, squaring her shoulders and lifting her chin. "My father had paid for us to have complete privacy to mourn. For four days, people gathered outside the hospital to pray for my husband, not knowing he was already gone. When the time came, we called a press conference and Cecil broke the news while we left through a side door. My parents tried to convince me to come back to California, but all that was left of Cosmo—it was all in our home. I couldn't leave it behind.

"My mother stayed with me in Nashville for several weeks. Every time we left, there was the press, without any qualms about how their presence might make me feel. They were kinder at first, would bring trinkets and bouquets and teddy bears, gifts and apologies that meant nothing. They didn't know him. They couldn't miss him. I did. Every moment of every day.

"I wanted to punish them, honestly, but I couldn't figure out any way to do it. The best I could come up with was giving them more spectacle, feeding their unquenchable thirst for drama. They wanted a madwoman, and that's what I was. I ripped up our gardens and left all the flowers in trash cans at the gate. I left the house barefoot, and chopped off my hair with a pair of kitchen scissors. I wore the same dress I'd worn to our wedding to the burial, and I relished every headline about my deranged behavior, because at least it seemed like proof that I had *some* control over who they said I was. After a couple of weeks, that stopped soothing the ache and all I wanted was to be alone. To feel my pain completely, without interruption. I sent my mother home, paid the staff, and let them go. Then I shut myself away. For two years, the only person I saw with any kind of regularity was Cecil.

"He'd come to check in every week or so that first year. After that, he went back to Switzerland, to Laura. He'd call to check in on me sometimes. I wondered if it was at my sister's request, but I never asked. He was my last connection to her, and deep down, I think I wanted to hold on to that.

"Two years after my husband's death, my father urged me to move back to the House of Ives. I obliged but I couldn't stand to be in the wing of the house where Laura and I had grown up together, and where Cosmo and I had spent so many nights, so instead I settled into Gerald's old rooms.

"When my parents told me that Cecil and Laura were getting married, I almost broke and called her. They'd fallen in love slowly, over years of friendship. His kindness and patience were exactly what my sister needed. But any happiness I felt for her always turned into more pain after a minute or two. My parents and Roy went overseas to witness the private ceremony, in their home. I stayed behind, alone in my empty mansion.

"The worst part was the day I found out my sister had given birth to a baby girl. And I'd missed it. The pregnancy, the delivery, the whole thing."

Surprise whizzes through me like a dozen bottle rockets. "She had a daughter? You're not the last Ives?"

"I am," she says firmly. "When I go, the name goes with me. Laura's made sure of that, in every way she could. She and Cecil changed their surnames, and they raised their daughter in Europe, far away from us. Away from the Cosmo fans and the media circus. They stayed in touch with my parents, but at a distance. It was the only safe way. Sometimes, when my mother and Roy came for dinner, she'd ask when I was going to forgive my sister, but the truth was, it wasn't a lack of forgiveness keeping me away anymore."

I shake my head, not understanding. "Then *what*?"

She thinks for a minute. Then she heaves herself out of her chair. "Come with me, Alice."

I follow her inside and down the hallway, to a shut door. She opens it to reveal a sparse office, with a desk, a computer, two chairs, and a thriving potted plant. In the corner, she opens the closet door, then steps back, gesturing toward a brown box on the top shelf.

"Oh. Sure." I step forward and pull it down, handing it over. She places it on the desk and, with shaking hands, lifts the lid off.

"What is it?" I ask.

She waves toward it, inviting me to look. Nervously, I lean over, without one single guess at what I'll find.

"Go on," she says.

I carefully lift the stack of yellowed newspaper clippings out of the box and begin to skim them. All of them about her, some from before Cosmo's death and some from after, but all of them damning.

THE IVES CURSE CLAIMS COSMO

"I BLAME PEG," COSMO'S CHILDHOOD FRIEND SAYS

THE LIES OF IVES: HOW PEG TRAPPED COSMO

There are dozens more. They call her Pushy Peggy and Me-Me-Me Margaret. They label her stuck up, sneaky, manipulative, catty. They accuse her of hating to share the spotlight with her husband. She's never photographed *leaving*, but instead *storming out*. She doesn't *wear* anything, but instead *shows it off*. They write about feuds with other beloved women in Hollywood, and in one especially sickening tabloid piece, an anonymous source says Cosmo was on the verge of leaving Margaret when he died. The headline reads: *If I Can't Have Him, No One Will.*

My stomach turns. I stuff them back into the box. "Margaret," I say gently. "You know all of this is bullshit, don't you?"

"Says who?" she replies evenly.

"*Stuck up? Manipulative?* Come on," I say. "These are all just old stereotypes about women. They might as well be calling you a Jezebel."

"*It's just a* story," she says bluntly, lowering herself into one of the chairs. "That's what I used to tell Cosmo. And I believed it. But after I lost him, and Laura . . . When you don't have the people who love you around, reminding you who you are, that story feels bigger and realer than anything else. You lose yourself inside the character with your name and face."

I want to reach out and touch her hand, or hug her, but I'm not sure she'd appreciate it.

I don't belong to you, I imagine her saying. And she's right. I'm just another person sitting here trying to collect her likeness and hammer it into something digestible for the masses.

"That's why I couldn't face my sister," she explains. "Because everything they said started to feel true. Like I was cursed. Like everything I touched was ruined. I was so damned ashamed. Laura hadn't come to see me after the accident because she knew she'd be in the blast zone. And as angry as I was with her for so, so many years, I couldn't stand the thought of taking the blast zone to her doorstep. So I stayed away. I spent my parents' twilight years with them. I buried my father, and then my stepfather, and then finally, several years later, my mother."

"And then, in 1985, I tried to disappear."

"Wait—you . . . *what*?" Nineteen eighty-five was *two decades* before she vanished.

"I booked a one-way ticket to London," she says. "It took about four days for coverage of *Cosmo's Widow Abroad* to make newsstands. From there, I flew to Miami. Same thing happened. After that, I made it two weeks in Providence, Rhode Island."

"Your *jet-setting* era?" I say in disbelief. Dove Franklin had thought she was just bored of mourning and thus burning through her money to pass the time. *I'd* thought those days were a sign of her healing.

"Ill-advised escape plan after escape plan," she confirms. "See, it was one thing when I was a socialite. But my husband, he was the stuff of legend. Following me around was the closest people could get to having a piece of him again, I guess. Eventually, I had to accept it was never going to end. So I went back to California and spent twenty more years in that house, locked away with my family's ghosts and their letters and their journals.

"Then one day, in spring of 2003, a woman shows up at my gate. Buzzes it again and again until I answer. Tells me she's my niece and she needs to talk to me.

"I tried to send her off, but she kept coming back. It's strange . . . she's a lot more like me than she is like Laura. Stubborn, obstinate. But Jodi's compassionate—just like my sister."

"*Jodi*," I breathe, the realization reverberating through me.

Margaret hardly seems to hear me. She goes on: "Eventually, I let her inside on the condition that once I heard her out, she'd leave me alone for good. She agreed. And then she told me that . . ." She pauses. "That my sister was sick."

She stops there, and I catch myself leaning forward, my breath held. "What'd you do?"

"I sent her away," she wheezes.

My heart twists, a rag having every last drop squeezed from it.

"I sent her away, and then, then I took all those journals and letters—Lawrence's and my father's and my own—and I put them in the grate, and I burned them. Like that might cut my ties to my family. Like it might finally make me into an island. Untouchable. Safe. Incapable of hurting anyone."

My heart cramps. Not just for all that lost history, those details gone up in smoke, but for the unbearable loneliness that now hangs around Margaret like a cloak.

"Jodi left a card behind, but I didn't touch it," she continues. "It had a phone number and her address scribbled on it. On some tiny island in Georgia. And I couldn't make myself burn it. The past? Sure. But some part of me, I suppose, kept holding on to the possibility of a future, no matter how hard I tried to stop. I'd just stare at that card on the console table every so often, until it was so thickly covered in dust I couldn't read it. But by then it was engraved in my memory."

I glance down at my notebook and damply ask, "So, that's why you wanted to disappear? Because if Margaret Ives stopped existing . . . you could have your sister back?"

"I already told you." Her knees creak as she stands. "The only person who gets that story is the one who writes this book."

Just like that, we're finished, and I have more questions than ever.

• • •

I DON'T SEE Hayden Thursday night. He's shut up in his hotel room finishing his proposal for tomorrow, and I've got my own to think about for Saturday.

As I drive home from Margaret's house, her story plays on a loop in my head. All those years alone, the foiled escape plans. *And Jodi.*

The way she and Margaret bicker makes more sense now—it's got a distinctly *familial* flavor—but her absence lately seems a little stranger, given the context. I'm dying for the rest of the story, and if I'm going to earn the right to hear it, I need sustenance, because I've got a long night of researching and writing ahead of me.

I stop by the grocery store and grab a frozen pizza for dinner, along with a jug of green tea, some Marcona almonds, a premade salad, and a bar of dark chocolate.

I drop the snacks and tea outside Hayden's hotel room, then scurry back to my car, texting him as I go: Something's at your door.

I get into my car and watch his door open, see him step out—*shirtless*, it should be said—look left and right, then grab the bags and head inside, head bowed over his phone.

This is sweet, he says, but I was hoping it was you.

We wouldn't have gotten anything done, I reply.

We would've made good use of the time, he counters.

Tomorrow, I tell him, and drive back to the bungalow in the woods.

At the kitchen table, I pour myself a glass of wine and listen to the printer in the other room churning out page after page of my notes while I sip. I always work better with something physical in front of me.

When the printer has finished, I carry the stack of pages back to the kitchen and sit, pen in hand, colorful highlighters at my elbow, to get to work. It's not like I'm starting from scratch. I have a pretty good idea of how I want to handle the proposal itself already.

The big thing is the sample pages. I should've been working on them all along, but I wanted to choose the strongest part of the story, and to do that, I felt like I needed as complete of a picture as possible.

But what I've got is riddled with holes.

There's so *much* material but very little that's fully fleshed out. I'm second-guessing my process now, but it's too late to do anything differently.

I pull out the notes on a handful of my favorite anecdotes and set them aside. I highlight Margaret's word choice in places, draw question marks around the things that interest me.

Then I shove aside my impostor syndrome and start writing.

Aside from a quick break to heat up the pizza, and several trips to the bathroom once my bladder is already full to bursting, I do nothing but write, read, rewrite, and edit until four in the morning.

I didn't mean to stay up so late, but I've got multiple usable writing samples now that I can revisit in the morning. Scratch that: in the afternoon. It's morning already, and it's time for me to sleep.

I scrub my face and brush my teeth, then collapse into bed, shooting off a good luck text to Hayden.

He responds immediately, because of course he's somehow already awake: Sleep well.

And I do.

I dream I'm riding in a dark blue 1958 Spyder, the top down, Hayden in the seat beside me, our hands tangled up. The road curves back and forth along the cliffs, and the sun shines down on us. He lifts our hands to kiss the back of mine, his pale brown eyes warm on me.

Alice all the time, he murmurs, and then I wake up.

• • •

HAYDEN SHOWS UP at my door on Friday night with champagne in hand.

"Shouldn't I be the one giving that to *you*?" I say. "You're the one who did his pitch today."

He kisses my cheek as I take the bottle from him. "You can bring the champagne tomorrow," he promises, following me inside.

I pour us each a glass, and we clink them together and drink. The light sweetness fizzes down my throat, my stomach warming immediately.

"How did it go?" I ask him.

He lifts one shoulder. "It went."

"That's all I get?" I ask.

He puts his glass on the counter and takes my waist in his hands, drawing me to stand right in front of him. "How's it been going here?" he asks.

"Okay," I say, then amend my answer. "Good, I think. I feel like I've done everything I can at this point, so it's either enough or it's not."

"It'll be enough," he says, smiling faintly.

I roll my eyes, but the truth is, his vote of confidence glides down between my ribs, warmer, fizzier, and more delicious than champagne. I lock my arms behind his neck. "You know what I think sounds nice?"

"I can guess," he teases, voice low.

I smile. "A walk."

He gives one hoarse laugh. "A walk," he says, "sounds perfect."

We wander along the trail for a while, then stop to have a drink on the patio at Rum Room. One drink turns into two, and then we need dinner to soak up the alcohol. We order every appetizer on the menu and share them between us.

By the time we're trekking home, the moon is high and silvery. This time, when we get to the place where the path runs behind my rental house and he kisses me—like he did that first time—neither of us pulls away. We crash into each other, hands greedy for bare skin and hair, tongues and teeth and lips eager.

I try to tell myself that no matter what happens tomorrow, this thing between us won't change, but I can feel the panic thrumming through our bodies, the fear that we're racing against a ticking clock.

I pull back, catching my breath, our foreheads pressed against each other in the dark. "What if," I whisper, "we did it together?"

"Did what?" he hums, his thumb running up and down along the small of my back, beneath my shirt.

"The book," I say. "What if we did it together?"

He tenses in my arms.

"It was just an idea," I say, trying to talk myself out of taking his reaction personally. It's not *wrong* for him to have a preference for how he works. It doesn't mean anything about how he sees me . . . does it?

"No," he says, the word a heavy stone in the pit of my stomach.

"Okay," I say.

"No, I mean, I already asked her," he says. "A week ago, I asked if that was something she'd be open to. She's not."

"Why not?" I ask, my brow furrowing.

"I don't know," he says. "But it's okay. You deserve this job, all on your own."

"Stop being so nice," I say. "You're allowed to want it too."

"I do want it," he admits. "I just want other things more."

He kisses me again, slow and purposeful. A kiss that feels like a promise. And then I take him inside and try to find every way I can to make my own promises.

And I keep an existing one.

Every time I almost tell him I love him, I drag the words back into myself, hold them tight. One more night. One more night and then I can say it, the whole wonderful truth.

33

IN THE MORNING, I tiptoe past a sleeping Hayden and go to the kitchen. I drink water while my coffee brews, then drink coffee while I pack up my laptop and notes.

I put my things by the front door, brush my teeth, wash my face, and then creep back into the bedroom to get dressed.

Despite my being as quiet as I could manage, Hayden stirs awake while I'm pulling my shirt over my head. He slits one eye open at me and gives me a sleepy smile that, to the untrained eye, might appear to be a grimace. "Hey," he croaks.

My heart swells in my chest. "I was trying not to wake you."

"I should get up anyway," he says, pushing himself up, the blankets coiled suggestively around his bare waist. "C'mere."

I go sit beside him, and he pulls me in against his chest, kissing the top of my head.

"I like waking up next to you," he murmurs.

"What about my snoring?" I ask.

"I like that too," he says. "Like a white noise machine turned all the way up."

I chortle and, with some effort, peel myself away from him. "You're welcome to use it anytime you want."

I get up and grab a hair tie and some bobby pins off the dresser, using them to pin my short hair up off my neck. The air-conditioning is doing all it can, but it's *hot* today, I'd guess, based on the temperature of the bedroom alone.

"What's this?" I hear him ask, some of the sleep clearing from his voice.

I turn around and find him holding the small framed mosaic I bought from the gallery down by the beach.

"That," I say, crossing toward him and taking the mosaic from his hands, "is *Nicollet*."

"No, I know," he says. "I meant, I've never seen anyone spell it like that, other than my mom."

I stare blankly back at him, my hand—and with it, the mosaic—dropping to my side. "That's your mom's name?"

He nods. "Spelled just like that. Two *l*'s, and no *e* on the end."

A small wave of dizziness passes over me, followed by that buzzing sensation in the back of my head, the feeling that I'm approaching something important. "Is it a family name? Someone's maiden name, maybe?"

"I don't know," he says.

"You've never asked her?" Even if they're not super close, that doesn't seem like him, to have not sought out that information. Or, honestly, even have had it offered freely.

"She doesn't know where it came from," he says. "She was adopted, but she'd already been named. The agency told my grandparents it would be best for her if they kept it. That's why she was always so anxious about health stuff, you know? Because she doesn't have a family medical history or anything. I thought I'd told you that."

"You didn't." The floor sways under me as questions start burbling up through my mind. "You mentioned the health anxiety, but not the rest."

He sits up straighter, his brows knitting. "Are you okay?"

"I'm . . ."

I don't know where that sentence was going. *Am* I okay? Am I seeing connections where there are none? Journalism will do that to you sometimes—make you view the world as a puzzle to be solved.

His mother has the same name as an old hotel the Ives family owned. So what?

The same name as the little sister Lawrence left home to save, and the name given to Ruth Nicollet Allen, a secret Ives baby. Slightly more coincidental, but ultimately meaningless.

But then there's what Hayden told me, about how he's gotten here.

He didn't track Margaret down. She tracked *him* down.

I close my eyes to stop the room from spinning.

"What year was your mom born?" I ask.

His forehead wrinkles. "What?"

"Just—when was she born?" I say, flustered.

He laughs uneasily. "Nineteen sixty-seven. Now are you going to tell me what all this is about?" He starts to rise, alarm written across his face. "Alice, are you okay?"

"I just—that reminded me of something, and—" I step back from him.

My phone alarm goes off then, shrieking out its warning that I have to leave this second or risk being late to my last appointment with Margaret.

I break out of the trance, though my mind is still reeling, my body alternating between flaming hot and ice cold.

"I'm running late," I stammer, hurrying for the door.

"Alice?" he shouts after me.

"I'll call you when I'm done," I promise without looking back, my face on fire. I grab my bag by the door, realize I still have the mosaic in my hand, and stuff it in on top of my computer. And then I run.

• • •

I SIT IN my car on Margaret's private street, sorting furiously through my notes. I'm no longer worried about being late. When she sends me a text reminding me that we agreed on 9:00 a.m. and it's now 9:07, I ignore it.

She's lied to me enough. I'm not going inside until I'm ready. Until I'm sure she can't lie anymore.

I find my notes from the day I confronted her about the Nicollet's name, a name she'd intentionally tried to hide from me. She'd told me that the name was a reference to Lawrence's little sister, the reason he'd headed west and the thing he'd given up, and she'd admitted Ruth was Gerald's biological daughter, and all of that had felt like such a grand reveal, a secret I'd unearthed. But what if that wasn't even the secret she was trying to hide? What if it was a distraction?

I page through the transcript of our conversation, and there it is.

Whatever you tell me, it doesn't have to go beyond this room, I told her.

Even at the time, her response seemed strange.

This includes the boy . . . I have two NDAs. So whatever I tell you, you can't take it to him. You understand that, don't you?

Every time the nondisclosure agreement has come up, the person she's been most concerned about has been Hayden.

Not me blabbing to *People* magazine for a price. But sharing bits of information with the other writer in the running. As if we've been getting different stories all along.

Which leads me straight to Hayden's uncertainty about this job from the beginning, his suspicion that she was lying. With every word she said. Keeping something from him.

That she wanted to talk to him—but not about *herself*.

About anything else. About *him*.

Like she wanted to *know* him.

My mind is spinning. I can't tell if this is just some weird hangover mixed with years of constant coffee chugging, or if I've stumbled onto something.

Nineteen sixty-seven. His mother is named Nicollet and she was born in 1967. Less than a year after Cosmo's death.

Nineteen sixty-seven. When Margaret sent her mother back to Los Angeles, let all of her staff go, and shut herself away in her and Cosmo's Nashville home. For two years. Seeing no one except Cecil Willoughby, their trusted family doctor.

Something else pings in the back of my brain, and I'm paging furiously through my notes again, back to Nina Gill's secret pregnancy.

Nine months would've been too suspicious. They had to drag it out. And publicize it, when they were able.

Nina had spent two years in the Alps.

A part of me still won't believe it. I thrust the papers into the passenger seat and pull out the mosaic next.

Nicollet: The person you'd do anything for. The only one who could make you give it all up.

Five by five, with tiny pieces of warm-toned glass. Translucent reds and ambers, golds, fitted into a tight spiral like a miniature galaxy.

The longer I stare at it, the more the feeling grows in me.

The truth. I feel it there, bursting to escape its cage.

I stuff the mosaic into my bag and get out of the car.

I enter Margaret's house without knocking.

"*Finally,*" I hear her call from deep within the house. I don't reply, don't take my shoes off, just let my feet carry me to the living room as if I'm on a track.

Like maybe I *don't* have free will. Maybe I was always going to end up here, from the moment I was born, and there was never any stopping it.

She stands from her rattan chair when she sees me storm in, her brows shifting toward her hairline. "Alice? Are you all right? You don't look well. If you're sick—"

I thrust the mosaic at her. Her eyes waver toward it. Her lips press tight, her face otherwise impassive, but I can see the wheels turning behind her eyes, calculating what I might know, all the reasons I might hold this out to her like an accusation.

There's really only one.

Her eyes finally lift to mine. "What is this?" she breathes.

"You tell me," I say.

She stares back at me, her face stony, and for the first time, I see it. *The resemblance.* The whole world rocks.

"Is Hayden your grandson?" I ask.

Another beat of perfect silence. "Who else have you talked to about this?" she says. "Because I'll remind you—"

"I have a nondisclosure," I cut her off. "I'm aware."

Her lips press closed. She doesn't say anything else. She doesn't deny it either.

"You have a daughter," I say.

"No," she says quietly. And then, in a low murmur: "I *had* one. For nine months, while I carried her. And I knew there was no way she could live. Not as herself, not the way we wanted her to." Her voice shakes. "Our daughter was born, and I held her in my arms for five minutes. Five minutes, and that was all it took for me to be sure that

I couldn't keep her. That I loved her too much. So I watched her be carried out of the room, and Nicollet Ives stopped existing."

"Cecil helped you." I force the words past the knot in my throat: "He helped you hide your pregnancy after the accident. Delivered her. Orchestrated the adoption."

"He was the only other person who knew," she says weakly. "The one who'd tested me. We'd only found out a week earlier, and..." Her throat bobs. "Cosmo was an anxious wreck. I'd started spotting. I knew it probably wasn't anything, but he wanted to be sure."

"There was no appendicitis?" I ask.

She shakes her head, eyes welling. "I should've made him listen. But he was in such a panic. And then—on the road... the paparazzi... he was so angry and scared. *What were we thinking?* That's what he kept saying. We both understood right then what it would be like for her. She'd never belong to herself. Never. And then..." She chokes over a sob. "Then he was gone, and I knew. I had to save her. Like I couldn't save him. That's what we did, Cecil and I. We saved her."

My mind swirls, a drunken carousel of hurt, sorrow, confusion.

And in the middle of it all, a tall, still figure.

"Does he know?" I rasp. "Have you told Hayden why he's really here?" A new thought crashes into my mind, knocking everything even further off balance. "If the job was always his, why even bring me here?"

"He doesn't know," she croaks. "And it *wasn't* his. The job... it didn't exist."

I pinch the bridge of my nose. "The book—"

"There wasn't going to be a book." Her jaw muscles leap, an expression that's *so Hayden* it makes my chest feel like there's a crack spreading down it. "I just needed *time*."

"Time?" I demand feebly.

"To get to know him," she says. "To see if . . . if she was happy. If there was a chance I might . . . that she might forgive me someday."

"You were messing with me." It feels like my lungs are folding in half, my heart crushed between them.

She stares at me, saying nothing.

"*Why?*" My voice rattles as it gains volume. "Why bring me here? Why do *all* of this?"

"Because he wouldn't come otherwise!" she cries. "I'd tried to entice him to the island before, and he didn't reply. So I gave up. I was okay with it. But Jodi wouldn't let it go. She sent you that damn email—"

"*Jodi?*" I say. "Why?"

"Because she's a meddler!" she says. "Because she thinks she's doing her mother's bidding! She figured with another writer in the mix, she could make Hayden see this as legitimate, as . . . as a story worth fighting for."

I try to hold back the angry tears rising along my lashes. "You were using me."

"At first," she replies. "But this whole thing . . . Alice, you changed my mind. You made me feel like maybe I *could* share my story. I thought if I told Hayden the truth . . . if he accepted it . . . then maybe we could write the book after all. Nothing about him or his mother, of course. We'd protect their privacy. But the rest—everything that happened to Laura, everything I wish the world knew about my parents. My *husband*—" She shakes her head, eyes tight. "And then he came here yesterday and told me he didn't want the job."

My heart trips over a beat. "*What?*"

Her eyes open. She looks as distraught as I've ever seen her, like somehow *this*, out of everything she's been through, was the blow she couldn't take.

I sway on the spot, lean against the nearest wall. "He already turned it down?"

"I wouldn't tell him about Cecil," she says. "And then he said it didn't matter, because he'd already decided he wasn't the right person for the job. But the truth is, he disliked me. From the beginning. I could tell. Jodi doesn't want to hear it—keeps storming out every time I cancel one of these little chats—but it's been clear from the start. That boy wants nothing to do with me, even as a *subject*. Even as a *paycheck*."

"He doesn't *know* you!" I half shout. "How could he? You've lied to him every single day for a month."

"I never lied to him," she counters. "I only avoided certain things."

"You have to tell him the truth." My chest throbs from the betrayal, from the unfairness. "You can't keep this from him."

She shakes her head. "He doesn't want the truth from me. He doesn't want anything from me. And neither does his mother."

"You don't know that," I fire back.

"I *do*," she says.

"*How?*"

"Because I saw her!" she all but screams back.

For a second the house falls eerily quiet. Then she takes a step toward me, her voice shrinking to a plea. "I waited until she was eighteen, and then I found her. Through an investigator. She was living in Indiana, with this beautiful family, and I thought—I don't know what I thought. I tried to let it be enough that she was alive, that she seemed happy. But I couldn't stop thinking about her. I needed proof."

"Proof of *what*?" I demand.

"That I'd done the right thing," she says. "That when I gave her up, there really wasn't another option. That's why I started trying to disappear. To see if I could do it. If maybe I didn't have to . . ." Her voice becomes garbled as emotion sticks in her throat. "If maybe I didn't need to let her go. And every time the paparazzi caught me, I found just... just a tiny fucking kernel of comfort. Because it meant I did the right thing. And every year when her birthday passed and they still hadn't found out about her, it made it all worth it. It was the only reason I could sleep at night. The only thing keeping me going. I was okay, finally, being alone. Until Jodi showed up."

Her jaw muscles twitch. "But after I sent Jodi off, the thought of my sister never let me go again. I'd been a shut-in for years at that point, but suddenly I couldn't take it anymore. Being in that house filled with ghosts. Everyone I'd lost. Everyone my family had ever hurt. I sold off Ives Media and got rid of the money, donated nearly all of it, and still I felt like that house, all that history, was suffocating me. So one day I just went out. And I wandered around town for hours, and no one spoke to me. No one even looked at me. Not a soul.

"I went to the beach, and the same thing happened. I kept waiting for someone to recognize me, but I'd stopped dyeing my hair or wearing makeup, and more importantly, I was sixty-seven years old. At some point, while I'd been hiding, I'd crossed that age where women turn invisible. From ingenue to femme fatale to old crone."

She gives a shred of smile, but I don't return it. My emotions are all over the place—anger, disappointment, hurt, sadness—and the last month's worth of conversations are a swirling, chaotic mess. Everything Hayden's told me about his mother, about her depression and the anxieties and hurts she passed on to him, is colliding with Margaret's story, and I just need a minute to breathe. To make sense of all of it and figure out what to do next.

But she's on a roll now, her story pouring out of her. "At the end of that day, I got back in my car to drive home, and I just couldn't do it. Not again. I headed east instead. Drove as far as I could, then stopped at a motel. Paid in cash, so I wouldn't have to use my name. In the morning I kept driving. And eventually, I made it to the address on that little card Jodi left behind. On a small island in Georgia."

Her voice cracks. "We had six months together, my sister and I. We were both such different people since the last time we saw each other, and somehow, still, it was like no time had passed at all. We still belonged to each other. Belonged *with* each other. Six beautiful, terrible months, and then she was gone, but not until she'd made me promise to tell Nicollet the truth.

"I would've agreed to anything Laura asked at that point," she says roughly. "But I knew she was wrong about it. The best thing for Nicollet now is the same as back then. I put it off as long as I could, but Jodi never let me forget. Finally, she hired a detective, and it turned out she needn't have bothered." She shakes her head on a laugh as tough and coarse as sandpaper. "Could've found Nicollet with one little Google search. She'd married a small-town politician and found her way back under the microscope. A smaller microscope, sure, but just as cruel as any. How's that for an Ives curse? I gave up an entire lifetime with her, and it wasn't enough to keep her safe."

"It's not too late," I say, vehement. "The only thing keeping you from her now is you. You have to tell Hayden. He deserves to know the truth. So does his mother, and his brother."

"The truth?" She scoffs. "Haven't you been listening these past four weeks? The truth hasn't been the story that shapes the world for a long time. I'm no one to him and his family, and that's for the best. So no, I'm not going to tell him. *And you're not either.*"

The last sentence slices through me. The implication. The threat. The millions of dollars I'd owe this woman if I broke our agreement.

There's a desperate, almost ruthless gleam in her eyes.

Suddenly, my whole body is sweating and my heart jabs at my chest like a woodpecker's beak, clumsy and forceful.

Margaret takes a half step toward me. "Hayden doesn't want to do this book," she says, "but we still can, Alice. I'm sorry for dragging you down here under false pretenses. I'm sorry I wasn't the woman you thought I was, and that this didn't play out how you'd hoped. But I'll do what I can to help you now, how you helped me. We might not be able to tell the whole truth, but we can add to the story. Right some of the wrongs of the past. That's what you were after, isn't it? Finally telling that story your dad always wanted to know?"

White-hot pain lances through me. "I'm not doing that."

Her right brow hooks upward. "What, you think all those celebrity memoirs tell the whole truth? Everyone's got secrets, Alice."

"It's not about that." I step back from her. "This is about your life. Nicollet's life." I swallow a thorny knot. "*Hayden's* life. He deserves a choice in all of this."

"He had one," she says, her voice pitching upward, like she's begging me to understand. "He met me. He doesn't like me. I can't change who I am, and I'm not going to change him either. So what good does it do to bust open his whole life? What good does it do anyone?"

It's so eerily similar to what I said to Hayden when he pressed me about talking to my mom, and now, from the outside, I hear how hollow it rings.

Because I also see how bright and damp her eyes are, see the tension in her shoulders and the way her hands fist at her sides, her knuckles white.

And after years of knowing her as sunny smiles and bright clothes and open-mouthed laughs, I finally see the truth of her. Everything that she's inherited.

Lawrence's guilt over failing the people he loved, and Gerald's anger over the love that always remained out of his reach, and Freddy's fear of not being enough for the ones who mattered most.

The terror of what happens if you ask for something someone's not able to give you.

And it seems so asinine, because she doesn't have the love she longs for now anyway. She's lonely. This house is *bursting* with loneliness, and she's so used to hiding away in it that she won't even let herself imagine things being different.

"Telling him would only make things worse," she whimpers. "Jodi's already furious with me, but I thought at least *you* would understand."

"I understand the story you're telling," I choke out, the fire dying down inside me. "But the truth is, you're just scared." I turn to go.

"Alice," Margaret says. "If you leave now, there's no going back, so *think* about this."

I pause for just a second at the mouth of the hallway. She looks so small and frail it breaks my heart. "See?" I tell her. "Our choices do matter." And then I leave.

34

THE WHOLE DRIVE back to the bungalow, I'm fighting tears, trying to make some kind of plan and coming up against all the same walls every time.

I can't tell Hayden the truth.

I can't lie to him.

My phone is full of messages from my friends, checking how the pitch went, asking for updates. I silence it and drive to the beach. Don't even get out of my car, just sit there with the front bumper pressed up against a dune, sobbing.

I'm not even totally sure why I'm so emotional.

I'm sad about losing the job, sure.

I'm heartbroken for Margaret. For the decision she made, and the love behind it, and how all that love congealed into a hard shell around her, keeping everyone out.

And I'm devastated for Hayden. For me.

When I'm all cried out, I drive home. I leave my laptop bag in the car and go inside, immediately start packing my stuff, ignoring the crying jags that start and stop at random.

I can figure out flights later. I just know I'm not staying here.

Around two o'clock there's a knock on the door. I go to open it, and the pain I feel at finding Hayden on my doorstep, *another* bottle of champagne in hand, is physical, a perforated edge down the middle of my heart. "I know we said you'd buy the champagne tonight," he begins.

"I'm not taking the job," I choke out before he can go any further.

His mouth drops open. "What?"

I swallow the jagged tangle in my throat. "I'm not taking it."

"I don't understand," he says.

"You should," I say. "You passed on it too."

Slowly, his face slackens. "Wait, are you *mad* about that?"

"You're the one who wanted me to 'know I earned it,'" I say, paraphrasing him, like it matters at all. Like any of this matters. I'm not angry with him, but I'm *angry*, and it's seeping into everything else, poisoning it. "And then you just withdraw yourself at the last minute. So which is it, do I deserve it, or did you think I didn't have a chance?"

He gapes at me. "Fuck, Alice. Of course I thought you had a chance. I also thought you'd do a better job than I would, and—and I didn't want this dumb shit to come between us."

"You didn't trust me not to resent you," I clarify.

His mouth jams shut. "I didn't want to put you in the position where you had to even consider it. And I didn't want the job that badly."

"And now I don't want it either," I say, tears burning in the back of my nose. Not now, not at the cost of the truth. Not at the cost of him. "Is that so hard to understand?"

"*Yes*," he says, vehement. "This is your dream job."

"Exactly! It was just a dream," I force out. "The reality isn't what I thought."

"You're *lying* to me, Alice." His voice strains with hurt. "What's going on?"

I shake my head, backing away from him as he moves closer, guarding that distance between us like it can do anything to protect my breaking heart. "I can't," I grind out.

"Alice, what is this?" he pleads. "Tell me. Tell me what's going on. If I did something to hurt you, then tell me how to fix it, and I'll do it, okay? Anything."

I jerk back from him as he reaches for me, trembling from the effort of not breaking into sobs. "I *can't*," I say more harshly. "Ask Margaret."

"I don't want to ask Margaret," he fires back. "Margaret's not important. You are."

"I'm sorry," I say, and then again, like I'm a skipping record, "*I'm sorry*. I can't give you any more than that. I can't—I can't make this make sense for you."

Not just because of the NDA, but because of Margaret. Because, no matter how furious I am with her, this is her story to tell. That's what I promised her before I knew the truth, and it's still what I believe.

"All you have to do is be honest," he says helplessly. "Just talk to me."

"Please don't ask me again," I whimper. "I don't have anything to say."

He stares at me, his disbelief curdling into a frustrated resignation. "So that's it?"

I want to tell him to stay. To beg him to.

But I already know it won't work. That he won't be able to let this go. That even if he could, for a night or two, this secret would eat away at this thing between us. Margaret will go back into hiding, and then, someday, she'll be gone, and if I *did* finally tell him myself then, how could he forgive me for lying to him for so long?

"Please go," I whisper.

He stares at me for a long beat, his dark eyes glazing with tears. "Goodbye, Alice," he finally chokes out, then turns and walks back down the path, away from me, while I try not to break.

Try not to call after him.

Try not to tell him now, in the worst possible moment, when all I can do is wound, that I love him like I've never loved anyone.

When he's gone, I shut the door and slump onto the floor, letting a fresh torrent of tears overtake me. I'm not sure how long it goes on—minutes or hours—but when I catch my breath and my hiccups settle, I pull my phone out and text my mom.

> Would it be okay if I came home for a while? I'm not doing well right now.

The dots appear to indicate she's typing back. She says what she always says.

> Sure.

● ● ●

UNDER THE HIDEOUS neon-green quilt in my childhood bedroom, I half-heartedly search for other jobs. Aging celebrities who might want to tell their stories, dating trends that could become articles for *The Scratch*, and restaurants back in Los Angeles that might need servers. Because if I'm being honest, right now the last thing I want to do is my current job.

I told my friends the bare-bones details—that I'm not moving forward with Margaret, that I'm spending a few days with my mom—but since then, I've been more or less ignoring their texts.

I think about calling Hayden, but what else can I say? I could assure him that I want to be with him, beg him to let this one secret sit, but if he ever found out, could he forgive me for knowing something this huge and keeping it from him?

Could he even *take* being in a relationship with someone he knows, in essence, is lying to him, every single day, the same way that Margaret was?

I play mental games with myself: *If he calls me right now, I'll tell him everything.*

I debate whether Margaret would ever forgive me, like it's a game of *he loves me, he loves me not*, and if I just happen to pluck a flower petal at the right moment, all my problems could go away.

After three days of moping, Mom walks into my room, flips on the lights, and grunts, "If you're going to be here, you might as well work."

I don't have a good argument for that.

I get dressed and meet her in the garden. I kneel beside her in the dirt, and without looking at me, she takes Dad's hat off her head and holds it out to me, one hand still digging with a spade.

My heart pings at the gesture, at the familiarity of it, the quiet care. I put it on and get to work.

For the next two days, we plant.

Irish potatoes and squash, more cucumbers, and snap beans. We prepare the soil for the upcoming cool season planting, clearing out the empty beds, turning the dirt with fertilizer. We take the broccoli seeds she started inside last month and plant them, along with collards and onions.

I feed the chickens, and I collect their eggs. I pick the ripe fruit from the stand of trees, and I manage the compost toilet.

I take short, scalding hot showers, and I help cook every meal.

My limbs ache, but my mind, finally, goes quiet.

On my fifth night there, we sit down to eat in near silence, the same way we've eaten every meal since I got here.

Across from me, at the far end of the old wooden table, Mom picks up her fork, then sets it down again. "Are you going to tell me what's going on, kid?"

"Do you *want* me to?" I ask, surprised.

She sits back in her chair, mismatched from mine, all of them found in trash heaps on curbs or at thrift stores and lovingly restored by her and Dad. "What the hell kind of a question is that?" she demands.

"Sorry," I say quickly, searching for a way to backtrack.

"Dear god, Alice," she says. "I know I'm not winning Mother of the Year anytime soon, but do you really think I'm *that* awful? That I'd see my kid in pain and not care?"

"That's not it at all," I say.

"If something happened," she replies, "you can tell me. If you lost your job, just say it."

"Sorry to disappoint you," I murmur, looking down at my full plate. "But no, I didn't lose my job."

"*Sorry to disappoint me?*" she says, aghast. "You think I want you to get fired?"

This just keeps getting worse and worse. I want to rush to smack a Band-Aid on it, to take back or explain away that little comment.

But the truth is, now that my mind is clear enough to think, the memory of what Margaret said keeps surfacing: *What good does it do anyone? He doesn't like me . . . I can't change who I am, and I'm not going to change him either.*

I push back from my plate and, with a shuddering breath, force the words past the thickness in my throat. "You've never respected my job. You don't respect me for doing it. You think it's stupid and shallow and a waste of time, and I'm sorry—I'm sorry I'm not like Audrey. I'm sorry I'm not saving the world, and I'm not living a perfectly carbon-neutral life, and I spend money on—on unnecessary things like manicures and candles and romance novels. But this is who I am, and even if you don't understand it, couldn't you just *pretend* for a few days a year that you respect me? That you *like* me? Because I can't figure out how to be anyone else, and it's lonely, it's so fucking *lonely* being the person who doesn't belong in this family."

She stares at me, agog, blank faced.

My chest heaves as I try to even out my breathing. My eyes, I realize, are glossed with tears, and I'm gripping my fork like a lifeline.

One second ticks by. Another. I wonder if she'll just pick up her fork and go back to eating, pretend this never happened.

I wonder if she'll scream. If she'll let *me* have it the way I just did to her.

Finally, she cracks: "*Oh, honey.*"

Her chair scrapes back from the table and she comes around toward me, crouching to wrap me in her arms. The simple contact, the tight hug with no casual backslapping, no rush to pull away, makes me start to cry in earnest. "You belong," she murmurs, kissing the top of my head. "Never doubt that."

"I don't," I argue, my voice wrenching upward.

My mom grips my shoulders in her hands, kneeling beside me. "Alice," she says calmly. "I respect you. I love you. I *like* you. But I don't understand you."

I blink away the tears, and her elfin features come back into focus. "Your dad . . ." She shakes her head and tries again. "When you were a tiny little girl, you were always glued to my side. All day, every day. Audrey was more independent, but you were my shadow."

I sniff, wipe my eyes. "I was?"

She nods. "And as you grew up, grew into yourself . . . I don't know how to explain this in a way that won't make me seem like an asshole, so I'll just say it. The first few years as a mom, it felt like you and your sister were pieces of my heart walking around outside my body. You were your own people, but you were also *mine*. It feels like a miracle, because it is. You had your father's DNA and you had mine, and somehow that made a whole new person who was both of us and neither.

"And then you started growing up, and you found new things to like. Things I'd never even really considered. Pieces of yourself that were all you. And you didn't need me anymore. It was amazing—it's what's *supposed* to happen. But it was terrifying too. To let you grow past me. Suddenly there were all these locked doors that used to be wide-open hallways."

"Mom, I didn't need you because I didn't *let* myself. Because Audrey was sick, and I thought that's what everyone wanted from me. For me to just . . . be okay. *Happy*. And I *was*. I figured it out."

"I know," she says. "And that breaks my heart. Because I wish I could've been there more. Not just when Audrey was sick, but since then too. Your dad would've . . ."

She chokes up again, but she forces herself onward. "Your dad *understood you*." Her voice squeaks, and her shoulders lift in a slight shrug. "He understood the things you love. He understood your sense of humor. He had access to pieces of you I couldn't get to, and I was okay with that, mostly. But when he died—god, Alice, I haven't been able to figure out how to be what you need. He always knew the right thing to say to you. He always knew how to cheer you up, or how to talk you down.

"And I want to be a good parent to you, but I can't be him."

"I don't need you to be him," I promise tearily.

"You deserve to have him," she says. "You don't know how many times I've wished it had been me instead."

"*Mom*." My heart cracks, shatters. I wrap my arms around her again. "Don't say that."

Her voice shivers out of her, wispy and ragged: "I miss him so much."

I shut my eyes, the tears still managing to pour through my lashes. "Me too," I squeak. "I should have asked him more. I should have written it all down. I should've recorded every stupid joke and every piece of advice. I should have taken videos of him singing in the kitchen while you cooked. I should have tried to know all of him while I had the time. Before it was too late."

My mom's embrace loosens and she sits back on her heels, swiping her own tears away. "Baby girl," she says. "It's *not* too late. What do you want to know?"

• • •

WE PROP MY phone up on the table with a stack of old books, set to video. I place my recorder next to it, both angled toward where Mom sits with a stack of old photo albums. I hit RECORD on each, then go join her at the table.

"Where should we start?" she asks me.

"The beginning," I say.

She opens album after album until she finds the book she's looking for. "Our commune days," she says, smiling affectionately at the first Polaroid of them, out in the sun, each in overalls, both skinnier and younger. He has his arm slung around her. He's wearing a different though not dissimilar wide-brimmed hat.

"You said he was ridiculous?" I ask her, and her smile widens.

"The most ridiculous," she says.

"Tell me everything," I say.

"Only if you'll do the same," she says.

I hold out my hand. We shake on it.

Then we take turns sharing our stories.

THE NEXT MORNING, I sit down at the desk in Audrey's room and start to write a letter.

After speaking with Mom, I know what I need to say. I can't control how it will be received, but I have to try.

I've just finished when I hear the pounding at the front door, followed by Mom's footsteps, and then a few overlapping voices.

The back of my neck tingles as I stand and make my way through the small house toward the laughter and conversation. In the entryway, I stop short at the sight of them, kicking off their shoes.

"Alice!" Priya squeals and bounds toward me, wrapping me in a hug.

"What are you *doing* here?" I say, flabbergasted, as Priya releases me.

"Your mom invited us," Cillian says, hugging me next.

I look over his shoulder toward my mom. "Did you go through my phone?" I say, more confused than upset.

"Of course not," Mom replies, seemingly a *bit* offended by the accusation.

"We exchanged numbers last time I was here," Bianca says, sidling up to hug me next. I hold on for a long moment, so grateful for these people who show up for me even when I don't ask them to.

"I'm glad you're here," I get out.

"Really?" Priya says. "Then *why*, pray tell, haven't you been texting us back?"

"It's a long story," I say.

"Would anyone like some tea or coffee?" Mom asks.

"I, for one, would *love* some, Angie," Cillian says, following my mom down the hallway, gawking at everything he passes and quickly throwing a look over his shoulder at me as he says, "It's so nice to *finally* be invited here."

"He's never going to let it go, that he was the last one to visit here, is he?" I say.

"If you die first," Bianca says, threading an arm through mine and turning me to follow him, "he'll mention it in his eulogy."

35

I CAN'T TELL them everything, but I tell them enough. That the job with Margaret imploded. That it took Hayden's and my budding relationship with it.

That it made me doubt myself and the work.

"We can lighten your load at *The Scratch* for a while," Bianca promises, "while you figure things out."

"I don't want to put anyone in a bad spot," I say.

"Alice. *You're* in a bad spot," Cillian says.

"It's fine," I say. "This really isn't that big of a deal, all things considered."

"Well, then stop considering 'all things' for a minute," Priya says. "This doesn't have to be the greatest tragedy to ever befall anyone. It doesn't even have to be the worst thing that's ever happened to you."

"Exactly," Bianca agrees. "You're hurting right now, that's what matters."

"I'm so glad you're all here," I say again, and when Cillian opens his mouth, surely to say something snarky, I add, "*especially* you, Cillian," and we all dissolve into laughter.

I show them around the property, let them take pictures with Marietta, the friendliest of our chickens.

Mom puts us to work for an hour in the afternoon, and afterward, we take turns using our house's one shower.

Cillian is craving pizza, so for the first time I can remember, *ever*, my mom agrees to order some. As we're waiting for the delivery, she and I make a peach crumble and set it out to cool while we eat dinner. After Mom goes to bed, we play three-quarters of a game of Monopoly, then agree that we hate Monopoly too much to play for another second.

"We should have a sleepover," Priya says.

"That's literally what this is, Pri," Bianca says.

"No, I mean, we should all sleep in the living room together," Priya says.

"I'm too old to sleep on the floor," Cillian says through a yawn.

"But I *hate* sleeping alone," Priya says.

"I'll sleep with you," Cillian offers, waggling his eyebrows.

"Never again," Priya says, because that actually *is* how their friendship began.

"I meant *platonically*," Cillian insists.

"It's either that or one of you takes Audrey's room and the other takes the couch," I say.

Priya pouts. "Why can't I sleep with you?"

"Because *I* already called it, within ten minutes of getting here," Bianca says.

"Fine," Priya says. "Cillian, you're back in."

"Well, now I'm not sure I'm up for it," Cillian says, and they squabble for a minute while we're all standing up and saying our good nights. In the end, he and Priya take Audrey's room, and Bianca and I tuck ourselves into my bed.

"You seem better," she murmurs sleepily as we settle in.

"You guys lifted my spirits," I say.

She shakes her head. "No. I mean, you seem somehow happier than you did before you left. More at peace or something."

It's strange, but she's right. I feel at once utterly heartbroken and also like a weight has been lifted off my shoulders.

I miss Hayden. I love him. But after sending that letter, I've done what I can.

I've done what I need to do to live a life without any more regrets.

"I'm thinking about writing a memoir," I whisper up to the dark ceiling.

Bianca turns over to face me. "Really?"

I nod. "About my parents. About everything they've taught me."

"That's a beautiful idea," Bianca says.

"It's not a Margaret Ives biography," I say. "There's no guarantee anyone will want it."

"You can't think about that yet," Bianca says. "Right now you just have to think about what *you* want to write about."

I want, I realize, to write about the same thing I've always wanted to write about.

"I want to write about love," I say.

Bianca nods. "Then do that. Write about love."

•   •   •

AFTER ONE LAST group hug, I deposit my friends in an airport-bound cab. Mom and I wave as they retreat, the sun setting brilliantly behind them.

I think, as I always do at sunrise and sunset, about the tiny mosaic in my bedroom.

The colors of *Nicollet*. The colors of *hope*.

Back inside, we set up the camera and recorder and get back to work.

A month goes by. I garden with my mother during the day, the recorder running as we talk. We listen to music while we cook at night, all of Dad's old favorites. Afterward we look through photo albums and watch old home movies.

I treasure every word she gives me. Not just the ones about my father, but the ones about her too. She was right when she said it wasn't too late to know him, but the thing I'm realizing is, it's not too late to know her either.

Sometimes, on very rare occasions when we wrap up work early in the day, we'll sit outside on the grass, drinking beer and darning socks while the sun melts into the horizon, painting everything with its glory.

Sunset, I learn, is my mother's favorite time of day. It relaxes her more than a hot shower or a glass of wine or anything else, to watch another day come to a close, everything in its right place.

We video call with Audrey when she's able, and she tells us about her work and asks us about ours.

My mother isn't a different person. I'm not either. But she asks me to send her a few of my favorite stories I've written, and sometimes, when she's reading them at night on the couch opposite from me, she even laughs. She pushes her wire-frame glasses on top of her head and looks at me and says something like "You're so much like him," something that makes me feel not just seen but *loved*, *liked*.

Theo texts me a couple of times, but when I give as little in our exchanges as he does, they quickly peter out. It's not a breakup, because it wasn't a relationship, and I'm okay with that.

I try not to think too much about Hayden, but he's everywhere. In one month, he invaded every facet of my reality. Like the Cosmo Sinclair song.

Hayden, Hayden, all the time.

I'm still doing work for *The Scratch*, but mostly short-form pieces, with phone interviews and email exchanges. Once, I go to Atlanta for a weekend to interview a chef, but mostly I spend that whole first month at my mother's side, her shadow once more but still my own person.

Five weeks after my friends left, I talk her into ordering pizza again.

"It *was* pretty good," she allows, then negotiates, "no more than once per month though."

We shake on it, and then I call the order in.

She's in the shower when it arrives, and I'm putting the finishing touches on a fresh salad. "*Coming!*" I shout in the general direction of the door, then rinse my oniony fingers and pat them against my legs as I jog toward the door.

I swing it open and the sunset blinds me for just a second, before the inky blot in front of me resolves into a person.

A tall, devastatingly handsome, walking, talking *glower* of a person.

"Hayden," I gasp, feeling vaguely like I've run at a dead sprint into a wall.

He stares at me, face hard and impassive as ever. "What is this?" he asks sharply, and holds up a piece of paper.

Nothing fancy. Notebook paper with blue ink scrawled across it, front and back. My handwriting.

For a split second, I go ice cold with the fear that I mailed the letter to the wrong person. Him instead of Margaret.

Then I realize the flaw in that theory. I don't even have Hayden's address.

"Does it look familiar?" he asks me.

I try to speak. No sound comes out.

When he realizes I'm not going to answer, his eyes drop to the front of it. He clears his throat and reads tersely, "'Dear Margaret, you asked me once if you could trust Hayden. I told you that you could, but that wasn't the whole truth.'"

"I know what it says," I weakly manage, but he goes on.

"'Yes, he has some walls up, the same as you do. And just like you, he has his reasons. He's careful about who he lets in, but when he does, he loves them wholly. He's blunt, and he's honest, but he's never cruel or unkind. He can be hard to read, but he doesn't play games.

"'He doesn't sleep well. He knows where every twenty-four-hour diner is within forty minutes of Little Crescent, and probably where all of them are back in his own neighborhood too. He's careful about his health—he doesn't have a complete family medical history to rely on, so he tries not to take risks.

"'He's funny, very funny, but because he's so dry about it, it might take you a while to realize that.

"'He never wears shorts. He's afraid of snakes but not so scared he wouldn't protect you from one if it came to it.

"'He's generous and thoughtful, and every second you spend not getting to know him is a second wasted. I don't know what your daughter will say if you ask again for a chance to know her. And I can't know for sure what Hayden would say either. But I know he takes life seriously. I know he's not the kind of person to put off uncomfortable conversations now and regret not having them later.

"'He is, I think, the most wonderful person I've ever met, and in the interest of full disclosure, I have a personal stake in whether you tell him the truth or not, because I love him with every fiber of my being, and as someone once told me, when you love someone, you do anything to give them what they need. You unmake the world and build a new one.

"'I've already lost him, but maybe you don't have to. Either way, he deserves the chance to say yes or no. He deserves to be asked. Your friend (I think, I hope), Alice Scott.'"

He stares down at the page for several seconds, and I stand there, trembling with nerves and raw emotion. Finally, his eyes lift to mine, his face etched with tension.

"How did you get that?" I force out.

"She sent it to me," he says. "Along with her own letter. Explaining what happened."

My eyes burn. My cheeks burn. My *skin* burns, even as my insides feel chilled.

"Is it true?" he says finally.

"What?" I whisper.

"Is it true?" he says.

"I'm sorry I couldn't tell you," I get out. "I *wanted* to tell you—"

"Is"—he steps in closer, the letter falling to his side—"it true?"

"About Margaret's connection to you?" I ask.

His chin moves to the left one inch. "That you love me?"

The tears break. "Of course it's true. How could it not be? I loved you almost instantly, before I really even knew you. Before I understood it. I trusted you, and I loved you, and I still do."

"Good," he says, taking another small step toward the open door. "Because I love you too. I love you so much, and I don't want to be without you ever again. I'll move to Los Angeles, I'll find a new job, whatever."

"*Hayden—*"

"Don't try to talk me out of it, Alice," he says. "Every time we try to protect each other, all it does is cost us more time together, and I'm not willing to lose any more. I want to be with you. Nothing else is going to matter to me more than that. Not at the end of my life. Not even now. Nothing will matter more than who I spent my time with, and I want it to be you. I need it to be you."

I've done more crying in the last two months than in the two years prior, and I'm determined to hold these tears back, to be cool, calm, and steady until the end of this conversation.

"*Okay?*" he says, ducking his head to hold my eyes.

"I love that plan," I whisper. "And I'm so grateful and honored. But there's a problem."

His brow rumples, an expression that hits my heart like one of Cupid's arrows. "What?"

"I'm not going back to Los Angeles," I say. "I'm staying in Georgia for now. Maybe forever, I don't know. I'm working on something new, and even when it's over, I think I'm going to want to be close to my mom, while she's still healthy. I love you so much, but I can't miss out on more time with her. I did that with my dad, and I need this, and I'm sorry, because if it was anything else—I'd give up *anything else*, but I don't think I can give up on this, and I know I can't expect you to wait for me, but I wish that—"

He takes my face in his hands while I'm still rambling. "*Alice.*"

"I'd love it if you interrupted me right now," I whisper, heart heavy in my chest.

He smiles. "I hear Atlanta's a great place to be a music journalist."

Just like that, my resolution not to cry snaps. Tears fall hard and fast, sliding down my nose, dripping onto my chin. "Really?" I ask wetly.

"Really," he says.

"Are you sure, because—"

This time he does interrupt me, our mouths colliding, my hands in his hair, his flat and firm against my back, molding me to him, drinking me in. I hold on to him as tight as I possibly can, the sunset scorchingly bright, all that hope gathered in one place.

We pull apart just enough to rest our foreheads together, his hand moving softly, lovingly up and down my back.

"When I let myself dream," he murmurs against my ear, "or it all comes crashing down—it's Alice, Alice on my mind. Alice all the time."

The Story

THEIR VERSION: Pulitzer-winning biographer Hayden Anderson teams up with celebrity journalist Alice Scott on salacious new Margaret Ives biography *From the Far Side of the World*.

• • •

OUR VERSION: It's a love story. Like everything I write, that's what it comes down to. That's what always matters most to me, about any interview subject: *Whom do you love? What makes your heart beat? For whom would you unmake the world, and how would you build a new one?*

We tell the truth, mostly.

Nicollet, though, is a casualty. It's the only way.

Hayden's mother doesn't want to be known, not in that way. But she's open to knowing her biological mother. Open, if not eager.

There's a path forward, and it will end wherever it ends. All they can do is walk it at their own pace.

Margaret's moving slower these days, moving less. She can't tend to her own garden, but Mom and I drive down to work in it often.

Hayden comes up from the city to meet us. Sometimes we take the airboat out and collect trash, bring it home and watch Margaret fit all these broken pieces together into something beautiful.

As much as I love my mosaic, I give it back to Margaret, and it sits in a place of honor on her mantel, until, one day, it doesn't.

"What happened to it?" I ask her while I'm dusting her bookshelves.

"Sent it off with a letter," she says.

I don't press her. She'll tell me more when she wants to, or maybe she won't.

She's being brave where it counts.

The book is a hit. The message boards go wild. Some of them are onto something, though just far enough off the mark to not figure out the truth.

Cosmo Sinclair is still alive, I SWEAR, you can just FEEL it in the way M.I. talks about him, one conspiracy theorist writes, and hundreds more upvote the comment.

In a way, he is. His memory will never be lost now. It was passed on to his grandson.

It will be passed on to our daughter.

We didn't expect it, but almost overnight, Hayden becomes the kind of man who sings to my pregnant belly, who sends dozens of "what about this name" texts over the course of the day, sometimes when we're working in our separate offices, four feet apart in our new home.

We don't settle on one until we're driving to the hospital, my contractions getting closer and closer.

In the hospital waiting room, my mother and Hayden's take turns pacing. Every thirty seconds, Jodi or Margaret or Cecil or Audrey or Priya or Bianca or Cillian or Hayden's brother, Louis, texts us some variation of *Is she here yet?!*

Until, finally, she is.

Laura Grace Anderson-Scott is born at 11:53 p.m. She slips in, just under the wire, on a Tuesday.

Half him. Half me. Entirely her own.

Hayden holds her against his chest with tears in his eyes—our whole world, packed into this tiny, impossible thing, and I've never felt anything like the love that spreads through my heart.

Like I swallowed the sun. Like it's breaking up every bit of darkness inside me.

I know I would do anything to protect her, anything to make the world better for her.

In that moment, I feel closer to my parents, both of them, than I ever have in my life.

And strangely, I find myself thinking about the meandering path of broken glass around Margaret's workshop. About the unicursal labyrinth.

I find myself thinking that maybe every bit of heartbreak in life can be rearranged and used for something beautiful. That it doesn't really matter whether I chose this path or I was born onto it, so long as I stop and appreciate the path itself.

Four months after Laura's born, once she finally starts sleeping better, I sit down with the notes I've spent years compiling with my mother and a blank document on my computer, a freshly brewed cup of coffee sitting at my elbow, where Hayden left it for me.

I crack my knuckles, and then I start to write.

Everything I want to tell her someday.

Not just the headlines, but the whole truth.

The good and bad, the magic and curses, all the blues and grays right alongside the reds and golds. I tell her the story about a love so powerful it remade the world for her. I welcome her to this great big beautiful life.

Acknowledgments

FIRST, I WANT to thank my readers, the ones who've been with me since the beginning and the ones who just picked this book up on a whim and made it to the end. It has been an immense joy, honor, and privilege to write for you. I'm grateful every single day. Today I'm especially grateful, though, because this book was a terrifying, exhilarating departure for me in so many ways, and to know how many of you have graciously followed me here to this new terrain is humbling. I hope you found something to love in Margaret, Alice, and Hayden's world.

I truly feel that I have both the best readers out there and the best publishing team in the world. First off, there's everyone at Root Literary, including but not limited to Taylor, Jasmine, Gab, Melanie, and Holly, who operate on a superhuman level while also being so kind, generous, and supportive. I would be utterly lost without them. The same goes for my Berkley family: Amanda Bergeron, Sareer Khader, Theresa Tran, Dache' Rogers, Danielle Keir, Jessica Mangicaro, and Elise Tecco. Huge thanks also to Sanny Chiu for another gorgeous cover, to Craig Burke for talking *Vanderpump Rules* with

Acknowledgments

me (and also being amazing at his job), and to the rest of the incredible PRH team, especially Christine Ball, Ivan Held, Jeanne-Marie Hudson, Cindy Hwang, Christine Legon, Lindsey Tulloch, and Claire Zion.

Another enormous round of thanks to my UK team at Viking, with a special extra shout-out to my editor Vikki Moynes and the rest of my team: Ellie Hudson, Georgia Taylor, Harriet Bourton, Lydia Fried, and Rosie Safaty. Huge shoutout to Holly Ovenden too for another brilliant cover.

So much appreciation to my unparalleled film agent Mary Pender and her phenomenal assistant Celia Albers, who have been endlessly supportive of me since the very beginning of our time working together.

There are so many booksellers, podcasters, reviewers, writers, and artists out there who have loved and championed my books and characters, and I wish I could thank you all individually, but this will have to do for now: Thank you, thank you, thank you a million times over for your kindness.

And lastly, as always, thank you to my family and my friends, especially Dottie, who sat beside me for every word. Thank you all for loving me on my best days and my worst. You make this life great, big, and beautiful. I love you.